TEARS OF BLOOD

TEARS OF BLOOD

A CRY FOR TIBET

Mary Craig

With a New Afterword by Mary Craig

COUNTERPOINT
WASHINGTON, D.C.

Library of Congress Cataloging-in-Publication Data
Craig, Mary.
    Tears of blood / Mary Craig.
        p.   cm.
    Includes bibliographical references and index.
    ISBN 1-58243-102-7
    1. Tibet (China)—History.   I. Title.
DS786.C7   1999
951'.—5—dc21   99-28444
                                                              CIP

Jacket design by Amy Evans McClure

Printed in the United States of America on acid-free paper that
meets the American National Standards Institute Z39-48 Standard.

COUNTERPOINT
P.O. Box 65793
Washington, D.C. 20035-5793

Counterpoint is a member of the Perseus Books Group

10 9 8 7 6 5 4 3 2 1

To the Tibetan people

and their non-violent struggle

for freedom

The word "genocide" must be used with care. Our world and our century have seen countless abominable massacres, and it is easy to slip into the use of the word to denote such atrocities. We should, however, restrict it to those crimes before high heaven which are truly designated by it. If we do so, and if we consider only the last sixty years, there are four such mass murders which can justifiably carry the terrible brand. They are: the Jewish Holocaust, the Stalin Terror, the bloodthirst of Pol Pot and the Khmer Rouge, and what was done to the people and culture of Tibet during the miserable lust for death and torture unleashed by the mad Mao Tse-tung under the name of "The Cultural Revolution."

BERNARD LEVIN, *The Times*, 7.9.90

Once identified with Shangri-La, a mythical place of peace and contentment, [Tibet] is now a dark and sorrowing land.

HARRISON E. SALISBURY, 1982

List of Illustrations

Lobsang Jimpa © Author

Monk during Lhasa riots of October 1987 © John Ackerly/ Tibet Image Bank

Sonam Tseten © Author

Tibetan demonstrators in Dharamsala © Raghu Rai/Magnum Photos

Monlam Chenmo; monks calling for Independence © Tibet Image Bank

Monks loaded into trucks after Monlam Chenmo protest © Tibet Image Bank

Christa Meindersma © Ron Schwarz/Tibet Image Bank

Chinese armoured personnel carriers in Lhasa © T.I.N./Tibet Image Bank

PLA soldier on roof top © D.I.I.R., Dharamsala/Tibet Image Bank

Tashi Dolma © Author

Gyaltsen Chodon © Author

HH the Dalai Lama holding his Nobel Peace Prize © Office of Tibet

President George Bush with the Dalai Lama © Author

HH the Dalai Lama with the Archbishop of Canterbury © Office of Tibet

Giant gilded yaks © Alex Stuart/Tibet Image Bank

Fireworks at the Potala © Alex Stuart/Tibet Image Bank

Members of the Tibetan Youth Congress © Office of Tibet

Contents

TEARS OF BLOOD

Foreword

The entry of Chinese Communist forces into Tibet over forty years ago was the first step in a campaign of outright assault on an independent peace-loving people, which continues unabated to this day. Under the slogan of liberation the Tibetan people and their entire way of life have been attacked, as a result of which over 1.2 million of them have died.

The Tibetan people have been humiliated and impoverished in their own land. Many thousands have been imprisoned, tortured and subjected to every indignity.

With the destruction of the several thousand monasteries and nunneries and the expulsion of the monks and nuns, not only were the repositories of our religion and culture lost, with their vast libraries and precious artefacts, but also the traditional education system. Nowadays, young people come out of Tibet unable to read or write their own language and so are cut off from their natural heritage.

The Chinese disregard for the Tibetan people has been compounded by the insidious policy of population transfer. As huge numbers of Chinese settlers are added to the already substantial occupying forces, the threat of the Tibetans becoming a minority in their own country is very real. Even now, poorly educated, unemployed and denied basic human rights, they are treated as second-class citizens.

Yet, their spirit is unbroken. It is the young people, who never knew the old Tibet, as much as the older generations, who put their lives at risk by continuing to demonstrate against Chinese rule.

We in exile have been fortunate in being able to preserve our religious and cultural traditions and educate our children, as well as learn about democracy and experiment with its procedures.

The Chinese refer to Tibet as part of the "motherland", yet in civilized societies if children were subjected to the kind of abuse meted out to the Tibetans, they would immediately be taken into safe custody. It should be recognized that never in their long history have Tibetans accepted that they were part of China.

At a time when the beacon of freedom and democracy is burning brighter in many parts of the world what the Tibetan people need is the protection of international concern and support. For this to be forthcoming it is essential that the world at large be aware of what has taken place in Tibet over the last four decades. This book makes it very clear and I appreciate Mary Craig for her valuable contribution.

December 19, 1991

Prologue

On 1 October 1949, Mao Tse-tung proclaimed a People's Republic in China. It signalled the end of a loosely structured Nationalist regime which had endured – bedevilled by civil war – for nearly forty years; and announced the arrival on the world scene of a centralized, highly organized, tightly controlled and aggressive dynasty ruled from Beijing.

As the new Chinese Communist regime set about expanding and consolidating its power, it quietly swallowed up the disputed outlying territories of its western neighbour, Tibet. Then, on 7 October 1950, almost a year to the day after Mao's proclamation of the People's Republic, 30,000 battle-hardened, self-confident troops of the People's Liberation Army invaded the heartlands of Tibet, to liberate it, they said, from its feudal oppressors and from Western imperialists.

Tibet's tiny, unprepared army had about as much chance as an ant against a rhinoceros; its defeat was never in doubt. The nations of the world looked the other way, as China had gambled they would. In 1950, the Cold War was just beginning and – as the Korean War had broken out in June – they had more pressing things to worry about. On 23 May 1951 during negotiations in Beijing, Tibetans were offered a choice: "peaceful liberation" by the Chinese, or annihilation by military force. Under this kind of duress, they chose "liberation".

Exactly forty years later on 23 May 1991, the Chinese staged elaborate celebrations to mark the anniversary of Tibet's "liberation", complete with singing, dancing, picnics and fireworks. It was, of course, all a charade. Plane-loads of Chinese armed police were flown into the Tibetan capital, Lhasa, to discourage the Tibetans from publicly showing their discontent. For to the people of Tibet, the day commemorated not liberation but national downfall. On the streets of Lhasa pamphlets were being secretly handed out calling for "tears of blood" rather than rejoicing. Twenty-third May 1951 was the day on which a nation with a 2,000-year-old civilization had begun its slide to the brink of extinction. But for the Tibetans to have shown openly that they were in mourning on that fortieth anniversary day would have been to court imprisonment or even death.

In all those 2,000 years, Tibet had come under foreign influence only twice, in the thirteenth (Mongol) and eighteenth (Manchu) centuries. This influence was benign, remote and caused barely a ripple on the unchanging surface of Tibetan life. As the ambassador for Ireland at the United Nations remarked, during the General Assembly debates about Tibet in 1960, "For a couple of thousand years ... Tibet was as free and as fully in control of its own affairs as any nation in this Assembly, and a thousand times more free to look after its affairs than many of the nations here". The coming of the Communist Chinese changed all that. Claiming that Tibet was rightfully theirs, they ruthlessly colonized it. Repression, famine and death became the order of the day.

In the first twenty years of Chinese occupation, 1.2 million Tibetans – one-fifth of the total population – are believed to have died, either by starvation (unknown before the Chinese came and changed the traditional agricultural practices), execution, imprisonment, torture or in conflict. (Tibet has been described as "a laboratory for torture techniques for the Chinese security forces".)[1] Thousands of Tibetans, including their leader, the Dalai Lama, were driven into exile. The Cultural Revolution of 1966–76 plumbed incomparable depths of savagery in Tibet and brought Tibetan culture and religion to the brink of destruction. "The holocaust that happened in Tibet", said Alexander Solzhenitsyn, "revealed Communist China as a cruel and inhumane executioner – more brutal and inhuman than any other Communist regime in the world".[2]

Only in the early Eighties did a brief taste of liberalization bring the hope of better things. But the hope had already turned sour by 1983, when Tibet began to be flooded with Chinese immigrants, and the indigenous inhabitants were outnumbered. Tibetan cities became indistinguishable from their Chinese counterparts. Tibetans found themselves second-class citizens with a second-class language, discriminated against in their own land. They had no legal representation, no freedom of speech, no permitted outlet for discontent. New buildings were for the benefit of the Chinese immigrants. In the Tibetan areas of towns, there was no running water or basic sewerage, and only rarely electricity. And outside the towns, there was little food.

In 1987 the bitter struggle for independence began in earnest. The last few years have seen an escalation of this distressingly uneven contest: naked power lashing out against non-violent protest. For what makes the Tibetans special is that they are a peaceful people; a deeply religious people, disinclined to use violence because it is against their Buddhist faith. Their determination to win independence by non-violent resistance makes their struggle unique in the world.

But how much longer they can remain non-violent when all the forces of repression are deployed against them is a question to which some Tibetans are currently addressing themselves. "How many more of us must die before we can retaliate?" some of them ask. There is a fear that one day in desperation the Tibetans will match violence with violence and thus precipitate a great cataclysm.

The Chinese claim (and the British government has actually echoed the claim) that Tibet is an autonomous region within the People's Republic of China. But, as Robert Barnett pointed out in an article in *The Spectator*, it is not what *we* would call auto-nomy: "Every law in Tibet is subject to Peking, and anyone who calls for anything that queries Peking's view of socialism, the Party or the annexation of Tibet is committing a capital offence.

These are not conditions which most people identify with
autonomy."[3]

The Chinese refuse to face the truth, that – with a very few
quisling exceptions – the whole Tibetan nation is behind the
independence movement. They prefer the comforting theory
that it is only a handful of "splittists" and reactionaries who are
causing trouble. Human rights, religion, nationality have
nothing to do with the matter, they argue; it is all down to the
interfering "criminal splittists". But to the Tibetans those three
things are precisely what the struggle is about. Their human
rights have for too long been trampled on, their religion all but
eradicated, their very identity as a nation threatened. First of
all, a rigid and unwanted ideology was imposed on them by
force; and when that was seen to have failed, they faced the
threat of being engulfed by a tide of Chinese settlers. And since
1987, the Chinese have been tightening the screw of their birth
control policies, extending to the Tibetans a programme of
forced abortions, sterilizations and even, allegedly, infanticide.

Does the rest of the world know or care that, in the name of
"liberation", the Chinese forced on Tibet one of the worst
occupations in history? That a vicious colonialism which
amounted quite literally to genocide was inflicted on that tragic
country? That the Tibetans are treated as slaves in their own
land, despised as stupid, ignorant, dirty savages? That one-fifth
of them have died through murder, starvation, disease or
torture? That the killing still goes on?

What, after all, have we in the West ever cared about Tibet, a
country which until the twentieth century was a blank space on
most of the world's maps, a mystery unsolved? A strange,
remote land, peopled by gods and demons, the fabled Shangri-
la, perhaps, where men lived forever innocent and time stood
still? Has that romantic image obscured reality and prevented
us from understanding that Tibet is no fantasy-land of mist and
magic; that behind those majestic peaks which isolate it so
effectively from an indifferent world, it endures the kind of
lonely martyrdom which ranks in this, our bloodiest of cen-

turies, with Stalin's persecutions and purges, the destruction of Europe's Jews by Hitler, and the blood-lust of Pol Pot in the killing fields of Cambodia?

Recently, there has been a shift away from total ignorance. Since June 1989 when the massacre in Tiananmen Square laid bare the moral bankruptcy of the Beijing regime, more and more people all over the world have begun to know of and sympathize with Tibet's desire for self-determination. Systematic discrimination is inflicted on Tibet by China, public champion of anti-colonialism yet the last remaining land empire in the world.

The nations impressively united under the banner of the UN to free Kuwait when it was invaded by its neighbour, Iraq. But what the Iraqis did to oil-rich Kuwait is exactly what the Chinese did to mineral-rich Tibet over forty years ago. Why the double standard? "We are no different from Kuwait", cries a Tibetan woman, anguish etched into her face, "why does no one help us? Are we some species of animal? Are we not human beings?"[4]

Would those same nations who stood firm against the infamy of Saddam Husain now be willing to call China's bluff? Or are we still, like Chamberlain and Daladier at Munich, mortally afraid of dictators, especially those we want to do business with? It is at least possible that China has so far remained deaf to calls for human rights within her borders because there has simply not been enough pressure on her to listen.

My aim in writing this book has been to tell the story of a forty-years nightmare through the testimonies of those who have lived through it. In the course of three visits to Dharamsala in Northern India – "Little Tibet" – I have listened exhaustively to the stories of refugees young and old, from all sections of society. Fresh waves of them arrive every week. It is their personal stories which flesh out the bare bones of contemporary history on these pages, their voices which tell of the disaster which has overtaken their land. I make no apology for being partisan. Since 1959, 110,000 Tibetan refugees have fled the

Chinese, and as the Dalai Lama says, "Often they cry, cry, cry, and I have to play the role of a mother, consoling them". They must have their say. The official version of events has for too long gone unchallenged.*

One way or another, time is running out for Tibet; it may soon be too late to save her. Pressure must be brought to bear on China now. Impossible? It would be well to remember, as Lord Grimond recently reminded us, "Appeasement did not work with Hitler. And it will not work with China".[5]

---

* Perhaps, also, it is high time that someone conducted similar extensive personal interviews with ordinary Chinese people, particularly those who live and work in Tibet.

CHAPTER 1

No Smoke Nor Dust

Tibet and China shall abide by the frontiers of which they are now in occupation. All to the east is the country of Great China; and all to the west is, without question, the country of Great Tibet. Henceforth on neither side shall there be waging of war nor seizing of territory ... Between the two countries no smoke nor dust shall be seen. There shall be no sudden alarms and the very word "enemy" shall not be spoken ... All shall live in peace and share the blessing of happiness for ten thousand years.

> Part of the peace treaty signed in AD 821/22 by the Kings of China and Tibet. Replicas were inscribed on obelisks set up outside the Chinese Imperial Palace and the Jokhang temple in Lhasa.

Tibet is not the tiny country most Westerners seem to imagine, but the highest country in the world, and one of the emptiest and most inaccessible. In places it soars for three miles upwards, its jagged peaks seeming to claw the sky, its air diamond-sharp, a towering wilderness at the heart of Central Asia, with an average height of over 15,000 feet above sea level. Even most of its towns are at around 11,000 feet.

Really, there are two Tibets. Traditionally, the name included areas to the west such as Ladakh, and huge kingdoms and tribal territories to the east and north-east, inhabited mainly by people of Tibetan race, religion and culture, and where the majority of Tibetans actually lived. This land mass, known as ethnic or Greater Tibet, rests on a high plateau which extends for over 2,000 miles from India, Pakistan and Afghanistan in the west to the foothills of China in the east and from Nepal in the south to East Turkestan (now the Chinese province of Xinjiang) in the north. In Western terms that is roughly equal to saying that it is as large as all the EEC countries put together. Or, for those of a different hemisphere, it is the size of California, Nevada, Utah and Arizona. It is a land of boundless diversity. To the north, west and south, some of the highest mountains on the planet act as a natural fortress to isolate Tibet from the rest of Asia, though only the north-west, the icy windswept, sterile desert of the Chang Tang, is completely uninhabited but for a few hardy nomads. It is "a wasteland of titanic mountains, vast empty landscapes strewn with shattered rocks, and utter desolation".[1] In the god-forsaken Chang Tang the winter temperature can fall to as low as minus forty-four degrees centigrade; while in summer the frozen wastes turn to slush and swamp.

Most of eastern Tibet was ruled over by independent kings or chieftains and in some cases by Muslim warlords, sometimes supported by China but owing allegiance to no-one but themselves. The north-east (Amdo) was infested by bandits and was approached only by the bravest souls, travelling in caravan for safety. In the east (Kham), some of the world's mightiest rivers gather force as they descend towards the great plains of China and South-East Asia: the Irrawaddy, Yangtse, Mekong, Salween among them, fed by giant ice-age glaciers. Here, where the formidable mountains of the Tibetan plateau begin their own descent into forests and fertile valleys, Tibet's frontiers were shadowy and uncertain, making her vulnerable to predators.

Before 1950, however, the name Tibet signified to neighbouring powers only that area which extended from the eastern borders of Ladakh as far as the Yangtse River: a political entity under the rule of the Dalai Lamas and their regents. This territory (known as U-Tsang and Western Kham) is all that remains today – it is what the Chinese mean when they speak of "Tibet".

Though the racial origins of the Tibetans are lost in the mists of legend, one thing is clear: they are not akin to the Chinese. Their features are sharper and less oriental. They are thought to belong to the same stock as the nomadic, fiercely independent ancient Turks and Mongols. Their spoken language is not directly related to Chinese, while their script is derived from mediaeval Sanskrit, with an alphabet rather than ideograms. The people of U-Tsang are for the most part short (though taller than the Chinese), with high cheekbones, flat noses, round heads and scarcely any body-hair. By contrast, the people of Kham and Amdo are tall, angular giants with broad shoulders and long heads. They wear jewelled daggers and wicked-looking knives slung on leather belts, for in temperament they are flamboyant, volatile and fierce, unlike the more easy-going and cheerful people of U-Tsang whom Heinrich Harrer described as "a happy little people, full of childish humour ... grateful for any opportunity to laugh".[2]

Over thousands of years, Tibetans have had to live at the dictates of their hostile geography and climate. As most of the high plateau is at the sort of altitude which rules out normal methods of cultivation – and therefore permanent habitation – almost half of her estimated six million people were nomadic herdsmen, breeders of huge herds of yaks, sheep, goats and ponies, roaming the steppe-lands in summer from one pasture to another within their tribal territories, and in winter, when much of the terrain was frozen and impassable, escaping from the ice and bitter winds of the high plateau to the more temperate foothills.[3] The nomads dressed in sheepskins and lived, guarded by fierce mastiffs, in vast black yak-hair tents which could accommodate as many as 200 people and protect them from even the most arctic temperatures.*

The rest of the people lived either in the south, in the area watered by the adolescent Brahmaputra (in Tibetan, the Yarlung Tsangpo) and its tributaries, or in the eastern province of Kham. They were farmers, herders or – a mixture of these two – agro-nomads. Their way of life was spartan, barely changing in the course of centuries; they lived in rectangular flat-roofed, stone and mud-brick houses in the river valleys between the high mountains, where, thanks to the altitude and the thinness of the air, the land supported only the hardiest of crops. The staples were highland barley (which grows even at a height of 15,000 feet) and a very few vegetables such as potatoes, radishes, cabbages and peas. The main item of food, tsampa, was a flour made from roasted barley; and all Tibetans ate it, either dry or mixed with liquid – milk or a brick tea imported from China – into a kind of dough to which were added butter and salt. This monotonous diet – anathema to the rice-eating Chinese of the plains – was occasionally supplemented by strips of dried yak meat, mutton or cheese, obtained from the nomads in exchange for grain.

Then there were the traders, who took goods to India, Nepal, Turkestan, Kashmir, Pakistan, Bhutan, Sikkim and China by yak or pony along the age-old caravan routes which criss-crossed Tibet in lieu of roads, exchanging Tibetan wool for cotton, manufactured goods and Chinese silks.

---

* The yak, a long-haired bison-type creature described by Paul Theroux as "like a cow on its way to the opera", is typically Tibetan and probably the most useful animal ever born. Able to live only at high altitudes, and subsisting solely on grasses and lichens, it is a powerful beast of burden and many other things besides. As well as being the main means of transport, the male yak was a source of meat, while the female dri gave milk, butter, cheese and yogurt. Its skin provided boots and saddlebags; its hair was the source not only of tents but of blankets, ropes and clothing; its bones were used for building houses, its backbone was crushed and mixed with gold dust for a female contraceptive; and its dung, when dried, was everywhere used for fuel and insulation.

Incredible though it may seem to modern secularized Westerners, almost one quarter of Tibetan males were celibate monks. In fact, the most significant thing about the Tibetans, that which set them apart from other peoples, was the way the Buddhist religion permeated their entire lives. It is impossible to exaggerate this factor, impossible to understand the Tibetans if its importance is not appreciated. Religion was not something reserved for one particular day of the week or for the ceremonies of birth, marriage and death; it was fundamental to their very existence, as necessary to them as breathing. By some standards it could be said that the people of Tibet had barely emerged from the Middle Ages, for they were superstitious, set great store by fortune-telling and horoscopes, and believed in a bewildering array of spirits and demons. They were unable to make even the smallest decision without consulting the omens. As Heinrich Harrer observed:

> The daily life of Tibetans is ordered by religious belief. Pious texts are constantly on their lips; prayer-wheels turn without ceasing; prayer-flags wave on the roofs of houses and the summits of the mountain passes; the rain, the wind, all the phenomena of nature, the lonely peaks of the snow-clad mountains, bear witness to the universal presence of the gods whose anger is manifested by the hailstorm and whose benevolence is displayed by the fruitfulness and fertility of the land. The life of the people is regulated by the divine will, whose interpreters the lamas are. Before anything is undertaken, they must test the omens. The gods must be unceasingly entreated, placated or thanked.[4]

What the Tibetans lacked in sophistication, they more than made up for in religious awareness. Every town or village throughout Tibet had its own religious centre, from remote caves and hermitages to monasteries the size of towns. The average village consisted of a monastery – the focal point of community life – with a few peasants' houses and a market clustering at its foot. Every house, large or small, had its own domestic altar stacked with devotional pictures and sacred objects. Even the nomads erected shrines, sometimes just in one corner of their tent, but often setting aside a complete tent for the purpose. All over the country were countless small monuments (Tibetan: chorten/Sanskrit: stupa) containing sacred relics associated with holy men of the past. And from every rooftop fluttered strings of prayer-flags.

Some monasteries, such as the famous "Big Three" of Lhasa – Drepung, Sera and Ganden – were huge university centres housing several thousand monks. It was these monks who preserved the artistic and literary heritage of the land, who absorbed the vast medical knowledge of their ancestors and were skilled in the understanding and use of herbs. Boys generally entered the monastery at the age of seven, but only the brightest were admitted to the higher learning; and only these would become teachers. The rest became builders, artists, craftsmen, cooks, housekeepers or servants. Though most were sincerely holy, many were there only because their parents had sent them:

> Many monks were only children offered up to the monastery in lieu of local taxes or debts to act as servants for the more important lamas. Other children were sent to the monastery as an act of devotion and others still because the monastery offered the only hope of education and advancement in a land which had no secular schools.[5]

Tibetan Buddhism is often mistakenly called Lama-ism, and many Westerners speak as though the terms "monk" and "lama" were interchangeable. But though it is true that some lamas are monks, not all monks are lamas, for it takes twenty to twenty-five years of study and meditation to qualify as a lama. The word lama means "guru" or spiritual teacher, and is applied to those who are authorized to transmit the Buddhist teachings (dharma in Sanskrit; chö in Tibetan) from one generation to the next. It is a distinctively Tibetan Buddhist belief that important lamas are reincarnated and can choose the manner of their rebirth.

The Mahayana Buddhist way of life which the Tibetans practise is based on unselfishness and compassion for others; and on the belief that whatever happens to us is the consequence of our own past actions; that through the practice of patience, tolerance, kindness and compassion, combined with a correct view of reality, we will achieve enlightenment and need no longer be reborn into a world of pain and suffering. There are those, revered as spiritually enlightened Tulkus (Incarnate Lamas) of whom the most outstanding are known as "bodhisattvas". These, following the example of the Buddha himself, have actually attained enlightenment, interrupting the cycle of rebirth, but have unselfishly chosen to return to earth in human form to help others along the path.

The outstanding example of a bodhisattva is the Dalai Lama, with whose status the West has no figure to compare. His secular authority is (or was, before the Fourteenth Dalai Lama went into exile) roughly similar to that of president and prime minister rolled into one. He has the political power of a king, but he is also a pope, the spiritual head of the Tibetan Buddhists wherever they may be found. The Dalai Lama, the present incarnation of Chenresig, the Buddha of compassion, the patron deity of Tibet, is not so much a god in the shape of a man as "a divine idea that has been realized in a human being to such an extent that it has become its living embodiment".[6]

In old Tibet religion held every place of honour. The deliberations of the National Assembly (consisting of fifty secular and monastic officials and presided over by a Council of four senior monks) were based on the Buddhist moral law as well as on civil law, and focused not only on the prosperity of Tibetans in this life but also and more importantly on their spiritual welfare in the next.[7] Politics and economics took a back seat.

In this strange theocracy administered from Lhasa, all land belonged to the state. Much of this had been granted in the form of hereditary manorial estates to aristocratic families or important monasteries. The government retained a few holdings for its own use, but most of the remaining arable land was leased in strips to small-holding peasants.[8] It was a mediaeval feudal society and whether he worked on government property, the monastic estates or on the lands held by the two hundred or so great aristocratic families, the Tibetan peasant was undeniably owned by his master. He had to render a certain amount of compulsory labour in exchange for holding his own bit of land; and give up the greater portion of his crops to his landlord, keeping only the barest minimum necessary for himself and his family. The landlord not only had the right to exact whatever rent he wished, but could also impose cruel punishments for failure to conform. Capital punishment and limb amputation were quite common in some regions. But it was not true, as the Chinese later claimed, that serfs who did not pay their taxes were routinely condemned to lose an ear or a hand. If it had been so, every Tibetan in the land would have been minus one or the other.

Life for the ordinary Tibetan was harsh, but it was not the unmitigated hell claimed by Chinese propaganda. Noone ever seems to have gone hungry: there was always enough surplus food stored in monasteries and government granaries to meet such emergencies as poor harvests and freak hailstorms. Everyone had warm, homespun clothes and adequate shelter. Generally speaking, the Tibetans were not aware of being downtrodden or exploited, and their enormous zest for life was undimmed by desire for a freedom they had never known. They celebrated festivals, danced, laughed, drank the local chang (barley beer), visited friends and relatives and regularly went on pilgrimage to well-known shrines and holy mountains.

"Tibetan society was far from perfect," Ugyan Norbu, a refugee belonging to a large nomad family in south-western Tibet, readily admits,

> but at the time we were very happy. With hindsight, of course, in the changed politics of the world, it was backward and left a lot to be desired. From a modern point of view we were isolated and ignorant. But we had simple tastes, and if our food and dress lacked variety, we didn't mind. We were attuned to it. I had no

schooling, but I remember hours of playing games with baby
yaks and goats; and fishing for tadpoles in the river. Our parents
told us how lucky we were to have so many good things in life,
especially our religion. Everything good was associated with our
religion. We may have been illiterate, but the monks used to
come to the village frequently and expound Buddhist principles.
Life was lived on a religious level.[9]

Despite the yawning divide in terms of money and material
possessions, there was so little resentment of the rich by the poor
that in all Tibet's history there had seldom been a popular
uprising. The fact that everyone believed in the Buddha's teaching encouraged at least a token generosity on the part of the rich
and an absence of envy on the part of the poor. By and large,
people were content with their lives. "Though in some ways the
situation resembled that of France before the Revolution, what
made the difference was the element of compassion", reflects
Tendzin Choegyal, youngest brother of the present Dalai Lama
and himself a recognized Incarnation*:

On some estates, it is true, the master might be a merciless slave-
driver, intent only on increasing his own wealth. But on the
whole, relations between people who worked the land and those
who owned it were something like that between father and son.
The peasants were looked on as people who had to be taken

---

* Technically it is more accurate to spell the name Tendzin with a "d" as
Tendzin Choegyal does, but today in English transliteration the "d" is
often omitted. His own story is worth a footnote. Some time after the
present Dalai Lama had been taken to Lhasa, his mother gave birth to a
son who died two years later. The lamas and astrologers advised that
rather than dispose of the child by water-burial (the established method
for young children), he should be embalmed, thus ensuring, they said,
that he would be born again in the same household. They also suggested
that a small identifying mark should be made somewhere on the child's
body. The next child born to the family was Tendzin Choegyal, who bore
the identifying mark, thus proving to everyone's satisfaction that the child
had been born again in a new body in order to embark on a new life.

care of, and the peasants looked towards the master as someone who took care of them. There was a tremendous human bond.[10]

Though some peasants undoubtedly resented the injustices of the system, there were many others who, despite the hardship of their life, had few complaints. Tenzin Atisha's family were serfs on an aristocratic estate in Western Tibet:

> We had a proper house with two bedrooms and a courtyard. My mother said they had never been without food or shelter. It was true that whenever Government officials came by, we had to provide them with horses, fodder, fuel and accommodation, and this was a great hardship. The worst thing for us was that if the crop failed we had to buy the seed for a new sowing, and the landlord charged us very high interest on it. But there was very little resentment. My parents used to tell me that this was our karma. We must have done bad things in our previous life and now were getting what we deserved. We accepted that – and I still accept it. In any case, it was not so hard for us as for villages further from Lhasa. In the east, some of the nobles and land-owners were a law unto themselves. There was nobody to check their excesses and they exploited the people.[11]

Over the centuries the monasteries had become very powerful. Owning one-third of the land, and exempt from taxation, they had amassed great wealth. Too much, claims Tendzin Choegyal:

> When Buddhism first came to Tibet, it was under royal patronage, it was a small growing thing that had to be carefully nurtured. But things changed, the ground became firm, and the whole system became a monster. Sometimes the monasteries which held too much land made too many demands on the peasants who worked on those lands, although technically speaking each monk was supposed to go and beg for his food. But many of them did exploit the people and fundamental change was needed.[12]

*   *   *

It was during the reign of the early kings of Central Tibet that Indian holy men gradually, beginning in the seventh century, brought Mahayana Buddhism to the country. It eventually replaced the old religion, Bon, though strongholds of the latter remain even today. Hugh Richardson, one of the foremost twentieth-century writers on Tibet, has speculated as to whether the once militaristic and ambitous Tibetans – between the seventh and ninth centuries they dominated an empire stretching from the Bay of Bengal in the south to China in the east – were tamed by Buddhism, or whether they had welcomed with relief a religion so eminently suited to their temperament and needs.[13] Whichever way it was, a formal peace treaty between China and Tibet in 821/2 established the border betwen the two countries and stipulated that "Tibetans shall be happy in Tibet and Chinese shall be happy in China." Thereafter the Tibetan rulers renounced militarism of every kind; and Buddhism slowly transformed society. The process was, however, gradual and not without setbacks. In the ninth century, the Tibetan king, Lang Darma, persecuted Buddhism almost into extinction, and little was heard of it for two centuries thereafter. It was the arrival of the great Indian teacher, Atisha, in Tibet, in 1042, which appears to have rekindled the embers of Buddhism. Within thirty years of his arrival, several important monasteries had been founded whose influence, wealth and power would reshape the course of Tibetan history.[14]

In the thirteenth century, Tibet fell under the sway of Genghis Khan and became part of the huge Mongol Empire which eventually embraced most of Asia and much of Europe besides. The lama leaders of Tibet offered a trade-off: spiritual counselling in exchange for patronage and protection against future aggressors. A few decades later, when Genghis's successor, Kublai Khan, conquered China and made it the centre of his Mongol Empire, he adopted Tibetan Buddhism as the official religion, continuing the special priest/patron relationship which suited both parties well and enabled the Tibetans to maintain both their non-militarist way of life and their separateness. Long before China regained its own independence from the Mongol Khans (in 1386), Tibet had broken its political ties with the Empire, but the unique priest/patron relationship with the Mongols endured.

It was Altan Khan in 1578, who bestowed the title of Dalai Lama ("Ocean of Wisdom", a Mongolian translation of the name "Gyatso") on Sonam Gyatso, abbot of Drepung, chief monastery of the Gelugpa sect which had come to predominate over its main rivals, the Kagyupa, in Tibet. And in 1642, the fifth Dalai Lama, with powerful Mongol support, united the whole of Central Tibet (U-Tsang) under his supreme spiritual and secular authority. To consolidate Gelugpa control, the "Great Fifth" gave his revered teacher, the abbot of Tashilhunpo monastery at Shigatse, the title of Panchen Lama ("Great Scholar"), recognizing him as having spiritual (but, it is important to note, *not* secular) powers equal to his own. These two, the Dalai and Panchen Lama, became henceforth the two most significant figures in Central Tibetan society, with the Dalai Lama predominating. The "Great Fifth" built the magnificent, thousand-roomed Potala Palace in Lhasa as his centre of government, and was revered as an incarnation of the all-merciful Chenresig, the saviour of mankind. The God-King had arrived on the scene.

When the Manchus became emperors of China in 1644, they too invited the Dalai Lama to be their spiritual guide in return for protecting his realm. It was the only formal tie between them. Between 1720 and 1792, the Manchus did in fact defend Tibet against incursions by both Mongols and Gurkhas; but although the emperors appointed two representatives (ambans) in the Tibetan capital of Lhasa, they did not incorporate Tibet into their empire. As the nineteenth century wore on and the increasingly degenerate Manchus were preoccupied with shoring up their own waning power, the ambans became little more than provincial officials, advisers to the Dalai Lama and his government.

The British, whose empire now embraced northern India and the Himalayan hill states, had come to understand this, since every agreement they reached with China over trading rights in Tibet came to nothing because the Tibetans simply ignored them. By the end of the nineteenth century, the British Political Officer in Sikkim had expressed the view that the Chinese had "no authority whatever" in Tibet and that China was "suzerain over Tibet only in name".[15] Lord Curzon, who became Viceroy of India in 1899, wrote to his Secretary of State in 1903 that, "We regard Chinese suzerainty over Tibet as a constitutional fiction – a political affectation which has only been maintained because of its convenience to both parties".[16] This was not entirely comforting to the British, who had no desire for a power-vacuum in Tibet which might be filled by Tsarist Russia.

For these were the years of what Kipling called "The Great Game", the high-risk power politics and gamesmanship through which Tsarist Russia and Victorian Britain competed for the mastery of (or at least a privileged foothold in) Central Asia.[17] Tibet's geographical position as the Roof of the World, a natural fortress overlooking India, China and Russia and keeping them apart, meant that no great power could ignore her strategic significance as a buffer state, or allow any rival to become influential there.

As the Tsar's armies advanced relentlessly across Central Asia towards British India, Britain became alarmed. Tibet was the key to victory in "The Great Game", yet Tibet remained stubbornly aloof. When intelligence sources indicated that the Russians might be seeking influence there, Britain decided to act. (No one seems to have considered the possibility that the Tibetans didn't want *any* foreigners interfering in their affairs). A British expeditionary force arrived in Tibet in 1904, in order to extract a trade treaty, by force if necesary. This army, led by Colonel Francis Younghusband, inflicted terrible carnage on a tiny Tibetan army armed with little more than matchlocks and prayer-wheels.[18] Yet, though the Tibetans were massacred in battle, the expedition was otherwise conducted in a relatively gentlemanly manner. There was no looting or raping; and above all, no disrespect shown to the Tibetan religion. (Ironically, the Chinese had for many years warned the Tibetans that the British would try to destroy their religion). After extracting an exclusive trade treaty from the Tibetan government in Lhasa, Colonel Younghusband thus becoming the first Western soldier to set foot in the Holy City, the British withdrew, leaving behind a small commercial mission in the town of Gyantse. The Thirteenth Dalai Lama, meanwhile, had removed himself to the safety of Mongolia.

The British venture upset China, where the Manchu government, rattled at having lost face, resolved on a new, aggressive "forward policy". In 1905, taking advantage of the Dalai Lama's absence – in fact they managed to delay his return from Mongolia until 1909 – the Imperial army advanced without warning into eastern Tibet, leaving a trail of slaughtered monks and lay Tibetans behind them. In 1910 they seized Lhasa. The Dalai Lama was again forced to leave Tibet, with the Chinese in hot pursuit and with a price on his head. But this time, significantly, he went to British India, taking refuge in the small Himalayan trading-town of Kalimpong. En route, he had written to British officials in India, "I now look to you for protection, and I trust that the relations between the British government and Tibet will be that of a father to his children."[19] It was a watershed in Tibetan history, and the friendship which blossomed between the Dalai Lama and Charles Bell, the Englishman assigned to look after him, sowed the seeds of what eventually became a real friendship between Britain and Tibet.

In Lhasa, the Chinese, plundering and pillaging, were meeting fierce opposition from the people. The city was saved by events in Beijing: the Chinese revolution led by Dr Sun Yat-sen in October 1911. With the Manchu dynasty overthrown, fighting broke out in the ranks of the Imperial army and quickly spread to the garrison in Lhasa. The Tibetans seized their chance to throw the army out of Lhasa and to regain many (though not all) of their lost territories beyond the Yangtse. When the Dalai Lama returned to Lhasa in triumph in 1913,

Sun Yat-sen's new republican government offered to renew his former priest/patron status. But the Dalai Lama had had enough. It was time for Tibet to break once and for all with the past and proclaim her independence, he replied, adding that China's colonialist hopes had faded, "like a rainbow in the summer sky".[20]

The Chinese did not want to let go; and the eastern borderlands continued to change hands like so many shuttlecocks. In 1913, at a conference at Simla in the Himalayan foothills, the British attempted to arbitrate between the Chinese and the Tibetans. Now *for the very first time* the Chinese were proclaiming that Tibet had been an integral part of China for 700 years; while the Tibetans produced an impressive amount of documentation to prove that it had not. Six months later, in 1914, after a bitter war of words, a compromise agreement was drafted, allowing China a nominal "suzerainty" – virtually a protectorate – over Tibet, while requiring her to respect and guarantee the latter's autonomy and refrain from interfering in her domestic affairs.

The Tibetans, though wary of the term "suzerainty", reluctantly concurred. But although the Chinese delegate initialled the agreement, his government refused to sign it. Tibet and Britain signed alone, China thus forfeiting in law any of the privileges she would have been granted. Among other things this meant – and in the light of what happened later it is important to spell it out – that China would *not* be recognized as "suzerain" over Tibet, nor be entitled ever again to claim Tibet as part of China.

Tibet was now independent. But did that independence have any foundation in law? Over forty years later, when Tibetan freedom and independence alike had been ground into the dust, the International Commission of Jurists stated that it had; that in 1912 there were "strong legal grounds for thinking that any form of legal subservience to China had vanished", and that Tibet had re-emerged "as a fully sovereign state, independent in fact and in law of Chinese control".[21]

Unwisely, the Tibetans subsided within the sheltering shield of their mountains and tried to keep the rest of the world at bay,

not understanding that times had changed and the world could
no longer be kept out. They would have been better advised to
step into the international marketplace and try to win sympathy
and friends among other nations. Had they joined the League of
Nations, for example, their subsequent history might have been
different.* Instead, they allowed their case to lapse, leaving it to
China to make whatever propaganda she pleased. It was a
decision which would cost them dear.

Only the fact that China was preoccupied by its own civil
wars enabled Tibet to enjoy thirty-eight years of independence.
After 1911, China disintegrated for a decade into a chaos of
battling warlords and local chieftains. Later, from the mid-
Twenties onwards, the fighting crystallized into all-out war
between the Kuomintang – the Nationalist government of
Chiang Kai-shek, who had succeeded Sun Yat-sen – and the
Communist guerrillas led by Mao Tse-tung.

In respect of Tibet, Nationalist China's aims were no less
imperialist than its predecessor's. The Lhasa government had
been unable to dislodge the Chinese permanently from the parts
of Kham and Amdo they had been hanging on to since 1905.
Chiang Kai-shek, though powerless to extend his writ any further within Tibet, continued to insist on China's right to rule the
whole country. The old Confucian view of China as the centre of
the universe, the hub of culture, the magnetic pole towards
which all peoples were irresistibly drawn and to which they
were fated to succumb, was deeply ingrained in the Chinese
psyche. It led China's leaders, whatever their political colour, to
assume that Tibet "had always been part of the Chinese fold
and was yearning to return to it".[22] More pragmatically, China,
whether imperialist, nationalist or communist needed Tibet (as,
to *their* lasting misfortune, it had needed Mongolia, Manchuria
and East Turkestan), to secure its uneasy western and northern
frontiers; and to gain control of the high Central Asian Plateau,

---

* They considered doing so, but backed off when told that the League
would not be able to defend them if the Chinese should decide to invade.

with easy access to India, the Middle East and European Russia. The stakes were enormously high. No matter who won the game in China, Tibet was certain to lose.

CHAPTER 2

A Breathing Space

The night will be long and dark.

Political Testament of the

THIRTEENTH DALAI LAMA

For the rest of his reign, the spectre of China would loom over the Thirteenth Dalai Lama (1895–1933). But that country's internal divisions gave him a breathing space in which to deal with his other pressing problem – to make Tibet strong and independent, by dragging her out of the Middle Ages and into the twentieth century.

He began with the monasteries, tackling corruption, discouraging the monks from involving themselves in secular affairs and increasing the number of lay officials in government. An intelligent and able man, a political realist, he overhauled the penal system, reformed and modernized the army, standardized taxation, abolished capital punishment and restricted the barbaric (and very un-Buddhist) cruelties with which even minor offences were liable to be punished. Education, hitherto reserved to the monks, was extended to the children of aristocrats and peasants alike, even if mainly on the level of the three Rs. He revived traditional Tibetan medicine and sent trained doctors to every part of the country. By introducing electricity, a mint for producing currency, postal services, telegraph and telephone systems, and even (in a country where even horse-drawn vehicles were a rarity and the only wheels were prayer-wheels), three cars,[1] he did his best to modernize Tibet.[2] He allowed the British to set up a garrison in Gyantse for the training of Tibetan soldiers,* enrolled Tibetan army officers into the British army in India, and even sent four Tibetan boys to Rugby School in England, hoping they would learn how to steer Tibet on a forward-looking course.

All this merely scratched the surface of the problem, for what was needed was fundamental social change. But even these relatively slight changes to the hallowed system were fiercely resisted by the more die-hard and ignorant government officials and ecclesiastics determined to hang on to their power. Says Tenzin Atisha:

> In 1924 when he opened a school in Gyantse with the help of the British, the nobles saw it as a threat to their power. They persuaded the abbots in the National Assembly that such foreign influence represented a danger to religion. The abbots then vetoed the proposal, and His Holiness could do nothing. In the same year, he tried to have a road built from the Chumbi Valley to Lhasa. But the aristocratic owners of asses and horses would have lost money if the road had been opened, so that plan too was defeated. Later on, there was a British teacher in Lhasa who taught his boys to play football. But there was a thunderstorm one day while the boys were playing and the abbots said the gods were angry. And that was that. If the religious institutions had had less power we might have had more progress.[3]

By 1931, the Dalai Lama's health was failing. In his last recorded statement, one year before his death in December 1933, he chilled Tibetan hearts with an apocalyptic warning. In Outer Mongolia, Bolshevik troops had killed the highest Incarnate Lama in the land, and 70,000 other monks; demolished Buddhist monasteries and conscripted the remaining

---

* The training was, of course, in English, with the odd result that the Tibetan army had such regimental music as "God Save the King" and "Auld Lang Syne".

monks into the Red Army. If Tibet refused to modernize, warned the Dalai Lama, she would undoubtedly suffer the same fate. The night, he warned, would be long and dark.

Had "the Great Thirteenth" lived, Tibet just might have had a chance. As it was, the loss of his strong reformist leadership at this dangerous time was catastrophic. The child into whom his consciousness was reincarnated was sought and found (in 1937) in the time-honoured way by a mixture of signs, dreams, oracles and incantations.* The new Dalai Lama, the Fourteenth, was Tenzin Gyatso, a three-year-old boy from a farming family in the village of Taktser, in Amdo, the north-eastern province ruled by a Chinese Muslim warlord, loosely controlled by Beijing.

Although the new Dalai Lama was welcomed with ecstatic adulation by the people, he was a mere infant and until he reached the age of eighteen, a Regent would run Tibet's affairs, in consultation with the Kashag (cabinet) and the National Assembly. It was (as it always had been) a recipe for disaster, as aristocrats and senior clerics schemed and plotted against each other in a shameless struggle for power. Old jealousies and feuds would be revived; corruption would return in force; and all of this, as the "Great Thirteenth" had foretold, could only weaken Tibet and lay her open to a land-hungry China.

Since their ejection from Lhasa in 1912, no Chinese official had been allowed to enter Tibet. But at the time of the Dalai Lama's death, a Chinese condolence mission was allowed to visit Lhasa. When the leader of this delegation returned home, he left behind two liaison officers with a wireless transmitter: a small but sure wedge in the door. Scenting danger, the Tibetans encouraged a young Tibetan-speaking British official, Hugh Richardson, to open a rival British Mission in Lhasa, with its

---

* For a detailed and enthralling account of these searches, see elsewhere, notably *My Land and My People*, the memoirs of the present Dalai Lama; or such publications as John Avedon's *In Exile from the Land of Snows* or Michael Harris Goodman's *The Last Dalai Lama* (see Bibliography).

own wireless transmitter and a willingness to keep a wary eye on the Chinese.

Tibet continued to underline its independence of China. She would take no part in Nationalist China's 1931 war with Japan; and when, after the Japanese bombing of Pearl Harbor, that war merged into World War Two, she clung to her neutrality, refusing to allow the Chinese to build a military supply road through south-west Tibet. (Nor would they let the USA use Tibet as a supply line.) The Chinese were belligerent about it, but the Tibetans would not budge. In 1942 the British Foreign Office observed somewhat ruefully that the Tibetans not only claimed to be, but actually were an independent people.

But Tibet's time was running out and the long shadow of history was creeping up on her. Had the British remained in India, the Chinese would most probably not have attacked. But when India gained independence on 15 August 1947, the British quit the subcontinent. Overnight, the British Mission in Lhasa became an Indian Mission, though, as Hugh Richardson points out, "the existing staff was retained in its entirety and the only obvious change was the change of flag".[4]*

Even at so late an hour, the present Dalai Lama believes that the day could have been saved, if the Tibetan government had shown any political sense. A gesture could easily have been made:

> When India got independence, our Tibetan government should have acted properly. In view of our centuries-old ties and for being ... a brother-country, we should have sent the biggest delegation to participate in the independence celebrations. If they thought I was too young, a twelve-year-old boy, then the Tibetan delegation should have been headed by the Regent. They should have met Mahatma Gandhi, Pandit Nehru, other

---

* In the following year, the Mission's surgeon was replaced by an Indian doctor, and an Indian officer joined Hugh Richardson for training.

Indian leaders and freedom fighters. This would at least have
registered our independent status as a nation.[5]

But the opportunity was lost, and soon there would be no more
time for gestures. After Japan's surrender in 1945, civil war had
broken out afresh in China between the Nationalists and
Communists, and it was now nearing its climax. Fearing trouble
from the Chinese officials in Lhasa (among whom were suspected Communist sympathizers), the Tibetans summarily
expelled the entire delegation, a crude panic measure interpreted by the Chinese, both Nationalist and Communist, as an
unforgivable insult. As it dawned on the Tibetans that the
Nationalists would be defeated, that the new China would be
Red, and that the Communists would be a more deadly threat to
their independence than ever the Nationalists had been, their
alarm grew, changing to panic as terrifying signs and portents
began to appear. A gilded dragon on the roof of Lhasa's
Jokhang temple dripped water day after day though the season
was dry and no rain had fallen. For weeks on end, a comet
blazed in the night sky, and as the previous confrontation with
China had been preceded by a similar phenomenon, many saw
in it an omen of war. Freak births among domestic animals were
reported; and when one night the capital of an ancient stone
pillar, erected at the foot of the Potala Palace to seal the peace
between China and Tibet, came crashing to the ground, a sense
of imminent doom was inescapable.

By 1949, advance units of the Chinese People's Liberation
Army (the PLA) had taken much of Amdo from the Nationalists
and were preparing to climb up to the mountainous gorges of
eastern Kham, which the Nationalists also nominally controlled.* By spring of that year, the entire mainland had been
"liberated"; and China's long civil war was over. Chiang Kai-
shek withdrew his demoralized forces to the island of Formosa

---

* Chinese warlords strove to absorb Kham into China from 1910
onwards, and had renamed the region from Kongpo to Dartsedo as
Sikang (Chinese for Western Kham).

and the Communists declared China a People's Republic. With the years of hardship and humiliation behind them, they were looking forward to a period of stability and the chance of a place in the sun.

Ever since their expulsion from Lhasa in 1912, the Chinese had hungered to return. Now, weary of fighting, they hoped to be able to strengthen their western border without bloodshed, relying on massive international indifference to whatever China might choose to do in its own backyard.

So the Chinese began testing the water, sending out radio bulletins which proclaimed Tibet to be an "integral part" of China and promised its imminent liberation from "the reactionary Dalai clique and foreign imperialists": its restoration to "the great motherland". Shuddering with apprehension, the Tibetans rushed to reorganize and strengthen their minuscule army. Realizing too late the folly of an isolationism which had allowed China to capture the world's attention and sympathy, they began at last to broadcast their own claims to independence on Radio Lhasa in Tibetan, Chinese, and English. Frantically, they dispatched delegations to put their case in the United States, Britain, India and Nepal, firing off telegrams beseeching the governments of those countries to receive them. "The replies were terribly disheartening", recalls the Dalai Lama:

> The British government expressed their deepest sympathy for the people of Tibet, and regretted that owing to Tibet's geographical position, since India had been granted independence, they could not offer help. The government of the United States replied in the same sense and declined to receive our delegation. The Indian government also made clear that they would not give us military help, and advised us not to offer any armed resistance.[6]*

---

* Although British officials on the spot had long seen that the Chinese claims to suzerainty over Tibet had no substance (e.g. see p. 35) the British government had always declined to contest the claims.

It was the negative response from Britain which distressed the Tibetans most. The British government, ignoring its moral and political commitments to Tibet, had lost no time in recognizing the new regime in Beijing.[7]

On 15 August 1950, while the people were still recovering from their fright over the comet, one of the worst earthquakes in history devastated southeastern Tibet. Whole mountains and valleys were displaced, and the Yarlung Tsangpo (Brahmaputra), diverted in its course by a huge landslide, inundated hundreds of villages, drowning thousands of people. For hours afterwards, "the sky glowed with an infernal red light, suffused with the pungent sense of sulphur".[8] "It was no ordinary earthquake", commented Robert Ford, the British radio operator employed by the Tibetan government in the border town of Chamdo. "It was as if the end of the world had come".*

In the face of this terrifying omen so near to the frontier with China, the Tibetans responded in their own unique way, as Heinrich Harrer reported:

> All the monks in Tibet were ordered to attend public services at which ... the Tibetan Bible was to be read aloud. New prayer-flags and prayer-wheels were set up everywhere. Rare and powerful amulets were brought out of old chests. Offerings were doubled and on all mountains incense fires burned, while the winds, turning the prayer-wheels, carried supplications to the protecting deities in all the corners of heaven. The people believed with rock-like faith that the power of religion would suffice to protect their independence.[9]

Watching them, Harrer reflected sadly that it would take more

---

* Ford was one of fewer than six Westerners in Tibet in 1950. Together they represented the "massive number of imperialists" accused by Radio Beijing of being the real rulers of Tibet. As Dawa Norbu (in *Red Star over Tibet*) commented later, the majority of Tibetans had never seen a white foreigner in their lives, and "imperialist" was a word they had never heard. "We wondered where in Tibet these oppressive Americans and British had been hiding".

than prayers to save them now: "I could not banish the thought that their touching faith would never move the golden gods. If no help came from outside, Tibet would soon be roughly awakened from its peaceful slumbers."[10]

India, like Britain, had quickly recognized the new Chinese regime, although she did try to point out that Tibetan autonomy was a fact. The Indian leader, Jawaharlal Nehru, did his best to defuse the gathering crisis, but the Chinese ignored his attempts. When Mao Tse-tung unblushingly assured Nehru that there was no question of using force against Tibet, India subsided into a relieved and convenient silence.

On 7 October 1950, 30,000 troops of the Chinese People's Liberation Army – the world's biggest and most successful fighting machine – attacked Tibet from six different directions at once. And Tibet had to face them alone.

CHAPTER 3

Divide and Rule, 1951

Power grows out of the barrel of a gun.

MAO TSE-TUNG

Blitzkrieg in the east of Tibet, a sharp, staccato little war in which the Tibetans were outnumbered ten to one. Though they fought bravely at river-crossings and mountain passes, how could an ill-organized, inexperienced army of fewer than 4,000 men armed with ancient flintlock rifles and a few howitzers withstand ten times their number of battle-hardened guerrillas equipped with the latest in automatic weaponry – and flushed with recent success?

The Lhasa cabinet, the Kashag, faction-ridden and corrupt, dithered this way and that. But they would not surrender without a struggle. "As soon as the Communists had come to power at the end of 1949", says Sonam Chophel Chada (then a twenty-nine-year-old District Commissioner in Kham), "the government sent a circular letter to all district officers on the eastern border, advising us to prepare for any emergency by raising our own armies".[1] With the enemy already at the gate, the Kashag appointed a new Governor-General for Kham and sent him to oversee the fighting in the east. The new man, Ngabo Ngawang Jigme, flamboyant and something of a play-boy, would become Tibet's most notorious "two-headed one" or collaborator. (It should, however, be remembered that most of these collaborators were acting under duress or out of fear, and did not cease to sympathize with the Tibetan cause.)

Sonam Chophel Chada, a relative of Ngabo's by marriage,

was persuaded by him to move to the provincial capital Chamdo as District Officer:

> I didn't want to go anywhere near Chamdo, but Ngabo told me not to worry, there would soon be peace, just as there always had been after China had attacked Tibetan territory. I believe Ngabo had already made up his mind to sue for peace, for even as the first reports of the Chinese invasion came in, he wrote to me again telling me not to worry, since peace would come shortly.[2]

Ngabo was not one of nature's heroes. Hearing that the PLA were only a day's march away from Chamdo, he abandoned his troops and fled. As one Tibetan remembers bitterly:

> The Chinese had only begun to cross the Drichu, [Upper Yangtse River, the de facto Sino-Tibetan border] and a Communist agent to run through the streets of Chamdo shouting, "The Chinese are coming! The Chinese are coming!" and Ngabo took off like a frightened rabbit.[3]

Before Ngabo cut his losses and ran, says Mr Chada:

> He called his servants together and told them to help themselves to his belongings, including his clothes. Then he set fire to all the government stores, destroying grain reserves, weapons, ammunition and clothes. He was censured later for doing that. They said he should have distributed those things to the Army.[4]

Fleeing westwards, Ngabo encountered an armed relief column which had been despatched weeks earlier from Lhasa.[5] To the soldiers' astonishment and dismay he ordered them to throw their weapons into a ravine and flee with him. Yet, reinforced, as they soon were to be, by about five hundred cavalry troops from the east, they could easily have retreated to the mountains and conducted a guerrilla campaign from there. With the mountains and rivers running from north to south, with neither supply lines nor motorable roads for armoured cars and tanks, guerrilla forces could have made life very difficult for Chinese troops already suffering from dizziness and snow-blindness because of the high altitude.

Many Tibetans believe they could have won such a campaign. Win or lose, Tibet would have shown the world that it was prepared to defend its independence to the death. But Ngabo was a frightened man with no stomach for confrontation, so he ordered his baffled troops to lay down their arms and surrender to a small force of Chinese. With that surrender on 20 October, military resistance came to an end.

Only then did the Tibetan government jerk out of its paralysis. When Ngabo's surrender was followed by an announcement on Radio Beijing that People's Army units had been ordered to advance into Tibet "to free three million Tibetans from imperialist oppression and to consolidate national defences on the western borders of China",[6] they were galvanized into doing what came most naturally to them in an emergency: they sent for the Oracles.* With one voice, the latter declared that the Dalai Lama, though still a minor of fifteen, should immediately be made head of state. And as this was what the people had been clamouring for, preparations were put in hand for the boy-monk's accession. It was clear that the Dalai Lama alone could give his country the leadership it needed so urgently. The boy protested at first, painfully aware of his own youth and inexperience. But in the end, "I could no longer refuse to take up my responsibilities. I had to shoulder them, put my boyhood behind me, and immediately prepare myself to lead my country, as well as I was able, against the vast power of Communist China."[7] He accepted, "with trepidation"; and despite the gravity of the situation, his accession in November was celebrated with great rejoicing throughout Tibet, as Heinrich Harrer told:

New prayer-flags fluttered over all the roofs and for a short time

---

* Deities who spoke through mediums – often monks – in trance.

the people forgot to think about the dismal future, and danced and sang and drank in a burst of old-time happiness. At no time had a new Dalai Lama inspired so much confidence and hope. The young king stood high above all cliques and intrigues and had already given many proofs of clear-sightedness and resolution. His inborn instinct would guide him in the choice of his advisers and protect him from the influence of scheming men.[8]

Alas, Harrer knew that it was all too late, that Tenzin Gyatso, the bright and idealistic young man, full of energy and promise, had come to the throne at the very moment when the gods had decided against him. "Had he been a few years older, his leadership might have altered the history of his country". For the young ruler was conscious of the injustices in Tibetan society, and was eager to bring about social change. "When I was a child of eleven or twelve", he told me,

My only playmates were the sweepers who cleaned the rooms of the Potala and the Norbulingka. They used to talk to me, tell me what was what, complain to me about various officials, about this or that lama. So I knew all about the exploitation – and I knew which officials were corrupt.[9]

"There was too much of a gap between rich and poor", says Tendzin Choegyal:

A gap in terms of money, possessions, education. Tibet had become decadent, it had contracted a form of cancer and was dying of it. It was like a frog which has been put in a cooking-pot with the water slowly being heated until the frog is boiled without even being aware of it. His Holiness wanted to make changes. But he was given no time.

The hopelessness of Tibet's case had become clear on the very day of the Chinese invasion, when the National Assembly had appealed to the United Nations for help, citing the invasion as "the grossest instance of the violation of the weak by the

strong". Briefly, the Chinese, who had already seized large
chunks of eastern Tibet and parts of the central area, paused to
see which way the wind would blow. They need not have feared.
Tibet was not a UN member state and was virtually unknown.
In the General Assembly, only El Salvador sponsored a move to
condemn Chinese aggression. The British, Tibet's oldest
friends, feebly claimed that the legal status of Tibet was "con-
fusing", and, together with the Indians, actually persuaded the
UN not to debate the issue, for fear of upsetting China! (Is it
possible that Britain was still playing the Great Game and
preferred to see China rather than the USSR expand its
influence in Asia?) India, which, out of fear for its own frontiers
and for the sake of peace in Asia, had already acknowledged
Tibet as part of China, expressed a forlorn but understandable
hope that the two countries would settle their grievances peacefully. The United States, heavily committed to a draining war in
Korea (and, in any case, hardly capable of moving an army over
the Himalayas), agreed that the question of Tibet should be
shelved. Evidently the "domino effect" – the theory which held
that political events in one place would trigger similar events in
another – on which American policy in South-East Asia was
based, held no relevance for Central Asia! "Our friends would
not even help us to present our plea for justice", the Dalai Lama
recalls sadly. "We felt abandoned to the hordes of the Chinese
Army".

By now the Chinese were deep into Tibet, and the National
Assembly urged the Dalai Lama to leave Lhasa in disguise, for
Yatung on the Indian border, from where he might plead his
country's cause. What could Tibet do but surrender? To continue fighting would guarantee a bloodbath. Flushed with victory, the Chinese could afford to appear generous. They called
on the Tibetan Government to send envoys to Beijing to negotiate a settlement.

The Dalai Lama, bereft of options, despatched Ngabo and a
five-man delegation to Beijing, with instructions to refer any
major decisions to the government in Lhasa. But, with Chinese
troops already occupying so much Tibetan territory, the

Tibetans held no bargaining chips and their proposals were simply ignored. It was made clear that the Chinese were there not to negotiate terms but to dictate them: the only choice presented to the Tibetans was between "peaceful liberation" and a continuation of the war. They were ordered to sign a package Agreement already drafted by the Chinese – or face further military action.

This "Seventeen Point Agreement on Measures for the Peaceful Liberation of Tibet" was an ambiguously worded document which appeared to offer a similar "two-systems" arrangement to that accepted for Hong Kong and proposed for Taiwan in the 1980s. The Chinese promised to leave Tibet's political system (and the authority of the Dalai Lama) intact, and to respect the religion, language and customs of the Tibetans. They gave a specific assurance that the monasteries would be protected and school education developed.

But the litany of guarantees was too vague for either comfort or credibility. Was it likely that a victorious Mao Tse-tung would tolerate the continued existence of an ideology so fundamentally different from his own? In any case, the general tenor of the Agreement was weighted against any kind of genuine autonomy for Tibet and was totally opposed to independence. It declared unequivocally that Tibet was a part of China and that henceforth all policy-making would be taken over by Beijing. Clause One stipulated: "The Tibetan people shall unite and drive out imperialist aggressive forces from Tibet. The Tibetan people shall return to the big family of the Motherland – the People's Republic of China". ("Reading this", the Dalai Lama wrote later, "we reflected bitterly that there had been no foreign forces whatever in Tibet since we drove out the last of the Chinese forces in 1912".) Other clauses required the "local government of Tibet" to give active assistance to the PLA forces entering the country; and to allow for the eventual absorption of the Tibetan army into the PLA.

The Tibetan delegates were insulted, abused and threatened with personal violence. When they protested they were not empowered to sign a treaty since they did not carry the Dalai

Lama's official seals, the Chinese simply produced facsimiles specially made in Beijing.

The Agreement was signed on 23 May, 1951. And at the moment that Tibet signed away its independence, the Dalai Lama and his government knew nothing about it. "We first came to know of it from a broadcast which Ngabo made on Beijing Radio", the Dalai Lama wrote:

> It was a terrible shock when we heard the terms ... far worse than anything we had imagined ... But we were helpless. Without friends, there was nothing we could do but acquiesce, submit to the Chinese dictates in spite of our strong opposition, and swallow our resentment. We could only hope that the Chinese would keep their side of this forced, one-sided bargain.[10]

The treaty was no more than a means to an end, a cynical sop thrown to the Cerberus of international opinion. Now they were in actual military possession of the country, the Chinese could disregard their paper promises and settle to the task of moulding Tibet to its role as a far-flung province of the People's Republic of China.

In October, with banners and framed posters of Mao Tse-tung and Chou En-lai held aloft, the first of twenty thousand crack Chinese troops marched into Lhasa to establish their military and administrative HQ. The people watched in dazed silence as the neatly uniformed Chinese entered the capital. They clapped, not in welcome, but following an ancient ritual for the driving away of evil spirits. Their enthusiasm was aroused only once, when the wind swept away a huge poster-portrait of Chairman Mao and ripped it to shreds.

*   *   *

With the arrival of the PLA in Lhasa, the oppression of the Tibetans began. Mao adopted the time-honoured policy of "divide and rule", following a pattern set by his Nationalist predecessors and the Muslim warlords. The eastern provinces of Kham and Amdo which contained most of the mineral wealth, were to be permanently separated from Tibet. Mao incorporated Amdo, despite its overwhelmingly Tibetan population, into the Chinese provinces of Qinghai and Gansu; and Eastern Kham into Yunnan and Sichuan. The remaining rump, U-Tsang and Western Kham, which alone would be recognized as Tibet, was itself divided into three separate regions: Central Tibet (U), based on Lhasa, under the control of the Dalai Lama – who now returned home; Southern Tibet (Tsang) round Shigatse, to be ruled by the Panchen Lama; and Western Kham surrounding Chamdo, the provincial capital. The Chinese explained that the guarantees offered by the treaty applied only to this rump. They had already begun to break faith. And if the Dalai Lama was unhappy, it was too bad.

In Kham, the first province to be "liberated", the Chinese had a built-in advantage. The attitude of the ferociously independent Khampa warrior-chiefs to rule by what they regarded as effete and arrogant aristocrats from Lhasa was about as enthusiastic as that of Plaid Cymru or the Scottish National Party to rule from London. Though most were loyal to the Dalai Lama and devout Buddhists, they detested the Lhasa officials who since the expulsion of the Chinese in 1912 had been treating them like dirt, while squeezing taxes out of them. Some Khampas openly expressed a preference for the Chinese. Alexandra David-Neel, the intrepid Frenchwoman who travelled through Tibet in 1927 disguised as a beggar-woman on pilgrimage, found that:

> Those tribes who have greeted the departure of the Chinese officials as meaning entire freedom for them do not feel in the least inclined to accept as governors men from Lhasa ... they strongly resent the appointment of governors or other dignitaries to rule over them, and especially their power to tax them and carry away to Lhasa the product of their levies.[11]

At the time of the Chinese invasion, some Khampa chiefs were actually conspiring to seize power from the Lhasa government. The Chinese, happy to exploit old grievances, persuaded some of the Khampas to collaborate with them, in exchange for vague utopian promises of tax-free independence. Even before the 1951 Agreement was signed, a military/political People's Liberation Committee was set up in Chamdo to administer the Kham area without reference to Lhasa. Consisting of Chinese soldiers and cadres (Communist officials), with a handful of Tibetan officials to give it respectability, it was headed by the flexible Ngabo who was now justifying Chinese interference in Tibetan affairs as "a scientific revolution".

The second regional centre, Shigatse, was the traditional home of the Panchen Lama, the Tashilhunpo monastery being his historic seat. Shigatse had a long tradition of hostility to Lhasa, stemming from a protracted religious civil war in the sixteenth and seventeenth centuries. Ever since the seventeenth century, the Dalai and Panchen Lamas had installed each other as spiritual leaders, with the older of the two becoming spiritual tutor to the younger. Yet rivalry and bad feeling had persisted, not between the Lamas themselves, but between their respective courts. The old Chinese emperors had skilfully manipulated these divisions; and, since the Revolution, so had both Nationalists and Communists. Because of a disagreement with the Thirteenth Dalai Lama, the previous Panchen had fled with his court to China, dying in Amdo – on the way home again – in 1937. A possible Incarnation had been found in 1944 near Xining, an important trading-centre on the frontiers of Amdo; and in 1949, in revenge for the expulsion of the Chinese Mission from Lhasa, the Nationalists recognized this boy as the Tenth Panchen Lama. (There were two other candidates in Tibet proper). A few weeks later, when the Communists captured Amdo from the Nationalists the boy fell into their hands, the perfect weapon against the Dalai Lama: a ready-to-hand alternative figurehead, a puppet under their control. To underline the fact, the eleven-year-old boy sent a telegram to Mao, inviting him to liberate Tibet.

In 1951, the reluctant Tibetan delegates in Beijing had been made to endorse this boy as the new Panchen Lama. A year later, disregarding the fact that the Panchen Lamas had never enjoyed political authority in Tibet, Mao returned the sixteen-year-old to Shigatse in triumph, with a large PLA escort and a status and power intended to match the Dalai Lama's own. He was given a governing body like that of Lhasa's Kashag; and his private army was enlarged and put on a formal footing. The puppet government thus installed in Shigatse was a clear warning to the Dalai Lama to watch his step.

The "peaceful liberation" of Lhasa would be trickier than that of Chamdo and Shigatse, but for this too the Chinese had a game-plan. While Tibet remained unpacified, there would be no talk of "class enemies" or of "democratic reforms" (Chinese-speak for redistribution of the land). Far from chasing the aristocrats and monk-officials from the corridors of power, the Chinese openly wooed them, assuring them that if they studied Communism and sent their children to Chinese school, they would be assured of ruling positions in the new society. They appointed twenty-nine leading Tibetans to the Chinese Buddhist Association, to teach them that the principal task of Buddhism was to serve the Chinese Communist Party and the Great Motherland.[12]

The ordinary people were put to work building roads, paid handsomely in silver dollars. Wangchen, a refugee now in India, remembers:

> In those days the Chinese were very polite, saying they'd come to liberate the Tibetans and improve their living conditions. When they'd done that, they would go home again. They built a hospital, to win over the people. Then they opened a Chinese school and paid the students in silver dollars. There was a song about silver dollars raining over the land of snows and the mountains of silver dollars being higher than the snow-capped peaks. But even then they were acting like imperialists, sending large numbers of Tibetan children for indoctrination to China, to train them as officials, so that one day it would be the Tibetans themselves who were seen to be oppressing the Tibetans.[13]

Inch by inch the Chinese tightened their control in Lhasa,

requisitioning or buying up houses (some aristocrats and
government officials were only too eager to sell, as indeed they
were eager to collaborate), setting up one military camp after
another as more and more soldiers were brought in. Wangchen
remembers the hundreds of tents going up and how the Chinese
killed yaks and cooked and ate the meat immediately, "so different from us Tibetans who dried the meat and stored it in
strips to eat throughout the year".

In accordance with the terms of the Agreement, the Dalai
Lama tried to ensure that the soldiers' demands for food,
accommodation and transport were met. Lack of roads and
airfields had prevented the invaders from bringing their own
supplies, and their constant demand for lodging and for 2,000
tons of barley to feed the troops caused havoc. By the spring of
1952 the fragile Tibetan economy was in ruins, inflation was
running at 500% and the city, for the first time in living
memory, had been brought to the edge of famine. Not only were
the regular state granaries emptied, but the emergency sur-
pluses held in reserve (in government and monastic store-
rooms) to safeguard this high-altitude people against crop
failure were almost exhausted too. These had taken years to
build up and would take years to replace. The price of food shot
sky-high, the cost of all but the most basic items soaring way
beyond the reach of most Tibetans.

The people began to show their derision and hatred for the
Chinese in the time-honoured way for averting evil:

> They began to clap and spit whenever they saw groups of
> Chinese soldiers. Children began to throw rocks and stones, and
> even monks would wind the loose folds of their gowns into a
> bunch and use it for whipping any soldiers that came near.[14]

A popular mass movement of dissent sprang up, known as the
Mimang Tsongdu or People's Party. On the whole it did little
more than put up posters telling the Chinese to go home; and
hand round anti-Chinese leaflets. It was neither well-organized
nor particularly effective, because the Tibetans had no previous

experience of underground activities to draw on. It irritated the Chinese, however – though not enough to persuade them to moderate their demands.

Truth to tell, the Chinese were disappointed. Filled with a romantic revolutionary idealism in which they saw themselves as the bringers-of-progress to an oppressed and backward people, they had naively expected the Tibetans to welcome them and their radical ideas. To them Tibet was a hardship posting, and they would have infinitely preferred to be somewhere else. Yet these barbarians, far from appreciating the sacrifice made on their behalf, sniggered at them and treated them as unwanted invaders. The soldiers were baffled by the mounting hostility in the streets. Believing they had genuinely tried to be friendly and co-operative, they were riled by the attitude of Lukhangwa, the Dalai Lama's lay prime minister, who had sensibly pointed out that the situation in Lhasa would improve only if some of the Chinese forces were removed. To Chinese complaints about the hostility, Lukhangwa drily replied, "If you hit a man on the head and break his skull, you can hardly expect him to be your friend".

Since both Lukhangwa and his co-prime minister, Lobsang Tashi, were staunch defenders of Tibetan independence and had always insisted that the invaders' demands were unreasonable, the Chinese hated them. When Mimang Tsongdu handed a six point memorandum to the occupying authorities, setting out the people's grievances and asking that Chinese troops be withdrawn from the city, the Chinese blamed the two Prime Ministers, accusing them of being "imperialist reactionaries" and of conspiring to prevent better relations between China and Tibet. They ordered the young Dalai Lama to dismiss them, assuring him that they would get the army to remove them if he would not. The young ruler caved in, to avoid bloodshed in the streets:

> I reasoned that if we continued to oppose the Chinese authorities, it could only lead us further along the vicious circle of repression and popular resentment. In the end, it was certain to

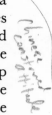

lead to outbreaks of physical violence. Yet violence was useless; we could not possibly get rid of the Chinese by violent means. They would always win, and our own unarmed and unorganized people would be the victims. Our only hope was to persuade the Chinese to fulfil the promises they had made in their agreement. Non-violence was the only course which might win us back a degree of freedom in the end, perhaps after years of patience. That meant co-operation whenever it was possible and passive resistance whenever it was not.[15]

Not only was the Dalai Lama not allowed to appoint successors to the deposed Prime Ministers but he was forced to imprison five of the people who had presented the petition to the Chinese. It was a bad time for him. Nevertheless, he had no intention of becoming a Chinese puppet – any more than he would continue bowing to the Tibetan old guard. He wanted to be his own man. In the period of uneasy truce which now ensued, he had the Kashag draw up a programme of educational reform and set about abolishing the principle of hereditary debt owed by a tenant to his landlord:

> This, I had gathered ... from my sweepers ... was the scourge of the peasant and rural community in Tibet. It meant that the debt owing to a landlord by his tenants, perhaps acquired as a result of successive bad harvests, could be transferred from one generation to the next. As a result, many families were not able to make a decent living for themselves, let alone hope one day to be free.[16]

But the Chinese blocked the proposals, fearing perhaps that they might unite the Tibetans and weaken the Chinese cause. The Dalai Lama's hands were tied. Deprived of the men he could trust, and with the Chinese infiltrating more and more of their own officials and bureaucrats into his government, the twenty-year-old god-king had never felt more alone.

CHAPTER 4

Act of Violence

A revolution is not a dinner party, the writing of an essay, the painting of a picture or the stitching of embroidery. It cannot be so refined, so leisurely and gentle, so temperate, kind, courteous, restrained, magnanimous. A revolution is an act of violence by which one class overthrows another.

MAO TSE-TUNG

The newly "liberated" people of Amdo and Eastern Kham had no love for the Chinese, at whose mercy they now lay.* In 1910, General Chao Erh-feng (called "Butcher Chao", from his penchant for wholesale massacre) had ravaged much of Kham, slaughtering monks and laymen alike; and in 1934, Mao's armies had passed through the easternmost borders of Kham on the Long March, seizing crops and livestock in support of a revolution which the Tibetans regarded as a purely Han Chinese affair.

The transformation of eastern Tibet into a Marxist state began slowly. "One day in 1952", says Lobsang Rinchok from Amdo,

a high Tibetan Lama came to our village from Beijing with some senior Chinese officials. I was ten years old at the time and I

---

* 92% of the present population of China belong to the Han race. 8% are of other nationalities, including Tibetans, Manchurians, Mongolians and Uighurs.

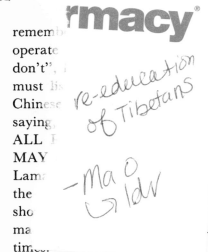

remem...   he Lama said we had to co-
operate...   be friends with them. "If you
don't", ... tears and you will suffer. You
must li... r great Chairman Mao". The
Chinese ... wall-poster in big gold letters
saying ... EME LEADER, PERFECT IN
ALL ... OF A GOLDEN COUNTRY.
MAY ... THOUSAND YEARS." The
Lam... Mao, and the Chinese official at
the ... the same. The Lama said we
sho ... actly. Then all the people were
ma ... Long Live Chairman Mao" three
times.

Such crude political re-education soon became a familiar part of everyday life, and at first it was conducted in a fairly low key. For the first year or so, the Chinese trod carefully, courting the landlords and chiefs, hinting at the possibility of independence if they would co-operate. Mao knew that Communism had few natural friends in Tibet and that a softly-softly approach was needed. He urged caution on the soldiers, restraint and courtesy towards their Tibetan "brothers" in order to win them over. Besides, until roads to Lhasa from China could be built, the PLA were unable to bring their tanks and armoured cars into Tibet; for the moment, therefore, it was imperative to maintain good relations with their hosts.

Far from exploiting the villagers, these PLA soldiers even brought their own meat and rice along with them. Never before had Chinese invaders behaved so well, and the Tibetans found it puzzling. Phuntsog Wangyal, son of a moderately prosperous peasant family in Kham and destined for the monastery, was six years old when the Chinese came to his village:

> I heard my parents talking in terrified whispers of sending us children away because the Chinese might capture us and take us to Beijing. They sent me to stay with an aunt in a nunnery up on a hill overlooking the valley.

From the hill one day I saw big white objects moving in the distance. I wondered if these were the Chinese. And I was right – they were horse-carts containing their arms and ammunition and so on, covered with a tent-like structure. Just like covered wagons. The soldiers accompanying the wagons were on foot.[2]

Naturally, at first he was very frightened:

But they were very nice, kind, smiling, giving us sweets. There were thousands of them in their army camp, but all of them in the beginning were extremely polite. They would knock on our door and ask permission to stay in our courtyard or wherever. Of course nobody dared refuse. Families would herd together in one room, while everywhere else was occupied by the Chinese soldiers. They would stay for a few days, then they would clean up and ask the lady of the house if anything was broken or missing. If you said you'd lost so much as a sweeping brush they'd give you silver dollars for a replacement.

Everyone was puzzled, because they had such a terrible reputation. They were disappointed, of course, that we didn't welcome them as liberators, but they had their own explanation of that. "We know why you're afraid", they said to us. "The KMT (Kuomintang/Nationalists) got at you with their lying propaganda. They told you that Communists are bad men who kill and rob. Well, you can see we're not like that at all".

Oh, they really had us fooled.[3]

To Aten, a nomad chief, the behaviour of the soldiers seemed irreproachable. They paid for the supplies they bought and "used threats only as a final resort". He tells how the soldiers went out of their way to help the villagers with the harvest and other rural chores, while their Commanding Officer cultivated the nomad chiefs:

He repeatedly stressed that the only thing the Communist

government wanted was to better the conditions of the ordinary man and remove the vices of the past. He made it clear that it was now the people who ruled and that we, the local leaders, were to play the most important role in the regeneration of our society.[4]

Everyone expected the occupation to be brief. As Aten said:

Chinese armies of many regimes had come and gone throughout our land. All of them had been brutal or tyrannical, yet thankfully indifferent, inefficient and corrupt. Of course, we expected some changes in the beginning, but then the Reds would settle down, reveal their all too human weaknesses and leave us alone.[5]

How could he have guessed that this time would be different? That this time the Chinese were there to stay?

They began deporting children as early as 1951. Villages throughout the east were forced to send at least fifty young boys and girls to China each year for education and indoctrination. Some of the older ones wanted to go, after seeing plays and films which painted a glowing picture of life in China. Others had to be forced. Deportation squads would arrive to seize the children, willing or unwilling, and load them into armoured trucks bound for China. Streets were sealed off by men with machine guns while a search was made for missing children. Frantic parents were told they had no right to interfere. Some of them managed to hide their children; some killed themselves when they could not.

Soon even babies were being taken from their mothers and sent to China. In Kham in 1954, for example, forty-eight infants under the age of one were seized by Chinese troops, to be taken to China "to learn about Communism" and to free their parents to work longer hours. Fifteen parents who protested were thrown into the river and left to drown. One other committed suicide.[6]

Lobsang Nyima from Kham went to a Chinese school in his province for two years:

One day the Chinese announced that everyone must go to China to study Communism. Two days later the teacher told us that since the Chinese Communist Party did not believe in the gods we must stop praying to them. I decided not to go to China. I tried to escape to India but I didn't know the way and was soon caught and taken back to school where they kept me chained by the legs.[7]

Tsewang Samten Ato, an eighteen-year-old Tulku (Incarnate Lama) from Kham, was one of many teenage youths sent to the Minorities Institutes in Beijing, Shanghai or Nanking, to learn about the infinite superiority of Chinese culture, and the "higher civilization" it represented:

Our monk's robes were taken away and we were dressed in Chinese coats and trousers. We were taken to a school where Chinese instructors spoke of Tibetan customs and the Buddhist religion with scorn. They tried to force us to give up our Buddhist beliefs ... When I contradicted the teachers and spoke up for Buddhism, I was given the punishment of standing for hours with a heavy log on my head in front of the whole class.[8]

Young Aten, though already married with children, was also sent to a Minorities Institute. In history classes he learned how China, with some help from Russia, had won the Second World War and saved the world from Nazi domination; how the rest of the world, apart from a distant country called America, had been liberated by the Chinese and had joyfully embraced Communism. Only people like the Tibetans were too backward and ignorant to do so. Listening to all this, most young Tibetans were stung into a sharp awareness of their own national identity. But they soon learned to keep their mouths shut when they heard of dissident students being shipped off to distant communes or labour camps.[9]

The roads to Lhasa, from Xining in the north and Chengdu in the east, were completed towards the end of 1954. (The Chengdu road, built at an average altitude of 13,000 feet, crossed fourteen mountain ranges and seven large rivers.) According to the Beijing press, the roads indicated "the concern and care which the Chinese Communist Party and Chairman Mao have for the Tibetan people".[10] But in fact the roads were built (often over prime farmland, and at great cost to human life) largely by Chinese and Tibetan political prisoners or Tibetan conscripts; and they were entirely for the benefit of the Chinese military machine. Only when the roads were built could the mountain be tamed and the Chinese bring in all the soldiers and weapons they needed to make the occupation of Tibet a reality. Only then could the Communist system be universally imposed.

With the coming of the new roads, Tibet's centuries-old trading habits disappeared. Itinerant traders were made to cut their ancient links with India, Sikkim, Nepal and Bhutan, in favour of an exclusive trade with China tightly controlled from Beijing.[11] The old casual Tibetan system of barter at outdoor markets was stopped, the markets were shut down and many Tibetans forced out of business.

If the road-building caused deep anguish among the Tibetan labourers, even worse were the compulsory extermination programmes which ordered them (on pain of beating) to kill insects, rats, birds and all kinds of vermin. These activities violated their profound belief in the sacredness of all sentient beings. Compassion is no empty word among them, it is a quality which illumines all of their relationships with the natural world. To them, animal life in all its forms was sacred. Vegetarianism, in this land of high altitudes and extremes of temperature, was never a real possibility for the Tibetans, who needed to eat the meat of yaks and sheep to survive. But they did not kill lightly. Whenever a herdsman found it necessary to slaughter for food, he would pray for forgiveness from the animals and perform rituals for their rebirth into a happier state of life. Phuntsog Wangyal recalls regular visits to a nomad camp with his parents: "They would kill a yak and cut it up and sell the meat to us. Before the killing, the nomads used to sit down and say prayers. Then they would put holy water on the nose or mouth of the yaks before killing them."[12] In old Tibet, there was even a law that forbade the taking of honey, since animals must not be deprived of their food. The government had banned a general building programme for fear of hurting the worms and insects. There were almost no exceptions to the rule of universal compassion:

> If at a picnic an ant crawls up one's clothes, it is gently picked up and set down. It is a catastrophe when a fly falls into a cup of tea. It must at all costs be saved from drowning as it may be the reincarnation of one's dead grandmother. In winter, they break the ice in the pools to save the fishes before they freeze to death, and in summer they rescue them before the pools dry up. These creatures are kept in pails or tins until they can be restored to their home waters. Meanwhile their rescuers have done something for the good of their own souls. The more life one can save the happier one is.[13]

"Slowly things began to change", remembers Phuntsog Wangyal:

> The first problem was the food. The Chinese had to eat and the villagers had to supply them with food. They paid for it, but inevitably prices went up, and soon the villagers couldn't afford to buy food for themselves. That was the beginning of big changes.

> The soldiers would move on and leave officials behind, political officers dressed in blue boiler suits. At first they seemed willing to work alongside the local leaders doing things in the old way. Then slowly they began criticizing everything, and inch by inch they changed everything. At that stage they were still keeping their hands off the monasteries because they knew how religious the people were. But there were re-education meetings in the villages all the time. Slowly you began to sense what they were going to do.

"Suddenly", says Rinchen Khando,

> it was the household servants who were being wooed. Overnight

the landlords had become bloodsuckers and exploiters and a few servants were threatened or bribed to support the Chinese accusations. Those who refused, who said their employers had been fair and humane were arrested on the spot. When the Chinese felt they had got rid of the opposition, they shifted their attention to the serfs – and to the criminal element. The pattern repeated itself there too. Only when they had arrested all those who stuck up for their employers, did they feel strong enough to move against the landowners and village chiefs. It was very clever.[14]

By 1954, many atrocities were being perpetrated by the Chinese in eastern Tibet, and the people were frustrated and angry. In the small Amdo town of Doi, for example, out of 500 alleged "serf-owners", 300 were shot in the back of the head in 1953 before a horrified crowd, who were warned that such would be their own fate if they opposed socialism.[15]

The liberators stood revealed as oppressors. "Anybody who opposed the Chinese was arrested", testified Dorje Tsering, a farmer from Amdo:

Innocent people were accused of various crimes and put in prison. Daily meetings took place where anybody and everybody was criticized for his previous behaviour. And at least ten people were shot every day after these meetings. Chinese soldiers were posted all around the village, and there was no way to run. Many people committed suicide. My own brother was one of them.[16]

Aten, the nomad, back from his education in China, was now a minor Party worker with a family to support. He was assigned to a team of investigators – army units, Party workers, specially recruited petty criminals and beggars – renamed "diligent ones" and "model citizens"[17] – who spread out through Kham and Amdo, making the head of each household declare the precise amount of his property and wealth. It was said to be for purposes of taxation, but the hidden aim, said Aten, was the confiscation of all lands, valuables and weapons: "Their smooth talk, their presents, and their silver dollars blinded us while they drew their noose around our necks. It was too late when we remembered the old adage: 'Beware of the sweet honey offered on the blade of a knife'." Through the unsuspecting zeal of Aten and his like, the Chinese were able to draw up lists of all the prominent people in any district – and the wealth they owned. "They were very thorough. They gave candies to little children while asking them questions about their parents and elders".[18]

It was when they were ordered to surrender their rifles that Khampa patience snapped. Throughout their history, the Khampas had had to defend themselves against the bandits who infested their lands and preyed on unwary travellers. "Tibet never had a police force", explains Tendzin Choegyal,

> You had to fend for yourself when you travelled. Sometimes the Khampa and Amdowa bandits rode out in groups of fifty or one hundred, just like cowboys in Westerns. When people made long journeys from Lhasa, they always travelled in caravan for protection. Bandits would never attack a large caravan, because they knew it would be armed. That doesn't mean that all the Khampas were aggressive or would kill unnecessarily. I've heard many of them say that on occasions when they could have wiped out a troop of bandits, they merely fired a few warning shots. But where there was real danger to life, then they would kill.[19]

The Khampa's rifle was a necessary extension of himself. Asking him to surrender it was like ordering him to commit suicide. Added to the onslaught on their religion, their possessions and their way of life, the confiscation of rifles was the last straw, the spark which exploded into rebellion.

The flash-point occurred at Lithang in south-east Kham. The Lithang monastery, one of Kham's largest and most famous, had been relatively undisturbed by the Chinese until 1955 when, with the new roads now complete, the first of many settlers had started arriving. (It was Mao's avowed intention to bring in four Chinese for every Tibetan). A few months later, the abbots of Lithang were ordered to carry out an inventory of the monastery's possessions. They refused; and called a meeting of village elders, urging them to take up arms against the Communists.

In February 1956 the men of Lithang made a surprise attack on the local Chinese army camp and managed to steal a supply of weapons before being driven off and forced to take refuge within the monastery. The Chinese laid siege to the monastery for sixty-four days, after which they made a proposal which was also a threat. If the monks and villagers surrendered, the Democratic Reforms would be postponed until the next Five Year Plan in 1958. If they did not, the Chinese would bomb them out. As the monks had never seen an aeroplane – an "Iron Bird" – let alone a bomb, they had really no idea what this threat meant. They rejected the Chinese proposal, and to their terror and consternation the monastery was bombed by Chinese jets. Over 6,000 people were inside at the time; and over 4,000 of them, men, women and children, were killed. It was the first step in a new Chinese scorched-earth policy which would end by uniting the whole Tibetan people against them.

Some of the survivors began the slow trek westwards to Lhasa, a three month journey over the high mountain passes. A savage revenge was taken on those who remained – in this and other villages. Thousands were arrested and executed. Thousands were driven out and huge numbers of Chinese settlers were brought in to replace them.

Hermits were dragged from the caves where they had lived for years to be interrogated and tortured. Not many of them survived. Shortly after seizing the monastery,

the Chinese brought two elderly lamas, former abbots, before the other captives. It was obvious, they announced, that the lamas were charlatans, for they had been unable to save the lives of their friends and relatives, and the time had come to see if they possessed the ability to save even their own lives. Boiling water was poured over the head of one of them, and then he was strangled; the other was stoned and then clubbed on the head

with an axe. During the next few weeks other lamas were cruci-
fied, incinerated, disembowelled or buried alive in full view of
horrified Tibetans. A few were simply locked up and left to
starve to death.[20]

"When the Chinese destroyed our monastery", remembers a
monk from Chamdo,

> they selected out for special treatment all the incarnate lamas,
> the teachers with high learning and the administrators. They
> accused us of all sorts of crimes which were not true. Then began
> a long period of torture when they tried to get information that
> we did not have. We were brutally beaten and forced to kneel on
> broken glass with our bare knees. Some who survived still cannot
> walk properly today because all the [tendons] of the muscles
> were cut. Then many were thrown on their backs on the ground
> and eight people, holding arms and legs, pulled them apart ...
> The torture also included tearing off the prisoner's ears and nose
> from his head. The Chinese would also poke their fingers into the
> prisoners' eyes and throw dirt into their mouths so that it would
> choke and suffocate them. And then they would laugh in our
> faces and say, "Now, where is your God? If he exists, call him".[21]

Throughout 1956 a rash of revolts erupted throughout Kham
– and soon, in Amdo too – as the pent-up resentment and misery
of the Tibetans boiled over into a boundless desire for revenge.
Ordinary people, weavers, tailors, farmers, laid aside their narrow clan loyalties to adopt a wider regional allegiance:

> Guerrillas, clad in shirts of parachute silk, wearing heavy charm
> boxes to protect them against bullets and living on dried meat
> and tsampa ... operated on horseback from mountain
> strongholds, ambushing – with flintlocks, swords and the occa-
> sional grenade – small PLA outposts and convoys coursing
> between the large, heavily garrisoned towns.[22]

As Chinese troops poured into eastern Tibet along the new
roads, Khampa horsemen, protected by their knowledge of the
wild, high-altitude terrain, wrought widespread destruction on

the enemy's life-line, ambushing supply columns and raiding military posts, damaging the prized new roads and bridges, cutting communications, seizing territory with ferocious bravura. When the Chinese recovered from the shock, they realized they had a new war on their hands, albeit an unequal one in which *they* could field armoured cars, tanks, automatic machine guns and military aircraft against the enemy's rifles, daggers and swords.

At first, many of the tribal chiefs, still trusting in Chinese promises of independence, refused to support the rebels. Then, one day, in the summer of 1956, the PLA Commander summoned 350 prominent Khampas and asked them to approve the introduction of the Democratic Reforms. After long discussion, a huge majority voted against the plan. Whereupon 210 leaders from Derge, the largest region in Kham, were summoned to Jomda Dzong, a fort lying to the north-east of Chamdo near the Yangtse River. Once the chiefs were all inside the fort, 5,000 Chinese troops surrounded it. The men were held prisoner for two weeks, until at last they agreed to authorize the Reforms. That night, however, all 210 of them broke out and escaped to the mountains to form a powerful guerrilla force.[23]

The Chinese now threw conciliation to the winds. Dropping all pretence of sweet reasonableness, they began to bulldoze through the Democratic Reforms. "One day", said Chime Namgyal from a family of agro-nomads in Kham, "they summoned us to a meeting and told us that the time for change had come. Marxism was going to be put into practice." They imposed new forms of taxation – on land, cattle, houses and monasteries; large estates were confiscated and local committees redistributed the land, forcing the peasants into collectives in which everything – land, herds, seeds, even the smallest implement – was held in common. The peasants now had to work where they were told, grow what they were told to grow; and they were paid in grain, according to the amount of work done. Most of what they grew had to be sold to the state. (Even the nomads had to sell their wool, butter, milk and yak hides direct to the Chinese). Only officials and Communist sympathizers would get the monthly maximum food allowance of fifteen kilogrammes of grain, whilst the most hard-working ordinary Tibetans could hope for no more than twelve kilogrammes. The people were told to eat less for the sake of the Motherland's economy – and they were ordered to stop wasting precious butter on butter-lamps for their religious rituals. When noone obeyed, recalls Chime Namgyal, "Chinese cadres came to our village to enforce the ruling. They banned the lamps completely and ordered them to be turned upside down." As far as the Chinese were concerned, Tibetan "barbarism" and "green brains" could all be blamed on a thousand years of superstition as exemplified by the butter-lamps.

Ordering all the produce to be turned over to the state, says Phuntsog Wangyal, was a very efficient way of controlling the people: "When you sell to the State, they give you a piece of paper saying that you have so much money in the bank. But the money is useless because you can't ever claim it." Wangyal had spent three years studying in Lhasa, but in 1955 had returned to Kham, to find that the Chinese had already forced the villagers into violent "class struggle":

I reached home late at night by truck. It was very dark, no moon. My mother came with a light. I could only see her face, but straight away I realized that though she was still a young woman she had aged terribly in the three years I had been away. She looked old and very pale. As soon as I came to the house she whispered to me to keep quiet. Then a neighbour came and he too signalled me to be silent. I realized that people there were no longer free and that they were very frightened.

Next day, on my way up to the monastery, I saw all the people working in the fields with red flags everywhere. Collectivization was well-advanced. You could sense the terrible fear without quite understanding it.

He pursued his monastic studies for three more years, and all the time things got worse:

The food that the monks ate had to come from the villagers. The monasteries didn't produce anything, the villagers had always provided for their material needs, while the monks and nuns provided the spiritual care, the prayers and so on. Now the Chinese had cut that system at its roots. They did not actually say that noone was to supply food to the monasteries, but they rationed all the villagers' food. They could not keep what surplus they had, because it had to be sold to the State. If my mother wanted to give me some food, she had to do so out of her own inadequate rations, because there was no ration for me. Food became very scarce and hard to find.

Before long the people were reduced by hunger to eating wild herbs, chopped-up leaves and the husks of wheat. Aten and some of his friends questioned a Chinese official explaining the new system:

We asked if there were to be any consideration for those who were either too young or too old to perform manual labour. He declared that all those below sixty years of age were capable of manual labour, while those beyond seventy could still be used to scare off birds in the fields.[24]

"How can you expect your labourers to work hard when they do not get enough to eat?" persisted Aten:

According to the system you have just explained, there will simply not be enough for a man to fill his stomach. In the case of old people, cripples, the sick and children, they will have to suffer even worse than the animals we kept before. In our land we may have worked our beasts during the day, but we let them eat as much as possible afterwards.

He [the instructor] replied: "Everyone is capable of working. The crippled can stitch, the blind spin wool. Even children can perform simple tasks. Anyone who expects food without working is a parasite and an enemy of the people."

By a combination of threats, bribery and blackmail, the Chinese acquired a network of spies and informers. It was part of the plan that nobody should feel safe, nobody should dare trust anybody else. Everyone feared for his or her own security and that of his family. Children were encouraged to report parents who did not conform to the "wise and correct leadership" of Chairman Mao.[25] Parents were subjected to abuse and torture, and many of them committed suicide.

It was dangerous merely to be able to read and write (a skill which many simple farmers had been taught by the local monks), since literacy branded a person as belonging to the "oppressing classes". Such people had to be eliminated. While filming in Tibet for Channel 4 TV, Vanya Kewley spoke to Thondup, the son of a simple peasant farmer, who at the age of nine had been forced to watch as soldiers marched his father, to the village square, scarcely able to walk from the beatings he had received. Here, after trying to extract a "confession" from him, they made him kneel with his hands tied behind him, and shot him at point-blank range in the back of the head – in front of Thondup, his brother and the whole village. And then, with the devastating barbarity for which the police and the PLA are still notorious, they asked the family for the price of the bullet, before allowing them to take the body for burial.[26]

Every evening, after a hard day's work in the fields, there were compulsory political lectures. Through their spy network, the Chinese now had the necessary information about everybody's class origins. They divided the people into classes: capitalists (a category which mystified the unworldly and apolitical Tibetans); landlords, aristocrats and high lamas; tradesmen and craftsmen; poorer peasants and nomads; serfs, agricultural workers and beggars. The first two groups were "enemies of the people". The lower categories were to be given positions of importance and made to destroy the higher groups. "Hatred is a great social leveller", Premier Chou En-lai had once advised; and the stirring up of hatred had become the most potent weapon in the Communists' armoury. "The enemy will not perish of himself", wrote Mao. "There must be a struggle between the peasant and landlord classes if you want your freedom ... To win a fight you have to fight."

The "struggle session" – known as "thamzing" – was the inhuman and sadistic method used by the Communist Chinese to break old loyalties and smash existing social patterns. It added a whole new dimension to the phrase "Chinese torture". In Tibet (and, in fact, throughout mainland China[27]) it was used to force people to denounce anybody of any authority: village headmen as well as lamas and landowners. The scenario for these "struggle sessions" comes straight off the pages of Kafka. The victims were brought bound or in chains to a public meeting place where they were accused of being exploiters and counter-revolutionaries, before being humiliated, beaten, tortured and – frequently – killed. The Chinese went from house to house, forcing everyone, even children, to attend the thamzing. Those who resisted were liable to be the next victims.

At the meeting place, hatred was skilfully whipped into a froth. A group of former serfs would be seated on the stage, and before the prisoner was brought in would have related in detail their sufferings (whether real or fictitious) at the hands of their old oppressors. The cadre in charge would rouse the audience to fever pitch, shouting slogans, playing on old animosities, activating new fears. His whole purpose was to teach the masses the techniques of the class war, to unleash their supposed resentment of former leaders. Thus he would summon members of the audience at random to the platform and make them (under pain of immediate retribution) add their voices to the crescendo of condemnation. "In this way", points out Fredrick Hyde-Chambers, poignantly describing a thamzing in his novel, *Lama*:

the masses themselves make the traumatic break with the old way of life, old loyalties ... The danger, as Mao pointed out, was that if the people were just passive onlookers, uninvolved, they might begin to sympathize with the person being punished. The cadre had yet to attend a thamzing in Tibet where the people reacted spontaneously. He never ceased to be amazed at their incredible, stubborn faithfulness to their religion. In such cases terror was the only way.[28]

Frequently, the families of the victims were forced to watch and applaud while their loved ones were hanged; and those who wept were beaten for their lack of revolutionary zeal. "Among other humiliations", says Lobsang Rinchok, "senior lamas and landlords were made to drink their own urine and eat their own excreta in public. It was done to the abbot of Labrang and to two famous freedom fighters, in front of twenty to thirty thousand people."[29]

When he speaks of thamzings, Aten is passionate, recalling how every shred of dignity was stripped from the victim, every humiliation heaped upon him by his own people, his own unfortunate children and loved ones:

> Often the accused was beaten, spat and urinated upon. Every act of degradation was heaped upon him and it killed him in more ways than one. When a man was through in a thamzing session, no one ever spoke of him again. He was no martyr for the people, because the people had killed him. His death lay in the hands of those who should have honoured and remembered him; but in their guilt, the people tried to forget him and the shameful part they had played in his degradation.[30]

After one of these brutal and brutalizing sessions, a Chinese general told the assembly that they were now fully liberated, and asked for their comments. Aten tells the story:

> At first no one spoke. Then an old man got up. "My name is Shanam Ma", he declared, "I am, as you can see, an old man and a poor one. There are a few things that have to be said here today, and it is best that I say them. Since I am poor, I have nothing to lose; since I am old, death will come for me soon anyway."
>
> "I have this to say to you Chinese: Ever since you entered our

land, we have been barely able to tolerate your behaviour. Now you try to force some new-fangled 'Democratic Reforms' on us, that all of us think are ridiculous and nothing but a mule-load of conceit. What do you mean you will give us land, when all the land you can see around has been ours since the beginning of time. Our ancestors gave it to us, and you cannot give it to us a second time. If anyone is oppressing us, it is you. Who has given you the right to force your way into our country and foist your irrational ideas on us? We are Tibetans, you are Chinese. Go away to your homes, go back to your own people. We have no need of you here."[31]

Another man, Apei Tsultrim, rose to support the old man. The whole assembly roared its approval. The following night, the General declared that the two men were "serf-owners" and ordered them to be arrested. They underwent thamzing and were severely beaten in public. What happened to them after that is unknown.

CHAPTER 5

Small Candle in a Storm

The building of a socialist society is the common object of all nationalities within our country. Only socialism can guarantee to each and every nationality a high degree of economic and cultural development. Our state has a duty to help all nationalities within the country to take this path step by step to happiness.

LIU SHAO-QI, Report on the Draft Constitution for the People's Republic of China, September 1954

Lhasa might have been on another planet for all it knew of the eastern nightmare. The Chinese imposed a strict black-out on news from the east, and so for some months – until the refugees began pouring in – the Dalai Lama remained in ignorance. In Lhasa he had his own problems, walking a tightrope with the Chinese: refusing to become the puppet leader they wanted yet trying to avoid confrontation. Matters had improved since the sacking of the two Prime Ministers and the resistance leaders' arrest, but the Chinese were still chafing at the open hostility shown them in Lhasa. They had refrained from introducing Democratic Reforms or interfering with the monasteries, yet their restraint had won them few friends among Lhasa's prominent citizens. And the ordinary people showed no gratitude at all for being liberated.

Their solution was to invite the Dalai Lama to China. After all, at twenty years old, he was still an impressionable boy, known to be fascinated by mechanical things. He would find plenty of modern marvels in Beijing and would return home filled with enthusiasm.

So in 1954, when the new Chinese constitution was being inaugurated in Beijing, the Dalai Lama was deputed to lead the Tibetan delegation. The Lhasans were appalled, convinced of a Chinese plot to kidnap and/or murder their leader and leave them defenceless. What could they do but resort to prayer? "We set off in four groups to the holy mountains around the city, to pray for his welfare and speedy return", says Dolma Chozom, then a young Lhasa housewife. Grief and lamentation followed the royal party as it left Lhasa in July, the mourners feeling quite certain they would never see their leader again.

The Panchen Lama had joined the party, since the Chinese missed no opportunity of presenting him as the Dalai's equal. The Lhasans made no secret of their contempt. Chinese posters announcing his arrival in Lhasa were smeared with dung, and ribald songs were sung about him in the streets. The Tibetan officials in the delegation refused to treat him as anything other than a senior ecclesiastic, despite Chinese attempts to invest him with political status.

Since the roads leading into China from Lhasa were not yet quite finished, the journey was beset with danger from floods and landslides; and the delegates spent much of their time knee-deep in mud. Once inside China, however, the young Dalai Lama enjoyed the informality with which he was treated, a refreshing change from the elaborate rituals of Lhasa. Meeting veterans of the Long March, he was pleased to find them open and friendly: "I developed considerable respect for them and admired their determination and self-sacrifice. They had faced so many difficulties and hardships, they'd really suffered to bring happiness to the Chinese people."[1] He was distinctly charmed by Chairman Mao, "a simple man of dignity and authority ... a strong magnetic force". The Dalai Lama admired Marxism, at least in its original form, as a system based on equality and justice for everyone and free of narrow nationalisms. At this point he still believed it could coexist with Buddhism:

The main concern of the original Marxists was a concern for working-class people ... the majority ... the less privileged ones. Insofar as they were seriously concerned about social justice, they were right. Their economic theory was mainly concerned with distributing rather than making money, whereas the capitalists put the emphasis on making money without caring too much how fairly it was distributed. In Buddhism, especially in its Mahayana form, we are trained to put others first – before oneself. That is similar to the basic ideals of socialism.[2]

He and Mao appeared to like each other. Mao actually conceded that Buddhism was good because the Buddha had wanted to improve the living conditions of the people. Then he spoiled the effect by thumping the table and shouting: "But of course religion is poison ... It undermines the race and retards the progress of the country".[3] (Religion had been officially endorsed by the new Chinese constitution, but all religious activities were to be closely controlled by state-run organizations).

Mao insisted that the Chinese were in Tibet only to help develop the country, and promised to withdraw when the Tibetans could go it alone. The Dalai Lama agreed that his country was backward, but begged to keep the Tibetan flag at least. Mao conceded that the flag was important. "He was very understanding", said His Holiness:

We once sat facing each other at a long table with other Chinese and Tibetan dignitaries. At one corner were two Chinese Generals. Mao pointed at them and said, "These men have been sent to Tibet in order to help you and serve you. If at any time their behaviour offends you, let me know and I will remove them."[4]

But Mao was grieved by the lack of gratitude shown by the Tibetans so far. His guest explained that change could not be rushed and that under pressure the Tibetans were more likely to explode than co-operate. Mao then told of his plan to set up a

Preparatory Committee for the Autonomous Region of Tibet (PCART), whose job it would be to prepare Tibet for gradual absorption (at her own pace) into the Chinese People's Republic. Though this would involve a further erosion of his own authority, the Dalai Lama welcomed the prospect of a working partnership with the Chinese.

Much of what he saw in China he genuinely admired, but he was not the naive pushover the Chinese had counted on. He was clear-sighted enough to keep a sense of perspective. For one thing, he began to see what lay behind the Chinese urge to control Tibet, a land known to them as Xizang, the "treasure house of the West", whose vast, unpopulated space and unexploited mineral, forest and animal reserves made it seem like El Dorado. And though at first dazzled by the efficiency with which People's China was being run, the human cost of that rigid, unbending control had not escaped him:

> Progress had cost the people all their individuality. They were becoming a mere homogeneous mass of humanity. Everywhere I went I found them strictly organized, disciplined and controlled, so that they not only all dressed the same but all spoke and behaved the same and, I believe, all thought the same.[5]

Though trembling at the thought of his own people being brought to this pass, he could not believe it possible, for "religion, humour and individuality are the breath of life to Tibetans and no Tibetan would willingly exchange these qualities for mere material progress, even if the exchange did not involve subjection to an alien race."

*   *   *

When, to his people's unbounded relief, the Dalai Lama returned home safely a year later, the face of his country had already changed. Two of the new arterial highways from China to Lhasa had been completed, and the city was choked with military trucks and cars, and the noise and pollution that came with them.

The PCART – which signalled Tibet's official carve-up and limited the Dalai Lama's writ to a mere "local government" – was duly inaugurated with banquets and parades in August 1956. Dawa Norbu from Sakya remembers it as "a grand festive day. An enormous portrait of Mao Tse-tung was set up, flanked by portraits of the Dalai and Panchen Lamas. Multi-coloured posters in Tibetan adorned all the walls. Long speeches were made, and all the children and the officials applauded dutifully."[6] The Committee was to consist of fifty-one members, all but five of them Tibetans. The Dalai Lama was to be Chairman, with the Panchen Lama – "Mao's Panchen", the Tibetans called him[7] – as Vice-Chairman, and Ngabo Ngawang Jigme as General Secretary. It could be, the Dalai Lama, suggested, "the last hope for the peaceful evolution of our country". But his hope was soon shattered:

> I had not made allowances for one essential fact. Twenty of the members, although they *were* Tibetans, were representing the Chamdo Liberation Committee and the Committee set up in the Panchen Lama's western district. These were both purely Chinese creations. Their representatives owed their positions mainly to Chinese support, and in return they had to support any Chinese proposition ... With this solid block of controlled votes, in addition to those of the five Chinese members, the Committee was powerless – a mere facade of Tibetan representation behind which all the effective power was exercised by the Chinese ... We could never make any major changes. Although I was nominally Chairman, there was nothing much I could do.[8]

Not only had two-thirds of old Tibet been swallowed up by China, but two-thirds of what remained was in the hands of Chinese puppets. In any case, all real power lay only with the Committee of the Chinese Communist Party in Tibet, and on that august body there were *no* Tibetan representatives at all. The set-up clearly breached Article Fourteen of the Seventeen Point Agreement in which Beijing had guaranteed not to alter the political system of Tibet nor to change the status, functions or powers of the Dalai Lama.

When the people realized their humiliation, they exploded in anger. Public meetings were held and protests sent to the Chinese authorities. The Chinese made the Kashag ban such meetings, a ban reluctantly signed by the Dalai Lama who knew that the Tibetans would ignore it anyway. Indeed the people were past caring about consequences, many of them believing that violence was the only option left. Posters sprouted all over Lhasa, mainly of the "CHINESE GO HOME" variety, though one compared Tibet to a small candle in a violent storm and others promised to "shed our blood and sacrifice our lives to oppose the Communists".[9]

Adding fuel to the flames, news of the terrible massacres in the east began filtering through. Passing through Kham on his way back from China in 1955, the Dalai Lama had sensed that something was badly wrong. There was a "boiling resentment" in the air which filled him with foreboding: "Among the Tibetans, I saw mounting bitterness and hatred of the Chinese; and among the Chinese ... the mounting ruthlessness and resolution which is born of fear and lack of understanding."

That was before the revolt had begun. When news reached Lhasa of the guerrilla risings in Kham and Amdo; the bombing of Lithang; the torture and execution of women and children whose fathers and husbands had joined the resistance movement; the sexual abuse of monks and nuns, the Dalai Lama wept. "I could not believe that human beings were capable of such cruelty to each other". The possibility of confrontation without end terrified him: "In those impregnable mountains, the guerrillas could hold out for years. The Chinese would never be able to dislodge them. Yet they would never be able to defeat the Chinese army. And however long it went on, it would be the Tibetan people, especially the women and the children, who would suffer."[10] Recalling Mao's promise to deal with any officials whose zeal had outstripped their humanity, he wrote to him:

I tried to explain the situation to him and how the officials were causing such suffering. I wrote both officially and unofficially.

But he did not reply – and the behaviour of the officials became even more aggressive. Then at last I realized what a huge gap there was between Mao's words and his actions. His promises were like a rainbow, beautiful but without substance.[11]

The Dalai Lama was not alone in protesting, he told me many years later (May 1990):

One Chinese general who protested that there were too many Chinese soldiers in Tibet was sent back to China in disgrace. Then there was another general who told Chairman Mao that so many Tibetans had been arrested there was not enough prison accommodation for them. Mao replied: "Don't worry. Even if you have to imprison the whole population, we'll find enough prisons."[12]

In a state of profound depression, the Dalai Lama was allowed to visit India (the Panchen Lama went too) for what might in happier circumstances have been a joyful occasion: the Buddha Jayanti, the 2500th anniversary of Buddha's birth. The three ministers who accompanied him told a group of Tibetan exiles in India that Tibet was like an egg placed under the raised foot of an elephant. The survival of the egg depended on whether the Chinese foot descended. The Dalai Lama seemed to share their pessimism. Discarding the set-piece speeches given him by the Chinese, he spoke publicly about large nations which swallowed up tiny, independent ones; and begged the world to take note.

Despondently, he told his host, Mr Nehru, that he might not return to Tibet, since he could do no more good there:

I said I was forced to believe that the Chinese really meant to destroy our religion and customs for ever ... All my peaceful efforts had so far been failures. But from India, I could at least tell people all over the world what was happening in Tibet and try to mobilize their moral support for us, and so perhaps bring a change in China's ruthless policy.[13]

But Nehru still dreamed of peaceful coexistence with China*
and, nervous of the implications of giving the Dalai Lama political asylum in India, he forcefully urged him to return. In New
Delhi, Nehru and the Dalai Lama both had talks with the
Chinese Prime Minister, Chou En-Lai. Chou, in conciliatory
mood, apologized for the excessive zeal of the Chinese soldiers in
Tibet and promised to do what he could about the situation –
provided the Dalai Lama returned home. The Chinese, he said
reassuringly, did not intend to foist unwelcome reforms on the
Tibetans, and he agreed that the PLA troops should gradually
be removed from Tibet. He did, however, warn that any serious
uprising would be violently put down.

With a heavy heart, the Dalai Lama returned to Tibet in
February 1957. In Lhasa itself the Chinese had been making
concessions. (Chou En-lai was being as good as his word.) Work
on the building of new barracks and a hydro-electric plant had
been discontinued. Mao had announced that since Tibet was
not yet ready for Democratic Reforms, he would postpone them
for at least five years. Some of the soldiers and most of the
political cadres whose job it was to enforce the reforms were
removed from Lhasa (although only in order to be sent east to
help discipline the rebels). Chinese newspapers positively wal-
lowed in self-criticism, deploring the excesses of "Great Han-
ism" and Chinese chauvinism.

But there was open warfare in Kham and Amdo, where the
Chinese had fourteen crack divisions but where the freedom
fighters too, under the command of Gompo Tashi Andrugtsang,
a Khampa trader living in Lhasa, were growing in strength and
daring. Encouraged by the Khampas' early successes, in
December 1956 Gompo Tashi wrote to various leaders
throughout Kham, urging them to sink their differences and
unite:

---

* India and China had signed an Agreement in April 1954 based on the
Panch Shila – Five Principles of Coexistence – through which peace in
Asia was to be assured.

The time has now come to muster all your courage and put your bravery to the test. I know you are prepared to risk your lives and exert all your strength to defend Tibet. I also know that the tremendous task that you have undertaken is a noble cause and that you will have no regrets, despite the ghastly atrocities committed by the enemy. In this hour of peril, I appeal to all people, including government servants, who value their freedom and religion, to unite in the common struggle against the Chinese.[14]

In July 1957, twenty-three Khampa chieftains, under cover of preparations for an important religious ceremony in honour of the Dalai Lama, met in Gompo Tashi's flat. They decided to abandon their historic mutual hatred and join together, calling themselves Chushi Gangdrug (Four Rivers, Six Ranges), an ancient name for Kham and Amdo. "What united us was our desire to fight back", one of them recalls. "There was no thought of whether we would win or lose. We just wanted to kill Chinese and get our country back".[15] They began to collect guns, ammunition and horses, to fight the war in earnest.

And now a new element entered the equation. The CIA stepped in, for its own purposes and as part of US covert operations against the People's Republic of China. They had begun aiding the Tibetans in 1956, parachuting weapons to the guerrillas near Lithang and Batang from a plane which reached Tibet by way of Burma. A handful of Khampa recruits had been airlifted to Taiwan for training in the use of sophisticated weapons and communications. After December 1956, when the US acquired C-130 Hercules planes capable of covering the long haul to Tibet from Bangkok with a load of up to twenty-two tons, it became possible to extend their field of operations. Flying low at night over the Himalayas, these planes could, without the aid of navigational beacons, locate remote drop zones and bring much-needed arms to the guerrilla forces.[16]

Though the Chinese had earlier denied there was any trouble, they now admitted that a revolt was taking place in Kham (or, as they called it, West Sichuan) but claimed that it was being successfully dealt with. The guerrillas were "Tibetan bandits", and a propaganda film showed a group of them in the mountains "proceeding with their reckless preparations for war". The laconic announcement failed to mention that much of Kham was now a wasteland, since China was bombing and shelling the monasteries from which the Resistance derived its support. The Chinese campaign in Kham was one of unparalleled savagery, their atrocities attested to in two reports (1959 and 1960) by the International Commission of Jurists. Entire villages were wiped out, with hundreds of public executions to intimidate the survivors:

> The methods employed included crucifixion, dismemberment, vivisection, beheading, burying, burning and scalding alive, dragging the victims to death behind galloping horses. Children were forced to shoot their parents, disciples their religious teachers ... Monks were compelled to publicly copulate with nuns and desecrate sacred images before being sent to a growing string of labour camps in Amdo and Gansu.[17]

And to prevent the victims shouting out, "Long live the Dalai Lama" on the way to execution, they tore out their tongues with meat-hooks.[18]

By the time the Dalai Lama arrived back in Lhasa in April, he knew that the situation was beyond saving: "I felt I was losing control of my own people. In the east they were being driven into barbarism. In central Tibet they were growing more determined to resort to violence; and I felt I would not be able to stop them much longer."[19] Under pressure from the Chinese, he sent a peace delegation to the freedom fighters but found the Khampas and Amdowas determined to go on fighting. Thousands of monks were revoking their vows of non-violence, vowing instead to fight the Chinese to the death.

The mountain passes and valleys were choked with refugees. And as ten thousand of these weary and exhausted travellers reached Lhasa and began pitching their tents on the outskirts, their tales of horror could not fail to fuel the city's mounting rage.

CHAPTER 6

The Elephant's Foot

[They], the council ministers ... likened Tibet to an egg placed under the raised foot of an elephant. The elephant was China, and the life of the egg depended on the elephant's action.

TSEPON W. D. SHAKABPA, during the Dalai Lama's visit to India in 1956

Lobsang Rinchok, the son of an Amdo chief, was fifteen when the risings began:

In our area there were two monasteries with about three hundred monks. Early in 1958 the Chinese arrested all the monks between eighteen and seventy-nine. We couldn't believe it. Then they came to our village and ordered all the villagers (about one thousand of us) to assemble in the village hall. We were instructed to remain seated unless our name was called out, and then to raise our hand and go outside. The Chinese started reading out a list of names, and my own name was on the list. I went outside and to my horror I saw that all those who'd gone out before me were tied together with ropes and were being beaten by the Chinese.

We were tied together in fives. There seemed to be prisoners wherever I looked, hundreds of them. On that first day, about one hundred Tibetans died from exhaustion, fear, shock – and the inability to keep up with the people they were tied to. Some of these were very old.

The Chinese took us to District HQ which had a huge forecourt. We were told (still trussed up) to sit down. Then Chinese

soldiers surrounded us with machine guns. I was sure we were
going to be shot; I was terrified and kept imagining the impact of
the bullet and the pain it would cause. Then they told us we were
prisoners on Mao's instructions. "You are criminals", they said,
"who have sucked the blood of the poor."

We were sent to prison, but the prisons were too small to
house us. So they sent us to empty monasteries from which the
monks had been driven out, and proceeded to treat us like
animals. We were herded into the monastery temples, packed so
tightly that we couldn't move. We sweated in the intense heat,
but there was no way out. We had to piss and defecate where we
stood, still tied together in fives.

We were kept like that for three days. Then the Chinese
allowed us outside, still tied up, to piss and shit. We saw that all
the religious objects of the monastery had been dumped in the
latrines for us to shit on. Soon the whole place was full of shit, we
were wading in it up to the ankles, then the knees, then the
thighs. All you could do was shake it off as best you could by
wiping your hands on the wall. Then of course you had to eat
what little food there was with the same unwashed hands. At
first we used to try to cover our eating hand with our jackets, but
before long the jacket too was thick with shit.

I was lucky, though. Three weeks later, they came and untied
my ropes because, they said, I was too young for such treatment.
Twelve months later, instructions came from China that the
prisoners were either to be released or executed. As I was under
the age of eighteen, and it was against the Chinese constitution
to execute a minor, I was one of the few released.[1]

The experience of Beri Laga, a woman from a distinguished
Khampa family, was similar:

The Chinese summoned all the leading Tibetans, including
about three hundred landlords and senior lamas, to a meeting.
We met in two huge assembly halls in a monastery, and as soon
as everyone was there, the Chinese ringed us round with soldiers
and took us prisoner. They divided us into groups of about thirty

and made us "struggle" with each other. If we didn't do this enthusiastically enough, and beat each other, they beat us. Two months later, we were given public thamzing, three or four of us at a time. We were badly beaten, then put in prison. They had arrested everybody who opposed them in any way. From my district alone, there were a thousand of us.[2]

When the local people refused to condemn any member of the highly respected Beri family, she was moved to another area. For two years in Kanze prison, Beri Laga was subjected to thamzing

almost all day and every day, and with four big public ones. It took one hour to get to the place of thamzing and the Chinese shackled me and threw me into a truck for the journey. My hands were bleeding and raw from the handcuffs. During one of the sessions, my hair was dragged out until the scalp bled. Sometimes my eyes were so swollen from blows that I was blinded. Once, when they returned me to the prison, they accused me of having lied. They tied my hands behind my back and strung me up by the thumbs on a hook suspended from the ceiling. I was left like that, with my feet off the ground, for a full twenty minutes. My arms were all but wrenched from their sockets, and, given a few more minutes, I daresay they would have been.

What happened to Topai Adhi, a twenty-five-year-old woman from Kham, was even more harrowing. As she would testify many years later before an International Tribunal on Human Rights in Bonn, her husband had been organizing resistance to the Chinese and had died suddenly, almost certainly by poison administered by the Chinese. With their men either dead or having taken to the mountains, the women of the village took the burden of resistance on themselves. Organizing a rota, they took food to their menfolk at night, at the same time informing them of Chinese movements. Inevitably, they were discovered. The Chinese came for Adhi one afternoon which she will never forget:

Six Chinese policemen came to arrest me. My son, Chime
Wangyal, aged three, and my one-year-old daughter, were with
me. As they tied me up with ropes, the baby gurgled innocently
on the bed, but my little boy kept calling my name and trying to
come to me. Every time he got near, the policemen kicked and
shoved him out of the way. Then when they began to take me
away, he fought even harder to reach me, but the police kicked
him viciously. I could hear him screaming from a long way off. I
wish I had died that day. It was the worst day of my life. I was in
prison for sixteen years and only on my release did I discover
what had happened. My little boy had become so hysterical that
he fell into the river and they left him to drown. The baby had
been looked after by a neighbour for a time, and after that, I
don't know.[3]

Like Beri Laga, Adhi was taken to Kanze prison where, during
interrogation, the policemen kicked and beat her with rifle
butts; "They also forced me to kneel on two pieces of sharpened
wood with my hands raised in the air. Whenever I lowered my
hands they hit my elbows with the rifle butts."

That year, 1958, all of China suffered from Mao's Great Leap
Forward – the drive to solve all the problems of the economy by
heavy industrialization. Everything non-productive had to be
expunged. Just how drastic the expunging was is vividly con-
veyed by Catriona Bass in her book, *Inside the Treasure House*:

Every citizen had to exterminate a weekly quota of birds, fleas,
rats or mosquitoes. Schoolboys were issued with catapults, the
girls with fly-swats. Deyang said that she would spend long
hours at the latrines with her friends, swatting flies to meet the
targets set by the leaders. Once a week they would have to queue
up with their jars to prove that they had killed their quota. It
was a lengthy process. Each pupil was made to tip his dead flies
onto the table and count them one by one before the class leader.
Later, when the targets were made impossibly high, they started
breeding flies themselves.[4]

As part of this same campaign, local Tibetan newspapers

began decrying Buddha as a reactionary. They said that since monks and lamas were "enemies of the people", they must either work or be exterminated. One hermit in Kham was locked up without food or water for five days. The Chinese accused him of being an exploiter and told him that God could look after him. After five days, the local people were summoned to view the corpse and told that if there'd been any truth in religion, he would still be alive. In another place, three monks were arrested, subjected to thamzing and thrown into a deep pit. The public were made to urinate on them while the Chinese urged the monks to fly out of the pit. Elsewhere, a monk who begged the Chinese not to use the Buddhist scriptures as toilet paper had his arm cut off and was told to ask God to give him another one.[5]

"The Chinese came to the monastery of Trakar Trezong in Amdo", recounts Lobsang Rinchok. "They shot the whole community, except for about one hundred young novices under fifteen who sheltered under the robes of the older monks and so escaped death. I saw the place in 1981. The blood was still there, and no grass would grow in the area."

The Chinese began to press monks to sleep with women, threatening them with death if they refused. One mill-girl in Kham reported that she was offered 100 Chinese dollars for every monk she could seduce.[6] At Dzokchen monastery, which had about 1,000 monks, a unit of Chinese ordered all the monks to marry. They tore down the images of Buddha and other deities, threw the scriptures onto the ground, forcing the monks at gun point to trample on them. Then they ordered them to give thamzing to their abbots and senior lamas. Knowing that during thamzing in other monasteries, elderly lamas had been made to fornicate with prostitutes, then were beaten, spat and urinated on, the Dzokchen monks refused. They attacked and killed the Chinese soldiers, rescued their lamas, set fire to the monastery – and escaped, like thousands of their kind, to join the guerrillas.[5]

One day in 1958, Phuntsog Wangyal's monastery was surrounded by soldiers with tanks and machine guns. The five

spokesmen sent by the abbot to argue with the soldiers were
arrested:

> They said they knew we had guns, and they demanded to have
> them. When the monks resisted, the Chinese cut off the water
> supply for three months. Fortunately, there was so much rain
> that we could collect enough for our needs. But even so. Eventu-
> ally, the monks gave in and agreed to hand over whatever
> weapons they had.

Not long afterwards, fourteen-year-old Phuntsog was told to
prepare to leave the monastery to join a guerrilla cavalry unit:

> I did not go to say goodbye to my mother, because I was afraid
> of putting her in danger. (I never saw her again.) We left one
> night when there was a full moon. The Chinese were guarding
> the bridge, so we forded the river. I could see my village in the
> moonlight, and knew it was for the last time. I felt very sad.

> There were about eighty of us (I was the youngest) and we were
> in the mountains for about eight months, with nine weapons
> between us. We often encountered Chinese units equipped with
> machine guns. On three occasions there was serious fighting and
> many of my friends were killed. Others were seriously wounded.
> When we eventually reached Lhasa, there were only forty-two of
> us left.[8]

Chime Namgyal from Trindu also fought with the guerrillas:

> In March 1958, a relative who worked for the Chinese warned us
> that all the chieftains and high lamas in our area were to be
> summoned to two separate meetings – one in Trindu, the other
> in Jyekundo – where they would be arrested. My father and
> another chief, Namka Dorjee, consulted their people. If they
> resisted the Chinese, they might be killed, they told them. So
> what did they want to do? The people said they would give their
> lives to resist those who attacked our religion. Besides, they said,

they were likely soon to die of starvation. "Better to die protecting our religion with our bellies still full than to stay here and die of hunger".

At the meeting in Jyekundo, all the chiefs and lamas *were* arrested. Nevertheless, when the Chinese discovered that we in Trindu were planning to form a guerrilla force, they pretended they wanted to negotiate. When negotiations got nowhere, the Chinese threatened the villagers with military force. Namka Dorjee told them to do their worst. "For eight long years we've lived with your policies, and nothing could be worse than that."

The villagers moved up to the nomad pastures and joined forces with another nomad chief, making about seven hundred in all. There was a well-fortified Chinese post nearby which they planned to attack, though since they were armed with only a few rifles and about fifty bullets, they knew the attempt was suicidal. When they counted forty-three military trucks approaching the Chinese post their hearts sank still further.

But next morning, when the trucks left to surround our village of Trindu, we ambushed them and fought with them till three in the afternoon. We were outnumbered and we had so few weapons, but we staked everything on our skill at hand to hand fighting. Three of the trucks got away, but we managed to capture the rest and all the Chinese (more than 700) were killed. The river was dyed red with Chinese blood that day. We lost nineteen and five more were injured.

So there we were with good ammunition and a supply of Bren guns. But, as no one knew how to drive the trucks, we siphoned off the petrol and then set fire to them. We intended to use the petrol for blowing up the bridge from Qinghai over the Yellow River. But in the end we blew up four Chinese posts instead.

More and more Khampas were joining the guerrillas. Before long we had 1500 men, together with some stray nomads and all the wives and children. We moved the latter to a safer place, an operation which took twenty days. Then we divided one thousand men into three groups and set them to guard the main

road while the remaining 500 set off towards Tindu. We fought
with the Chinese for fifteen days, to gain control of the stores,
schools and offices. Many of our men were killed, but the rest
remained in good spirits.

Meanwhile, the Chinese in the mountains had brought in
reinforcements and a Chinese flag was flying on the new military HQ up there. The rebels cut off their water supply. But
their triumph was short-lived.

Suddenly we saw a long line of trucks, hundreds of them,
approaching the village, loaded with cannon and even tanks.
The Chinese had sent reinforcements and had encircled and
killed the thousand men guarding the approach roads. And now
they proceeded to fire the cannons at every house in the village
that was not flying the red flag – about half of all the houses.

I watched this slaughter from the western side of the hill. All
the inhabitants of those houses, and all the domestic animals
were killed. The Chinese announced that the rebels should surrender since they had no chance against nine hundred new military trucks. But we went on fighting for three days more. I had
started off with thirty-six men, but only three were left, when we
finally decided to escape. We had to presume that all the rebels
in the other groups were dead.[9]

Refugee and nomad camps were machine-gunned and bombed
from the air or massacred on the ground. Aten reports coming
upon a nomad camp, on his way to Lhasa, and meeting a scene
of total devastation:

Blood-stained and rotting corpses of men, women and children
lay sprawled across the ground in grotesque and pathetic positions. The big tents were slashed to ribbons and the rags fluttered wildly in the evening breeze. There must have been at least
four hundred corpses ... I saw a woman lying on the hard earth
clutching a baby. Both of them were dead, a dog was savagely
tugging at the leg of the baby. But even in death the mother
refused to give up her child. Words cannot describe all that I saw
that day ...[10]

The Chinese were thoroughly alarmed by the growing strength of Chushi Gangdrug, which was rapidly changing from a regional to a pan-Tibetan force. By the early summer of 1958, members of Chushi Gangdrug had joined forces with the old resistance organization of Lhasa, Mimang Tsongdu, to create a unified guerrilla army based in Lhoka, the mountainous area to the southeast of Lhasa. Not only, wrote Andrugtsang, was everyone's personal safety at stake, but the whole Tibetan way of life was being extinguished: "Individual freedom had become nonexistent since the Chinese invasion and the Communist doctrine was being barbarously enforced. Patriotic people felt there was nothing left to hope for or live for. We were rebelling not from choice but from sheer compulsion."[11]

The Khampa and Amdowa refugees had continued to flood into Lhasa. Then the Chinese raised the tension a notch higher by conducting a census and decreeing that no non-Lhasan would be allowed in the city without an identity card bearing name, age and place of birth and signed by a Chinese official. The refugees, already afraid that the Chinese would put the blame on them for the rebellion in the east, were convinced they were about to be arrested. A mass exodus began, as all the able-bodied (some of them with their families) decamped to join the guerrillas at their new headquarters in the mountains.

Now began the most intense phase of the fighting. With ever more volunteers joining them, the rebels notched up successes in a dozen bloody battles and daring raids near Lhasa itself. They attacked Chinese convoys and military camps to steal arms and ammunition, and in the process killed hundreds of Chinese. In a memorable attack in late January 1959, a PLA garrison at Tsethang, south east of Lhasa, was wiped out. The Chinese authorities complained furiously to the Dalai Lama and promised a terrible revenge. "Like all invaders", he wrote, "they had totally lost sight of the sole cause of the revolt against them: that our people did not want them in our country, and were ready to give their lives to be rid of them."[12]

Fearing that the Tibetan army might decide to join forces with the rebels, the Chinese military urged the Dalai Lama and his government to ban the Resistance forces and send Tibetan troops into action against them. Aghast at the prospect, His Holiness stalled for time, claiming that the army was too small, too inexperienced, and finally that if they were ordered to fight their own countrymen, they might well join them instead.

His own attitude to the rebels was still ambivalent and he could not give them his unqualified approval. Part of him clung to the belief that whatever the violence being used against the Tibetans, "it could never become right to use violence in reply". Yet, as he recalls in his memoirs,

> Part of me greatly admired the guerrilla fighters. They were brave people, men and women, and they were putting their lives and their children's lives at stake to try to save our religion and country in the only remaining way they could see. When one heard of the terrible deeds of the Chinese in the east, it was a natural human reaction to seek revenge. And moreover, I knew they regarded themselves as fighting in loyalty to me as Dalai Lama: the Dalai Lama was the core of what they were trying to defend.[13]

He was in a classic double bind, with the Chinese suspecting him and his Cabinet of supporting the guerrillas, while the guerrillas considered them mere tools of the Chinese.

But the Chinese had no such hangups and they threatened to use the full weight of the army if the Tibetan government would not act. Eventually a five-man delegation was sent to promise immunity to the rebels if they laid down their arms. The latter, predictably, ignored the request – and the five delegates abandoned their mission and joined them. It was, admitted the Dalai Lama, difficult to blame them.

The situation was out of hand. The rebels were in control of almost all southern Tibet and large parts of the east. While the Tibetan government continued to hope that moderation would yet save the day, the Chinese were steadily building up their forces – and preparing for all-out war:

> The Chinese were arming their civilians and reinforcing their

barricades in the city. They declared that throughout the country they would only protect their own nationals and their own communications: everything else was our responsibility. They summoned more meetings in schools and other places, and told the people that the Cabinet was in league with the "reactionaries" and its members would be dealt with accordingly – not merely shot, they sometimes went on to explain, but executed slowly and publicly. General Tan Kuan-sen, addressing a women's meeting in Lhasa, said that where there was rotten meat, the flies gathered, but if you got rid of the meat, the flies were no more trouble. The flies, I suppose, were the guerrilla fighters: the rotten meat was either my Cabinet or myself.[14]

The stage was already set, and the actors in place, for the bloody last act of the tragedy. And it would be the Chinese who raised the final curtain.

CHAPTER 7

Uprising in Lhasa, 1959

When the Iron Bird flies and horses run on wheels,
The Tibetan people will be scattered like ants across the world.

Eighth-century Tibetan prophecy

Losar, the Tibetan New Year (which, rather like the Western Easter, is a moveable feast, usually falling in February/March) was traditionally the signal for three weeks of prayer and merry-making. Despite the tense political situation, the dawn of 1959 was no exception. Thousands of expectant pilgrims, traders, artisans and officials poured into Lhasa for the festivities; plus about 17,000 monks arriving for the Great Prayer Festival (Monlam) which followed Losar. With the 10,000 refugees camped outside the city, there were about 100,000 people in Lhasa, more than double the usual number.

During the Great Prayer Festival that year, the twenty-four-year-old Dalai Lama was to take his final religious examinations, in a series of taxing debates which would make him a Doctor of Metaphysics. It was the culmination of twenty years of study, and so preoccupied was he with his forthcoming ordeal that when the Chinese pressed him to attend the National People's Congress in Beijing in April, he did not hesitate to plead the examinations as an excuse for delaying a decision.

On 1 March, the night before his last examination, the Dalai Lama was in his private apartments in the Jokhang temple when two junior Chinese PLA officers demanded to see him. Their mission seemed a trivial one: to fix a date for him to attend a performance by a new dance troupe from China in the military camp. The invitation – a barely disguised command – had been issued by the military commander some time earlier, and the young ruler had indicated that he would accept. Now they wanted him to name the day. But the Dalai Lama, with more pressing matters on his mind, persuaded the officers to go away, promising an answer after his exams were over.

Next day, having covered himself in glory during the debates, he won his doctorate. Three days later, with thousands of devotees lining the route, he returned from the Jokhang to his summer palace – the Norbulingka – in a noisy and colourful procession, always one of the highlights of the Tibetan year. The one ominous note this year was the absence, for the first time since the invasion, of any Chinese in the procession.

To avoid giving offence, the Dalai Lama agreed to attend the theatrical performance on 10 March. On the 9th, the Chinese summoned Phuntsok Tashi Takla, the Dalai Lama's security chief, to their military headquarters to finalize the preparations for the visit. To Takla's astonishment, the Chinese presented him with a list of demands. The Dalai Lama was to go to military headquarters in complete secrecy, without either his ministers or the twenty-five-strong armed bodyguard which usually accompanied him; and no Tibetan troops were to be stationed beyond the Stone Bridge which marked the outer limits of the army camp.

These commands alarmed the Dalai Lama. It was ludicrous to suggest that the visit could be kept secret; everyone knew about the invitation and the minute he left the Norbulingka word would get round and the whole of Lhasa would turn up to watch him go. If he broke his promise to attend, the Chinese would "lose face" and exact an unimaginable revenge. On the other hand, to accept their conditions would mean further humiliation for himself and his government. That, however, could be borne and was certainly preferable to the alternative. He decided to agree to the Chinese proposals, despite his worries about what the Tibetans would do when the news leaked out. They would probably insist on following him into the

Chinese camp, and that might provoke a bloodbath. To forestall such a contingency, he arranged for traffic restrictions near the Stone Bridge next day.

That did it. The news swept the city like a dust storm. For the angry Tibetans there could be only one explanation: the Chinese were intending to kidnap the Dalai Lama and abduct him to China. Speculation was already rife, since in the past week Radio Beijing had announced that His Holiness would be attending the Congress in Beijing in April. As in fact he had made no promises, the announcement implied that the Chinese were determined to get him there at any cost.

The Khampa refugees stoked the unease, recalling how in four different areas of Kham senior lamas had been lured to a seemingly innocuous social occasion, after which they disappeared or were known to have been executed. Justified or not, fears for their leader's safety escalated. By nightfall of the 9th, thousands of angry, frightened men, women and children, armed with sticks, clubs, kitchen knives, bottles and anything they could lay their hands on, had streamed out of the city and were surrounding the Norbulingka, ready to defend His Holiness to the death. "You must understand", Phuntsok Tashi Takla reminds us, "that the relationship between the Dalai Lama and the people is unique. He is as close to them as their own heart."

By the morning of the 10th, almost 30,000 people were camped with their cooking pots and blankets before the two huge stone lions guarding the Norbulingka's entrance. They had elected a committee of sixty or seventy leaders and had sworn an oath that if the Chinese attempted to make the Dalai Lama go to the military camp, they would barricade the palace and keep him in. The mood was ugly – and getting uglier – as they chanted "CHINESE GO HOME" and "TIBET FOR THE TIBETANS". A Tibetan official who arrived in a car driven by a Chinese soldier was set upon and narrowly escaped with his life. Phakpa, a monk-official known to be a collaborator, was less fortunate. When he arrived on a bicycle, in Chinese dress, the crowd believed he had come to kill the Dalai

Lama and stoned him to death, yelling and cheering as his body was dragged away.

Sonam Chophel Chada saw it happen. Arriving in Lhasa that very day, he had been swept along by the momentum of events. Hastily changing out of his official district officer's robes into ordinary Tibetan dress, he put a pistol in his pocket for protection and made his way to the Norbulingka, reaching the gate just as officials of every kind were meeting in emergency session inside the palace:

> A colleague recognized me and told me to go in, but the meeting had already started so I hesitated. As I stood just inside the gate, I saw Phakpa approach, and saw the crowd fall on him and stone him. I watched in horror, but when I wanted to go and calm them down, my colleague held me back, saying, "They are so angry, nothing and no-one will stop them now".
>
> As we stood there, frozen, another official came out and took me in to the meeting.[1]

Appalled by the murder, the Dalai Lama was in a state of considerable stress:

> I felt as if I were standing between two volcanoes, each likely to erupt at any moment. On one side, there was the vehement, unequivocal, unanimous protest of my people against the Chinese regime; on the other, there was the armed might of a powerful and aggressive occupation force. If there was a clash between the two, the result was a foregone conclusion. The Lhasan people would be ruthlessly massacred in thousands, and Lhasa and the rest of Tibet would see a fullscale military rule with all its persecution and tyranny.[2]

Anxiously, he sent three Cabinet ministers to tell the Chinese that he would not after all be attending the concert. He made sure that the crowd knew of his decision, so that they would calm down. Several thousand people did indeed return to the city – but only to hold public meetings and organize anti-

Chinese demonstrations. A large volunteer force was left behind
to guard the Norbulingka.

Inside the Chinese camp, the Dalai Lama's message was
received with unconcealed anger. The military commander,
General Tan, accused the Tibetan ministers of being hand in
glove with the resistance movement and threatened to use
whatever drastic measures were necessary to crush "the
imperialist rebels" once and for all. Nevertheless, after some
delay, a truncated version of the entertainment went ahead.
Tendzin Choegyal, the Dalai Lama's thirteen-year-old brother,
an Incarnation of very high standing, was among the guests:

> There were about ten of us from Drepung Monastery and we
> knew nothing of recent events. We had arrived in all innocence
> at about ten in the morning, eager for the entertainment due to
> start at eleven. On the way we had to cross the road which led to
> the Norbulingka, and we saw hundreds of people going towards
> the palace. There did seem an awful lot of them, and they
> seemed very excited, but I decided they must be going to line the
> route to get a glimpse of His Holiness.
>
> In the camp, there was definitely an atmosphere. All the
> Chinese were armed, and so were those Tibetans who were
> known to be friendly towards them. There was one who used to
> be a friend of my brother Lobsang Samten. When he came in I
> shook his hand and with my left hand made to embrace him. I
> could feel the pistol under his gown. They knew something was
> going to happen alright, and they had planned their response.
> You could feel it in the air; all their former friendliness had
> vanished.
>
> We went on waiting, people kept coming in and out of the
> military camp, and then we heard that there was some kind of
> disturbance, that a man had been killed. After that they said His
> Holiness wasn't coming because the people had stopped him,
> but that the show would go on regardless. I didn't feel
> frightened, but I did feel that something terrible was about to
> happen.[3]

Early that afternoon, the visitors left by car, preceded by a

Chinese armoured vehicle. Tendzin Choegyal, however, did not complete the journey and would never again return to Drepung:

> My mother had sent a servant to the intersection of the roads, and when he saw me looking out of the car window he beckoned the Chinese driver to stop. My mother, he said, wanted me to go home rather than to the monastery. I got out of the car and walked the remaining distance. The gate was closed, which was very unusual, but when the gatekeeper saw it was me, he opened it. My mother was watching through an upstairs window, and when she saw me she was so relieved she clapped and burst into tears.
>
> Soon after I arrived, there was a telephone call from my brother-in-law [Phuntsok Tashi Takla] who was in charge of His Holiness's bodyguard. He wanted to know if I was safe. By this time the servants had told me about the rising and I was very excited and full of thirteen-year-old bravado. I said, "Isn't it marvellous what the people have done?" He hung up abruptly – the Chinese had installed the phones themselves and almost certainly had the lines tapped.
>
> Before going to bed that night, I looked for my old .22 rifle. To my dismay I found I had only one bullet left. It wouldn't be much good. Nevertheless, I loaded the gun and slept with it by my side. Early next morning, at His Holiness's request, my mother and I moved to the Norbulingka.

At six in the evening, the government officials, together with the Dalai Lama's bodyguard and the leaders chosen by the crowd, unanimously declared an end to the Seventeen Point Agreement, adding that Tibet no longer recognized Chinese authority and was therefore once more independent. As Sonam Chophel Chada explained, "The Chinese had breached the Agreement in every conceivable way, so we declared that it was no longer valid. From now on, we said, Tibet must be left to the Tibetans and no Tibetan official must have any further contact with the Chinese."[4]

Tibetan army units stationed in Lhasa immediately removed their Chinese uniforms and joined the crowds round the Norbulingka dressed in Tibetan khaki. They brought all the weapons they could find and handed them to anybody who knew how to use them. Auxiliary units of volunteer fighters were being organized by members of all the trades and even the monasteries. Then news came in that the women of the city – from young girls to grandmothers – had taken to the streets and were shouting for Tibetan independence. "We had formed a Tibetan women's group", said Dolma Chozom, whose husband was away fighting with the guerrillas; "We said that Tibet belonged to the Tibetans and the Chinese should leave. We wrote a memo to the effect that the Chinese had illegally occupied our country and were destroying its culture, and I was one of those who presented it at the Indian and Nepalese Legations."[5]

The Dalai Lama continued to plead for calm, but his appeals fell on deaf ears. Lhasa was fast turning into a potential battleground. Nervous householders went to ground, preparing for a long siege. They built stockades, lined their flat roofs with barbed wire, barricading themselves in with sandbags and sacks of salt. The air was thick with a disastrous euphoria, for by now the Tibetans were believing themselves invincible. They would evict the Chinese from Lhasa, they believed, as they had driven out the Manchus in 1912. Now, as then, the women would complete the rout of the enemy by stoning them from the rooftops. No one paused to reflect that the Chinese rout in 1912 had only been possible because of the revolution in China; that the Chinese troops today were orderly and well trained; and that they were even now setting up sophisticated mortar and machine-gun emplacements, encircling the whole Lhasa valley with heavy artillery. What chance did the Tibetans have with their antiquated mortars, one small World War One cannon and their battery of rifles, sticks, stones and knives? The People's Liberation Army was leaving nothing to chance in its approaching showdown with the People.

For the next few days, Lhasa seethed in uneasy ferment. Still hoping against hope, the Dalai Lama tried to ease the tension by writing a series of conciliatory letters to the Chinese. Later they would use the letters as "proof" that he had been the victim of a "reactionary clique" who had forced the pace of events. But the Dalai Lama claims that he wrote the letters only "to prevent a totally disastrous clash between my unarmed people and the Chinese army." Phuntsok Tashi Takla agrees that at that stage negotiation was – or seemed – still a possibility: "We weren't considering escape. At most we thought that maybe if we could get His Holiness to the Potala he'd be safer. But the crowds round the Norbulingka made that impossible."[6]

His Holiness met with the people's elected leaders, pleading with them to calm the passions of the crowd. In a last ditch effort, he even wrote to Ngabo (now more than ever aligned with the Chinese), offering to hand himself over if it would prevent the massacre of his people.

On the morning of the 17th, as he waited for Ngabo's reply, a hundred Chinese trucks were seen approaching the city from the north and east. "Within the palace", wrote the Dalai Lama, "everyone felt the end had come". He consulted the Oracle who shouted, "Go! Go! Tonight". Just then two mortar shells were launched at the Norbulingka and exploded in the gardens. After that, the Cabinet decided that the Dalai Lama must leave and preparations for the escape were instantly put in hand.

Two hours later the escape began. It had to be kept secret, not only from the Chinese but from the crowd outside the palace. They would have attempted to follow him, and then the massacre would have begun in earnest. Writing a last message for the leaders of the people, begging them not to initiate violence, the Dalai Lama prepared to depart. "We decided we'd have to leave in small groups", says Phuntsok Tashi Takla:

We sent a few trucks back and forth to the Potala as a sort of smokescreen, to make everyone believe that life was going on as usual. Then we sent one or two people on ahead to alert the guerrillas on the far side of the river Kyichu, and a pilot group to make sure the river crossing was practicable. We were going to need horses, so they were sent over, one or two at a time, to wait on the south side of the river. It was all rather haphazard, we were very uncertain of success, but what choice did we have? We risked death by going, but if we stayed, we risked death too.[7]

First to go were the Dalai Lama's tutors and the four members of the Kashag, hidden under a tarpaulin in the back of a lorry. They were followed in the early evening by his mother, sister, Tsering Dolma, and thirteen-year-old brother, Tendzin Choegyal, ostensibly setting out to visit a nunnery on the other side of the river. To young Tendzin it seemed like a great adventure when his mother told him to change from his novice monk's robes into lay dress. When he first saw his mother and sister disguised as Khampa soldiers, he burst out laughing, to the irritation of his elders. He takes up the story:

> We left the palace by one of the west gates. As we left, a cool wind was blowing, and there was a sliver of moon. My mother, who had an arthritic knee, rode on a donkey but the rest of us walked until we came to the north bank of the Kyichu. At the river there was a ferry rather like a wooden horse-box. We crossed over in this. As we waited for the others, I walked along the bank until my monastery, Drepung, came into view. I prostrated myself three times and prayed that one day I would come back. Then I rejoined the group. There were people pacing up and down, horses neighing, a lot of noise. To my relief, I heard that His Holiness had successfully crossed the river without being spotted by the Chinese.[8]

The Dalai Lama did not share his brother's teenage thirst for thrills. For him, the leavetaking was a heartbreak. He went to his chapel to pray, then, returning to his rooms, replaced his monk's robes with a soldier's uniform and fur cap:

> As I went out, my mind was drained of all emotion. I was aware of my own sharp footfalls on the floor of beaten earth, and the ticking of the clock in the silence. At the inner door of my house, there was a single soldier waiting, and another at the outer door. I took a rifle from one of them and slung it on my shoulder to

complete the disguise. The soldiers followed me, and I walked down through the dark garden which contained so many of the happiest memories of my life.[9]

With his escort he crossed the park, removing his glasses to aid the disguise. "I groped my way across the park, hardly able to see a thing".[10] When they reached the gate, he could sense in the darkness the great mass of people surrounding it. "But none of them noticed the humble soldier, and I walked out unchallenged towards the dark road beyond".[11]

"This was, without a doubt, the very worst part of all", shudders Phuntsok Tashi Takla who had sole responsibility for His Holiness's safety:

Between the Norbulingka and the river, there was a stretch of sand. We sank into it as we walked and progress was terribly slow. It seemed to take an eternity. In the dark we mistook trees and branches for men, and were convinced that the Chinese were waiting for us. Still, we were glad that the moon was not very bright and more than grateful for the clouds that kept covering it. Every time the clouds cleared we prayed for them to return.[12]

It was an epic mid-winter journey, with the danger of discovery by the Chinese at each and every step. Crossing the Kyichu by coracle, the Dalai Lama was certain "that every splash of the oars would draw down machine-gun fire on to us".[13] But the crossing went smoothly and on the far side of the Kyichu, he was able to rejoin his family, his ministers and the thirty Khampa freedom fighters waiting with ponies to take them to safety.

I put my glasses back on – I could bear sightlessness no longer – but then almost wished I hadn't as I could now make out the torchlight of PLA sentries guarding the garrison that lay only a few hundred yards from where we stood. Fortunately the moon was obscured by low cloud and visibility was poor.[14]

Phuntsok Tashi could now relax slightly and trust the Khampa
guerrillas to protect them.

In separate groups, to avoid detection from the air, the party
rode south for a night and a day, crossing Che-La, a 16,000 feet
high mountain pass still covered with winter snow and ice.
"Our horses took one step up and slid back four", recalls Tendzin Choegyal:

> My mother was alright going up, but coming down we all had to
> dismount and walk. It was terrible for her, because she had such
> bad legs. One of our escort held her left arm, another her right,
> they were almost holding her off the ground, half lifting, half
> dragging her along.

By noon the next day, they had crossed the Tsangpo
(Brahmaputra) River by ferry and were marching south across
some of Tibet's most difficult and lonely terrain towards the
mountain area controlled by the freedom fighters. An escort of
about 350 Tibetan soldiers had been assembled, and the escape
party now numbered about one hundred people. Almost all of
them, except the Dalai Lama himself, were armed, including, as
His Holiness related in his memoirs,

> the man appointed as my personal cook, who carried an enor-
> mous bazooka and wore a belt hung with its deadly shells. He
> was one of the young men trained by the CIA. So eager was he to
> use his magnificent and terrible-looking weapon that, at one
> point, he lay down and fired off several shots at what he claimed
> looked like an enemy position. But it took such a long time to
> reload that I felt sure he would have been made short work of by
> a real enemy. It was not an impressive performance.[15]

Khampas guarded their rear, and each day small guerrilla
bands would appear from nowhere to check their progress
towards the Sabo-La pass:

> At the top it was very cold and snowing a blizzard. I began to be
> deeply worried about some of my companions. Although I was

young and fit, some of the older ones amongst my entourage
found the going very difficult. But we dared not slacken the pace
as we were still in grave danger of being intercepted by Chinese
forces.[16]

It was not the Dalai Lama's intention at that stage to press on
towards India, but to halt near the border and try and reopen
negotiations with the Chinese. But along the way, on 24 March,
he received the shattering news that the catastrophe he had
striven so hard to prevent had finally happened. Lhasa lay in
ruins, and thousands of its people had been killed:

> We knew, as soon as we heard the dreadful news, that there was
> only one possible explanation. Our people – not just our rich and
> ruling classes but our ordinary people – had finally, eight years
> after the invasion began, convinced the Chinese that they would
> never willingly accept their alien rule. So the Chinese were try-
> ing now to terrify them, by merciless slaughter, into accepting
> this rule against their will.[17]

*   *   *

Nobody in Lhasa would have expected the Chinese not to react
in anger. But nobody could have imagined the ferocity and
savagery of their actual response, nor the carnage that would
result.

The secret of the escape had been well kept, and forty-eight
hours had passed in an uneasy lull. The Chinese were still
unaware of the Dalai Lama's departure when at two o'clock on
the morning of 20 March, while most of the Tibetans slept, they
began shelling the Norbulingka from their fortified emplacements. Blinded by smoke, the Tibetans could see neither who
was attacking them nor where the missiles were coming from.
They had no previous experience of bombs. Before the morning
was out, hundreds of dead and wounded lay among the blazing
ruins of the palace and its temples. The PLA drove home their
advantage with tanks and armoured cars, beating back the

poorly armed Tibetan defenders, driving them towards the river whose strong spring currents swept many of them away. Unsure of the whereabouts of the Dalai Lama, the soldiers began a search for him among the corpses. Not until the next day did they learn that he had gone. Immediately, but too late, they sent out troops and spotter planes in pursuit. Putting the best possible face on their failure to find him, they announced later that evening that he had been abducted by reactionaries. "When we heard this", wrote Dawa Norbu, "we breathed an audible sigh of relief, and murmured, 'Thank God, the Precious One is safe. Now we shall be alright.'"[18]

As artillery pounded the Potala, the Medical College on Chokpori Hill and the great Sera Monastery, the Tibetans erupted into street by street fighting, trying to lob homemade petrol bombs into Chinese buildings from behind hastily erected barricades made of furniture and torn-up flagstones. They were picked off and slaughtered in their thousands by Chinese snipers firing from protected positions on the roof-tops. As monasteries, schools and many ordinary buildings were obliterated by shells, more than ten thousand survivors ran for refuge to Lhasa's most sacred building, one of the holiest shrines in all Asia, the Jokhang cathedral.

Just after dawn on the 22nd, the PLA shelled the Jokhang, machine-gunning the civilians camped in the square in front of it. Three Chinese tanks approached the scene. By midday, as flames leaped from the doomed Cathedral, corpses lay in mounds around the tanks. Throughout the city, between ten and fifteen thousand lay dead.

Two hours later, the three-day orgy of destruction was over. So was the revolt. Some managed to escape to the mountains to join the guerrillas. The majority could only stay and await their fate. "We had been sheltering in a cellar", said Wangchen:

We had guns but we didn't know how to use them. We'd piled sandbags in front of the door to keep the Chinese out. But at the end, the Chinese were putting ladders up to the walls, climbing up into the houses, ordering people to surrender, arresting many of them. They took all our guns and ammunition and arrested nine of the fourteen in the house.[19]

As Ngabo's hated voice boomed over the loudspeakers, ordering the survivors to surrender, white scarves fluttered in the air. Long lines of prisoners were led away to an uncertain fate, while over the blackened Potala Palace the red flags of the Chinese People's Republic were already flying. "Look at your precious palace carefully", the prisoners were told. "It now belongs to us".[20]

*   *   *

When the Dalai Lama, still on Tibetan territory, heard that the Chinese had (on 28 March) dissolved the Tibetan government and taken complete control of Lhasa, he formally repudiated the Seventeen Point Agreement and proclaimed a new provisional government. Then, realizing that the PLA were preparing an all-out attack on the guerrillas in the mountains, he decided at last to ask the Indian government for political asylum.

There was still another range of mountains to cross before India was reached, and there was very little fodder left for their exhausted pack animals. They needed frequent halts in order to conserve their energies, and progress was extremely slow. As they crossed the Karpo-la pass, the last one before India, a nasty shock was in store. They were spotted by a reconnaissance plane, a fact that made everyone nervous:

If it was Chinese, as it probably was, there was a good chance that they now knew where we were. With this information they could return to attack us from the air, against which we had no protection. Whatever the identity of the aircraft, it was a forceful reminder that I was not safe anywhere in Tibet. Any misgivings I had about going into exile vanished with this realisation. India was our only hope.[21]

The Indian government had already signalled its readiness to receive the Dalai Lama, and the party was free to proceed. "The night we reached the Indian border", recalls Tendzin Choegyal,

> it rained heavily. We were accommodated in tents and the one His Holiness was in leaked and his bedding got soaked. The water ran in rivulets down the inside. The fever he'd been fighting off for days developed into a chill and then into dysentery. I was with him and saw him become weak and ill. Next day he was too sick to ride. It was not until three days later that we were able to cross over into India.

As soon as the Dalai Lama was fit enough to travel, his companions loaded him onto the broad back of a dzo, a placid animal, a cross between a yak and a cow. On this lowly beast of burden, "in a daze of sickness and weariness and unhappiness deeper than I can express", on 31 March 1959, Tenzin Gyatso, the Fourteenth Dalai Lama, left his country and went into exile.

CHAPTER 8

"Springtime has Come to Tibet", 1960
(title of a Chinese propaganda film)

It suddenly struck us that Tibet was no more our country; that we were no longer free Tibetans; that we were under alien overlords, the Chinese Communists. The land of Snows, the land of lamas, the land of eternal mystery had passed away. Losing one's country was like suddenly losing one's parents.

DAWA NORBU, *Red Star over Tibet*

Among the Tibetan exiles already in India who turned out to greet the Dalai Lama was Lobsang Nyima, overcome with emotion:

When we saw him looking so haggard and ill, we couldn't help weeping. We were angry with the Chinese for causing him so much suffering. Fifteen of us got together to discuss the situation, and we decided we must return to Tibet and continue the fight. We bought good horses from India and set off, with five guns between us, and a few swords.[1]

The Khampa guerrillas who had escorted the Dalai Lama and his party to the frontier had immediately returned to continue the now hopeless struggle within Tibet. From this time onwards, the whole military might of the PLA was brought to bear against the Khampas and the volunteer fighters, abandoned now by the CIA, their only source of weapons being what they could capture from the enemy. There were no friendly neighbouring states to offer them the arms they needed: India, Nepal and Bhutan were themselves scared of sharing Tibet's fate if they offended China. One hundred thousand crack Chinese troops swept through the Lhoka area, relentlessly occupying towns and villages, destroying some of them, cutting the guerrillas off from their supply base at Kalimpong.

The experience of Lobsang Nyima and his friends when they returned to Tibet, gives some idea of the unequal odds:

> We discovered that 600 freedom fighters had been encircled by six battalions of Chinese – both infantry and cavalry – near Gyantse. We linked up with another group of Tibetans and decided to help them break out of that encirclement. Somehow we broke through the circle and let the guerrillas escape – but only at the cost of being surrounded ourselves. There was no way out. Two of my friends and I decided to fight to the death, but we told the rest of our group to surrender. One of my two friends was killed, the other one and I were wounded. We were captured by the Chinese and taken to Shigatse, and from there to prison in Lhasa.[2]

About 32,000 people were killed in the fighting around Lhoka. The morale of the survivors, cut off from friends and supplies was understandably low. Further resistance was useless. Though isolated units continued to operate throughout the area, on 21 April 1959 the Chushi Gangdrug leaders abandoned their Lhoka-based HQ and escaped to India. Before long the Chinese had taken control of all the main passes over the Himalayas, the principal avenues of escape for Tibetans fleeing to India or Nepal. When they managed to seal the borders all armed resistance came to an end.

Lhasa was in the grip of a military dictatorship. Those who had not managed to flee faced the full fury of the Chinese. The execution of the "ringleaders" began immediately. Most of the able-bodied men and boys – whether merchants, peasants, nomads, monks, soldiers, government officials or aristocrats –

were arrested. Many were deported to the gulags of the "Tibetan Siberia", the northern wilderness of the Chang tang; others were kept in or near Lhasa as a free slave-labour force. Some just disappeared. "It seemed", said Pema Saldon, "as though every family was searching for relatives who had disappeared. Many of these had simply been shot. Most of the women were hawking food around the various prisons, hoping to find the whereabouts of their loved ones."[3]

Tashi Palden, a monk, was one of about 500 monks, women, children and beggars who, prodded and pushed with bayonets towards the devastated Norbulingka Palace, found their way blocked with corpses:

> There were bodies everywhere and we couldn't avoid stepping on them. Some of them moved as we trod on them. The Chinese locked us into a cattle shed and left us without food for two days. But the people were beyond caring about food, they had lost all hope. All the bodies in the Norbulingka were collected and burned the day we arrived there. It took three whole days for them to burn.
>
> We were classified in groups according to where we used to belong, such as the various monasteries, regiments of the Tibetan army, etc... Then one of the Chinese officers addressed us: "You people have caused us a great deal of trouble, even though we came here to liberate you. We know you used to think that Chushi Gangdrug would drive us out easily because most of them were full adults whereas most of our soldiers were in their teens. Even your women had the cheek to demonstrate and tell us to clear out. Well, now you know what our soldiers and weapons are really like. So I hope it is clear to you that you stand as much chance of getting your independence as you do of seeing the sun rise from the west."[4]

The Chinese had put out their own version of events. Tsering Dorje Gashi, a Tibetan student in Beijing, reports that as early as 18 March (before the bloodshed had even begun), his class at the Minorities Institute was told:

the rebels are spilling blood and destroying everything with utter disregard for the sufferings of the populace ... the PLA of the Tibetan Military Region did not fire a single shot at the rebels. Chairman Mao and the Chinese Central Government were patient and did everything to bring the rebels to an understanding.

Later it was instilled into the students that the revolt was a class struggle, not a struggle between two nations, and though the violence of its suppression was to be regretted, nevertheless the outcome was happy:

The rebellion has quickened the pace towards a good future, and the Tibetan peasant-serfs will see the days of democratic reforms sooner than expected. The suppression of the rebellion has hastened the process of transforming the semi-feudal, semi-dynastic and semi-barbarian Tibetan society into a new socialist society. A bad condiiton has been turned into a good condition.[5]

The inhabitants of Lhasa saw little good in their condition as the Chinese, dropping all pretence of peaceful liberation, proceeded to remould Tibetan society. A massive military presence buttressed the change-over to Chinese-dominated bureaucracy. The Tibetan government was dissolved on 28 March, its functions transferred to the Preparato Committee for the Autonomous Region of Tibet (PCART), with the twenty-two-year-old Panchen Lama as its acting chairman, backed up by Ngabo Ngawang Jigme and "the patriotic few", those upper-class Tibetans who had thrown in their lot with the Chinese. (The Lama had signed a telegram to Mao, approving this step.) The Committee was a puppet controlled by the Chinese Communist Party and by the Tibet Area Military Command. These powerful organizations were led by three Chinese generals, to whom every Tibetan, however senior, was answerable.

Further reprisals and executions took place, as people slowly began to emerge from their cellars, to find PLA squads systematically searching the houses of "rebels", evicting their

families and sequestrating their property. The pragmatic
Sonam Chophel Chada decided to surrender, "since the
Chinese were threatening dire consequences to those who
didn't. I'd thought about killing myself, but had decided against
it. I wanted to go on working for my country, but how could I do
that if I was dead?"

Pema Saldon's family were luckier than most: "The Chinese
were scaling the walls and ransacking all the houses. They
searched all the men for weapons and arrested most of them.
But my father was a fat man and it was obvious he could have
done no fighting. So they left him alone."

Dawa Tsering, then a small child remembers going out for
water with a khata (white scarf) tied to his bucket: "I didn't
understand at the time ... but I knew that if I went out without
a khata I'd be shot."[6] He remembered the bodies too. "One day
I had to go to the Norbulingka with my mother and I saw them
... piles and piles of bodies reaching up to the branches of the
trees. Burning. PLA men were pouring petrol over them and
setting light to their hair."[7]

Lhasa was divided into north, south and east districts each
with its own zone and neighbourhood committees and smaller
block committees, all of them controlled by collaborators.
Families were labelled according to three broad categories: the
very rich (those who had more than 50% of their income after
expenditure); the middling rich (25%–35%); and the poor.
"Enemies of the people" were those who opposed the regime
and could come from any of the classes; they were criminals to
be hunted out of existence. With one collaborator/informer
allotted to every ten inhabitants, no one dared voice any criticism since no one knew whom he could trust. "Everyone was
under surveillance", says Wangchen, who was then thirteen;
"conversations were listened to. They even listened outside windows. Anyone seen talking to a group of friends was accused of
trying to bring back the old serfdom." For Pema Saldon, "There
was an atmosphere of tension and mistrust, of something dreadful that might happen at any minute."

A curfew was imposed. Lhasa's inhabitants were made to

carry identity cards at all times and could no longer move freely from one part of the city to another. Military control posts were set up all over Lhasa, the approach roads were heavily guarded. Investigating teams were sent into every part of the city to question people about their involvement in the revolt and about their class background. The houses of "rebels" were systematically commandeered and their owners forced into outhouses or sheds. "They locked the door", said Wangchen, "and stuck a large poster over it saying it was government property. All our family was herded into a small, dark room in someone else's house. On the 27th we were accused of belonging to the aristocracy and were denounced publicly before an assembly."

All precious stones and metals were confiscated and sent to China, whence they would find their way to the antique markets of Hong Kong and Taiwan. Furniture and carpets were given to Chinese civil and military personnel. The Chinese made great play of taking from the rich to give to the poor, but when the poor were summoned to their neighbourhood committee offices to receive their share of the loot, they were given "a haphazard array of broken chairs and tables, empty boxes, worn-out garments and an occasional tea-pot".[8] "Meanwhile", continued Wangchen, "we 'enemies of the people' were sent to do the most menial jobs in the city. We were accused of having 'old minds' and of resisting change. So, to cure us, they started by giving us big sticks and ordering us to go and kill all the dogs we could find."

At the compulsory meetings held daily by every block committee for the hundred or so people under its jurisdiction, everyone was required to denounce these "enemies of the people" and subject them to the dreaded thamzing. "In those early days, they had thoroughly brainwashed the poor and could manipulate them any way they wanted", said Pema Saldon. "Thamzings were carried out first in one part of the city, then another, morning and evening. Many atrocities were permitted during these sessions. Many were killed, many others committed suicide. Some just died of shock or heart failure."

It was through thamzing that the people of Central and

Southern Tibet were now forced – like their compatriots in the east – to "make the revolution". The unrelenting class struggle, artificially stoked by whipped-up hatred, was carried out with unspeakable cruelty. It set workers against employers, peasants against landlords, monks against their abbots, students against teachers and children against parents. "Those who held positions of authority in society", commented John Avedon, "were automatically seen to possess them, not on the basis of merit, but ... for the sole purpose of oppressing the people".[9]

The poorer Tibetans were helpless pawns, constantly egged on beyond endurance and assured that thamzings were in their own best interests. They may well have had genuine grievances against some of the victims, but those grievances were blown up out of all proportion, and led to unimaginable excesses:

> Burying alive, wrapping the accused in a blanket and setting it on fire, suspending him from a tree and lighting a bonfire beneath, hanging, beheading, disembowelling, scalding, crucifixion, quartering, stoning to death by the whole group, small children being forced to shoot their parents – all these methods were suggested (by collaborators) and subsequently employed, as reported in case after case to the International Commission of Jurists.[10]

The family of Kunga Thinle, formerly assistant secretary to the Dalai Lama's senior tutor, was subjected to thamzing because of their relationship with him: "My father was arrested, all our property confiscated. He was eventually released, but the torture, imprisonment and humiliations proved too much and soon after he, my eldest sister, my brother and my niece committed suicide together by jumping in the river."[11]

On 30 April, the Panchen Lama declared to the world that the "rebellion" in Tibet had been put down, that order had been restored and the democratic reforms established. He made no reference to the vast army of prisoners nor to the huge and growing death toll. In the three months that followed the rising, 18,600 Tibetans were said to have been killed.[12] On 1 October

1960, Radio Lhasa claimed that 87,000 "reactionaries" had been eliminated in Central Tibet following the Lhasa Uprising. Sixty-nine thousand of these had been executed in a period of seventeen days in and around Lhasa.

Within a year, many thousands would die as a result of thamzing, while survivors were often permanently maimed, blinded, or made deaf. Dead bodies began appearing in rivers and in unfrequented spots. Many prisoners starved to death, because their relatives were forbidden to bring them food. Lobsang, a monk brave enough to be interviewed by Vanya Kewley for her Channel Four film,[13] had been arrested and sent to prison in the north-east:

> For twelve hours a day, every day, we had to do hard labour, in the mines, building bridges, in all weathers, without food, without proper clothing, without sleep. If we fell down, they would beat us until we regained consciousness. Even when we had broken limbs from the beatings and the torture, we still had to work. There was no medicine, no doctors for the prisoners. To the Chinese we were less than animals. We would get frostbite because we had nothing to protect our hands and feet. Sometimes it was so cold that the flesh on our hands would tear off and stick to the shovels ...
>
> To make us change our thinking and support Chinese rule in Tibet, they hung prisoners upside down in empty rooms and beat them with batons. Sometimes they forced other prisoners to do the beating, so that the Chinese would not have to take the blame.

Small wonder that Dr Tenzin Choedrak, the Dalai Lama's personal physician, arrested immediately after the revolt and sent to a gulag near the border with Inner Mongolia, found that of the 300 Tibetans imprisoned there just two years earlier only two were still alive:

> Hard work coupled with meagre rations and subhuman conditions of work soon caused physical deterioration ... Amidst

famine, we lost our sense of shame and dignity . . . we ate ropes, leather bags, anything we could lay our hands on . . . the men in our prison ate rats, frogs . . . some even ate the worms that were found in excreta . . . A seventeen-year-old Chinese youth killed his mother to get the four kilos of barley she had in her safe-keeping . . . Another Chinese killed an eight-year-old boy and ate him . . . Within three years, two-thirds of the Tibetans imprisoned there were dead.[14]

Though religious freedom was still officially allowed, its days were clearly numbered, for religion gave Tibetans their distinctive identity and must therefore go. The softening-up process was under way. "We were constantly told that religion was poison", recalls Pema Saldon. "'You have been fooled for too long', they said. They insisted the Dalai Lama had used religion as an excuse for opposing the Great Motherland. Tibet, they claimed, had never been independent, but at least now it was free. 'We have liberated you', they said."

It was made clear that there was no place for superstition in the new society and that anybody clinging to Buddhist practice would do so at their peril. "Reeling from shock after shock", said Dawa Norbu,

we were forced to see our orderly Buddhist universe collapse into chaos, both in mental and physical terms. The Chinese Communists, full of revolutionary zeal and utterly without any human sentiment, deliberately set out to prove to us that what we believed in was nothing more than a mirage.[15]

On the pretext that the monasteries had supported the revolt, the Chinese moved in for the kill. "Soon after the revolt", says Yeshe Gompo, who was then a novice monk at the Drepung monastery,

the Chinese began closing down monasteries and arresting the high lamas and abbots. Those abbots who had opposed the Chinese were arrested, subjected to thamzing and sent to prison.

Many died under torture, others committed suicide. All the
monks, even the boy novices, were divided into classes and the
poorer ones had to give thamzing to their "oppressors". The
property of the abbots was confiscated and handed out to the
poorer monks. I was only a boy, but I was summoned to a public
meeting and accused of oppressing the people and living off their
toil. We were made to attend re-education meetings every day,
and were constantly humiliated.[16]

After suffering thamzing, the monks were bound and taken off
by the truck-load to the new labour camp outside Lhasa, the
hydro-electric station, Nachen Thang. Tashi Palden was among
them. One day he and a number of other monks were told to
smarten themselves up for an audience with the Panchen Lama.
They were taken to a ruined monastery where there were a
number of Chinese soldiers and officers. To their surprise, they
were each handed an unloaded gun:

One of the officers said to us: "We're here to make an important
documentary film about the uprising. You must display anger
and other emotions exactly as you felt them at the time.
Anybody who does not take the matter seriously and who ruins
the film by smiling or looking bored will be dealt with severely."
So we enacted mock battles ending with some of us pretending to
be dead and the rest emerging from the debris of the monastery
with raised hands. We were then told, "When you go back, you
must tell no one that you have taken part in a film ..."[17]

In Nachen Thang a few days later, the Chinese promised a film
which "would prove conclusively that monks had taken part in
the fighting". Only then did Tashi Palden and the others realize
how they had been set up. The film was subsequently shown
throughout China and to fellow-travellers in the West.

Yeshe Gompo, like most of his fellow-monks, was made to
attend lectures on his obligations to the new Tibet, before being
sent back to his village to work for a living in the fields, and to
marry. He was told he would get no food if he stayed. "But those

who were prepared to marry", he said, "were congratulated and rewarded". Such people were called "progressive", while those who clung to the old ways were "conservatives with unpurgeable old green brains":

> On the day I was leaving I went back to my room to collect some tsampa. (People were not allowed to provide food for the monks any more, so we were hungry.) The Chinese were there and forbade me to take anything away. Everything had to be left behind. In theory, the monks who stayed were allowed to practise their religion, but everything possible was done to discourage them. They were subjected to endless indoctrination and harassment. One thing they frequently did was to lock the monks in a house with a group of women for several days, so that they would lose their virginity. By 1961, there were only thirty monks left in Drepung, once the biggest monastery in the world.

By the end of 1959, in the great monasteries of Drepung, Sera and Ganden, only a few aged caretaker-monks were left. And in the ancient monastery of Samye, the first Buddhist foundation in Tibet, out of 500 monks only thirty-six old men remained.[18]

Then began the wanton destruction of most of Tibet's 6,524 monasteries and temples. The Chinese would claim later – when they realized they had gone too far – that this wholesale destruction was the work of the Gang of Four and the Cultural Revolution of the late Sixties. But it is a well-authenticated fact that most of the monasteries were destroyed between 1959 and 1961.[19] The destruction, says Phuntsog Wangyal, was systematic:

> First of all, special teams of mineralogists were sent to religious buildings to locate and extract all the precious stones. Next, metallurgists arrived and marked all metal objects which were subsequently removed. Then trucks were sent from local army headquarters, the walls were dynamited, and all the wooden beams and pillars were taken away. Clay images were destroyed in the hope of finding precious objects inside them. Finally,

whatever remained – bits of wood and stone – were removed by local people.

In an interview with Vanya Kewley, the monk, Lobsang, told her how the Chinese had stripped the Sera monastery of whatever remained of its religious artefacts – the silver butter-lamps, the long horns used in religious rituals – and loaded them onto ninety-seven three-tonne army lorries. "The lorries always left for China in the dead of night when there were few witnesses around to record the fact".

Centuries-old monastic libraries were turned into assembly halls and store-rooms. According to Chomphel Sonam, a monk official from Shigatse, the precious scriptures were either burned as fuel, mixed with manure or used as wrapping in the Chinese shops.[20] In the rural areas they were used as toilet paper, while the engraved or carved wooden blocks and covers were turned into chairs, floorboards and farm implements.

It was only now that the Chinese, to justify what they had done, began making exaggerated claims about the corruption and cruelty of the old system, the "atrocities" committed by the former landlords and monastic officials. There had been "no human rights" in Tibet prior to 1950, they claimed. Such charges were undisputed in the West, particularly by those who saw the Chinese Communist system as a shining social experiment. But, as Hugh Richardson points out:

> they bear little or no relation to the accounts of conditions in the country and the way of life of its people as reported by experienced and authoritative foreign visitors ... It might also be asked why, if such oppression did in fact exist, it had not been mentioned, let alone removed, in seven years of Communist domination of Tibet.[21]

In a letter to a friend in 1948, one of those "experienced and authoritative foreign visitors", the writer/mountaineer Marco Pallis, referred to the corruption that existed in Tibet, but was sure that "these people are still far happier and healthier and more human than is the average with us".[22] And Dawa Norbu insists that, though the serfs may indeed have regarded some of the aristocrats as social parasites and exploiters, no-one had ever thought of the monks like that and no amount of Chinese propaganda could ever persuade them to do so: "The lamas formed one of the constituents of the Buddhist Trinity, and when they were persecuted the masses mourned."[23]

Large numbers of immigrants flooded into Lhasa from the overcrowded areas of China, given rights which were utterly denied to the Tibetans. Their prime task was to create a new city tailored to the needs of Mao's China and their own. It could be done on the cheap since all the materials were available, just waiting to be confiscated or purloined. They built a variety of enterprises: a power station, a cement factory, a broadcasting station, a people's hospital, a guest house and an exhibition hall. Building progressed at a rapid pace. How could it not, with an unlimited labour-pool of prisoners and under-paid, under-fed, conscript Tibetans at their disposal?

> If there was any construction work to be done, whether building a bridge, factory, or road, the prisoners were made to do it. People were made to pull horse-carts and iron ploughs in the fields alongside yaks, and carry boulders on their backs. Their feet, hands and backs turned into one big sore and bled. But they had still to continue with their work.[24]

Many of the men and women who had been released from prison a few months after the rising were employed in humping rocks and shovelling soil. Thirteen-year-old Wangchen was sent to a work-gang at the hydro-electric station. "We were given huge baskets to fill with earth and had a quota to fill every day. We had to carry one basket on our heads and another in our hands, and our backs were soon covered in sores. The land frequently subsided, and once fourteen workers were buried alive."

All this at a time when there was near-starvation throughout the land, for reasons which lay in mainland China. From 1959

the Chinese economy was in dire trouble, thanks to the disastrous Great Leap Forward policy, which had urged the
peasantry on to impossible efforts in the interests of rapid
modernization. It had led to a rift with the Soviet Union, which
subsequently cut off vital grain supplies to its former ally.
Recent harvests in China had been poor; serious famine resulted
and millions starved to death. To feed the remainder, Tibet's
harvests were seized as soon as garnered; she was made to
replace Soviet Russia as the bread-basket for the Great Motherland. The average Tibetan's diet was cut by two-thirds, and in
the ensuing famine (which lasted well into 1963), tens of
thousands died. "Rations were terribly scarce", says Wangchen. "We were reduced to eating intestines filled with animal
blood. Even a bowl of rice was a rare luxury." Allowed only a
few pounds of grain a month, people in the cities ate cats, dogs
and insects:

> Parents fed dying children their own blood mixed with hot water
> and tsampa. Other children were forced to leave home to beg on
> the roads and old people went off to die alone in the hills.
> Thousands of Tibetans took to eating the refuse thrown by the
> Chinese to the pigs each Han compound kept, while those
> around PLA outposts daily pieced apart manure from the
> soldiers' horses, looking for undigested grain. Even for Tibetan
> cadres, normally better-fed than the population at large, meat
> and butter were unavailable, salt and black tea being the sole
> supplement to barley grain.[25]

Matters were worst of all in the prisons. From Drapchi and
Taring prisons in Lhasa alone, two or three cartloads of corpses
were taken daily for burial or for use as manure on the fields.
"But people were not allowed to say that those deaths were
caused by starvation", remembers a nun, Lobsang Wangmo,
who had been arrested for giving food to escaping "reactionaries". "If they were caught saying so, they'd be severely
punished".[26]

As Tibetans died from starvation and exhaustion, the Beijing

LEFT *Thubten Gyatso, the 'Great Thirteenth' Dalai Lama, shortly before his death in 1933*

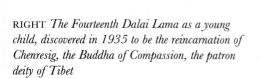

RIGHT *The Fourteenth Dalai Lama as a young child, discovered in 1935 to be the reincarnation of Chenresig, the Buddha of Compassion, the patron deity of Tibet*

ABOVE *Chinese troops entering Lhasa through the Western Gate, 1951 (now destroyed)*

BELOW *On an official visit to New Delhi in November 1956 the Chinese Prime Minister, Chou En-Lai (right), meets the Dalai Lama (left) and the Indian Prime Minister, Jawaharlal Nehru (centre)*

ABOVE *The Potala Palace in Lhasa*

BELOW *Phuntsok Tashi Takla, Tibetan historian and HH the Dalai Lama's security chief at the time of the escape from Lhasa in March 1959*

BELOW *A contemporary photograph of Tendzin Choegyal (aka Ngari Rimpoche) younger brother of HH the Dalai Lama*

ABOVE *March 1959. The difficult escape from Lhasa. In the foreground on a white pony is HH the Dalai Lama disguised as an ordinary soldier. The route led over many snowbound high passes*

BELOW *May 1959. Newly arrived Tibetan refugees at the Missamari Camp, India*

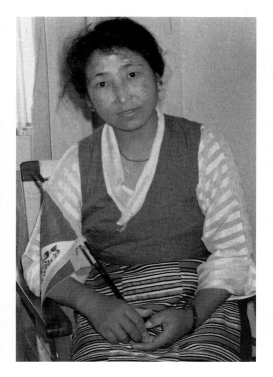

ABOVE *Pema Saldon*

ABOVE *Beri Laga*

BELOW *Topai Adhi*

BELOW *Yeshe Gompo, former Drepung novice-monk, expelled from his monastery by the Chinese in 1959*

LEFT *The Tenth Panchen Lama, 1938-1989*

RIGHT *Ganden Monastery, near Lhasa, in 1949. Built in 1417, this centre of learning housed more than 5,000 monks. It was reduced to ruins during the Cultural Revolution of 1966-69*

BELOW RIGHT *Some of the rebuilt Temples of Ganden. In the 1980's they began to rise from the ruins*

BELOW *Bylakuppe settlement in S. India, seen from the rebuilt Sera Monastery*

ABOVE *Throughout the forty years of occupation, the Chinese have continued to cut down the forests of Tibet and send the timber back to China*

BELOW *Chinese poster proclaiming the government's birth control policies - 'control the population increase and civilise the country'*

People's Daily and the New China News Agency sang of the glories of the "socialist paradise on the Roof of the World". Lhasa's streets and parks, once named in accordance with Tibetan culture and religion, were renamed in Marxist fashion: Great Leap Forward Street, Liberation Street, Sunshine Street. The Norbulingka Gardens became the People's Park; the sacred Chokpori Hill was rechristened Victory Peak. Before the revolt, Tibet's most famous medical school had stood there; but now it sprouted radio antennae and was being used as an ammunition dump. As Paul Theroux would one day write, the Chinese were incapable of seeing that this did not represent progress. They "could not understand why anyone would prefer an old Buddhist Medical College to a tall new TV antenna bolted to a ferro-concrete block".[27]

The spurious glamour of the new Lhasa could not disguise the stark truth that the shops were all closed, the market was empty and "even the best-kept buildings showed signs of the decay which would, within a few years, reduce the Tibetan quarter of Lhasa to a slum".[28] Tibetan society was confused and uncertain. Life had to go on somehow, and many had resigned themselves to their fate: there were Tibetan cadres, factory workers, teachers working for the Chinese. Others carried on some small-trading or worked in handicraft centres, but most were press-ganged into the projects which by no stretch of the imagination could be said to benefit Tibetans. The broadcasting station was used by the Chinese for propaganda purposes and became an instrument of oppression; the products of the cement plant and the coal and coke factory were used for the most part by the Chinese: no Tibetan was given any cement for house-building or coal for either cooking purposes or fuel. Even in the hospital, Chinese and Tibetan patients were treated in different sections. Treatment was free, but for the Tibetans, it usually amounted to no more than a routine injection.

Yet the Panchen Lama, speaking to the Standing Committee of the National People's Congress in Beijing in December 1960, could describe the situation in Tibet as "wonderful", with "prosperous scenes of labour and production" visible wherever

one looked. One wondered where exactly he *was* looking. For, as
Tashi Palden reported, "The work got harder and harder and
the food became worse and worse". People were committing
suicide by jumping into the Tsangpo River.

In the rural areas around Lhasa, life for the poor had at first
seemed to promise a better world. Teams of Chinese officials
with China-trained Tibetan "interpreters" to help them,
descended on the villages and set up village councils manned by
the former landless peasants. Debts and taxes owed by these
tenants to their landlords were scrapped and all records of loans
publicly burned on huge bonfires round which everyone had to
gather and applaud and shout slogans. The poorer peasants
could scarcely believe their luck, especially when the land was
redistributed amongst them.

But a few of them were uneasy. "Our hope of a happier future
was mixed with a certain fear", wrote Mrs Dondub Chodon,
then an eighteen-year-old from a family of serfs and relatively
enthusiastic about the new regime. "We had never seen a
Chinese before. We wondered whether they really spoke the
truth, whether they could be trusted and how many soldiers
they had. Above all, we wondered about their real aims in
coming to our land and hoped that they would not stay too
long."[29]

They were soon disillusioned. When the houses of the rich
were broken up, everything happened as it had in the cities.
Most of the animals were taken by the local Chinese. The gold,
silver and other valuables were carefully collected (for transpor-
tation in trucks to China), while the poorest peasants were given
the leftovers. Dawa Norbu's family, small-time traders, received
nothing, but his sister, Donkar, who was classified as a proletarian, was given "two old silk shirts, a pair of old ornate shoes
worn by some senior lama on festive occasions, a huge, cumber-
some ant-eaten box, two tables with missing legs, one wooden
saddle, an old blue brocade chuba and an odd glove."[30] He
heard one peasant say that the Chinese had eaten all the meat
and given the Tibetans the bones. "The only democracy in the
democratic reforms was the right of the Chinese masters to

'liberate' the Tibetan people from their wealth, works of art and priceless religious relics", wrote the ex-student from China, Tsering Dorje Gashi.[31]

These Buddhist peasants were told it was the old regime, not bad karma, which was the root cause of all suffering, the source of every imaginable evil. Now that the landlords had been dispossessed, the peasants were remorselessly instructed in the art of recognizing "enemies of the people" and of inflicting thamzing on them. They had no choice but to take part, since if they did not, they would themselves be subjected to the process. At the assemblies, as they waited for the "bad people" to be brought in, they had to sing revolutionary songs and shout slogans such as "We, the people of Tibet, must unite to exterminate the reactionary upper strata". This was done "to arouse our animal instincts, so that we might appear as aggressive as tigers before the helpless wolves".

The thamzings were a harrowing ordeal for everyone concerned:

> We had one thamzing after another, of every type: the extermination of rebels and their associates; the extermination of feudal government and its running dogs; the extermination of landlords and their agents. If the Chinese working personnel observed any aristocrat not yet humbled, or discovered any counter-revolutionary, they called for a thamzing rather as we used to call the butcher to slaughter our sheep.[32]

Nor did it stop there. As in the cities, when the people had been roused to fever-pitch against the former "serf-owners", it was time to set them at loggerheads with each other, to foment the endless class struggle in which everyone was required to betray everyone else. It cut across the grain of the Tibetan temperament, for, whatever class they had been born into, Tibetans felt an instinctive sympathy with one another.

To speed up the social levelling, compulsory Mutual Aid Teams were established in which about ten families not only shared their newly acquired land and the work of sowing, growing and harvesting, but also pooled their property, farm implements and animals. Former landlords were not eligible to join these collectives. Nobody was allowed to consort with them, or even talk to them; they were generally issued the worst bit of land and, if they were lucky, a single plough animal with which to work it. Lobsang Rinchok was a "class enemy", deprived of both privileges and protection: "When there was rough or unpleasant work to be done, we were the ones to do it: cleaning out latrines, carrying officials' luggage on our backs."[33] Beri Laga's fate was similar. She was driven out of her late husband's house and made to work in the fields:

> Everyone else had a half-hour rest period both morning and afternoon, but we did not. When everyone went home in the evening, we had to continue working until sundown. And we received the barest minimum of food. The Chinese introduced a reward system of stars, but no matter how hard we worked (and we certainly worked harder than anybody else) we never got any stars. We were always at the back of the queue for food.[34]

All the people had to work excessively hard, and their attendance was meticulously logged to preclude the possibility of shirking. During lunch breaks and after work in the evening, they had two-and-a-half hours of compulsory indoctrination classes. The only holidays were China's national days. Through the co-operatives, the Chinese "made us work, talk, eat, cry and sing as their almighty Party wanted."[35] Conversation, even jokes, had to conform to the Party line. And to add insult to injury, they had to sing as they worked. "We want to weep", the workers lamented, "but we are made to sing".

They no longer had any peace of mind or body. Though the Tibetan respect for all forms of sentient life was deeply ingrained in their psyche, they were compelled now to kill dogs and flies. The Chinese said that this was on the grounds of hygiene, but the Tibetans knew it was one more attack on their beloved religion. They had already been told that to visit the monasteries or invite monks to perform their time-honoured family rituals was to reject the new order. In each village, the Dalai Lama was publicly held up to ridicule and abuse. The Chinese would gather the people together and tell them that their former leader was an evil man and that they must reject him. On one such occasion, an old man got up and said that the Tibetan people could never reject the Dalai Lama since he symbolized everything that was Tibet. The people cheered and clapped. But that night the old man was taken away and was never seen again.[36]

Through the collectives, efficiency undoubtedly increased and agricultural production improved by leaps and bounds. But even if the Tibetan peasant had received a fair reward for his labour, the price he paid would still have been too high:

> In the old days there had been a time for everything – for merry-making as well as hard work. The seasonal work days were exciting, enjoyable events in the farmers' calendar and the labourers used to look forward to feasts washed down by chang, and to songs and laughter ... But hard work without freedom of the spirit was deadly monotony, and without adequate food it was veritable torture.[37]

Drinking was now "anti-Motherland sabotage".

Though the harvests got better, the peasant got less and less, as the fruits of his toil were consumed by the People's Liberation Army troops on the spot or despatched to China. "No one had enough to eat, not even enough for one meal a day. The peasants were made to grow rice instead of their own staple crop, barley, because the Chinese didn't like barley. Without barley, the Tibetans were reduced to living on herbs and nettles."[38]*

"We told them wheat wouldn't grow so high up, but they wouldn't listen", a farmer told Vanya Kewley.[39] "They wanted to grow wheat for their noodles because they didn't like our tsampa made from the barley which is so well-suited to this climate."

Thousands starved. Lobsang Chophel, a Tibetan living in

Australia, recalls an uncle telling him that "in the early 1960s there was a daily death toll of 150–200. They were literally in hell – the anguish, fear and hunger made ghosts out of them. My uncle said, 'When we awoke in the mornings we were scared to call the person sleeping next to us for fear he might be dead.'"[40]

The Chinese had little sympathy to spare. "People who died of starvation or sickness were said to be unworthy of life, since they were unable to make a worthwhile contribution to their country", claimed Pema Lhundup, a refugee in India.[41] By the end of 1961, even as the Chinese proclaimed that the Tibetans had welcomed their unusually high production figures with "pure ecstasy", and that a million serfs were celebrating with song and dance, over 70,000 of those ecstatic serfs had died or were dying from starvation. The survivors described Chinese policy as the torture of "the wet leather helmet", which, as it dried out, became tighter and tighter until finally it crushed the victim's skull.

---

* Stephen Corry, Director General of Survival International, an organization which works for the rights of threatened tribal peoples, reported: "Far from providing the poor with enough to eat, the overwhelming evidence suggests that the Chinese totally disrupted an essentially self-sufficient society and caused, through their brutality and colonialism, massive food shortages and widespread hunger as the masses were put to work to feed their new masters."

CHAPTER 9

The White Crane Flies South

The white crane is the bird of the north,
Born there, yet he flies south.
The north is not an unhappy land
But winter ice has gripped the blue lakes.

TIBETAN FOLK SONG

When in April 1959 Nehru told the Indian Parliament that the Dalai Lama and his party had arrived safely in India, they cheered him roundly. There was a strong wave of popular sympathy for the Tibetan leader which Nehru dared not ignore. Besides, as it had been at Nehru's insistence that the Dalai Lama had returned to Tibet in 1956, he must have wished to make some sort of amends. But how to tread the tightrope between assisting the Dalai Lama and not offending the Chinese? After 1950, China had kept up the pressure on the Indian government, constantly accusing Nehru of aiding imperialist schemes to prise Tibet from China's grasp. In April 1954, China and India had signed an Agreement known as the "Panch Shila" or Five Principles of Coexistence. "Tibet was murdered", wrote Dawa Norbu, "and upon its grave the Panch Shila were engraved".[1] He was right. Nehru set great store by the Agreement, and it led him to exercise a strict censorship on news about Tibet, thus preventing the outside world from learning about Chinese atrocities there. At that very time, the Chinese were urging him to expel the Tibetan refugees who had already settled in India (mainly around Kalimpong, the old terminus of the Lhasa–India trade route).

So when he offered asylum to the Dalai Lama and expressed a

cautious sympathy with him, the Chinese were furious. They
trundled out all the old accusations of expansionism and of
being in cahoots with the Tibetan reactionaries in India who
had fomented the Lhasa revolt and abducted the Dalai Lama.
"It astonished me yet again", the Dalai Lama wrote in his
memoirs,

> to see how the Chinese blamed everybody they could think of for
> the revolt – like an injured dog which snaps at everybody. At
> different times they had tried to put the blame on the totally
> imaginary imperialists, the Tibetans who were living in India,
> the Indian government, and the "ruling clique" in Tibet, which
> was now their description of my government. They could not
> allow themselves to recognize the truth: that it was the people
> themselves, whom the Chinese claimed to be liberating, who had
> revolted spontaneously against their liberation, and that the rul-
> ing class of Tibet had been far more willing than the people to
> come to an agreement with the Chinese.[2]

Though Nehru, like every other Indian politician, knew that
welcoming the Dalai Lama made India more vulnerable to
attack by China, he could not ignore the groundswell of popular
feeling. He did, however, assure the Chinese that the Dalai
Lama would be restricted to his religious functions while in
India, with no opportunity to engage in politics or in propaganda on behalf of Tibetan independence.

Despite his fears, Nehru was determined to give as much
humanitarian aid as he could to the Tibetans. Once the
exhausted party had reached Tawang, the district HQ for the
North-East Frontier Agency (NEFA), the generosity of the
Indian government knew no bounds. "From the moment we
entered Indian territory", says Tendzin Choegyal, "they provided us with everything we needed:

> While we were at Tawang, planes used to come, Dakotas and
> DC10s from the plains of India. They dropped food and all sorts
> of other things. I used to go and watch the planes come in very

low and drop sackloads of rice, just half-full so that they would not burst open on contact with the ground. Then the planes would regain height and drop crates of tinned foods and cooking oil by parachute. Sometimes the parachute failed to open and the crates hit the ground with the force of a bomb. I remember oil spraying everywhere in a huge fountain.

It was terribly hot, and we had come from Tibet in winter clothes, in boots and fur hats. Our officials asked the government of India for more suitable hats for us, and next day they dropped a plane-load of trilbies. It was heart-warming that a country that had so few resources of its own could be so generous to strangers.[3]

Along the road, the Dalai Lama received a telegram of welcome from Nehru; and on reaching Tezpur was mobbed and cheered by a crowd of journalists eager for the "story of the year". Here the party was at last able to stop walking and board a special train for Mussoorie, a former British hill-station in the Himalayan foothills north of Delhi. Cheering crowds lined the route.

Three days later, Nehru came to visit the Dalai Lama in Mussoorie, the visit reflecting the Indian leader's anxiety and ambivalence. Though he posed for affectionate photographs with his "true old friend", the Dalai Lama found Nehru "a bit of a bully". The Indian leader made it clear that he would not jeopardize his non-aligned status in the world nor run the risk of a Sino-Indian war by recognizing the Dalai Lama's newly proclaimed government of Tibet. Nehru remained adamant on that, though opponents and colleagues alike accused him of cowardice and appeasement.

For two months, out of gratitude to Nehru, the Dalai Lama stayed silent. But the thousands of refugees still streaming over the mountain passes into Nepal, Bhutan, Sikkim and India, brought spine-chilling evidence of the Chinese determination to destroy the old Tibet in the wake of the Lhasa revolt. Overwhelmed by their revelations of murder and mass destruction, the Dalai Lama decided to ask the international community for help. At a press conference on 20 June, he at last spoke out, expressing his deep gratitude to India but able no longer to keep silent on the wanton destruction of his country. He insisted that China's aim was to exterminate his people, their religion and their culture; and he called for an international commission to investigate the reports of atrocities brought by the refugees. Then, formally repudiating the 1951 Seventeen Point Agreement on the grounds that the Chinese had broken every one of its terms, he said he would return to Tibet only when the country's pre-1950 independence was guaranteed. "I was sure", wrote the Dalai Lama in his memoirs,

> that people would realise that my story was nearer the truth than the incredible fiction put about by the Chinese. But although my latest statement received wide coverage, I had underestimated the power of an efficiently conducted public relations campaign such as the Chinese Government was able to carry out. Or perhaps I overestimated the willingness of mankind to face the truth about itself. I believe that it took first the evidence of the Cultural Revolution, then the sight of the 1989 Tiananmen Square massacre on its television screens before the world fully accepted the mendacity and barbarism of the Communist Chinese.[4]

Responding to the Dalai Lama's plea for an impartial inquiry, a body of respected lawyers, the International Commission of Jurists, launched an investigation both into the question of Tibet's independence and into the reported atrocities. Basing their inquiries on statements taken almost exclusively from the poorer sections of society, they reported that human rights had been violated in Tibet in sixteen different ways, including murder, rape, torture, destruction of family life and deportation.[5] They concluded that Tibet had indeed been a sovereign and independent state before the Chinese invasion; and that China had by genocidal acts systematically tried "to destroy in whole or in part the Tibetans as a separate nation and the Buddhist religion in Tibet".[6]

The lawyers' findings gave the Dalai Lama heart to have another go at the United Nations. By the end of September 1959, Ireland and Malaysia had agreed to take up Tibet's cause – on the ground of Human Rights abuse – and the Steering Committee for the fourteenth session of the General Assembly debated the issue at some length. "On the basis of the available evidence", it reported, "it would seem difficult to recall a case in which ruthless oppression of man's essential dignity has been more systematically carried out".

But those were the frosty days of the Cold War, when Communist China was not a member of the United Nations,* but when the Soviet Union and its satellites could be relied on to champion every Communist cause and veto every Western one. The Communist bloc complained that raising the "non-existent" Tibetan question was blatant interference in China's internal affairs. The US was determined not to be seen stirring the pot, and the British remained non-committal. In spite of this, a majority voted to include the issue on the agenda of the General Assembly, where a vague resolution was passed in Tibet's favour. (The voting was forty-five to nine with twenty-six abstentions, one of them Britain.) China was not mentioned by name, but the Assembly called for "respect for the fundamental rights of the Tibetan people and for their distinctive cultural and religious life". There was not a word about the two issues which lay at the root of the problem: Tibetan independence and sovereignty. The Dalai Lama had hoped for some constructive action; but he had to be content wth encouraging words – which needless to say left the Chinese unmoved. (A year later, and again in 1965, with more reports of atrocities and murder being brought by fresh waves of refugees from Tibet, he tried again. The UN expressed "grave concern" and "deep anxiety" for the Tibetans, but did not call for any action.)

---

* China was represented at the UN by Chiang Kai-shek's ousted Nationalist government which had taken refuge on Formosa (now Taiwan).

By the end of June 1959, before the Chinese had contrived to seal the borders, nearly 20,000 refugees had streamed over the Himalaya from Tibet. Most were ragged and destitute, driven to flee their country by starvation and terror, and by loss of hope. Although the Chinese proclaimed that the rebellion in Lhasa had been the work of upper-class reactionaries and that the refugees were all from the upper strata, they were, on the contrary, mainly the common people of Tibet, the yeoman farmers and the landless peasants whom the Chinese had claimed to liberate, but whose lives they had destroyed. "Once the revolt in Tibet was over", wrote Dawa Norbu, "everybody felt their life was broken beyond repair".[7] "Before the Dalai Lama left", agrees Ugyan Norbu, "escapees had just wandered around from one part of Tibet to another seeking refuge. As long as he was there, there was still hope. But when he went, our happiness – and our security – flew out of the window."[8]

Many more tried to escape than succeeded, for the journey was fraught with dangers. Those who lived close to the borders – where Chinese control was not yet complete – had to cross uncharted peaks 24–25,000 feet high. Others fought their way from Kham or Amdo in the teeth of the Chinese army; and their losses were enormous. Of one group of 4,000 which left Tibet in June, only 125 remained on arrival in India.[9] Families were separated from each other or watched each other die. Without exception, the escape routes were strewn with bodies, bullet-ridden, starved or frozen to death.

For the survivors, the nightmare did not end with their arrival on friendly soil; it merely entered a new phase. The refugees were hungry, often seriously wounded, affected by the heat and the low altitude, bewildered and confused by events and by intense culture shock. They had arrived, moreover, at the start of the hottest season, wearing winter boots and heavy robes. The injections they were given against cholera and typhoid nearly finished them off. Tendzin Choegyal remembers that, "everyone was sick, everyone was crying with pain, even tough old warriors".[10]

The Indian authorities rose to the occasion magnificently.

The new arrivals were accommodated in hastily erected tents in two large transit camps in the Himalayan region: Missamari, near Tezpur, and Buxa Duar, a former British prisoner-of-war camp near the border with Bhutan. All the Indian political parties supported an unofficial Central Relief Committee which provided food, clothing and medical supplies, and co-ordinated the efforts of various international relief agencies. (News of the Tibetans' safe arrival had brought sympathy and support from many parts of the world).

At the crowded Missamari camp, life was hazardous: the water was contaminated, there was no sanitation and in the damp heat of the rainy season malaria was rife. The Indian diet of curried potato, dhal and rice wrought havoc with the digestion of people used to a frugal mix of barley, butter and dried meat. "India was so much hotter than Tibet, and they had difficulty in acclimatizing themselves", says Kesang Takla. "They missed their tsampa and tea and as they could not afford meat they soon suffered from protein deficiency. Their health deteriorated and many of them died."[11]

An epidemic of amoebic dysentery carried off scores of the very old and very young. It did not seem as though the Tibetans would long survive in India. They were dying not only of dysentery but of tuberculosis, influenza, scabies and severe malnutrition. "We couldn't concentrate on rehabilitating them", says Mrs Takla, "it was a question of mere survival and then of finding them a job, any job."

As the Tibetans did not want to continue depending on the Indian government's charity, gradually the able-bodied, including a large number of monks,* were moved to road-construction camps in the Himalayan foothills, where India was building

---

* Only 7,000 of more than 600,000 monks and a few hundred of Tibet's 4,000 incarnate lamas had escaped. The survivors set up monastic communities and collected all the scriptures they could find. But the death rate among the monks was extremely high, many of them dying from TB. With each death centuries of scholarship were lost.

new military roads to its northern border with occupied Tibet.
But in the heat of India, this was unhealthy work for mountain
people. When the Dalai Lama visited the road-camps, he was
heartbroken:

> Children, women and men were all working side by side in
> gangs: former nuns, farmers, monks, officials, all thrown
> together. They had to endure a full day's hard physical toil
> under a mighty sun, followed by nights crammed into tiny tents
> ... Though it was a bit cooler than in the transit camps, heat and
> humidity still exacted a frightening toll. The air was fetid and
> thick with mosquitoes. As a result sickness was universal and
> often fatal.[12]

The Tibetans were particularly vulnerable to any infection that
was rife among the Indians, especially tuberculosis. Lacking the
necessary antibodies, hundreds died.

They died not only from disease but from heartbreak and
despair also, as time went by and it became apparent that they
would not be returning immediately to Tibet. The Dalai Lama
knew that the Tibetans' only hope was to accept this and to plan
some kind of positive self-supporting future in India. After giving religious teaching to a crowd of 2,000 weeping Tibetans in
December 1959, he tried to instil a new courage into them: "For
the moment Tibet's sun and moon have suffered an eclipse, but
one day we will regain our country. You should not lose heart.
The great job ahead of us now is to preserve our religion and
culture."[13]

With the aid of foreign relief organizations, carpet-weaving
centres were set up in Darjeeling and Dalhousie, where about
600 refugees could find employment. But the most positive hope
for a settled future came when the Dalai Lama was offered land
for resettlement around Dharamsala, a Himalayan ghost-town
perched on the Dhauladar range on the northern fringe of the
Punjab. Established by the British in the 1860s as a summer
retreat, Dharamsala boasted a small town, McLeod Ganj, an
Anglican church and more than a hundred bungalows. It would

have become the summer capital of the Raj, had not an earth-quake devastated it in 1905, and the British chose Simla instead. Dharamsala's decaying bungalows were eventually entrusted to a Parsee family, the Nowrojees, owners of the General Store in McLeod Ganj. For years, Mr N. N. Nowrojee tried to dispose of the bungalows, even offering them free of charge to schools, organizations and the like. But in vain. Then, hearing that the Indian government was looking for a residence for the Dalai Lama, he seized his chance. Nehru was delighted with the "for-gotten ghost-town wasting in the woods", and offered it to the Dalai Lama.[14] The latter believed that Dharamsala – a day's journey from Delhi – was too isolated; but he also saw its pos-sibilities. "It was open and there was more room to expand". He accepted Nehru's offer.

He moved there in April 1960 with a large number of refu-gees. Here, with a permanent base at last, the battle for survival could begin. Here the Tibetan leader would strive night and day to prevent the collapse of the refugee community and to shape a new, more modern Tibet.

When the Dalai Lama had first fled to India in 1950, a treasure in gold, silver and ancient coins had been brought out with him and deposited in Sikkim. This he now transferred to a bank in Calcutta, converted it into currency and used it as a seed-fund for projects to help the Tibetans. It was time to dis-card some of the over-elaborate ceremonial of the past. But what was valuable in Tibetan culture had at all costs to be preserved: the performing arts, literature, medicine, religion, painting, metalcraft and carpet-making. The Tibetan Dance and Drama Society was founded, to keep alive traditional regional dances. The Tibetan Medical Centre followed, to manufacture and dis-pense ancient herbal remedies, and train a new generation of Tibetan doctors. And finally, the Library of Tibetan Works and Archives received what was left of Tibet's literature and Buddh-ist scriptures.

But rehabilitation was the most urgent problem. Though the climate of north India's hill towns suited the Tibetans more than the plains, there was not enough available land to accom-

modate them all. Nehru canvassed the southern state governments for help. In response Karnataka, in September 1960,
offered an uninhabited stretch of jungle at Bylakuppe west of
Mysore, and to this remote area, in December, a group of about
seven hundred Tibetans were sent. The task was a daunting
one, the land being a jungle wilderness which had to be cleared
with axes and machetes before anyone could live there. On the
night of their arrival, the new settlers almost despaired. "We
forced ourselves to eat", one of them later told John Avedon,
"but we all felt so frightened and forlorn that no-one could
speak. Many people sat helplessly on the ground crying to themselves. We could hear the calls of wild animals in the jungle and,
unlike in Tibet, you couldn't see a thing. Wherever you looked
there was nothing but trees."[15]

Settlers begged the Dalai Lama to send them somewhere else,
anywhere else. But there was nowhere else to go. Within a week
they had begun felling the trees and burning the forest.

> The heat was the worst. For two years, day and night, smoke
> and fire covered everything – even during the monsoon. Then we
> would work all day in the pouring rain and come home at night
> to find our tents blown down. Under these conditions many
> people died. They would recall Tibet, look at where they were
> and just give up.[16]

"Over and over again I counselled them to have faith and to
persevere", remembers the Dalai Lama. "They did, and I am
proud of them".[17] Though many died in the attempt, some of
them trampled to death by elephants maddened by the loss of
their habitats, early in 1962 the first settlers moved into more
than a hundred brick houses with tiled roofs. With new groups
of 500 sent down at six-monthly intervals from the north, the
flourishing farming community at Bylakuppe would gradually
take shape. It would become a model for thirty-four other large
agricultural co-operatives in South or North-East India built on
equally forbidding terrain. Its 5,000 acres came to support a
population of 10,000 in eighteen villages and six monasteries.

Meanwhile, for the Dalai Lama, the most acute problem was what to do with the many orphaned children whose parents had died in the transit camps or in the road-camps. Thousands of abandoned, mostly sick, children were roaming the transit camps in search of food or family. It was the other side of a tragedy which threatened the Tibetans with the loss of an entire generation. In Tibet itself, many thousands of children had been taken away to be brainwashed in China; and now in India, the refugee children, particularly the very young and vulnerable, were dying in droves.

Less than three weeks after arriving in Dharamsala, the Dalai Lama decided to set up a nursery for the destitute orphans and the children of those who were too ill to cope. The Indian government placed two dilapidated bungalows in Dharamsala at his disposal. The first batch of fifty-one starving and sick children arrived on 17 May 1960 and His Holiness's elder sister, Tsering Dolma, undertook to look after them in the new nursery. They were soon overwhelmed, wrote the Dalai Lama: "Almost before we knew where we were, 800 tiny children had been handed over to our care".[18] Children poured in from the itinerant road workers' camps in Kulu, Sikkim, Bhutan and Nepal. Though the Indian government provided some rations, and other individuals and voluntary organizations helped in different ways, life at the nursery was very hard, as Kesang Takla who worked there in the Sixties recalls:

Every day we had fifty or sixty coming across the border. There was a lot of malnutrition, sores, diarrhoea, and the children were very unhappy. Somehow we had to accommodate them all. Some of them needed special care or to be sent immediately to hospitals. We used to put six or seven children crossways on each bunk, and those who had no bunks slept on the floor. It was so hard to get enough of everything, even the most basic necessities were in short supply. But everyone was highly motivated and worked very hard. None of us worried about office hours or whether we had a Saturday off.

But in spite of all our efforts some of the children died; and sometimes infections – like scabies, for example – would spread through the school like wildfire. We had to give all our attention to just surviving.

Top priority had to be given to the children's physical needs, but by 1962 care was also being taken to provide them with a basic education in a stable atmosphere. The problem of education was well understood: the Dalai Lama knew that if the Tibetan children were to be equipped for a twentieth century world, their education could not be limited to the teaching of religion and philosophy, they must have access to vocational skills, to science and technology. Every effort must be made to give them the kind of sound education their parents had lacked.

On the children in India rested Tibetan hopes for the future. On their behalf the Dalai Lama proposed to Nehru an ambitious scheme whereby residential and day schools would be set up, jointly staffed by Indian and Tibetan teachers. The medium of education would be English, but Tibetan would also be taught, plus Hindi or the local dialect of whatever Indian state the Tibetans had settled in. Nehru responded with characteristic generosity, and the scheme was promptly put into action. Children were taken from the nursery at Dharamsala and sent to other schools; and three residential schools for older children were set up in Mussoorie, Simla and Darjeeling. Within four years there were seven residential schools for about 500 children each, four day schools in the settlements, three transit schools at the road-construction sites, and a number of grant-aided schools. By 1966 almost 7,000 young people had been rescued from the road-gangs. In the years to come, almost all these children would place their considerable talents and skills at the service of the refugee community.*

In the Dalai Lama's vision, the new Tibet would not be isolated from the world as the old one had been, and it would be a democratic community. The old feudal system had no place in

---

* According to Kesang Takla, they form 60–70% of the present administration in Dharamsala.

the new world in which the Tibetans found themselves. The introduction of democratic procedures was both the realization of a personal dream and part of his strategy to enable the Tibetans to overcome the trauma of their exile. The social reforms which the Chinese had prevented him from introducing he was now free to implement. One of the first things he did on arrival in Dharamsala in April 1960 was to set up his government, with a Cabinet under whom were six ministries: Home Affairs, Foreign Affairs, Religion and Culture, Education, Finance and Security. An office in New Delhi served as a liaison with the Indian government and with the various international relief organizations.

In the summer of 1960, with the help of Indian lawyers, the Dalai Lama began to draft a new liberal democratic constitution based on Buddhist principles and on the Universal Declaration of Human Rights. Elected representatives were to play the major role in a government which would be socialist in inspiration, with an emphasis on the common good and a fair distribution of wealth. At last Tenzin Gyatso could help the poor and down-trodden, welcoming the fact that such a constitution would involve a decrease in his own powers and status. "I am convinced", he wrote at this time,

> that government should always be by the will and through the co-operation of the people. I am ready to do whatever tasks my people ask of me, but I have no craving whatsoever for personal power or riches. I have no doubt at all that in this spirit, and under the guidance of our religion, we shall mutually solve whatever problems confront us, and make a new Tibet, as happy in the modern world as old Tibet was in its isolation.[19]

He would brook no delay, calling for informal free elections to an Assembly of People's Deputies immediately. There were no candidates as such, but all the refugees – even those in the road-camps – wrote down the names of those from their own region whom they respected most. In the circumstances, it was no surprise that the thirteen elected deputies turned out to be important lamas and aristocrats – the Tibetans still had a lot to learn about popular democracy. Nevertheless, a start had been made.

Unfortunately, the Tibetans were still paying for their ancient isolation – and for the West's refusal to believe ill of China. The refugees found to their dismay that no one believed their accounts of what was happening in Tibet, the implication being that they were merely anti-Communists with a vested interest in denigrating the Chinese experiment. In the West, newspapermen and influential academics were uniformly hostile. "When the reporters pressed us for facts and figures", complained Dawa Norbu,

> we were upset that they would not believe that we had suffered so much. We wished at times that we could turn our hearts inside out and show them ... The questioners were sceptical and incredulous. We thought that the world would believe in our honesty. We are a dying people, and lies seldom come from the mouth of a dying person.[20]

CHAPTER 10

Liberating the Neighbours, 1962

Liberation is like having a wet leather cap put on one's head. The quicker it dries, the tighter it gets, until it kills you.

After the Lhasa Uprising the Chinese knew they would never be able to govern by consent in Tibet or anywhere else; military force alone could carry their revolution into Central Asia. India would be next; Nehru would pay the price of his wilful blindness. Dawa Norbu recalls being summoned to a public meeting to hear the Chinese say: "What is India to us? Nothing! We can march in whenever we please". The speaker proceeded to underline the point: "The duty and ultimate goal of every Communist is to overthrow the bourgeoisie and to create an international republic. Asia is our special task. The patriotic people of China cannot rest until we have liberated our neighbours."[1]

From 1959 onwards, the Chinese in Tibet were getting ready to strike their southern neighbour. They had 250,000 troops in southern Tibet and the high plateau was now a strongly militarized area. Using exclusively Tibetan labour, they built a network of roads linking their army units in Chamdo, Shigatse and Rudok on the Himalayan border. Then – day and night – the Tibetan conscripts constructed observation posts, airfields and supply depots, or carried on their backs supplies and artillery sent in from China for the front-line troops. They did so, said Wangchen, "with one Chinese battalion in front and another behind in case any Tibetan tried to escape". (When the "porters" were killed in action, their families were awarded a

certificate of honour to hang over their doors.) Fresh troops
were brought in from China, causing a further drain on local
food supplies, since the soldiers fed off the Tibetan harvests
while the Tibetans themselves had their rations cut even more.

Nehru's dream of coexistence with the People's Republic of
China was about to be shattered. The rape of Tibet in which he
had weakly acquiesced, had deprived India of a peaceful buffer
between itself and China and rendered its northern regions open
to attack at any time. During the Fifties Nehru had appeared
terrified of China, but the revolt in Lhasa had changed all that.
When he welcomed the Dalai Lama and protected the Tibetan
refugees, Nehru – whatever his public rhetoric proclaimed – was
declaring he would no longer be pushed around.

The attack nevertheless took him by surprise.[2] At five a.m. on
20 October 1962, Chinese guns opened fire on a small Indian
border garrison in the North East Frontier territories, an area to
which China (in the name of Tibet) was laying claim. It was, in
fact, part of the old ethnic Tibet, but had been signed away to
the British at the Simla Convention, and when the British
departed, India had held on to it. The Chinese now told the
Tibetans that they would be failing in their sacred duty if they
did not try to recover these Tibetan lands. PLA troops poured
through, capturing with ease 14,500 square miles of North East
Frontier territory.

Tibetans paid literally with their own blood for the war. At
first, blood donors were cajoled with the promise of twenty-five
yuan, half a pound of butter and a pound of meat. But when
there were no takers for this special offer, it was withdrawn and
all Tibetans between the ages of fifteen and thirty-five were
ordered to give blood, one and a half times the standard
amount. ("Enemies of the people" were made to give even
more. Chinese settlers were exempt.) Since many were already
on the edge of starvation, the bloodletting simply finished them
off.

Most of the PLA soldiers in Tibet had been there – without
home leave – since 1950. Using a mixture of carrot and stick, the
authorities offered Tibetan women extra food and clothing

coupons if they would marry these men, at the same time saying it was a criminal offence to resist marriage with Chinese soldiers "who have travelled so far from home for the sake of Tibetans". Some women gave in, though they knew that any child of the marriage would be brought up as Chinese. At the same time, wholesale sterilization was carried out on Tibetans of both sexes in the interests of birth control. Tibetan cadres were the first to undergo the operations in the Lhasa Municipal People's Hospital, and to speed up the process, inexperienced Chinese medical students were let loose on them: "Many cadres emerged paralysed below the waist or having lost control of their bladder. A number, admitted to the hospital for unrelated conditions, discovered that during surgery they had also been sterilized."[3]

The campaign lasted six months, and when it ended, on 21 November, the Chinese claimed victory. In truth China's psychological victory was enormous, for she had shown India to be a "paper tiger", incapable of defending its territories. (Herein lay a clear message for the Tibetan refugees: Do not think you will ever be safe from us in India.) The territories themselves were apparently irrelevant. Having milked them of their propaganda value, China handed them back to India, which promptly renamed them Arunachal Pradesh.

Nehru, understanding at last that he'd been living in a fool's paradise, abruptly abandoned his precious non-aligned status and turned to the Americans for help. The Tibetans, in fact, had got there first. When, in April 1959, the guerrilla leader, Gompo Tashi Andrugtsang, abandoned his National Volunteer Defence Army HQ in the mountains of southern Tibet, it was not because he was giving up the struggle but that he hoped to continue it more successfully from elsewhere. In fact, on arrival in India, Gompo Tashi immediately consulted wth Gyalo Thondup, the Dalai Lama's eldest brother, to find ways and means of continuing the fight. In the absence of aid from any other quarter, the two men decided to accept further help from the CIA. It did not occur to the Tibetans that the Americans were using them in the new Great Game of world power politics, in which the US was concerned only with undermining Communist China. But even if it *had*, they had no other card to play.

The CIA undertook to train – secretly, at Camp Hale in Colorado Springs – about five groups of one hundred Tibetans, representing all the districts of Tibet's three provinces. Once trained in the art of subversion, they would be parachuted into their native areas to organize resistance cells which could link up with the NVDA troops in India.

Ironically, the resistance inside Tibet would be powered by those whom the Chinese had themselves educated as the future leaders of the country. The children sent to China in the Fifties had been groomed to take over the running of Tibet from the "upper strata reactionaries". And – until 1957 – these young Tibetans were on the whole content with their role as leaders-in-waiting. In that year, however, the liberal Hundred Flowers Movement, which had allowed and even encouraged Chinese intellectuals to criticize the regime, was succeeded by the ruthless and bloody suppression of all criticism. During this reign of terror, which stamped out every vestige of freedom in China, the Tibetan students lost all sympathy for the Communist system and moved into opposition. During the disastrous Great Leap Forward of 1958, it is estimated that 60% of them underwent thamzing, as a result of which many died.[4] By the time the students returned to Tibet to take up their positions, most of them were fanatically anti-Han Chinese. "Thus", says Avedon:

> while required to rely on Tibetans to administer the country, China was in fact putting in place those who would soon lead Tibet's burgeoning underground. Well-versed in both Marxist ideology and Chinese administration procedures, the cadres learned to carry out orders while seeking promotion to higher office from which they could more effectively undermine policy.

It was true that the Chinese would for a number of years yet have many collaborators, the "loyal Tibetans" who through conviction, cowardice or self-interest stayed close to the corridors of power; and some of the peasants who had been rocketed from serfdom to positions of relative authority. There would always be those who could be either bullied or bought, but the elite student trainees would not be among them. By 1962 almost 3,000 of them had been dismissed as unreliable; many were either in prison or dead.

*   *   *

US air support for the Tibetans ended abruptly on 1 May 1960 when a CIA U-2 reconnaissance plane was shot down inside the USSR and its pilot, Lieutenant Gary Powers, fell into Soviet hands. As relations between the Superpowers nose-dived, President Eisenhower ordered a ban on any further intrusion into Communist air-space. There would be no more supplies for the Tibetan guerrillas.

After Eisenhower, it was John F. Kennedy who inherited the Secret War in Tibet and who had to decide the fate of the partisans. Kennedy's ambassador in New Delhi, the economist J. K. Galbraith, disliked what he dubbed the USA's "spooky activities" inside Tibet, and was all for cancelling any further efforts on behalf of these "deeply unhygienic tribesmen". Kennedy compromised by moving the operation from India to Nepal.[5]

Throughout the second half of 1960, former Khampa guerrillas were collected from their various road-gangs and trekked through the jungles of Nepal to the new operations base in Mustang, an isolated mountain-kingdom right on the edge of the Tibetan plateau. Officially part of Nepal, its culture was Tibetan; and it was here that the CIA began training the Tibetans in the techniques of modern combat. Mustang could be approached only from the south, by means of a deep, almost impassable gorge. But it possessed the considerable strategic advantage of being close to the Xinjiang–Lhasa road which ran along the northern Himalaya to Ladakh, and from there to Xinjiang and the Sino-Soviet border. From such a vantage-point, once they had established their own network of camps and supply depots, the guerrillas could easily launch raids on

Chinese army posts to capture much-needed weapons and food supplies for their own use.

Then came the 1962 Sino-Indian War. Even before it was over, India had sought CIA help in arming its northern border. In this the Tibetans proved invaluable. On "the Roof of the World", Tibetans were far more accustomed to the cold than the Indians, and far more able to withstand the effects of high altitude. On 13 November 1962, the Special Frontier Force came into being, a Tibetan unit under Indian control, charged with the task of patrolling the Himalayan border; and of preparing to return to Tibet as paratroop commandos should the fighting break out again.

Tibetans eagerly left the road-gangs in order to enrol in this new secret regiment based somewhere near Dehra Dun. After six months basic commando training, an embryo Tibetan army 10,500 strong and with its own officer corps was developed. Thanks to them, India was able to build up a network of bases from Ladakh to Assam. But though the border remained tense for the next few years, China did not invade again.

China was worried both by the constant raids by Tibetan troops from Nepal and by the fact that hundreds of Tibetans were still escaping during the summer months and telling the world about the atrocities committed by the Chinese in their villages. By the end of July 1960, the number of refugees had grown to 60,000. They were driven out by hunger and misery, but their grief was more for the desecration of their religion than for themselves. The Tibetan peasant's very life had been overturned. "There is no hope either for our life in this world nor for our life in the next", Dawa Norbu's mother had lamented before taking the decision to try and escape.

The Chinese continued to exhort the Tibetans to tighten belts around famished stomachs. Since they owed indemnities to the USSR which had to be paid in grain and borax, prisoners were taken in their thousands to the borax mines, and in their thousands died. In the vast gulags in the north-east there was no mercy. Not only were prisoners forbidden to speak to each other, they were even banned from exchanging glances. Starv-

ing, they ate worms, leather and flies, the monk, Lobsang, told
Vanya Kewley:

> Some, and I was one, had to pick bits of vegetable out of human
> faeces and eat it. Some ate the flesh of rats and dogs ...
> sometimes we also had to eat ... the corpses of human beings. By
> using what little strength remained in our bodies, we crushed the
> long bones of the dead prisoners and drank the juice as well ...
> There was no choice. Most people died slowly and painfully of
> starvation.[6]

The camp statistics would claim that they died from hard
labour, for it was forbidden to speak of death by starvation.
Everyone, the authorities insisted, received "ample
sustenance"; and they punished anyone whom they caught
stealing cabbage leaves, bones or fruit peelings from the refuse
tips. "The Chinese then moved the bodies by lorry to quiet
corners between hills and buried them in deep holes. This happened all over Tibet. There are so many secret places with big
graves and piles of Tibetan bodies. They are still there. Go and
see them on your journey."

Frequently, in the course of beatings, Lobsang Rinchok told
me, prisoners' arms and legs were broken, but they received no
treatment:

> Often the Chinese would not allow the prisoners to sleep, and as
> a result they died. Or they were made to sit outside naked in
> mid-winter. There were many suicides – prisoners would impale
> themselves on spikes, cut their wrists with rusty nails or throw
> themselves into the river during exercise time. If two or three
> prisoners were tied together, they would all jump.

In Dartsedo prison, in eastern Tibet, Topai Adhi, like other
female prisoners, was consistently raped: "If we had resisted, we
would have been punished or sentenced to death. There was no
choice but to comply. Immediately after sexual intercourse, to
ensure against pregnancy, we were forced to drink an infusion of

musk." With starvation conditions prevailing there too, the prisoners subsisted on one mug of the worst quality tsampa porridge three times a day:

> Prisoners would rush to the wooden food bucket for any left-overs, they would put their hands in the bucket, they would lick it. The Chinese guards would stand and watch us, laughing at our struggles. Prisoners would also rush to gobble up used tea-leaves, thrown at us by the guards, for the sheer fun of seeing us scrabble. Dying Tibetan prisoners ate grass, roots and even worms. Every day, at least ten of us died.

Suicide – a terrible sin for a Buddhist since it severely reduces the possibility of good future rebirths – was seen by many as the only way out. Lobsang Rinchok remembers a couple from his village in Amdo who simply climbed to the top of a high mountain and threw themselves off:

> And there was another couple who had the man's eighty-year-old mother living with them. One night they warned her not to get up if she heard strange noises. Then they covered her with blankets, tucking her in so that she couldn't move. The old woman noticed that they were wearing their best clothes. Next morning she found that they had hanged themselves.

CHAPTER 11

"Big Rock on the Road", 1964

There is nothing to fear if one is doing one's rightful duty of preserving one's country's culture. This Mao Tse-tung guaranteed many times to me.

THE PANCHEN LAMA, 1964

By 1965, whether the people liked it or not, the Tibetan Autonomous Region (TAR) was about to be formally inaugurated. Everything was ready, there were between thirty and forty thousand supposedly compliant Tibetan cadres waiting to take over the running of Tibet – all of them, however, answerable to the military regime. (So, where was the autonomy?)

But according to the two Chinese generals who held supreme power in Tibet, one man stood in the way of progress, "a big rock on the road to socialism". This one man, hard though it is to believe, was the arch-collaborator himself, the Panchen Lama![1]

Many exiled Tibetans had long despised Lobsang Trinle Lhundup Chokyi Gyaltsen, the Tenth Panchen ("Great Scholar") Lama, as a mere puppet of the Chinese. Indeed, shortly after the Lhasa Uprising, while other monasteries were being scheduled for destruction, the monks of the Panchen Lama's Tashilhunpo monastery were given favoured treatment and promised immunity from attack.

Yet the Chinese had already begun to entertain doubts about their protégé, not least because his father was suspected of providing arms and horses to the Khampa rebels in 1958. After the Lhasa Uprising, though he became Acting Chairman of the

PCART and made all the right propaganda noises about the rebellion being liquidated and the democratic reforms implemented, the Panchen Lama began to see things in a different light. Before 1959, he had been a boy, too young to understand what he was doing and saying at the behest of his masters. Lhasa 1959 forced him to grow up; and from then on the puppet-masters found him less compliant and more demanding. He asked for the restoration of religious monuments damaged during the fighting in Lhasa, and arranged for the transfer of sacred images from the Potala to the Jokhang cathedral where the Tibetans could more easily protect them. Whenever he received pilgrims or gave a teaching, he referred to the Dalai Lama as Tibet's true leader, and insisted that Tibet's future should be for the Tibetans to decide. Poker-faced, he would quote Mao's assurance that the Chinese were there only to help and would go home when they were no longer needed.

The Chinese were confused by this change of tack, but they continued to pay lip service to his nominal authority. Sonam Chophel Chada who attended a course of political re-education in Lhasa found the Panchen Lama to be one of the indoctrinators. One day he came to address the group, which consisted of seventeen others from Lhasa and ninety-seven monks from Tashilhunpo. Speaking in Tibetan, he began by praising the Chinese and their achievements. Then without changing expression, he quickly went on:

> Look at your fellow-students on this course. There are very few from the old Tibetan administration. And do you know why? It's because they knew how to serve their true master. They are in India learning to fight the enemy. Look at all of you here, my own followers from my own monastery. You're well looked after. But what you have in reality is an empty bowl in the service of the Chinese. It is a shameful state of affairs.[2]

Mr Chada could scarcely believe his ears: "He said all this right in front of the Chinese, and the only reason they didn't retaliate was because they hadn't understood a word." To Chada the Panchen Lama had seemed no more than a Chinese lackey, but this little episode changed his mind.

At the end of 1960, while the Panchen Lama was in China to extol the success of the Democratic Revolution in Tibet, the Chinese surrounded the monastery of Tashilhunpo and arrested all 400 of its monks. They were accused of complicity in the Lhasa revolt, and a handful of them were publicly executed. Several committed suicide and the rest were deported to the salt and borax mines in the north – where most of them would die.

The Panchen Lama was deeply distressed by this attack on his beloved monastery, but not until a year later did he himself opt for open defiance. In September 1961, he set out for Beijing to attend the Twelfth National Day celebrations. By then, he was no longer under any illusions about what had been done to Tibet. The country was a vast slave-labour camp, a land of famine, a graveyard with thousands dead and dying. Hungry and demoralized, the people of Lhasa came to bid him goodbye as he passed through their murdered city, begging him to intercede with Chairman Mao for food and medicines for them. The sight of them stirred him into action, and by the time he arrived in Beijing, he had prepared a 70,000 character document for Mao, detailing the sufferings of Tibet and deploring the insensitive and authoritarian behaviour of the Chinese occupation forces. He begged the Chinese to stop persecuting his countrymen and pleaded for their food rations to be increased. He asked for more institutional care for the elderly and infirm; for real religious freedom; for an end to the mass arrests and to the mindless destruction of sacred manuscripts and artefacts.

Mao, with the easy charm which once had captivated the Dalai Lama, appeared to concur, and even had pamphlets printed and circulated within Tibet promising imminent improvements. But the promises had no substance. On the Panchen Lama's return to Tibet early in 1962, he was summoned by the authorities and told that nothing had been or would be done. Moreover, it was their turn to make demands: "We have until now told the world that the Dalai Lama was kidnapped by reactionaries", said General Zhang Jin-wu, Secretary of the Work Committee of the Chinese Communist Party in Tibet:

> We did this, to allow time for the Dalai Lama to return. He has, however, decided to work hand in glove with the Indian government. You must therefore take his place and assume the Chairmanship of the PCART. You must live in the Potala Palace and openly denounce the Dalai Lama as a reactionary.[3]

For the Panchen Lama, the moment of truth had arrived. He refused point blank, stating that he was neither able nor willing to replace the Dalai Lama, and would certainly not denounce him. Instead, he publicly advised the Tibetans to do what they could to preserve Tibetan culture, religion and respect for their exiled leader. "The Tibetan cultural heritage goes back more than a thousand years", he told them, "but the changes in culture cannot be carried out in the same way as land reform. There is no reason to destroy everything. To preserve and protect our cultural heritage is the responsibility of every Tibetan."

Dismayed by this volte-face, the Chinese banned him from teaching in public, and emphasized his fall from grace by seizing the few caretaker monks left at Tashilhunpo and subjecting them to thamzing before a kangaroo court in Shigatse.

After that, there was no longer any question of where the Panchen Lama's loyalties lay. He had regained the affection of the Tibetan people, but from then on, he was not allowed to appear in public except as a silent figurehead at official events. Then one day in March 1964, he again occupied the centre stage, with a last chance to retrieve his position. The occasion was the Great Prayer Festival (Monlam) which in old Tibet used to be spread over three weeks but was now reduced to one day. Ten thousand people, including the few remaining monks in Lhasa, packed the town hall to hear him speak. In an atmosphere heavy with emotion, they listened to him appeal for freedom of religion and greater cultural freedom for the Tibetans – but it was not this they were waiting to hear. They knew that the festival had been convened for one purpose only: the Panchen had been ordered to condemn the Dalai Lama.

He would not. Defiantly, he proclaimed that the Dalai Lama's survival was a sign of hope for Tibet: "Today, while we are gathered here, I must proclaim my firm belief that Tibet will soon regain her independence and that His Holiness the Dalai Lama will return to the Golden Throne. Long live His Holiness the Dalai Lama."[4]

He no longer cared that he might be signing his death warrant. Eyewitnesses report that all the Tibetans present, including the youngsters trained in China, wept to hear this brave testament of faith. Their last suspicions vanished; they no longer doubted that here was the true reincarnate Panchen Lama. "Mao's Panchen" had become a symbol of revolt.

It was equally obvious to the Chinese. Faced with such open defiance, they had no option but to brand him a reactionary traitor – and to close Tashilhunpo to the public. He was imprisoned along with his tutor, Ngulchu Rimpoche, while the two top Chinese generals flew to Beijing to consult with Mao and Chou En-lai over what should be done with them. The upshot was a vicious "Thoroughly Smash the Panchen Reactionary Clique" campaign intended to uncover the Panchen's "crimes against the people" and plots against the motherland. He was denounced as "a big rock on the road to socialism" and reference was made to a secret guerrilla army with which he had planned to launch an underground war against the Chinese. Those who were suspected of heeding his call to defend Tibet were immediately rounded up. Pema Lhundup, a farmer from Western Tibet who had joined in a local insurrection was arrested and subjected to thamzing:

A meeting was called at the ruins of the Menthang Monastery, and all the people were made to march there carrying red flags, beating drums and cymbals. I was summoned for a public trial which lasted a whole day. In the afternoon, the Chinese read out a list of my crimes, how while transporting ammunition I had thrown several bags into the river, and how I intended to help the resistance commit acts of sabotage. Throughout the proceedings I was beaten continuously, my hair was pulled and my teeth kicked out. I was bleeding heavily through my nose.[5]

The Chinese released the farmer, saying they had decided to be lenient with him this time. But they continued to hound anybody who had had the remotest connection with the Panchen Lama. The wife of one of his followers was related to Dolma Chozom. Dolma had only recently been released from a Lhasa prison, but now she was interrogated about the Panchen Lama's treasonable activities:

> I told them I had no connection with him, and that as everyone knew he was pro-Chinese, *they* presumably knew more than I did. How could I know anything, leading the kind of life I did, working all day and having to report each day to the area police? They had confiscated everything I had and I was given no pay. One of the Chinese interrogators got mad and went for me with the butt of his rifle. But the officer stopped him. Not out of human feeling, though. He said he didn't want me beaten senseless before I'd given them the information they wanted. But I knew nothing at all, and they had to let me go eventually.[6]

The Panchen Lama's public trial began in August and lasted seventeen days. In the course of it he was humiliated, vilified and physically abused. Those with a grudge against him were encouraged to come forward and testify. On the third day, General Zhang raised the temperature of the assembly a few notches: "If you squeeze a snake its intestines come out", he said provocatively:

> But to kill a snake it is necessary to crush its head. If we squeeze the Panchen by thamzing, many hidden reactionaries and enemies of the state will be forced into the open. If we kill the Panchen, the whole reactionary clique will collapse like a house whose foundations have been destroyed.

John Avedon describes the confusion that ensued:

> Cadres sprang from their seats and began to slap, punch and

kick the Panchen Lama, who was pulled from his chair and brought to the centre of the stage. The spectacle of seeing one of Tibet's highest lamas beaten by his own people deeply disturbed the majority of delegates. No matter how often they were urged, they could not bring themselves to join in.[7]

A woman from Amdo struck the Panchen Lama in the face, while Chinese officials abused him and a Tibetan activist made obscene gestures at him. But through it all, he stood by what he had said to the Tibetans in his past sermons. At one stage, he bared his breast in utter disgust at the way the trial had been rigged, and invited the Chinese to shoot him then and there. Ignoring the invitation, they produced an unlikely charge-sheet of his "crimes", which included murder, cohabiting with his brother's wife, participating in orgies and stealing from monasteries. He was accused of wanting to restore the old serf-dom; of criticizing China in the 70,000 character letter he had sent to Mao; of declaring open support for the Dalai Lama and of misleading the masses. Most seriously of all, he had raised a secret army to fight against the state.

The punishment had been decided in advance. In November, the Panchen Lama, his parents and what was left of his entourage were thrown into heavily guarded closed trucks and driven out of Lhasa en route for Beijing. In December, Chou En-lai informed the Third National People's Congress that the Dalai Lama, "an incorrigible running-dog of imperialist and foreign reactionaries who has organized a bogus government and a bogus constitution",[8] was unfit to be Chairman of the PCART; and that the Panchen Lama would no longer be Acting Chairman, though his name would remain on the list of members. In the following August, when the Cultural Revolution had already started, the Red Guards raided his house and took away all his property. He was charged with having "organized a counter-revolutionary clique on behalf of the serf-owning class and engaged in wild activities against the people, the motherland and socialism".[9] To all intents and purposes, the twenty-seven-year-old lama then simply disappeared, though his infamy was not allowed to be forgotten. Years later, a student told Catriona Bass of an anti-Panchen Lama exhibition which had been set up in Lhasa:

> They showed lots of photographs of so-called counter-revolutionaries. The guns that they were supposed to have been going to use were laid out on tables, with the coded messages and pictures of foreign spies who, they said, were helping him. We all had to go to the exhibition, the whole of Lhasa, unit by unit. We were told to learn from his mistakes.[10]

Only after his reappearance in October 1977 was it discovered that the Panchen Lama had spent the next ten years in solitary confinement in China's top security prison, Qin Cheng. He had been tortured and beaten and would carry the scars with him for the rest of his life.

*   *   *

There was no further obstacle to Tibet's becoming an official Chinese satellite. Ngabo Ngawang Jigme was on hand to replace the Panchen Lama as figurehead Chairman of the People's Council of the Tibetan Autonomous Republic. One year after the Panchen Lama's trial, the Chinese propaganda agencies claimed that Tibetans were flocking to the polls in a state of joyous excitement, dressed in their finest clothes and bedecked with flowers, celebrating "the first free expression of the voice of the Tibetan people". Reality was, of course, quite different: the free elections were a myth. The Tibetans were summoned in groups to vote for a candidate on a pre-arranged list, and only when the "right" one had been unanimously chosen, were they allowed to go home.

On 1 September 1965, the TAR came into being amid the usual Communist razzmatazz. *China Reconstructs* worked itself into a lather of dewy-eyed emotion:

> With the bright red ribbons identifying them as people's

deputies fluttering on their breasts, they walked into the meeting hall with heads held high, representatives of their emancipated people. During the nine-day session, with tears of emotion in their eyes and smiles of triumph on their faces, they spoke of their past misery and present happiness and expressed the deep love of Tibet's million emancipated serfs and slaves for the Chinese Communist Party and Chairman Mao.[11]

That joy, if it existed at all outside the fantasies of the myth-makers, would soon be changed to a limitless despair. For, whatever the glib talk of "past misery", nothing in the Tibetan experience had ever come within a million miles of the misery which the Great Proletarian Cultural Revolution was about to unleash on them.

CHAPTER 12

Exceeding all Limits

To right a wrong it is necessary to exceed proper limits, and the wrong cannot be righted without the proper limits being exceeded.

MAO TSE-TUNG, *On Going Too Far*

The word Hell is too soft . . . to describe what happened in those years.

HARRISON E. SALISBURY[1]

It had begun in China proper as yet another wild lurch of the pendulum – from left to right and back again – in the bitter power-struggle between the radical Mao Tse-tung and the more moderate Liu Shao-qi. For a few years after Mao's Great Leap Forward policy had fallen flat on its face, he was out in the cold. But by 1965 he was back, determined on all-out class war and the elimination of internal opposition. In August 1966 Mao launched the Great Proletarian Cultural Revolution in order to take an axe to China's cultural past.

It was a period of collective insanity, of legalized murder and mayhem. Brigades of young Red Guards, monstrous clones created by Mao's wife, Chiang Ching, and licensed to exceed all limits, rampaged through China, supplanting the existing Party organizations by Revolutionary Committees composed entirely of Mao's disciples, dedicated to his utopian plans. The "Four Olds" – old ways of thinking, old culture, old habits and old customs – must give way to the "Four News" (or the "Four

Cleans"), which were whatever Mao pronounced them to be.

All of China was terrorized by the Cultural Revolution, but the sufferings inflicted on Tibet were unparalleled elsewhere. Tibet was an irresistible challenge to the destroyers. Impatient at the slow pace of change there, at the continuing power of religion, at a culture that was redolent of the Middle Ages, the Red Guards planned to throw out the present regime and bulldoze through a full socialist programme, regardless of local conditions, temperament or needs.

In July 1966, a small band of Chinese Red Guards arrived in Lhasa to light the revolutionary fuse. Their programme was what one might expect of a band brash young hooligans given licence to roam where they would and inflict whatever damage they chose:

> We, a group of lawless revolutionary rebels, will wield the iron sweepers and swing the mighty cudgels to sweep the old world into a mess and bash people into complete confusion. We fear no gales and storms, nor flying sand and moving rocks ... To rebel, to rebel and to rebel through to the end in order to create a brightly red new world of the proletariat.[2]

Because the Cultural Revolution was essentially a cut-throat struggle between the pro and anti-Mao factions within the Chinese Communist Party, many young Tibetans joined in to let off steam and for the pleasure of watching the Chinese tear each other to pieces. There were Tibetans in both factions, but none of them really knew what it was all about, nor could they have imagined the horrors into which it would lead them. They, no less than the vast majority of innocent Tibetans became tragic victims of the Cultural Revolution. For their religion, their culture and their way of life actually *were* the battlefield on which the rival groups fought for supremacy.

It was on 25 August 1966, after their inaugural rally in Lhasa, that the Red Guards first showed their true colours. Urged on by the Chinese and intoxicated with excitement, bands of China-educated Tibetan youths invaded Tibet's holiest place, the Jokhang cathedral, and indulged in an orgy of desecration, destroying and mutilating the irreplaceable treasures stored there. (Ironically, it was here that the Panchen Lama had arranged for many of the artefacts from other monasteries to be brought for safe-keeping.) For days, the young fanatics rampaged round the courtyards, burning ancient scriptures, beheading the Buddhas, smashing and defiling centuries-old images. Finally they destroyed part of the temple itself, renaming the monastic quarters Guest House Number Five, turning the outer areas into a pig-sty and slaughterhouse, and setting up their own headquarters in the chapels and storage rooms.

Then followed a ruthless assault on Tibet's remaining monasteries. By the time the Cultural Revolution was over, very few of the original 6,254 monasteries, temples, hermitages, and shrines remained; and these were in a state of terminal decay. In their place came communes. As far back as 1962 the Tibetans had been ordered to request collectivization, though this was the last thing anyone wanted or needed in a land where such huge expanses of land lay unused, except by the nomads to pasture their vast herds. Knowing what had happened in the east, most Tibetans in the TAR feared that communes would spell the death of whatever freedoms and possessions still remained to them.

With the coming of the Cultural Revolution (the Cultural Annihilation, some called it), the drive to establish communes was stepped up. By the end of 1966, almost every village in Tibet had been communized into tightly organized production teams of 100 or so families holding the land and everything on it in common. (As in the east, farmers were paid a basic ration of grain and were forced to sell their produce to the state at very low fixed prices.) In theory, such egalitarianism sounded admirable, but in practice it was a recipe for disaster. Many of the former serfs who had rejoiced in the breaking-up of the old estates now felt they had lost everything they had gained. All animals, tools and equipment had to be surrendered – compensation was promised but never paid. The peasants were ordered to plant rice or wheat (which the Chinese preferred) instead of the barley which alone thrived at such high altitudes and in such impoverished soil. (Inevitably these crops would fail.) Grain was allotted according to work-points given only after excessively long hours of work. The Tibetans, wrote Tsering Dorje Gashi, were "bees collecting honey with no benefit to themselves";[3] the communes were a prison to enslave the people under Mao's rule. It was the Chinese who gave the orders and made the decisions:

> Every day [the Tibetans] had to get up before break of dawn and work until they absolutely could not see in the dark ... In the night, they had to attend marathon lectures where Marxism-Leninism and the thoughts of Mao Tse-tung were tirelessly preached ... From within, the communes are a literal hell on earth.

Protest was useless. The army was sent in to reinforce the orders and arrest protesters *en masse*.

As for the nomads, their lifestyle was the polar opposite of collectivization, and they were particularly badly hit by the arrival of communes. For thousands of years the nomads of Tibet had nurtured their sheep, goats and yak herds, all of them able to graze at 15,000 feet in impossible conditions. The yak gave wool, milk, cheese and meat which could be bartered with the peasants for grain. But the Red Guards forbade barter and slaughtered most of the animals, allowing the nomads to keep only a few for their own use. Dondub Chodon, the former serf who had given a tentative welcome to the new regime, tells of a woman who killed a ewe without permission and was paraded round the commune with the bleeding sheep's head hung round her neck as a warning to others.

Mrs Chodon was given an intensive course in political re-education, and made a political officer in her village. But she was already disillusioned, seeing all too clearly that the "great change" which was supposed to make ordinary Tibetans masters in their own house, would end by giving power over the land and everything and everyone in it – to the Chinese. "The inescapable fact", she wrote, is that now everything in Tibet is the private property of a few Chinese rulers in Beijing: the hills, the forests, rivers and green fields, the animals, precious minerals and even human beings – to do with as they please without fear of judgment. Can a Tibetan say what he likes, eat what he likes, live as he wants and go where he wishes? No![4]

Within the communes, all movement outside of house or field was forbidden; permission had to be sought even to gather firewood in the surrounding area; while to take a day's leave to visit a sick relative required a battery of official signatures.

Wangdu Dorje, a farmer in South Tibet, was summoned with his fellow villagers to a lecture by a Chinese general. "The reactionary people won't die", the general explained, "unless the masses destroy them, just as the dust in the room won't go, unless we sweep it out".[5] Mrs Chodon has a similar memory: "One day two Chinese and six Tibetan officials came to our commune and selected thirty young Tibetans from the (lowest) class who held Party membership. These thirty recruits were then appointed as Red Guards and told what they should do."[6] What they had to do was implement the slogan: SMASH THE FOUR OLDS – those "poisonous weeds" of the past. ("The four Olds are all things Tibetan, and the four News are whatever the Chinese say".[7]) In their task they were to be "pitiless, wrathful and zealous", denouncing anyone, even their own parents, who stood in their way. They began, she records, by:

> destroying all the small shrines and pulling down the prayer flags. Then they confiscated all religious objects and articles, even prayer beads. They destroyed all religious monuments and paintings in our area. They took the statues in the Tradruk Dolma Lhakhang and sold them to the Chinese antique shop in Tsethang and burnt all the ancient holy scriptures.

All references to religion were forbidden – it was as if Buddhism had never been. The people were forced to "show their contempt" for the old society and the "corrupt" monks.[8] The demolition was carried out – by Tibetan Red Guards – to the accompaniment of music and drums and much agitation of red flags. "The Tibetans did it, the Chinese just stood around and gave them orders", remembered Kunsang, a poor farmer from South Tibet:

> When one of the destruction teams tried to get into the Lhalung Monastery, the caretaker monk stood guard near the door and would not budge. The Chinese accused him of having an "unreformed brain" and dragged him out of there. The monastery was then torn apart brick by brick before the eyes of the caretaker – who later went completely insane.[9]

Kunsang managed to hide in his house while the mob destroyed a shrine outside it: "They ground the stones to small pebbles and laid them on the street".

The vandalism was not as random as it seemed. Dolma Chozom recalls that when the Red Guards began destroying the temples and monasteries, they first removed all the silver and gold objects and sent them to China. (In the late 1960s, many precious religious objects from Tibet were offered for sale in the international markets of Hong Kong and Taiwan.) "The people were then ordered to remove the stone or clay images and throw them into the latrines or onto the ground. Some of my neighbours refused to do this and they were tortured to death."[10]

Dayang, a Tibetan friend, told Catriona Bass of how, during a fuel shortage in Lhasa, the work-units had sent out teams to forage in the monasteries:

> She remembered returning from Ganden once, their truck piled high with altars, pillars, window-frames, books, musical instruments, cauldrons, ladles – anything they could lay their hands or axes on. At the work-unit most of it was distributed as firewood but some things were kept. The elaborately carved covers of religious books were used as washboards, she said. Children made writing slates out of broken-up altars. And the drums and cymbals, which had for centuries been beaten in offering to Buddhist deities, were used at parades to honour the man who

tried to destroy them. Dayang's laughter was bitter as she marched round my room shouting ... Long Live Chairman Mao! punching the air with one hand and rattling an imaginary ... ritual drum in the other.[11]

Lamas and other "reactionaries" were forced to assist in the destruction of the precious objects and were routinely humiliated. In Lhasa it was reported that all high lamas and government officials had been paraded through the city wearing dunces' hats, with Chinese guards whipping them along.[12] Chomphel Sonam, a monk in Shigatse, was one of many who reported celibate monks and nuns being forced to have sexual intercourse in public.[13] Many of these were made to marry, others committed suicide. Yeshe Gonpo, the ex-monk from Drepung, had long been harassed for his unwillingness to eat meat, drink, smoke or go with women. The head of his neighbourhood committee accused him of having "an old mind and old thinking": "He said I was still secretly a monk. They made me look after the pigs, clean out the latrines, do all the most menial jobs they could think of."[14] It was a grave charge. Anyone found possessing a monk's robes or scriptures or performing religious ceremonies, was deprived of his grain coupons, classed as an "agent of the serf-owners" and subjected to thamzing:

> The Chinese and the Red Guards charged that all Tibetans keeping old objects were guilty of trying to resurrect the past, they were the enemy within. Tibetans found lighting incense were charged with attempting arson and paraded in dunce caps. All people murmuring silently were denounced for being superstitious.[15]

Gyaltsen Chodon, a small child at the time, confirms that "no one was allowed to say prayers or light butter-lamps or keep images in their homes. Even to move the lips in prayer was a crime. But my father had been a monk before the Chinese sent him away from his monastery, and he read the scriptures and taught me prayers in secret."[16] When Gyaltsen's father was caught giving food and clothing to a high lama hiding in a cave, both he and his wife were punished by thamzing. The Chinese charged them with "feeding a useless mouth", and stripped the family of all opportunities and privileges. A woman from a commune near Shigatse speaks of the whole village being made to throw its prayer wheels into the river. "We saved a set of prayer beads by hiding them in the roof", she says.[17] Despite the draconian new laws, many people managed to hide their images and scriptures: some in the hills, others in trunks indoors, taking them out to venerate at intervals – at risk of their lives.

The changes spared no one, and life for ordinary Tibetans became a living hell. They were at the mercy of informers who might at any moment denounce them, and whether the accusations were true or false was immaterial. "There was no law to protect the innocent", wrote Dondub Chodon, "people had no-one to guard their rights. Fear and desperation ruled our land".[18] Many chose to kill themselves rather than endure the humiliation and terror of thamzing.

The Tibetans were in massive, collective shock. The prayer flags which for centuries had adorned every roof; the stone monuments erected at every high pass; the heaps of stones engraved with sacred mantras, marking the entry to every town, village or monastery; the rock paintings, the prayers chiselled on to rocks all over the Tibetan countryside; the prayer-wheels and the "windhorses" which released prayer into the skies on countless tiny bits of paper; the rhododendron and juniper wood burned as incense; all disappeared, replaced by the Thoughts of Chairman Mao in vivid scarlet paint. "The Red Guards swept through the land like madmen and destroyed everything", says Mrs Chodon:

> They came from house to house and forced everyone to buy Mao's portraits and painted his sayings all over the walls. Everybody was required to carry Mao's *Red Book* at all times. They stopped anyone any time and made them recite Mao's *Thoughts*. If anyone failed, then he was detained.[19]

Incarnate lamas were made to catch fish, kill pigs and sheep.

Ordinary Tibetans who had spent their lives protecting all sen--
tient beings from harm, were ordered to kill dogs on sight,
especially the Lhasa Apsos considered typical of the old society.
Soon all the Apsos had been beaten to death with sticks or
stones, shot or poisoned. Even cranes and ducks were missing
from the rivers. Nine- and ten-year-old children were made to
kill flies, rats and dogs. They were

> sent out in groups to hunt birds. In the evening they are required
> to submit their kill to the Chinese. The competitive spirit is
> encouraged and those declared the least ardent bird-hunters are
> subjected to brutal punishments. Insults and punishments are
> also given to the parents for breeding "reactionary" offspring.[20]

"The reasons for the killings [were] two-fold", says Mrs
Chodon, "to display a lack of compassion and disregard for sin,
and to remove a drain on the economy, as dogs are said to eat
man's food."

There was to be no more "merry-making among friends and
relatives"; no more drinking of chang, the beloved barley-beer.
Old-style festivals and fairs were banned and anyone recalling
them to the young must be denounced: "No Tibetan was to
speak of there being freedom and happiness in old Tibet. If a
Tibetan was heard in the unrevolutionary act of praising the
'dead past', he was liable to incur ... thamzing and imprisonment."[21] Tibetan proverbs, phrases and folk songs were forbidden; in their place came unfamiliar Chinese songs stuffed with
quotations from Mao. Everyone had to speak the new revolutionary language, an artificial Newspeak mix of Chinese and
Tibetan which few Tibetans could understand.

Mrs Chodon recalls an old man with a good-luck swastika on
his door undergoing thamzing to "make him new". The same
went for those who still exchanged good luck scarves (khatas).
"Please" and "thank-you" were forbidden, as was the ancient
Tibetan habit of sticking out the tongue and clucking in respect-
ful greeting. Not even names were sacrosanct. Large numbers of
Tibetans were ordered to change their names to Chinese
equivalents, each with one syllable of Mao's name included.

When parents resisted, their children were given names denoting their house number, date of (or weight at) birth, or the age of their father. "As far as Chinese administrators were concerned", comments Avedon, "many of Tibet's upcoming generation were literally no more than numbers".[22]

Old Tibetan cooking utensils of brass, bronze and copper were confiscated, even though aluminium pans were scarce, expensive and nowhere near as good. Both men and women were forbidden to wear their hair Tibetan-style. If they refused to cut off their long plaits – "dirty black tails of serfdom" – roving squads of Red Guards did it for them.* Women were stripped of the simple conch bracelets that were basic to a Tibetan woman's dress. Henceforth, said the Chinese, instead of wasting time on rings and ornaments, the Tibetans were to devote themselves to memorizing and repeating the *Thoughts* of Chairman Mao.

The Red Guards even smashed the flowerpots, so that the Tibetans would not be able to enjoy the colourful flowers they loved. Anything which once had gladdened the heart was taboo, even the wearing of the chuba, the traditional Tibetan garment. In its place came the charmless buttoned-up blue boiler-suit and Chinese peaked cap.

"The People's Commune is a Golden Bridge to Socialism where there is no oppression or exploitation", rhapsodized a Chinese slogan. "It is a socialist paradise". But though the system with its work-points and heavy taxation may have worked in China, in Tibet it reduced the population to near-starvation, with the grain ration running out months before the year's end.

All power lay with the local Communist party which answered directly to the rulers in Beijing. "It was far far worse than the revolt of 1959", says Pema Saldon:

---

* Not all Red Guards had the stomach for this sport. Dawa Tsering admitted to Catriona Bass that he had been too shy. "Other Red Guards would take people by the head and just cut their hair with a knife. I couldn't do it. When they complained, I let them go". (*Inside the Treasure House*, p. 200).

That one lasted only three days. The Cultural Revolution went on for seven years in all. Not only did everything have to be destroyed but the whole of the Tibetan past had to be denounced. If an "old" object was found in a family, it was hung around their necks, they were dunce-capped and paraded around the streets, with Tibetan boots hung around their necks. The Tibetans became paupers because people just hurled anything old or precious into the rivers. They tipped in cartloads of stuff. Those people were praised by the Red Guards, who encouraged others to follow their example. My family parted with every single piece of jewellery, their pearls and gold all went into the river.[23]

"Anyone who'd been educated simply disappeared," continues Mrs Saldon,

either to prison or death. The high lamas were made to dig latrines and carry huge basketfuls of excrement to manure the land. Nuns were sent to do domestic chores, and the whole social order was stood on its head. My own father who had been a moderately well-off trader, was sent for "reform through labour", and had to drag a cart loaded with bricks. Every day he had to write a self-criticism and write a progress report on his political development. My mother, in poor health, was sent as a sorter to a yarn co-operative. As a small child, I was alone most of the day, with no food in the house. My parents returned only to sleep.

All who resisted or disobeyed the Chinese in any way at all had to face a People's Court and subsequently thamzing. Tsering Youdon was a child living in Kham when she witnessed her father, a farmer of moderate means, being condemned:

I was very small and didn't know what any of it meant. But I was taken to a huge assembly of all the people in the village. My father was accused and all the Tibetans present were made to

beat him. Some of them couldn't bear to see this and put their
hands in front of their eyes. When I saw my father being beaten,
I cried.

They didn't take him away, but kept him in the village and
worked him to death. He couldn't work as hard as they wanted,
so they kept beating him. They broke his right arm, but refused
him medical treatment, while continuing to make him work. Not
long afterwards he died.[24]

Every former landowner underwent this "reform through
labour". Or worse. The treatment of Lobsang Rinchok who had
been born into an aristocratic family was not untypical:

They put a paper dunce's cap on my head, a very long, high one,
in three sections. On one, they wrote my name, and on the other
two my crimes: 1) I was a landowner and 2) I had belonged to a
monastery and had even been regarded as an incarnate lama. As
well as the dunce's hat, they strapped a wooden plaque to my
chest with iron bands, with my whole history written on it. Like
this, I (and others like me) had to go round the villages and
towns shouting that we were reactionaries who had fought
against Mao. If we didn't do this, the soldiers beat us. The
Chinese assembled all the inhabitants of one group of houses,
then another, then another, and forced them to give us thamzing. They had to do it, or get the same treatment themselves.
Some of the Tibetans died during these ordeals.

Sometimes they treated you like a football, kicking you from
one to the other. One day, something in me snapped. I wanted to
die and figured that if I protested, the Chinese would shoot me.
They didn't like to be argued with. So I said, "You accuse us of
being dogs, jackals, hyenas, bloodsuckers. But the poor people
are being treated far worse by you than ever we treated them,
and it is you now who ride around on fine horses." I waited –
and hoped – for the bullet in the back of the neck, but it didn't
come. Instead, they sent someone for a horse's bit and forced it
into my mouth. They brought a hammer for the purpose and I
thought they were going to knock my teeth out. Then someone

said, "Why not put a saddle on him as well?" They did this, and made the Tibetans take turns in riding me like a horse.[25]

He was sent back to his home village and given the job of collecting the communal excreta. One day he escaped, but was caught and arrested:

Then for twenty full days, I was put into thamzing, sometimes with the occupants of just one house, sometimes two at a time. It was so terrible that I began to wish they'd move me to district HQ and shoot me. So I pretended I was mad, uttering profanities, kicking and biting the Tibetans who were persecuting me. The Chinese simply tied my legs and my outstretched hands to a pole, so that I couldn't move.

Beri Laga too wore the dreaded dunce's hat:

If I wanted to walk even only a few yards I had to ask officials for permission, tell them where I was going and why, and report back again. Workers were given five days holiday a year, three days at New Year, two for the founding of the Communist state. But even on those days we "hats" had to work. Nobody was allowed to talk to us. Frequently they put the dunce's cap on us and made us parade through the streets shouting our "crimes".

Once a year we had to face a twenty-four hour thamzing. Each time it was the same. They told the story of who you were and your supposed crimes, and said, "Look at her, she's still not learned her lesson. She's working to destroy the Chinese government". I was made to kneel on a wooden plank. A wooden bar was placed across my shoulders and I had to sit for hours like that, bent over, hands tied behind me.

One day, the Chinese threw me out of the truck on the way to thamzing. One of my kidneys was ruptured, and I was in bed for four months. As soon as I was out of bed, they sent me back to work again.

Another Tibetan woman saw her parents forced to confess

"crimes against the people" at meetings orchestrated by hysterical Red Guards. As the old couple stood on the platform, children, paid a silver dollar to do so, threw stones at them. "The hardest thing was to see people paraded through the centre of town on the way to execution. Some boys and girls who were taken were not even tall enough to see over the sides of the trucks. But they were tall enough to be shot."[26]

As the in-fighting between the Red Guards intensified, so did the atrocities and the bloodletting. Thamzing was often followed by gang rapes and public beatings.

> Women were stripped, bound, and made to stand on frozen lakes under guard. A man and his daughter ... were compelled to copulate in public ... classed Tibetans were left tied in gunnysacks for days at a time ... whole families were made to stand in freezing water for five hours, wearing dunces' caps, heavy stones strapped to their legs. A wave of suicides swept over the country as many Tibetans, sometimes in family groups, chose to kill themselves by leaping from cliffs or drowning rather than die at the hands of Chinese gangs.[27]

According to a new wave of refugees escaping in the confusion to India,

> Tibetans were routinely mutilated, their ears, tongues, noses, fingers and arms cut off, genitals and eyes burned. Boiling water was poured on victims hung by the thumbs to extract information they were thought to possess concerning rival factions. Crucifixion was also employed: on 9 June, 1968, the bodies of two men were dumped in the street in front of ... the old Lhasan jail, riddled with nail marks, not just through the hands, but hammered into the head and the major joints of the torso.[28]

Enemy of the People Number One was the Dalai Lama, the "wolf in monk's robes" who had escaped the Chinese clutches. During the Cultural Revolution denunciations of him reached the level of hysteria. In December 1968, Radio Beijing described

him as a "political corpse, bandit and traitor". An article in the
Beijing Review described him as "an executioner ... with honey
on his lips and murder in his heart".[29] Straining credulity even
further, the same article alleged that the Tibetan leader "used
thirty human heads and eighty portions of human blood and
flesh each year as sacrificial offerings" during religious services
to draw curses down on the People's Liberation War. Lodi
Gyatso, a nomad from Western Tibet, remembers being told
that the Dalai Lama was "a red-handed butcher who subsisted
on the people's flesh".[30] Every night, at the political meetings,
says Dolma Chozom, "the Chinese ordered us to speak out
against the Dalai Lama, but most of us refused. We said, 'He is
our god, our leader'. I was severely beaten for saying this. A
Chinese official picked me up and threw me to the ground and I
lost consciousness."[31]

"Who master-minded the revolt?" was the standard question
at the nightly meetings; the obligatory answer being: "The
Dalai Lama". The next question followed immediately: "What
type of life did he lead?" The unfortunate Tibetans knew the
answer to that one, too: "He was a pleasure-loving lama who
loved women, gold and silver and who sold out his country to
the imperialists". Those who did not join in the chorus of
denunciation, says Dondub Chodon, were described as being
"infected with blind faith and empty hope", and on the pretext
of relieving them of a regrettable mental burden, they were
subjected to thamzing and made to confess to "wrong
thinking":

During these meetings, everyone had to cry out, "The gods,
lamas, religion and monasteries are the tools of exploitation; the
three serf-owners made Tibetans poor; the Chinese Communist
Party liberated us and gave us food, clothes, houses and land;
the Chinese Communist Party is more kind than our own
parents. May the Chinese Communist Party live for ten
thousand years. May Mao Tse-tung live for ten thousand years.
The crimes of the three serf-owners who ate the flesh and drank
the blood of the people are bigger than the mountains and can-

not even fit in the skies; from this day forward we will destroy them."[32]

Years later, in his memoirs, His Holiness referred ruefully to this period:

I became the focus of the Chinese Government's bile and was regularly denounced in Lhasa as someone who merely posed as a religious leader. In reality, the Chinese said, I was a thief, a murderer and a rapist. They also suggested that I performed certain quite surprising sexual services for Mrs Gandhi![33]

The ex-monk Yeshe Gonpo was goaded beyond endurance. The Chinese, having prepared a lampoon on the Dalai Lama to be performed in public, ordered him to stand on stage and translate it into Tibetan:

I told them I couldn't because my Chinese wasn't good enough. Then they threatened me with terrible punishments if I refused. But they couldn't make me do it. Something in me snapped, and for a while I lost my reason and went mad. My parents and elder sister all died at about this time, of exhaustion, hunger and despair. I wanted to die too.[34]

To compound their misery, starvation was rife. Not among the Chinese, however. One man who got a job as cook in a Chinese administrative office reported that he had to prepare three meals a day, using rice, flour, mutton, yak-steak, pork, chicken, butter, eggs and vegetables. Regardless of such discrepancies, the Chinese dared to tell the Tibetans that they were happy, that they lived in an ideal world, ordering them, at the political meetings, to compare yesterday's "bitter past" with the glorious happiness of the liberated present. But the Tibetans had a proverb, "When you have known the scorpion, you look on the frog as divine". Even those who had welcomed the destruction of the old society would willingly have exchanged the present for the past. Using a kind of double-speak which the

people had invented to preserve their sanity, one man spoke up:
"Throwing away all the dirt and rubbish of the old society", he
said sardonically, "we are implementing the 'three cleans' of the
new society. On the one hand, we make the outside clean by not
wearing any bourgeois clothes. On the other, we make the inside
clean by eating little. Thirdly, the new society is so good that
even without people it remains clean."[35]

It was a new Dark Ages, claimed Dondub Chodon:

> Human beings need friends, freedom, trust and filial bonds to
> make life worth living. But under the oppressive Chinese rule
> Tibetans have no friends, no relatives to rely upon, no confidant
> to trust and no filial bond to cherish. No one is allowed to
> socialize. If two people are intimate, the Chinese suspect con-
> spiracy; if you lend things you are accused of opportunistic
> designs. If in a family the parents and children love one another,
> the Chinese tell the children that their parents have old ideas,
> that they must be helped by opposing their mistakes, that they
> must report on their parents.

But one man found the courage to protest in a public meeting:
"Eating the tsampa destroyed by frost, the people let out loose
stool; eating the rotten radishes, the cattle let out loose stool;
remembering the bad old days, the people let out tears."[36]

Mao had come near to achieving his aim. "To right a wrong",
he had written in the essay – On Going Too Far – which launched
the Cultural Revolution, "it is necessary to exceed proper limits,
and the wrong cannot be righted without the proper limits being
exceeded". His followers had taken his words at face value and
had fashioned them into an epitaph for Tibet.

CHAPTER 13

A Chinese Vietnam, 1969–1976

"It was a mistake", a Chinese official told me
... "What happened in Tibet was an excess".
It was not an outrage in Chinese eyes.

PAUL THEROUX, *Riding the Iron Rooster*

By 1967 Topai Adhi had been in prison for nine years; and
believed that nothing worse could befall her. She was wrong:

> One day twenty of us were escorted to a room with chairs and
> several coal stoves. We were given several mugs of a very sweet
> drink which (we learned later) was meant to increase our blood
> supply. We couldn't understand why they were being so nice to
> us. But soon, with the heat from the stoves and the drink perspir-
> ation began to stream down our bodies and our faces became
> bright red. Within an hour, Chinese doctors came and took a
> whole bottle of blood from our left hand. Since we were in a
> terribly weak physical state, our bodies swelled up and we fain-
> ted. Three of my friends died instantly. I myself have suffered
> chronic fainting fits ever since.[1]

The blood was almost certainly intended for the military front.
China had convinced herself that a nuclear holocaust was
imminent, and that, surrounded by hostile neighbours – India?
the USSR? – she was immensely vulnerable. By October 1968
the whole of China was on a war alert. The Tibetan Volunteer
Army in Mustang discovered signs of a massive Chinese military build-up along the Himalayan borders, complete with
secret bases, underground troop bunkers, missile-tracking

stations and supply depots. China's main nuclear base was said
to have been moved from Xinjiang Province (too near the USSR
for comfort) to Nagchuka in Central Tibet, 165 miles north of
Lhasa. China had virtually completed its network of military
roads and bridges which linked all the districts of the TAR.
Tibet had become a bristling fortress with military bases spring-
ing up in every area and every village teeming with troops.
Major airfields had been built – all but one for the exclusive use
of the PLA. All towns were being readied for attack from the air:
trenches and fall-out shelters were dug, hospitals evacuated,
civil defence exercises rehearsed.[2]

Tibetans were reluctant participants. Farmers were conscripted into the PLA as auxiliary units. In communes along the
border zones, young people were organized into a two-tier
people's militia. In the top tier (to all intents and purposes, the
new officer class) were the *burtsen chenpo*, the enthusiastic but
largely illiterate local activists whom the Chinese trusted more
than the China-trained cadres. Two of these activists were
assigned to every unit, with the task of weeding out spies,
counter-revolutionaries, Tibetans who thought of escaping to
India; or anyone else who still opposed Chinese rule. They were
given up-to-date weapons, while the ordinary conscripts in the
second tier had clubs or wooden staves. The latter were meant
to hold the fort at home when the activists were called away to
war.

Age was no protection. Thirty-five- to forty-five-year-olds
were to go to the front as labourers and transport workers, while
the forty-five to fifty-fives would carry medical supplies, remove
the wounded and bury the dead.[3] The expendable "useless
mouths" – the fifty-five to sixty-fives – would be sent to the front
as cannon-fodder: "Unarmed, they were to attack ahead of the
regular troops in human waves, absorbing the enemy's fire".[4]

In the countryside, life became even more intolerable. Besides
their long day's work in the fields and their compulsory evening
study of *The Thoughts of Chairman Mao*, Tibetans were coerced
into building roads and bridges and collecting manure – all on a
starvation diet. Meat, butter and oil were very scarce,

and grain-rationing was so tight that no matter how hard they tried, the month's supply would never stretch beyond twenty days.

"My parents were weak from hunger and exhaustion", Lobsang Jimpa told me. "They worked from seven in the morning till ten at night while we children were left in the care of neighbours. Then after ten they had to attend political meetings. Only after midnight did they get any rest."[5] "We were starving", a young woman told me. "We had to eat whatever herbs and roots we could find, tearing our hands in the process. Some of the herbs were poisonous and our faces all swelled up."[6] Namgyal, a student in Lhasa at that time, had to do manual labour also, unpaid, because students were expected to support the commune. Hours of study were followed by political re-education, often involving thamzing:

> If someone confessed at these sessions, his food points were cut. If he didn't confess, he was guilty of the crime of not confessing, so his food points were still cut.

> In autumn, we only had three hours sleep before harvesting began. If a mother had a baby, she had to take it with her and feed it in the field – and her work points were reduced for the amount of time it took her to feed her baby. The commune leader collected the grain after the harvest and divided it up. He siphoned off a large amount for "the common good" – but we never discovered where it went.[7]

Villagers in Tingri, a village in West Tibet, complained to the Chinese authorities about the shortage of food. Ngodup, a poor farmer who later fled to Nepal, recalls, "We pointed out that in the old society, when everybody was doing whatever they were good at and exchanging their products with each other in barter, there was never any scarcity. They said we were at it again, 'spreading the old poison' and assured us things would soon get better."

Far from taking pity on the hungry Tibetans, the Chinese

concentrated on amassing immense reserves of food for the army; and they even refused to cut the amount of grain the Tibetans were forced to pay as a communal tax. There was "war-preparation" tax; "love the nation" tax; "grain surplus" tax; and "anti-famine" tax, all of which were deducted at the time of harvest. After the harvest, complained Mrs Chodon, "you can see the Chinese carting away our grain on lorries on various sweet-sounding pretexts."

The PLA had in addition turned their machine guns on the once sacrosanct Tibetan wildlife, slaughtering and eating the herds of wild asses which had once roamed free and untouchable over the Land of Snows.

*   *   *

Goaded beyond endurance, the Tibetans, even those who once had welcomed the Chinese social revolution, eventually struck back. The first open revolt came in 1969 in Nyemo, ninety kilometres west of Lhasa, triggered by a much-respected nun, Tinle Chodon. In an oracular trance she cried out that the Chinese were wiping out Tibetan religion and culture and the time had come to rise against them. Her words acted as a catalyst. The people of Nyemo rushed in a frenzy to attack a Chinese military post, killing soldiers and officials and slitting the mouths of known spies and informers. Some of the Chinese officials escaped to Lhasa and reported that a major revolt was in progress. They were right: the trouble spread like wildfire to twenty-nine different districts of Tibet.

The Chinese did not at first, however, realize the significance of what had happened at Nyemo. They believed it was just another twist in the feuding between the Red Guards. But Nyemo marked a watershed, the point at which the left/right struggle in the Communist Party became past history, and the struggle of Tibetans versus Chinese began. When the Chinese belatedly came to understand this, their reaction was extreme: orders were sent out to all twenty-nine district authorities to execute the ringleaders of the revolt. Tsering Wangchuk, a

Tibetan cadre, was told by Chinese colleagues that the order had come from the very top:

> Many of them told me they had been sickened by what they saw. Some of the victims were hacked to pieces with axes. The Chinese cadres said the carnage was completely inexcusable.
>
> I myself went to Nyemo and discovered that eighteen of the ringleaders had been shot at a public sentencing rally. The authorities' only regret was that they'd been unable to catch six others who had escaped to the mountains. Nyemo was a ghost village: there was no one left there but old people and women. Most of the young people were dead or in prison.
>
> The Chinese in the village were terribly tense, and all their cadres had to carry guns. I remember once, when the Chinese cadres were asleep, there was a sudden noise and they all leaped up and aimed their pistols. But it was only a mouse. They were so afraid for their lives that if one of them wanted to relieve himself during the night, he would wake all the others and make them go outside with him.[8]

In eastern Tibet, such outbreaks were not at all unusual – the Chinese had long since given up hope of subduing the wild men of Kham and Amdo. But now the whole of Tibet was in ferment. As fast as trouble was extinguished in one place, it would break out somewhere else. In Lhasa itself unrest flared into violence after a group of Tibetan youths had accidentally killed two Chinese soldiers in a brawl.[9] With 300 military police in hot pursuit, the youths took refuge in the Jokhang cathedral, and when ordered to surrender their weapons claimed they did not have any. In terror, they swore they were loyal Communists of impeccably low-class origins, and they held up copies of *The Thoughts of Chairman Mao* as they hopefully chanted a quotation: "The army and the people are one; nothing under the sun can separate them". The army, unmoved by this appeal to class solidarity, began shooting, bayoneting and clubbing the youths inside the Jokhang. Twelve died, forty-nine were injured, and the latter were denied medical attention until a team of Tibetan

doctors arrived to take them away. The survivors began singing
a defiant song of the Tibetan Underground:

> Do not mourn, people of Tibet,
> Independence will surely be ours.
> Remember our sun,
> Remember His Holiness.

After this new desecration of Tibet's Holy of Holies, anti-
Chinese sentiment grew apace. Acts of civil disobedience
multiplied, culminating in June 1969 in a symbolic mass
defiance as the entire population of Lhasa publicly celebrated
the Buddha's birthday.

In the summer of 1970, there was a major revolt in south-
western Tibet. It spread to sixty of the seventy-one districts of
the TAR and claimed the lives of 12,000 Tibetans and more
than 1,000 Chinese soldiers. A full-blooded purge aimed at
weeding out all opposition in every part of Tibetan society now
began. The mistrust long felt by the Chinese for the Tibetan
cadres turned to implacable hostility when it became clear that
the latter had played a leading role in the uprisings. Thousands
of them were removed at a swoop. Police terror reached unprecedented heights as security police files on every Tibetan were
carefully scrutinized. As John Avedon recounts:

> Thousands were arrested in surprise night-time raids, taken to
> prisons and submitted to interrogations. In each area, groups of
> ten to twenty were singled out as examples to receive one of three
> fates: thamzing, imprisonment, or public execution. The photos
> of those to be executed were posted around each district, the
> requisite red X marked across their body or face, their crimes of
> "anti-party and anti-people activities" listed beneath. The
> executions themselves took place on large public meeting
> grounds where the victim, a wire pulled tight round his or her
> neck by a Chinese guard (to keep them from yelling a last word
> of defiance) would receive a bullet to the back of the head.
> Immediately thereafter, their family members, assembled at the

head of the crowd, would be made to applaud, thank the Party for its "kindness" in eliminating the "bad element" from among them and then bury the still warm and bloody corpse, unceremoniously and without covering, in an impromptu grave.[10]

Wangchen was among those arrested. Charged with inciting revolt in the districts of Lhorong and Phenbar and with forming an underground organization, he was sent to prison for four years:

During that time. I was kept kneeling for fifty-eight days, with my hands in the air, manacled and with ice-blocks on them. They fed me every fifth day, a small bowl of tsampa and cold water, but for the rest of the time I went hungry. One day while I was chained in the cell, with fine wire strung round my fingers, I was told to stretch out my hand to the grille to receive my food. When I did so, a guard hit me several times with a bayonet. I was beaten every morning at reveille and again in the evening. I had no bedding, nothing in the cell but a urine bucket, and a crack in the floor to pour the stinking slops through. I discovered later that the man in the next cell had no such crack and therefore no way of disposing of his excrement. The contents of his bucket simply overflowed all over the floor and froze solid. As they gave him nothing to drink, he was forced to drink the "ice".[11]

Prisoners were not allowed even to talk to each other, the monk, Lobsang, told Vanya Kewley: "If we did, we were accused of plotting against the state and knives were stuck into prisoners' testicles. Those whose testicles were knifed did not die easily. Some did not die easily after their throats were slit either ..."[12] Whilst in prison, Lobsang Nyima saw thirty-four Tibetans executed, and then thirteen more, including three High Lamas:

We were forced to watch, and I was put into the front row. By then the area round the prison was one big grave and there was no more room. So the Chinese began throwing the bodies from a great height into the river. During the executions they dug a pit and made the victims stand in front of it, so that when they were shot they would fall straight into it.[13]

Yet no brutality could douse the flame of rebellion, and fighting was still going on two years later. In 1972 after 500 Tibetan youths who had demonstrated in the name of Tibetan independence were executed in Kongpo Tramu in Central Tibet,[14] *The Times* of India carried the headline: "CHINESE FACING VIETNAM IN TIBET".[15]

*   *   *

But China was changing, concerned now to improve its image in the outside world. Belatedly the Beijing authorities recognized that the Cultural Revolution in Tibet had boomeranged against them, destroying every vestige of international goodwill. In 1972, in another erratic swing of the political pendulum, they tried to undo some of the damage,* lifting the ban on wearing Tibetan clothes and proclaiming "Four Freedoms": freedom to worship; to buy and sell privately; to lend and borrow with interest; and to hire labourers and servants. Two years later, a group of forty Tibetans was actually encouraged to make a pilgrimage to Bihar in northern India where the Dalai Lama was to preach.

They even released some prisoners. When they let Wangchen go, the authorities did not refer to the supposed crime for which he had been arrested. Though his flesh was swollen and puffy and he could not walk properly, he was sent straight back to his old job with a construction unit – "still on the blacklist and still forbidden to talk to anyone else". Lobsang Rinchok was also

---

* Money had already been provided for repairs to the Jokhang Temple, the Potala Palace and Drepung Monastery in Lhasa.

released. Escorted to his village by about one hundred soldiers, he was made to confess his crimes yet again before a public assembly, and had to swear he was now a "new man" who was prepared to work with the Chinese. Nevertheless, discovered by the police in possession of a small newspaper picture of the Dalai Lama, he was re-arrested. "Another meeting was called and my crime exposed. 'He promised to become a New Man, but he has not changed at all', they said. I replied: 'Well, His Holiness is my leader and I respect him with all my heart. Kill me if you want, but you can't change me'."[16] Whereupon, they beat him unconscious. He was ill for a month, during which time he was visited every day by the Chinese, to make sure he wasn't shamming. As his strength began to return, he escaped yet again, this time to join a lama friend in hiding. He spent the next few years "in a small underground cellar where there was just room for me to sit, covered over with mats, rushes and stones".

The continuing reverence for the Dalai (and Panchen) Lamas irked the Chinese who initiated a new smear campaign. At the nightly political meetings the two men had to be denounced, while the authorities set out to prove them arch-fiends. Touring exhibitions displayed "a rosary of 108 cranial bones, purportedly made from 'victims' sacrificed to the Dalai Lama, as well as grenades and machine-guns collected by the Panchen Lama for his attempted uprising".[17]

As the tenth anniversary of the inauguration of the TAR (September 1975) approached, the Chinese invited a group of "Western" media people to Tibet. They were mainly (but not all) known sympathizers with the regime, like the writer, Han Suyin, and the film-maker, Felix Greene. The visitors were accompanied by plain-clothes security police and Tibetans were allowed to meet them, provided that they did not talk politics. "If asked about independence they were to say that it would not be a good idea because life was bad under the old society".[18]

Some of the truth did penetrate the rose-tinted spectacles. When they returned home, the foreign journalists reported: that the Jokhang now only functioned as a museum; that religion had been discouraged to the point of near-disappearance; that the great monastery of Drepung which had once housed 10,000 monks now had only eleven crippled old men in robes; and that the only manifestation of native culture tolerated by the Chinese was the "revolutionary opera" whose music may have been Tibetan but whose lyrics were literal translations from Chinese originals.[19]

If the visit of the media people was something of a circus, other arrivals in this same year cast a far longer shadow. One day Radio Lhasa announced casually that Chinese settlers were coming to Tibet. Until now, there had been only the PLA soldiers and a certain number of cadres and technicians. The Red Guards had come with the Cultural Revolution, but even these had caused no significant shift in the balance of population. Tibet may have been smaller than it was in 1949, but it was still recognizably Tibetan. But for how much longer? In 1962, Mao had sworn to settle ten million Chinese in Tibet. Now, twenty-three years later, he began to turn the threat into reality.*

The face of Tibet underwent a radical change, as the ugly, featureless cement and corrugated-iron buildings beloved of the Chinese grew up within and around every Tibetan city. Tibetan labourers built them, but the houses and offices were solely for the use of the settlers and of some of the Tibetans who worked for the State. From the start, it was obvious that the lucky recipients would be privileged far beyond the dreams of ordinary Tibetans. They would have piped electricity, while the Tibetans would have at best a fifteen to twenty watt lamp bulb. They would have running water, double the ration of rice and wheat, and access to consumer goods in special shops. In the areas of medicine and education, the Tibetans' inferior status would be particularly heavily underlined. While the settlers were offered free medicines and hospital treatment, the natives

---

* By 1982, Tibetan sources would estimate that one-third of the inhabitants of Central Tibet were Chinese.

had to rely on the crude ministrations of the "barefoot doctors" – an off-shoot of the Cultural Revolution when teenage primary school students were given a two to six month crash course in basic medicine and let loose on the communes with (at best) a first-aid kit of thermometer, stomach pills, laxatives, cough mixture and aspirin. According to Mrs Chodon, Tibetans were often reduced to selling their blood at the nearest hospital in order to buy food and clothing.[20] Only the bedridden and seriously ill among them were given medical treatment. Anything less serious did not merit even a day's absence from work, and absence in such cases was punishable by a heavy fine.

As for education, for Chinese children it was guaranteed. But in rural areas, at least, Tibetan schools were almost non-existent. "There are schools", stated Kunsang, a poor farmer from Tingri who fled to Nepal in 1974,

> but they don't have many students. That's because parents can't afford to send their children to school. Only the tuition is free. Clothes, meals, books and stationery have to be provided by parents, which of course is often impossible. So the children stay at home, collect yak dung and wood to sell to the Chinese, and pick wild herbs to supplement the family's diet.[21]

Many Tibetan children, therefore, including some who were debarred by reason of their former high social class, received no education of any kind. "My parents needed me as a herder", said Tashi Dolma, when I spoke to her in Dharamsala. "We lived on a points system and they needed the points I could earn in order to buy food. Even as a young child I started work at dawn and returned only at nightfall."[22] Dalha Tenkyong from Gyantse received no education at all: "My father was sent to prison and I had to go and work in a quarry because my mother couldn't afford to keep me. The Chinese discriminated against children whose fathers were in prison. Even when they worked well, they got less food than other workers."

In the towns, all schools were geared to Chinese needs. Lobsang Jimpa attended primary school from 1973–9. Priority was always given to the children of Chinese settlers, and it was very difficult for the Tibetan majority to secure even 50% of the total number of places. The education provided was given in Chinese by Chinese teachers for the benefit of Chinese children. For Tibetans like Lobsang Jimpa it amounted to little more than an indoctrination course into Chinese Communism:

> We had to learn by heart *The Thoughts of Chairman Mao* and study Marx–Engels. In the mornings we had four periods of forty-five minutes: one in Chinese Language; a double period of Political Theory; and P.E. In the afternoons we did Chinese History, particularly the Sino-Japanese War and the Second World War. After that, we either cleaned the school or sang Chinese songs. Then after a period of Elementary Science, the day ended with the hated "struggle session". That meant that we all had to accuse each other of crimes such as not cleaning up properly, not studying well or saying rude things about the Chinese. (If any one of us had dared say that Mao was an evil tyrant, he would certainly have been executed on the spot.) One day, I was accused of holding a pen over Mao's picture while studying the *Thoughts*, and of allowing a drop of ink to fall on the Chairman's face. Life was made very difficult for me over the next three weeks, even though I pleaded that I loved Mao and had merely dropped off to sleep. I had to undergo thamzing, first in the classroom, then in front of all the students in the school, and later I had to write endless statements of loyalty. My "confession" was posted up in the school for a whole week.[23]

But, though Lobsang Jimpa could not know it, Mao's days were numbered. In September 1976, "the Great Helmsman" died. He had in fact long been ailing, the country being virtually run by his wife, Chiang Ching, and a group of aggressively radical left-wing associates, soon to become infamous as "The Gang of Four". Within weeks of the Chairman's death, Chiang Ching and her henchmen were arrested and put on trial. When the moderate, Deng Xiao-ping, assumed power, Tibet began to believe that the worst was over. Had not the Nechung Oracle predicted at the beginning of the decade that when Mao died, everything he had built would dissolve into dust? It was an old Tibetan custom to take down the picture of someone who had died. Enthusiastically, the Tibetans set about removing the countless portraits of Mao which for ten years had defaced every corner of their living space. It was too much for the Chinese, who made a great many arrests. The celebrations would have to wait.

Ends and a Beginning:
The Tibetan Exiles, 1963–1973

Since the mid-Sixties the exiles had been cut off from all contact with their homeland, except for the odd snippets of out-of-date information passed on by itinerant traders from Nepal. They knew little about the Cultural Revolution that had brought their compatriots to the edge of the abyss; nothing of the desperate revolts. An impenetrable darkness separated them from their loved ones and their own past.

But among them a kind of miracle had occurred. No longer bewildered and helpless, the Tibetans had adapted vigorously to their new situation. "They confirmed my belief in the tremendous power of a positive outlook when coupled with great determination", the Dalai Lama later wrote.

Not all of the Tibetan refugees had stayed on the Indian subcontinent. Some had gone further afield to found small communities in Switzerland (the largest), Canada, the USA, France and the UK. To look after the interests of the widely scattered Tibetans – and to give their host countries some insight into Tibetan culture and way of life – the government-in-exile opened offices in Kathmandu, Zurich, New York, Washington, Tokyo and London. The Tibetan diaspora was taking shape.

But the majority had stayed in India. Nehru had died in 1964, and his successors, Lal Bahadur Shastri and Indira Gandhi, had continued to support the Tibetan exiles. Life in Dharamsala was spartan, the people were poor, but they were free. The government-in-exile, though its organization was somewhat ramshackle and its accommodation primitive, now comprised several hundred individuals in different, ever growing, departments. The Dalai Lama knew that it was vital for the Tibetans to have a workable constitution, even if no other nation would feel free as yet to recognize it. Some of the older, deeply conservative families bitterly resented the move away from the old system, regarding their leader's democratic principles with suspicion. But the majority of the refugees agreed with the Dalai Lama that in the new freedom changes must be made and equal opportunities become available for all. The search for democracy was part of the search for survival in a modern world.

The draft constitution was promulgated on 10 March 1963, and in the elections for the Assembly of People's Deputies which followed, Tibetans were introduced for the first time to the mysteries of the ballot box. Three years later, they were enabled to vote for candidates chosen by election committees; and within ten years (1975) they could choose their own candidates in primary elections. But though the younger Tibetans, like the Dalai Lama, wanted more – and more radical – political change, the old conservatives refused point blank to go any further.

In 1970, frustrated by their elders' refusal to move with the times, a group of five idealistic young Tibetans – Lodi Gyari, Tenzin Tethong, Sonam Topgyal, Tenzin Geyche and Jamyang Norbu – conceived the idea of a Youth Congress which would be democratic in every sense of the word, with a leadership which was both forward-looking and accountable to public opinion. The Dalai Lama gave the idea his blessing and provided the funds for an opening conference which was attended by 500 enthusiastic young Tibetans. For the first time since the exile, there was, claims Jamyang Norbu, "an organization which knew what it wanted to do; which was not a court organization, not regional, not sectarian. It was something new: it was national."[1]

The group which started the Youth Congress belonged to the first generation of Tibetans to have received a modern education outside Tibet. They were able to assess the problems of their own society without being hamstrung by a heavily ritualized culture. "They saw", said Lhasang Tsering, a future chairman of the Congress, that in future there would be two sets of young Tibetans. One inside Tibet, born under the Chinese, with no knowledge of freedom, never having seen the Dalai Lama. The other, born in exile, knowing nothing of the Chinese, nothing of Communism, and having never set foot in Tibet. How could one reach them all? We are not only in exile, we are scattered in exile, all over India, all over the world. So those young men who founded the Congress felt the need for a movement which would provide a forum to bring people together, to pool their ideas, channel their energies.[2]

The Youth Congress saw itself as a much-needed "loyal opposition". As such it was unwelcome to the Tibetan cabinet (Kashag) who, as Jamyang Norbu put it, "did not want any kind of opposition, loyal or otherwise".[3] Not without reason, the Kashag felt threatened by these young people who knew more than they did about the modern world. There were bound to be squalls ahead.

The Tibetan Children's Village (TCV) had overcome its teething problems*; and students from the various Tibetan schools in India and Nepal were already making good. "The children are your most precious resource", Nehru had told the Dalai Lama. And so it was proving. Through education, Tibetan youths, fluent in English and Hindi, were acquiring skills undreamed of by their parents. Ugyan Norbu, for example, while at school in Simla, was one of eighty Tibetan boys and girls sponsored by a Danish group to receive further education in Scandinavia. After six months basic education in Denmark, the girls went to Sweden, the boys to Norway. Like many of his friends, Ugyan Norbu wanted to become a teacher. But a taped message from the Dalai Lama changed their minds. "We are not just one big family," he reminded the young Tibetans, "we are trying to rebuild a nation. You are free to study whatever you like. But remember that most of your fellow-countrymen are

---

* On the death of Tsering Dolma, the Dalai Lama's older sister, in 1964, the work had been taken over by his younger sister, Jetsun Pema.

in settlements and urgently need to be taught modern farming methods."

Within two weeks, fifteen of the boys had asked the Norwegians to help them study agriculture. Until that time, says Ugyan Norbu:

> We had thought of farming as something sinful. We believed that in ploughing the land you would have to kill insects, and that was a sin for us. We didn't give much thought to the fact that we didn't mind eating what the farmer produced. Anyway, when that recording was played to us, we all rethought our plans.[4]

The generous Norwegian authorities set up two agricultural courses for the young Tibetans, and two and a half years later, in 1968, after studying tropical as well as general farming, they returned to India. "We were not highly qualified", says Ugyan Norbu, "but we had a lot of enthusiasm and at least a little practical experience".

They were very welcome. The new settlements were growing rapidly, and more and more Tibetans had been taken out of the road-gangs to join them. In the South Indian settlement at Bylakuppe, for example, there were now 3,200 people, struggling to survive but highly motivated and no longer sunk in despair. They had built themselves brick houses and were keen to master the agricultural skills necessary for the tropics. Conditions still left much to be desired, and the refugees were far from self-sufficient; but they had cleared the land and – thanks to various charitable organizations – most of them were receiving basic medical care. What is more, and it could not fail to gladden Tibetan hearts, many of the great monasteries, such as Ganden, Drepung and Sera were being rebuilt in the tropical climate of South India.

Ugyan Norbu was sent as agricultural supervisor to the settlement in the State of Orissa:

> Two of us went there. I was in charge of fifteen tractors and thirty-two drivers, with three thousand acres to plough. None of

the Tibetans in the settlement knew how to drive and I had to teach them. We really achieved something. Having tractors made all the difference. Before we came, 10% of the land was unused, but once they had tractors it could all be used. We introduced all sorts of crops, many of which were totally unknown to the Tibetans.

*   *   *

Throughout the Sixties, the Americans had continued to support the Tibetan guerrillas operating from Mustang and had backed the UN resolutions calling for "respect for the fundamental rights of the Tibetan people". But they had always stopped short of recognizing Tibet's right to independence from China. In 1971, with American support, Communist China was admitted to the UN. When, a year later, US President Richard Nixon "played the China card" and visited Beijing, the atmosphere between the two countries warmed perceptibly. This new *rapport* with China meant that the Americans dropped Tibet like a hot brick. For the Tibetan fighters in Nepal, as the former guerrilla, Lhasang Tsering, remembers all too clearly, the betrayal was a mortal blow:

> The CIA withdrew their support from us and the Chinese began to put pressure on the Nepalese who then encircled our camp. We could have fought them; we were ready to fight them. We had arms, we knew the terrain, we were battle-hardened, and we were volunteers with nothing to lose. But then a twenty-minute taped message arrived from His Holiness, pointing out that there were at least 12,000 Tibetan refugees in Nepal, we had nothing against the people of that country, and that in any case violence and bloodshed were always wrong. He asked us to disband.
>
> Most of our leaders were Khampas. When they heard the voice of His Holiness asking them to surrender their arms, some of them went away and cut their own throats.[5]

The request caused anguish among the guerrillas. "How can I

surrender to the Nepalese when I have never surrendered to the Chinese?" cried one of their leaders, who a few days later cut his throat.[6] Some, however, reluctantly decided to disarm. But the Nepalese, who had promised immunity in exchange for a surrender, now reneged on that promise, entering Mustang, seizing Tibetan property and arresting the disarmed fighters. A group of about forty fled in order to continue the fight. But shortly afterwards, they fell into a Nepalese ambush near the Indian border and most of them, including their leader, General Wangdu, were killed.

In this sad and inglorious way, a guerrilla war which had been bravely fought for almost two decades came to an end.

CHAPTER 14

"This is Plain Colonialism", 1979

Discriminated against at every turn, Tibetans are condemned to be second-class citizens, living in shame in their own country, and it is very difficult for them to see the Chinese policy towards them as anything but one of apartheid *and out-and-out racism.*

PHUNTSOG WANGYAL in *The Tibetans: Two Perspectives*

After Mao's death in 1976, the Gang of Four was blamed for everything that had been done to Tibet over the last ten years. But their departure from the scene did not improve conditions in Tibet. Chinese settlers continued to pour in, and, a quarter of a century after the invasion, the TAR was still controlled by hard-line Communist officials who spoke no Tibetan, ate no Tibetan food and lived in total isolation from the Tibetan people.

Nevertheless, throughout China, the wind of change was beginning to blow away the years of radical experimentation. China's moderate leaders were eager to show the USA that they could modernize the country and overhaul her economy.

In this changed scenario, Tibet – one-quarter of the entire territory of the Chinese People's Republic – presented a whole range of problems. It was a drain on resources, a Third World region in China's backyard; although it had vast mineral and ecological wealth it had made no attempt to exploit these for the benefit of the Motherland. Tibet swallowed up Chinese manpower, money and effort, and the settlers hated life on the high plateau with its threat to health. Moreover, the country was ungovernable: no-one in his right mind could claim that the Chinese had won the hearts and minds of the Tibetan people. The Tibetan cadres were proving inefficient or worse. There were no leaders of any use – neither the Panchen Lama nor Ngabo Ngawang Jigme could unite the Tibetans behind them. Nor, for that matter, did the Chinese entirely trust them.

Grudgingly, the Chinese administration recognized that only one man could unite and lead the Tibetans, the man they most loved to hate, the Dalai Lama. They needed him, partly because in their newly acquired taste for international approval the very existence of a Tibetan government-in-exile was embarrassing. But also because he alone would be able to halt the continuing unrest.

Since the massive outbreak of 1972, discontent had rarely been off the boil; and minor revolts by "class enemies" had continued throughout the Seventies. The Chinese had given up hope of subduing eastern Tibet – in 1977 a convoy of over 100 PLA trucks had been ambushed, looted and set on fire in that region. And round Lake Kokonor in Amdo in July, 20,000 Tibetans had risen in revolt, many of them being killed. But in central Tibet too sabotage and subversion had become the norm. The situation was out of hand.

In mid-1977, Ngabo Ngawang Jigme, now a high-ranking member of the administration, but residing in Beijing, announced that China would welcome the return of the Dalai Lama and his refugee followers – as Chinese citizens, of course. To lend the offer some credibility, Beijing softened its line towards Tibet. In Lhasa, on the Buddha's anniversary, older Tibetans were permitted to circumambulate the sacred pilgrim routes around the Jokhang temple. The ban on national dress was lifted and Hua Guo-feng, Mao's designated successor, even called for a revival of Tibetan customs.

Unfortunately, the still aggressively radical local Party had no use for such softness. Whether from ignorance of the instructions or sheer bloody-mindedness, they paid no attention to them – and indeed stepped up the terror. A new campaign – the

"Three Antis" (anti-small business, anti-pilferage and anti-bad elements) clawed back some of the recently granted "Four Freedoms" and resulted in thousands of arrests and mass executions, twenty being reported killed in Lhasa alone on 1 August.[1]

But Beijing's plans went ahead. On 25 February 1978, the Panchen Lama was suddenly released – after fourteen years of imprisonment in a top-security jail. And when Hu Yao-bang, the new General Secretary of the Chinese Communist Party, publicly admitted that the Cultural Revolution had been a disaster for China, it began to look as though real change could be at hand.

Admitting that "mistakes" had been made in Tibet, Deng Xiao-ping suggested a meeting with the Dalai Lama, to discuss his return. The latter, concerned solely for the happiness and wellbeing of his people, did not object. A pragmatist, he knew that the only hope for his country lay in some sort of compromise with China. Yet he was wary. "As the ancient Indian saying goes", he wrote in his autobiography, "when you have once been bitten by a snake, you become cautious even of a piece of rope".[2]

On 10 March 1978 (the anniversary of the Lhasa revolt), he tested the temperature of the water by calling for freedom of movement into and out of Tibet. Surprisingly, Beijing gave permission for Tibetans not only to correspond with their refugee relatives but even – for the first time since 1959 – to visit them.

In November, thirty-four elderly prisoners, mostly former officials in the Dalai Lama's administration, were publicly released from prison where they had been held for nineteen years. These men were, according to the Chinese, "the last of the rebel leaders"; and they promised to reinstate them, find them jobs, or even, should they so desire, enable them to emigrate. Such benevolence, however, was not completely disinterested. Paraded at a public assembly, the ex-prisoners issued an official invitation to all exiled Tibetans to come home, with no questions asked. (The refugees, while welcoming the sudden change of tune, greeted this ploy with considerable reserve, though fifteen young men did apply immediately for visas just in case it was genuine. Their application was in fact turned down because they had described their nationality as Tibetan rather than Chinese.)

The Panchen Lama's role in the unfolding drama soon became clear: his was the voice which in February 1979 called on the Dalai Lama to return from exile. It was also clear that since his "re-education" – for which he had publicly and profusely thanked the Chinese – the Panchen had resumed his role of official mouthpiece. "I can guarantee that the present standard of living of the Tibetan people in Tibet is many times better than that of the old society", he said, fooling nobody.[3] (Undoubtedly, though, it was many times better than life in a Chinese prison.)

In his 10 March speech that year (1979), the Dalai Lama urged the Chinese to "accept their mistakes, the realities and the right of all people of the human race to equality and happiness".[4] Within a week the Chinese moved to even more dramatic concessions, removing the "black hat" designation of 6,000 "class enemies",* and releasing almost 400 more long-term prisoners, many of whom had been incarcerated for twenty years and more.†

Lobsang Nyima, Beri Laga, Topai Adhi and Lobsang Rinchok were among the beneficiaries. Lobsang Nyima returned to

---

* In 1963, Tibetans had been classified into ten grades beginning with the most guilty. Landlords, their families, and senior lamas were public enemies number one and were given "black hat" status. They were marked men – and women.

† This was far from being the end of the story. In March 1979, an article in *Time* magazine reported on a "vast prison system" existing in the Chinese province of Qinghai, formerly the part of Tibet known as Amdo. An American imprisoned there for two and a half years believed that half the province's estimated four million inhabitants were either prisoners or forced labourers. ("The Gulag that Mao Built: the West gets its First Glimpse of a Vast Prison System", *Time*, 26.11.79. Quoted by Phuntsog Wangyal in *The Tibetans: two Perspectives on Tibetan–Chinese Relations*.)

his village a free man, but found it something of a Rip van Winkle experience. "Most of the people I had known were dead and a new generation was walking round dressed in Chinese clothes. When they told me the horrible things that had been done in the village, I knew I could no longer stay there."[5] Beri Laga had survived her prison experience, amazing even the Chinese guards by her tenacity. "They found it incredible that I was still alive", she told me, "and even more incredible when I said it was because of my religious faith. I had prayed night and day to the Three Jewels to come through the ordeal; and my faith kept me going".[6] Topai Adhi had been released from prison in 1974, but, as a "black-hat" outcast, was forbidden to communicate with people or even to raise her eyes from the ground. Working long hours at a brick factory, in the evenings she had all manner of menial tasks to perform. "I was looked down on and bullied by everyone", she said.[7] With her "black hat" status at last removed, she was sent to a construction site, relieved that "at least we didn't have Chinese holding guns at our backs, and we did receive a little pay."[8] Lobsang Rinchok was ordered to Xining to receive his certificate of release:

> At yet another large assembly, so reminiscent of earlier thamzings, the criminal charges against me were dropped and the "black hat" designation taken away. A banquet was even held in my honour, a fact that was announced over the radio for maximum effect ... They even said they'd give me back-dated pay from 1963, 48,000 yuan, but I told them to forget it. "I've survived till now, and will go on doing so without help from you", I said. Whereupon I was summoned to District HQ to be told I'd insulted the Party.[9]

To discover what conditions were really like and to re-establish contact between the refugees and their compatriots at home, the Dalai Lama suggested sending a fact-finding mission to Tibet, on the understanding that his representatives must be allowed to go wherever they wanted and speak to anyone they chose. China agreed. Events then moved with breath-taking speed until on 2 August 1979, a delegation of five members of the government-in-exile – from all three provinces of Tibet, each of them familiar with the old country but open to the modern world as well – left Dharamsala for Beijing. There they spent two weeks planning a four-month journey across roughly 2,500 miles of Tibet.

The outcome was a bitter disappointment to the Chinese. In his autobiography written ten years later, the Dalai Lama reflected on how badly they had misread the situation:

> I still do not quite know what impression the leadership in Peking expected the delegation to have of the "new" Tibet. But I think they were convinced that they would find such content-[ment] and prosperity throughout their homeland that they would see no point in remaining in exile . . . It was fortunate that they were so certain of themselves. For, whilst the first delegation was in Peking, the Chinese authorities accepted my proposal that this mission should be followed by three more.[10]

"At this stage", a former Tibetan cadre confirmed, "the Chinese really believed their own propaganda. They thought that in Tibet they had created New Soviet Man and were delighted to have the opportunity of showing off 'the socialist paradise on the Roof of the World'."[11] In spite of evidence to the contrary, they believed that most Tibetans had rejected the Dalai Lama. Just before the delegates arrived, the authorities organized meetings in many parts of Tibet, begging the people to hide their dislike and be polite to the visitors. The Tibetans were specifically asked not to throw dust and stones at them!

What actually happened shocked the Chinese to their ideological core. For from the moment the delegates' white Toyota minibuses arrived on the Tibetan plateau, in the mainly nomadic area of Amdo, they were mobbed by ecstatic but grief-stricken crowds, weeping and wailing. "The Tibetans", wrote Heinrich Harrer, gathered in huge numbers to convey to the sixteen emissaries of their lama-king their tokens of love and their expressions of despair. Thirty years of brutal Chinese oppression had failed to shake their profound faith. Secretly they produced their prayer-wheels from their hiding-places, brought out *khatas*, wept and touched the visitors. It was a demonstration of allegiance such as no-one had dreamed of.[12]

The visitors themselves were taken aback. Their hosts had warned them, for their own good, not to open their windows nor speak to the people; but events simply took over. "It was unbelievable", said the Dalai Lama's brother, Lobsang Samten:

Everywhere people were shouting, throwing scarves, apples and flowers. They broke the windows of all the cars. They climbed on the roofs and pushed inside, stretching out their hands to touch us. The Chinese were screaming, "Don't go out! They'll kill you!" All of the Tibetans were weeping, calling, "How is the Dalai Lama? How is His Holiness?" We yelled back, "He's fine. How are you?" Then, when we saw how poor they were, it was so sad, we all started crying too.[13]

It was Lobsang Samten who recounted the incident which best characterizes this extraordinary return:

One day we stopped in a small village for lunch. A crowd gathered before the guest-house, but Chinese guards kept them out. We were waiting to eat when a young Tibetan man some-how got in the door. He was very young, about twenty, and very strongly built. A great robust fellow - a real Khampa – bare-chested, in a sheepskin robe, with long hair. He didn't give a damn about the Chinese. He walked right past them up to our table, stopped and just stared at me. He was trembling violently all over. Then he burst into tears. Tears, I mean, were just rolling out of his eyes. I tried to console him. "Don't worry", I said, "I know how you feel." He didn't say a word. He squeezed my hands tightly, stared at me, then just turned round and walked out.[14]

To the horror of the Chinese, thousands of children and young people were among the crowds asking for blessings and begging for pictures of the Dalai Lama – "Chairman Dalai". Some of the scenes were so emotional that even the official Han guides were in tears. As for the exiles themselves, they were overcome by grief when they saw the poverty and misery of these stunted and malnourished people, their compatriots. "Most were just in rags, like beggars", said Lobsang Samten, adding:

> We were so shocked that after a few days none of us could eat or sleep. We remembered life in the old Tibet. We thought of our freedom in India and compared this to what had happened in our country. All the while, the Chinese kept shamelessly repeating propaganda about improved conditions and how joyful the people were. We were furious.[15]

The year 1979 had, in fact, seen the worst crop failure in modern times, owing as much to bad agricultural policies as to bad weather. Rations were so meagre that the Tibetans were once more on the edge of starvation, yet they were still having to hand over at least 1,000 pounds of grain in annual taxes.[16] Aware of this, the visitors were unimpressed by the model villages they were shown, with food in plentiful supply. The Tibetans had already told them it was all eyewash: that as soon as the visitors had gone, the butter and meat would be collected from the market stalls and carted away.

Bewildered by the totally unexpected turn events were taking, the Chinese reported on Radio Lhasa that the Amdowas, unable to conceal their hatred of the "reactionary" visitors, had openly attacked them with dirt and stones! At the same time, the Amdo authorities warned Lhasa of what to expect. Lhasa replied loftily that "thanks to the high standard of political training in the capital", they did not foresee any problem.

As the party drew near to Lhasa, the people were told to tidy up the city, dress in their best clothes and speak only when spoken to. They were to look happy, and, if asked, state emphatically how much better life was in the new Tibet than in the old. Women, deprived for years of their finery, were given pink and blue ribbons to braid into their hair.

On 29 September the delegation arrived in Lhasa to meet with an almost frantic reception from a huge crowd. Photographs taken on that first morning show streets packed with well-wishers, despite an explicit warning to stay indoors. Though many *did* stay at home, 17,000 Tibetans (some with coats over their heads, to avoid identification) stormed the Jokhang temple where the delegates had gone to worship. Chinese security personnel were trampled on and the temple gates were broken in the stampede. Each day, the chaotic scene was repeated, with men and women shouting "Long live His Holiness", throwing white scarves into the air, struggling to speak to or touch the delegates. In all this euphoria, tragedy of some kind was inevitable. On 1 October, a fifty-six-year-old gardener's wife and mother of seven, Tsering Lhamo, so far forgot herself as to shout, "Tibet is independent". She was arrested, subjected immediately to thamzing in her own neighbourhood, beaten, thrown into prison and tortured. Hearing this news, the delegation threatened to leave Tibet forthwith if the woman was not released. In some nervousness, the authorities released her – at least until the visitors had left. (She was then rearrested and subjected to drastic electric-shock treatment which reduced her to the state of a vegetable. Her son, imprisoned with her on the charge of putting up a wall-poster, had his jaw broken and deformed, as Amnesty International Report 1983 testifies).

From then on, the Chinese were taking no chances. In Shigatse, in Sakya, in Gyantse, the entire population was sent out to the fields by dawn so as to be out of the way when the delegation arrived.

By December, the delegates were back in Dharamsala, with "hundreds of rolls of film, many hours of recorded conversations and enough general information to occupy many months of collation, distillation and analysis."[17] As well as this, they brought more than 7,000 letters from Tibetans who had seized their first opportunity in more than twenty years to write to their families in exile. One of these letters was for Phuntsog Wangyal, a reply to one he had himself sent a few months earlier:

> When I heard that it was possible to send letters I could hardly believe my ears. I wrote a letter but I didn't even know who to send it to. I decided to address it to all of my family: my mother, two aunts, an uncle and several cousins. I got a reply from one of my cousins, who told me that almost everyone else was dead. There was no one left of my parents' generation, and only one or two of my aunt's children were still alive. Of course, my cousin did not dare tell me how they had all died.[18]

The delegates had been sickened by the near-destruction of their culture. Tibetan dance troupes performed for them, wearing Chinese costumes and Chinese make-up. Even the old folk-songs had gone, the only songs allowed being paeons of praise to Mao set to Chinese tunes. Infinitely worse, they had been told repeatedly of:

> years of famine, mass starvation, public execution and gross and disgusting violations of human rights, the least of which included the abduction of children either into forced labour gangs or for "education" in China, the imprisonment of innocent citizens, and the deaths of thousands of monks and nuns in concentration camps. It was a horrific litany, graphically illuminated by dozens of photographs of monasteries and nunneries reduced to piles of rubble, turned into grain stores or factories or cattle pens.[19]

It was all blamed on the Gang of Four. "Whenever we saw the ruin of a monastery or nunnery", said Phuntsok Tashi Takla, "they said, 'Oh, we didn't do that. It was the dreadful Gang of Four. We're improving things all the time. Come back in four or five years time, and see what a difference there will be' ".[20] But to the delegates it was obvious that the improvements were not for the benefit of Tibetans. In many places an old Tibetan town had been surrounded by a Chinese "new town", and, as Lobsang Samten observed of Tashikyl, the Tibetan part was "like an open grave":

> Its buildings were in total disrepair, its streets muddy and impassable. The people lived in dark, decaying rooms with barely any furniture or utensils and no running water and only intermittent electricity. On the other hand, the Chinese quarter, though itself showing signs of neglect, was newly built, its inhabitants far better fed and clothed than the Tibetans.[21]

In the new factories – making cement, leather, woollen fabrics, textiles, dairy products – the Chinese held all the top jobs, all the low-paid, heavy, dirty jobs being reserved for Tibetans. The produce was labelled "Made in China" and was destined for China, or for sale in Nepal and Hong Kong. There was electricity, but for the Chinese sectors only; roads, but mainly for the military, affording them an essential means of keeping control; vehicles, mostly heavy trucks belonging to the Chinese government; consumer goods, which the Tibetans could not conceivably afford.

On the medical front, large numbers of Tibetans were suffering from spinal and kidney ailments, the result of working overlong hours in the fields, poorly clad and in all weathers. They suffered from malnutrition; from heart and lung complaints unknown before the advent of the Chinese; and from nervous troubles caused by the ever-present terror of informers and of the "knock on the door".[22] Yet there were scarcely any trained doctors and rural Tibetans had to rely on ill-equipped "barefoot" doctors whose incompetence was a danger to life. Hospitals had been built, it was true, but they discriminated in favour of the Han settlers. As for education, it was, for Tibetans, a perversion of what the word should mean, since it was programmed only in the interests of the Chinese. Little Tibetan was taught (particularly in the east), most books were in Chinese and the vast majority of teachers had not themselves progressed beyond primary level.

Though new intensive farming methods had led to one or two spectacular harvests, the imposition of the commune system, crushing taxes and long hours of work on an empty stomach had contributed to years of famine. Moreover, the Chinese refusal to allow any land to lie fallow in the interest of rotating the crops, plus their insistence on replacing the highland barley by rice and wheat had led to the rapid erosion of the fragile topsoil and turned much of the land into desert. Nothing of this would ever be admitted, however. Tsering Wangchuk, a Tibetan cadre who had risen to being a reporter with Radio Lhasa, says that:

> crop failures, avalanches, heavy snowfalls, were all news so long as they were natural disasters. But crop failures that were the result of Party policy – we were never allowed to report on those. If the Party was wrong, you had to hide the fact. Our job was to prove that the Party was always right.[23]

The delegates' unequivocal thumbs-down to what they had seen in Tibet shocked and angered the Beijing government. They made it clear that they would not welcome public criticism from outsiders. So the Dalai Lama, unwilling to risk a new blood-bath for his long suffering people, decided not to publish the findings. There was, however, to be a second delegation in May, followed by a third a month later; and possibly a fourth and fifth later still.

The second fact-finding mission was led by Tenzin Tethong, a founder-member of the Youth Congress who now ran the Office of Tibet in New York. Phuntsog Wangyal, who headed the tiny Tibetan community in Britain, was also a member, along with the president of the Youth Congress and the Dalai Lama's representatives in Japan and Switzerland. All five were men in their early thirties. ("I wanted", said the Dalai Lama, "to ... gain an impression of how the situation in Tibet appeared to people whose perspective had the freshness of youth".[24])

This time the Chinese armed the police in Lhasa and other major cities with guns, chains and electrical stunning equipment. The ban on alcohol which had been in force since 1959 was lifted, presumably to encourage Tibetans to drink themselves senseless during the visit. There was no question this time of recommending courtesy. The rules were strict and specific: no one was to meet the visitors at all, on pain of being punished like Tsering Lhamo. "If they were encountered by accident", recounts Avedon,

> the people were not to smile, cry, shake hands, stand up if seated, remove their hats, offer scarves or invite them to their homes. The *logchopa* [reactionaries], it was said, would hand out "independence badges", small medals bearing the Tibetan flag. These should be thrown on the ground and stamped on. Pamphlets were then issued, outlining approved answers to questions the visitors might ask, while party cadres were given a crash course in Tibet's history as an integral part of China.[25]

The Tibetans took no notice. Despite the threats, it was the story as before, the delegates were mobbed throughout Amdo and Kham, with whole groups of people, wearing cast-off Chinese military outfits, prostrating themselves on the road to stop the Toyotas, or venerating lumps of soil over which the minibus tyres had passed. Thousands begged for the "independence badges" the Chinese had warned them about, but which, to their disappointment, did not exist. Children of ten and twelve offered flowers, saying, "May the sun of Buddha's teaching rise again"; and a group of twelve-year-old girls brought along pictures of themselves for "Chairman Dalai" to see. Mothers presented their babies, begging the visitors to give them long-forbidden Tibetan names, since their actual names represented only their birth weight or their father's age at the time they were born. "When you see and hear this kind of thing", said Tenzin Tethong, "it tugs at your heart-strings. It makes a very powerful impression".[26]

Like their predecessors in the first group, the visitors noted that much of the land had turned to dust, no longer providing abundant food for the local wildlife. And what had happened to the animals themselves? Where once there had been bears, eagles, wild geese and duck, black-necked cranes, wild yaks, deer and gazelles, there was now – apart from a few isolated preserves in Amdo – a total absence of wildlife. In all their travels they saw only one rabbit and a few marmots. (Jetsun Pema Gyalpo of the third group which travelled a month later, was also dismayed by this change. She could remember the herds of deer and wild asses which would accompany caravans for hours on their long journeys in which one was far more likely to meet gazelles, deer and antelope than human beings. But now there was nothing, not even, though it was the season for them, the famous white cranes of Tibet.) There were notices prohibiting the killing of animals, but local inhabitants said this had never inhibited the Chinese. As reported to Phuntsog Wangyal,[27] a favoured method was to "drive a motor-cycle and sidecar into a herd of deer, machine-gun the whole herd and then collect the carcases in a jeep".

Road signs were in Chinese, most places had Chinese names and there were no maps of Tibetan areas. The names had been sinicized during the Cultural Revolution, and few Tibetans could now remember where the old places were.* The distinctive scriptural texts and holy images that had once been carved or painted on hillsides, had everywhere been replaced by *The Thoughts of Chairman Mao*.

When in June the group entered Kham, they found the landscape almost unrecognizable: mutilated hillsides, which once had been alive with vast forests. Eastern Kham had suffered rampant deforestation, with hundreds of truck-loads of timber daily trundling east to southern and central China. (In thirty years, it was said that the Chinese had been cutting down trees

---

* The standard name for Tibet, as for China itself, was now "Motherland", no longer the Tibetan *Bo*. The term *Bopa* (Tibetan) had given way to *Borig* (of Tibetan race). Tibetan history had been reduced to a matter of fairytales and legends, the very word for history (*gyalrab*) being reserved for Chinese history only.

twenty-four hours a day, and had replaced virtually none of them.*)

Here in Kham, Phuntsog Wangyal at last discovered the fate of his family. It was a harrowing litany:

> My mother had been killed as early as 1959, soon after we had left. She was arrested, along with various other people in the village. They were all tortured, to find out who had organised our escape. And of course to find where they had hidden their "treasures". But no one had any treasures left. So the Chinese just went on beating and torturing them. I met a woman who had been in the same cell as my mother, on the first floor of a house that had once belonged to a wealthy landowner. All the prisoners had their arms tied behind their backs; and as a result nobody could use their hands to eat their food. They had to eat the way dogs do, licking it up. It wasn't real food, anyway, just slops. By then, my mother had lost all her hair – it had been pulled out. She looked like death apparently, but was still alive.
>
> My mother tried to kill herself, which for a devout Buddhist is a terrible thing. It was difficult, because they were all tied up and had no belts or anything. There was just a single ventilation hole in that first floor room. My mother got up there and jumped from it. But she didn't die. It was what we call karma: what you are destined to suffer, nothing can stop. They took her back to the cell, and just left her there to die. Then they threw her body in the river. I met somebody who had seen her body stuck in the river. He took it out, cut it into pieces, and scattered it for the birds, as we have always done in Tibet.[28]

Phuntsog Wangyal finished his blood-chilling story and said bleakly:

> I couldn't cry. Everybody else was hearing the same sort of story. Your own was nothing particularly special. I didn't even feel angry. It wasn't the Chinese who had done these things: they

---

* The Information Office in Dharamsala estimated that since 1959 China had earned 33 billion US dollars from the sale of Tibetan wood.

had got Tibetans to do them. They had to obey orders. If they refused, they were killed.[29]

In three and a half months the group saw temples and monasteries in only three places: Gyantse, Shigatse and Lhasa. Not surprisingly, the monastery to which he had once belonged was no more:

It had housed 3,000 monks, but when I looked, there was no sign of it. You would not have believed that it had ever been there. There wasn't even a foundation stone left. The villagers had been forced to take it away stone by stone, to uproot everything. Some of the sacred Mani stones had been used for building toilets, others for pavements, so that the villagers had to walk on them. The monks had been taken away, mainly to labour camps where they were given minimum food and maximum work until they died.

Wangyal's house had long since been burned down, but his village was still there, deprived, like most other villages, of electricity and running water. He asked his hosts why. "We could ask as many questions as we wanted", he said, "because we were an official delegation":

The Chinese kept telling us how they'd improved everything. Well, they'd built a good solid bridge over the river to take their own tanks. But the bridge the people use all the time was in a terrible state of repair. It was the same everywhere, Tibetans were just not getting access to the improvements. There were modern hospitals with modern equipment, doing operations. But the Tibetans were always in the minority of those allowed to go there. Villages were worse off than before. At least in the past they had had their herbal medicines. But all that was swept away in the Cultural Revolution, and nothing had been put in its place. The people in the villages were really suffering.

On their way to Lhasa, the delegates met numbers of vagrant

children who had left home because their parents simply could not feed them. They were also told of children being reduced to stealing the slops from Chinese soldiers' pigs.[30]

It was the end of July when they arrived in the capital, to be greeted with the same mixture of agony and ecstasy as their predecessors. A huge crowd waited for them outside the gates of Number One Guesthouse where they were to stay. "I think people had been anticipating our visit for weeks", said Tenzin Tethong:

> We were already notorious, chiefly, I suspect, because of our youth. The Chinese were dumbfounded and the Tibetans fascinated by the fact that the Dalai Lama had entrusted this mission to such young men. To the Tibetans it was a revelation that we were well-educated and able to talk to the Chinese on equal terms.[31]

Next day the streets leading to the Jokhang temple were packed solid with people. It took the group an hour or more to get through and the area round the temple itself was even more difficult. "People were struggling just to touch us. They were crying, shouting, throwing scarves in our direction". After visiting the main temple and shrine rooms, they went on to the roof – and looked out onto a courtyard jam-packed with people. "We *had* to speak to them, tell them who we were, who'd sent us and why", states Tethong:

> We told them we'd report our findings not only to Dharamsala but to the world. We said we'd been promised progress but had found only destruction and deprivation. We said that the concern of the exile community was not merely its own survival but the preservation of Tibetan culture and traditions. We encouraged them to hold fast to their religion and culture so that the hopes of His Holiness might one day be realized.

It was the same wherever the delegates went. That evening, so many people turned up at the Guesthouse that the Chinese put a guard on the door to keep them out. Nothing daunted, they surged back before dawn, "calling out our names, insisting on seeing one of us, anyone. All they wanted was to tell us about their sufferings. They told us of pain, death, torture, starvation, discrimination. They were distraught with grief".[32]

Next day, emotions boiled over when the delegates went to visit what remained of the beautiful monastery of Ganden – the name means Joyful Paradise – on a mountainside thirty miles or so outside the city. Seven thousand people were there on the hillside, ferried in by eighty-four trucks driven by Tibetans. (Later, many of these truck-drivers were arrested.) "Look what the Chinese have done to our Ganden", they kept crying. And indeed, nothing had prepared the delegates for the sight that met their eyes: they looked up and saw that the great monastery had simply been blown off the face of the earth. It was a blasted, bombed-out hulk which looked as though it had been destroyed 500 years ago rather than a mere twelve.

There in the ruins, before makeshift outdoor altars and images which had lain hidden for years, a prayer service was held. The delegates made emotional speeches and from thousands of Tibetan throats rose the long-forbidden cries for freedom. It was rumoured in the city that the Tibetan flag would be raised next day. With a group of Western journalists also in the capital, the authorities were understandably jumpy.

On the next day, when the delegates' minibus arrived in the city, the crowd went berserk. The journalists rushed to the scene in time to hear Phuntsog Wangyal address the Tibetans. "May the Dalai Lama's hopes and aspirations be fulfilled", he said. Immediately a young man leapt to his feet crying, "Long live His Holiness, the Dalai Lama", and the crowd took up the cry with passionate enthusiasm. The journalists tried to speak to the demonstrators, but were prevented by the police.

It was too much for the Chinese. The situation, already dangerously out of hand, was threatening to become worse by the minute. Though by doing so, they risked putting paid to future discussions with the Dalai Lama, the authorities first confined the delegates to their rooms, then expelled them from

Tibet. For form's sake, it was a Tibetan who did the expelling. "By your actions", Sonam Norbu, one of the Tibetan vice-chairmen of the TAR, admonished them, "you have deliberately incited the Tibetan people to break with the Motherland, and to sever their ties with their elder brothers, the Han Chinese. This ... will not be tolerated". An unambiguous threat was transmitted to the Tibetans. Do not forget, it warned, "the Dalai Lama's envoys are like the white cranes: they come and they go. But *you* are like frogs in the well and you have to remain".[33] "You can't reason with such people", sighs Tenzin Tethong, "they know what they want and are determined to get it. They posted police all round the Guesthouse and wouldn't allow anyone near us. That same day they took us to Lhasa airport and flew us out to Chengdu."

The third delegation had already been on its way for over a month, and was authorized by Dharamsala to continue. The official reception given to this third group (sent to investigate education and led by the Dalai Lama's sister, Jetsun Pema Gyalpo, head of the Tibetan Children's Village in Dharamsala) had from the start been less than warm. Hostility simmered between the Chinese and the visitors, and at times threatened to erupt. Writing later of her own impressions, Jetsun Pema Gyalpo commented: "Wherever we went, they tried to deceive us with false 'facts' and figures, and also did everything to stop us from getting in direct contact with our own people."[34]

In the rural areas, the vast number of school-age children seen working in the fields led them to suppose they would find no schools. This proved to be so, though they had a hard job getting their hosts to admit it. In many places they were told that schools were "closed for the summer", a strange admission in a country which almost came to a standstill during the paralysing cold of winter and had to make up for lost time during the warmer weather. Elsewhere a fake nomad school was staged for the delegates' benefit; and another school was "closed for lunch" at ten in the morning, with all its classrooms stacked with timber.[35] At first, said Jetsun Pema, "we insisted that we should visit the school just to see the empty school buildings. Then I realized that [this] was their way of saying, 'There is no school', or, 'We don't want you to see this school.'"

Despite all attempts to prevent them, in 105 days the group managed to visit seventy primary, middle and high schools and for the most part found the standard of education abysmally low. There was a 70% illiteracy rate among Tibetans. "But what can you expect when many of the teachers have not studied beyond two years of primary school?" asked Jetsun Pema. Almost 70% of the teachers were Chinese. The Tibetan language was almost a thing of the past and few children spoke it correctly. In Kham, little Tibetan was taught, while in the TAR it was restricted to primary schools only, and then as a vehicle for Marxist-Leninist-Maoist ideology. While Tibetan children were taught to despise their own culture, an alien ideology was the main subject offered to them at all levels.

In October this group too returned to Dharamsala with its report. "Its findings made clear", wrote the Dalai Lama,

> that although there had been a slight improvement in the standard of education over the past twenty years, this was not much of a blessing, for it seemed that, to the Chinese, the real value of reading was to enable children to study the thoughts of Chairman Mao and of writing to enable them to produce "confessions".[36]

Thirteen-year-old Lobsang Jimpa's experience over this period would bear out that assessment. "Unless you knew Chinese", he explained, "you couldn't get beyond primary level". During an examination (in Chinese), the boy scrawled a big zero on the page, followed by the words: I WANT TO LEARN TIBETAN. Angered by this "open rebellion", "the Chinese called an assembly of the whole school to give me thamzing. I was accused of sedition, the teachers beat me one by one, and the students were all made to cry out: 'Shame on you, shame, shame, shame.' Then I was expelled."

Together, the three delegations drew up a depressing cata-
logue of China's thirty-year legacy in their country:

- 1.2 million Tibetans, one-fifth of the population, had been
  killed or died of starvation.
- 6,254 monasteries and nunneries had been destroyed, their
  precious contents either melted down or sold for foreign
  currency.
- 60% of Tibet's literary heritage had been burnt.
- Two-thirds of the country had been absorbed into China
  proper, with only central and a part of eastern Tibet being
  given the name of Tibet.
- Amdo (Qinghai) had become the world's biggest gulag, with
  a reputed capacity to intern ten million prisoners.
- One in every ten Tibetans were in prison. One hundred
  thousand were in labour camps.
- Entire mountains had been denuded of their forests and
  Tibet's unique wildlife had been wiped out.[37]

A 2,000-year-old civilization had been brought to the brink of
destruction, they concluded, to promote China's unchanging
goals: to transform the region into a military bastion dominating
Central Asia; to exploit its vast mineral, animal and forest
reserves; and to remould the Tibetan people in their own image
and likeness.[38] Tibet was now China's largest Inter-Continental
Ballistic Missile base. Two years later, according to a Reuter
report in *The Times* of India (25.8.82) Tibet's Communist Party
supremo, Yin Fa-tang, claimed that the biggest reserves of
uranium in the world were locked inside the mountains of Tibet,
along with untold quantities of borax and iron ore. "Although
their true value will not be known for years, the hidden wealth of
this huge land mass ... represents an enormous resource bank
for China's future".

It was a warning of things to come. But in the short term it
seemed that the Tibetan longing for change might be answered.
On 22 May 1980, while the second and third delegations were

still on Tibetan soil, Hu Yao-bang, Deng Xiao-ping's heir apparent, arrived in Lhasa on a fact-finding mission of his own. The local officials did their best to mislead him by feeding him disinformation, and using the old "model village" strategy. Wangchen knew one old lady, for example, who "had her house decorated and stocked with food and furniture. Hu was brought to visit her and was very impressed by her unexpectedly high standard of living. How could he know that as soon as he had gone, officials would come and take everything away again?"

This old trick was practised many times over on the Chinese leader. But Hu finally saw through the play-acting and was appalled by the distorted picture he had been given. He publicly expressed shock at the grinding poverty, implicitly admitting the failure of Chinese economic policy in Tibet. Not attempting to hide his anger, he wondered aloud whether the 7,500 million yuan sent from Beijing for developing Tibet had been thrown into the Yarlung Tsangpo river. He went even further. According to the December 1980 issue of a Hong Kong publication, *Emancipation Review*, "Hu Yao-bang said one thing that no one in China has ever dared to say: *"This is plain colonialism"*. Fuming at the way the radical left had turned Tibetans into second-class citizens in their own land, he sacked the Party leaders, replaced them with more pragmatic and moderate men, and introduced a six point plan intended to improve the living standards, social conditions and fundamental freedom of the Tibetans. Eighty-five per cent of the Chinese cadres in Tibet were to be withdrawn within three years, their places to be taken by Tibetans.* Taxes were to be abolished for at least two years; some private enterprise would be permitted; and peasants would be allowed to plant their native barley again. Efforts were to be made to revive and develop Tibetan culture, education and science. And Hu promised to restore the Tibetan economy to its pre-1959 level within three years.

---

* There were at the time 120,000 Chinese civilians in the TAR.

It was almost too good to be true. Time alone would tell whether this was in fact a new dawn, a clever application of whitewash or merely the latest move in the deadly chess of Chinese politics.

CHAPTER 15

From Liberalization to Apartheid, 1980–1983

The Chinese government now acknowledges the failure of its minorities policy and is committed to making amends. It must be judged by results.

CHRIS MULLIN, 1981

Were the bad times really over? Was a fresh start to be made? The second delegation encountered widespread doubts – even among Communist Party officials. No one dared appear enthusiastic about putting the reforms into practice for fear of being denounced if the tide should turn again, reported Phuntsog Wangyal.[1] Far better to keep one's head down and do nothing.

Signs and street-names in both Chinese and Tibetan made an appearance in the cities. Ten thousand Han cadres were sent back, their jobs taken by Tibetans. But with more PLA soldiers coming to replace the departing cadres, the Tibetans could see little difference. "The blue Chinese are leaving", they shrugged, "but the yellow ones are coming in their place". There was no question of reducing the military presence. ("Of course Tibet isn't Chinese", a Chinese cadre admitted to visiting journalist, Jonathan Mirsky, "it's important strategically. We've got to keep the Russians and the Indians out. And US missile bases".[2])

But some repressive policies *were* being reversed and daily living was slightly easier. The hated daily political meetings were reduced to two hours once a week, with only one member of each family obliged to attend. For the first time in twenty years, people could move outside their own villages, though travel beyond a ten-mile radius still required a permit. Farmers were allowed to grow their beloved barley and to obtain loans with which to buy farm machinery.

"After Hu's visit, there was certainly an improvement", Pema Saldon agreed, but with a note of reservation in her voice:

> The Tibetans recaptured a little of their identity. We were allowed to wear the chuba again, sing Tibetan songs. Tibetan began to be taught in the schools, even if it was only for three hours a week. But it was a luxury subject; and it meant that Tibetans were unable to study English which was becoming very important in the school curriculum. If you wanted to go on to study science and technology, English was essential. Tibetan was useless for getting jobs. Worthwhile jobs were available only for those who could read and write Chinese.

Kelsang Namgyal was a film editor, working for the Chinese propaganda machine. "Our job", he told me,

> was to make propaganda films about the great liberalization of Tibetan language and culture. We made about twenty-five short propaganda films in sixteen or eight millimetre for the rural areas, the point being to show that even entertainment could now be provided in the Tibetan language. At the time we had to say that Chinese officials in Tibet were busy learning Tibetan. But that was all eye-wash.[3]

Though Tibetan was to be taught during the three years of primary school, all secondary education was in Chinese by Chinese teachers. Catriona Bass, an Englishwoman who spent sixteen months teaching in Lhasa, writes:

> Once they had made it to middle school, Tibetan children would find that, in effect, what they had learned at primary school was useless because they could not express it in the language their teachers understood. From then on, lessons would continually be

held up while the teacher taught the necessary words of his language before he could communicate the lesson ...

All over China students use the same textbooks, and the final exam which determines whether you can sit for university entrance or not depends on completing all the books in every subject. Children in the Tibetan classes could never hope to finish the number of books each year. So, in the final exam, which is a national exam, they would encounter even more problems than on graduating from primary school. Now, not only would their classmates be using their mother-tongue, they would also be answering questions on topics which the Tibetans had never studied.[4]

With poor school results, Tibetans found the job market virtually closed to them. Sixteen-year-old Namgyal from Lhasa experienced the despair familiar to all Tibetan youngsters. "All the school-leavers in our district had to take a final exam in Chinese", he said:

> I was one of only four who passed. Even out of the four, only one was given a job. The rest of us were ordered to go from village to village reading the newspapers aloud to an assembly of villagers. If we'd refused, our work points would have been reduced and we were afraid of being subjected to thamzing.[5]

Pemba, an intelligent Tibetan boy from Lhasa, was even worse off:

> I had three years at primary school, where I was taught Chinese, Maths and Tibetan. But from the age of eleven, I had no more schooling. There was nothing I could do. I fetched water for my parents, did some domestic chores and played with the other kids who were in the same boat: hide and seek, hopscotch, things like that.[6]

In the religious field, there was some relaxation and a huge upsurge in religious practice. In 1979 the Jokhang temple was reopened and other monasteries and temples – in both closed areas and those open to foreign visitors – were being partially rebuilt. It was, however, difficult to get permission and the work was usually paid for and carried out by the Tibetans themselves, with the Chinese taking the credit when it was completed! The Beijing authorities ordered the return to Tibet of crate-loads of gold and copper artefacts which had been taken to various provinces in China during the Sixties. Over 1,300 ancient statues were recovered at this time.[7] Among them (found in a junkyard in the suburbs of Beijing) was the mutilated upper half of one of Tibet's two most sacred statues: a Buddha already old and revered when it was brought to Tibet in the seventh century. During the Cultural Revolution in Lhasa it had been hacked in two, its gold and jewel-encrusted torso sent to Beijing to be stripped down, its lower half tossed aside as valueless.* Now, in 1979, the two halves were soldered together.

Talks were continuing about the Dalai Lama's return to Tibet, though the Chinese were increasingly anxious to impose limits on his future status – to protect their own sovereignty. In April 1982, Phuntsok Tashi Takla was one of a three-man team of Tibetan negotiators from Dharamsala who went to Beijing in the hope of finding a compromise. After weeks of argument the two sides were as far apart as ever. "They kept on repeating: 'Tibet is part of China'", says Mr Takla,

> and they refused to discuss independence at all. They certainly wanted the Dalai Lama to return, but they didn't think they'd allow him to live in Tibet. He'd be better off in China, they said. We tried to tell them that the Dalai Lama wasn't actually the main issue, that we were concerned more for the happiness of six

---

* The repaired statue was reinstated in its original home, Lhasa's restored and renovated Ramoche Cathedral in 1985.

million Tibetans. But though we argued for hours on end, we got nowhere.[8]

Instead of addressing the real issues facing the Tibetan people, complained the Dalai Lama, "China ... attempted to reduce the question of Tibet to a discussion of my own personal status".[9] When the delegates had returned to Dharamsala, the Chinese issued a statement, denouncing them as "splittists" and "reactionaries" who were hated by the Tibetan people. The Dalai Lama began to doubt whether the new Chinese policy really was any better than the old. He recalled an old Tibetan saying: "Before your eyes they show you brown sugar, but in your mouth they put sealing wax".[10] But he still wanted to return to Tibet, even if only for a visit; and hoped to send an exploratory team to Lhasa in 1984 to prepare the way.

Though pictures of the Dalai Lama were still seized from visiting Tibetans at the border – and promptly destroyed – his image was again hanging on Tibetan walls, flanked, for caution's sake, by those of Mao and Lenin. Religious reform was still half-hearted. "We could prostrate, erect altars in our homes, visit the temples – if any had been rebuilt near us – go on pilgrimages without having our ration cards taken away, fill the sanctuary lamps with yak butter and murmur our mantras", commented Pema Saldon, "but we weren't allowed to put into practice in our daily lives the Buddhist teachings we received". On a visit to Lhasa, journalist Nick Danziger was struck by the pageantry: "Barkor Street seemed peopled with characters who might have stepped straight out of a medieval morality play. Men dressed like court jesters, complete with cap and bells; lamas who blew strange trumpets made from human femurs ..."[11]

But, as John Avedon remarked, "The effect is to make Tibetans look like a backward, superstitious race, bowing down in blind faith before demonic idols – exactly what the Chinese Commulnist Party wants, for both internal and external consumption".[12] Whatever the outward tokens of religious tolerance, official attitudes were unchanged. *Basic Study Guide No. 55* published by the Information Office in Chamdo (April 1980) offered this advice for Communist Party and Youth League members:

> Religion is a tranquillizing poison used by capitalists to oppress people ... We have to stop religion in that it is blind faith, against the law and counter-revolutionary ... Anyone interested in being a member of the Communist Party or Communist Youth Organisation cannot practise religion. It is the duty of the Communist Party to try to persuade members who have a slight faith in religion to give it up. If they refuse, the Party should expel them ... Our policy has never changed; the recent relaxation is not a new policy. Whether the Dalai Lama returns or not, we must carry out our policy on religion ... Under this present freedom of religion people go on pilgrimages, practise religion ... take youngsters to religious places and try to teach them religious ideas. Some schoolteachers even try to use their position to talk about religion. All these activities are contrary to rules laid down in the Constitution.[13]

None of this gave much hope of real change. Religion was scheduled to die out as society evolved. Government employees or teachers were punished for praying in public. ("But we prayed in secret just the same", says ex-cadre, Tsering Wangchuk, "in public, we went into the temples, smoking cigarettes to show our contempt for religion. But when we thought no one was looking we went back there to pray. Even some of the convinced Communists did this.") Monks who dared teach the *dharma** to the people were denied their food-ration coupons; children were forbidden to pray in school; traditional Tibetan holidays like the Dalai Lama's birthday were not to be publicly observed.[14]

Though the monasteries and nunneries were again able to recruit novices, the numbers were restricted by quota. (In Lhasa, Ganden – which once had housed 3,300 monks – was allotted 300; Sera, formerly home to 5,500, was allowed 400;

---

* See ch.8, note 23, p.338.

Drepung – once the largest monastery in the world with over 10,000 monks – was given 450.[15]) According to official directives, the novice had to be eighteen, politically acceptable and appointed by a government committee, the Religious Affairs Bureau – which was also responsible for the administration and day to day running of the monastery. (In practice, however, people frequently managed to circumvent the rules.) Abbots were appointed by the same Bureau, and many of them were men who had renounced their vows – or over whom the administration had some hold.

It was impossible for monasteries to function as the centres of learning they once had been. According to a monk now in exile in Dharamsala, the novices were in the position of children admitted to a school "where there is no classroom, no teacher and no books".[16] With an entire generation of learned monks liquidated, the number of those qualified to teach was few indeed and the new novices could frequently neither read nor write. Even if their days could be devoted to scriptural study, there was little prospect of their being able to accomplish the twenty years of study considered necessary for the understanding of Buddhist philosophy. In fact they had little time for study and meditation. Lobsang Jimpa, expelled at thirteen from his primary school in 1979 for demanding to learn Tibetan, in 1982 became an "unofficial monk" at Sera monastery. That is to say, he was one of a substantial underclass who because they were under eighteen or from too high a social class – or politically suspect – had not received formal government permission to enter a monastery, but who were admitted at their own or their families' expense. Speaking about monastic life under Chinese control, he told me:

> Monks are allowed only three days a month in which to study religion, the eighth, fifteenth, thirtieth days of the Tibetan month. The rest of the time they must do manual work. Every day from eight a.m. till six p.m. we worked in the fields or on building work in the monasteries. Then in the evenings we had to attend political indoctrination meetings.

There is a great shortage of scriptures and of teachers. Almost all the older monks had died – committed suicide or been executed. The Chinese gave the monastery no subsidy, the monks had to support themselves by their own efforts and by donations from individuals.*

All rebuilding was carried out by the monks themselves. Study had to be slotted into whatever gaps there were in the timetable. If foreign visitors began asking awkward questions, such as why so much rebuilding was necessary, everything could be explained with a sigh and a reference to the infamous Gang of Four. No one dared mention that most of the destruction had taken place years before the Cultural Revolution – or the Gang of Four – had been heard of. Nor were the tourists told that the money they left before the altars would go directly into an account at the Bank of China, to be cashed only by officials.

At the hub of China's plans for developing Tibet was tourism. For the first time, foreign tourists – bringers of valuable hard currency – were arriving in Tibet in large numbers and with itineraries fixed in advance. They had to come in supervised groups via Chengdu in Western China, and stay in accommodation which for the most part was Chinese-owned and run (with Tibetans employed only in menial positions). Many of these early visitors were sympathetic to the Chinese socialist experiment and so those who kept their eyes skinned and found Tibetans to talk to received a nasty shock. They saw for themselves the crushing of Tibetan culture, the landscape littered with ruins. A few of the more intrepid went further. Award-winning Indian travel writer, Vikram Seth, wrote of his meeting with a young woman whose mother had died of a broken heart after the arrest of her husband:

My father was guilty of "contradictions between the people and

---

* In a few monasteries that are "national monuments", such as the "Big Three" of Lhasa, the monks do receive a small stipend.

the enemy" [the young woman told him grimly], while the murderers and rapists [in prison with him] were only guilty of "contradictions among the people". We're safe now, but we are ruined. We have almost nothing. Most of what we had was confiscated ... As for the family, look at my eldest brother, grief-crazed. And my younger brother is like a madman: he wanders round here and there and can't do any work. My father too ... mention my mother and he can hardly speak for grief. And who can say, a year, or two, or five, and politics will change again and people will look at us as before. It is not just the Gang of Four who did this to us.[17]

Sadly, the girl's fears were justified; politics would indeed change again before long. Another visitor, Heinrich Harrer, was reasonably optimistic in 1982, but a year later, when he came to write about his return to Tibet, the hope was already waning.[18] (It may be that the promise of 1980 was doomed from the start: its architect, Hu Yao-bang, was dismissed from his post six years later, partly because of his "softness" over Tibet.)

Discontent was never far from the surface, but resistance had been forced underground, because so many thousands of dissidents had been arrested or executed.* Secret independence groups had grown up, composed largely of poorly educated younger Tibetans, disorganized and with few resources, but enjoying a good measure of popular support. The independence movement had not as yet assumed dangerous proportions, but, as a reflection of Tibetan unease and desperation, it was enough to worry the authorities.

In May 1982, 115 dissidents were arrested in Shigatse. They

---

* In 1983 the Office of Information and International Relations in Dharamsala claimed to have established the following statistics: over 1,200 million Tibetans had died as a result of the Chinese occupation: 173,221 had perished in prisons and labour camps; 156,758 had been executed; 432,705 had died fighting; 342,970 had died of starvation; 92,731 had died of torture; and 9,002 had committed suicide. (*Present Conditions in Tibet, 1990*)

were not, of course, referred to as dissidents (a term not in any Communist vocabulary) but as delinquents, pornographers and black marketeers. In Chinese terminology, "pornography", apart from having its usual sexual connotations, is a blanket term for everything which undermines Communist ideology and "splits the Motherland". All talk of Tibetan independence threatened the unity of the Motherland. It was counter-revolutionary and since 1951 had in many cases been a capital offence.

1983 was the year when the dream – such as it was – died; when the Tibetans finally gave up even half-believing Chinese promises, and when the Chinese decided to tighten the screw. They began to flood Tibet with Chinese. This was, after all, the proven method which China had used to overcome opposition in other minority areas where it had been a deliberate, conscious policy. In Manchuria, for example, only two to three million Manchurians remained in a land settled by seventy-five million Chinese; in East Turkestan (called Xinjiang by the Chinese) the 200,000 Chinese who had been there in 1949 had grown to seven million, more than half the total population; and in Inner Mongolia, there were 8.5 million Chinese compared to two million Mongolians.[19] Tibet could now expect a similar fate. As John Gittings wrote in *The Guardian*, "The assumption behind sinicization is that of a superior culture, so deeply embedded in Chinese consciousness that their paternalism verging on racialism is mostly unconscious and therefore all the more resistant to reform."[20]

The independence groups were stirred into action. Although most of these favoured non-violent, passive resistance, there was a certain amount of random violence. Suddenly the Chinese found it unsafe to walk the streets. In May 1983, seven Chinese tourists travelling in a minibus in south-west Tibet were robbed and strung up; in June three more were lynched in Lhasa. In July, while Chinese officials were letting it be known that they were no longer interested in the Dalai Lama returning to Tibet in any capacity at all, his birthday was defiantly celebrated in Sakya and Lhasa. Youths handed out leaflets, claiming there were 2,500 political prisoners in Tibet's jails and telling the

Chinese invaders to go back where they came from. Forty foreign journalists visiting Lhasa in August were body-searched by airport police in case they should be carrying copies of the leaflets.

The journalists found a city virtually under siege, with thousands of Chinese soldiers patrolling the streets, and official posters everywhere warning of armed subversion.[21] But the dissidents they met were armed only with the written word. "They roamed the bazaar at night", reported Michael Weisskopf in the *International Herald Tribune*, "quickly slipping notes to the visitors and dashing off. Several letters were addressed to the United Nations from 'the people of Tibet'. One letter, partly written in English, urged Beijing to 'stop genocide, stop butchery' in Tibet."[22]

In August, a twelve-month anti-crime campaign was launched throughout China. In the last week of August, the Tibetan authorities imposed a curfew and launched a savage round-up of "criminals". Over the next six weeks, every household in Lhasa was searched and though nobody is sure of the exact figures, it was estimated that 500 were arrested.[23] In Chamdo, 1,000 were said to have been arrested at random off the street, with smaller numbers claimed for Gyantse, Shigatse and Tingri. On 13 September, 370 Tibetan monks working on the restoration of Ganden were surrounded by one thousand Chinese troops, beaten up and flung into trucks. (An old monk and former abbot was beaten to death.) By November, 750 Tibetans were said to be in Lhasa prisons, fifty of them chained in solitary confinement. It seemed beyond doubt that many others had been sent to the gulags in the north, from which few would ever return.

On 27 September 1983, six "counter-revolutionaries" were publicly executed in Shigatse, with the whole population in compulsory attendance. (The Chinese had reverted to their former practice of severing the prisoners' vocal chords to prevent them speaking out against their captors.) When a list of their crimes had been read out, the victims were shot in the back of the head. On 1 October, six executions were said to have taken place in Lhasa, all the victims being political activists. An eyewitness described one of the executions thus: "The victims were lined up and shot in the back of the neck. Wangdu did not die immediately and had to be shot three times. When his family members rushed to collect his body, they were made to pay ten RMB* [about twenty-five pence sterling] for each bullet used on him."[24] The relatives had to thank the Chinese publicly for eliminating "anti-social, reactionary elements".[25]

On 4/5 October twenty-one people were said to have been executed in police barracks in Lhasa. Fears of a new dark age engulfed the Tibetans, now once again in terror of the "knock on the door". When news of this fresh bout of repression reached Dharamsala, refugees demonstrated in Delhi and throughout the Tibetan settlements in India and Nepal. But the Dalai Lama, who had half-expected the Chinese about-turn, recognized that there was a new factor in the situation which might in the long run benefit Tibet: journalists from many countries were on the spot and could see the situation for themselves.

The outrage expressed by other countries when the journalists' reports were published underlined the Western failure to comprehend that in Deng Xiao-ping's China, economic and political reforms were held to be completely separate. The former was a necessity; the latter not in any circumstances to be contemplated. When, in the wake of this fresh outburst of criticism, the Chinese let it be known they were to implement more liberal policies, it was economic policies they meant: the communes would be disbanded, cultivators would be allowed to hold their land for thirty years, farmers could own their livestock and no longer be obliged to hand over more than half their meat, barley and butter produce by way of tax to the state. Privately owned enterprises would once again be allowed, as would trade with China, India and Nepal. These reforms, it

---

* RMB (*renminbi*) or yuan.

must be admitted, benefited nomads and traders enormously. But they did *not* herald the onset of greater political freedom.

Were the farmers happy? Well, maybe for a time, until they found out that the changes actually worked against them. As one of them told Vanya Kewley:

> The Chinese say one thing to the outside world, but inside the story is very different. They say they have liberalized their policies in Tibet and have given Tibetans more freedom and more land. This is partly true. Yes, we can grow barley again. Ownership of some land is now allowed, but if a group works very hard, they are officially only allowed to sell through the Chinese system, and if they exceed the official quota, they have to deposit the profit in a Chinese bank. Once this has been done there is no possibility of the family withdrawing their savings, say for an emergency, if someone has to have an operation ...
>
> Yes, some of us have been given a little land, but seeds and fertilizers, which we have to buy from the Chinese shops, are so expensive that in the end it is not enough to give a family even one meal a day. We have to buy everything in the shops run by the Chinese: things for the land, the clothes I am wearing, even my shoe-laces. The Chinese charge us very high prices, but we have no option.[26]

Offsetting the concessions was the dramatic new impetus being given to Chinese immigration. In September 1983, the official *Beijing Review* urged Chinese nationals to settle on the Tibetan plateau in large numbers because of the need for skilled and unskilled labour to develop a "backward" and "barbarian" country. Although in Amdo (Qinghai), Chinese settlers already outnumbered the Tibetans three to one, Tibetans still outnumbered Chinese in the TAR. It was to the TAR that the Chinese now attempted to lure their own excess population – for the most part the young and ill-educated – despite their conviction that Tibet was a frozen desert peopled with uncouth savages. Irresistible inducements were offered to workers willing to sink their prejudices and migrate: higher wages – two, three and

sometimes even four times what they could earn at home; inter-·
est-free loans; guaranteed housing and plenty of home leave. For
the professionals, there were three-year, renewable contracts,
short working days at twice the salary at home, and home leave
every eighteen months. For those prepared to intermarry and
settle permanently on the high plateau, in small businesses or
farming, for example, there was the promise of a 10% increase
in their retirement pension.

The blandishments proved impossible to ignore, and in its
February 1984 issue, the *Beijing Review* piously claimed that
Tibetans were now "fighting shoulder to shoulder with large
numbers of Han Chinese who have sacrificed the comforts of
their home towns and dedicated themselves to modernizing the
Tibetan areas".[27] In May, Radio Beijing announced that over
60,000 Han "experts" – the vanguard of a huge future workforce
– were on their way to Tibet. By July, 20,000 more –
"engineers" and "contractors" – had arrived in Shigatse. The
new immigrants were to be employed on a string of new construction projects, fourteen in 1984 and forty-two in 1985:
hotels, cinemas, a sports stadium, hospitals, power stations and
factories. The authorities set about enlarging the existing facili-
ties for air traffic: an ambitious programme of airfield construction was embarked on, to enable larger aircraft to land in Tibet.
(These improvements would, of course, also hasten the economic integration of Tibet into China.) "Everything was done to
encourage the new arrivals", said ex-cadre, Kelsang Namgyal,
bitterly:

> Naturally they got far higher salaries than we did. But in addi-
> tion they were given lots of allowances which never came our
> way. One of them was to compensate for Tibet being at a high
> altitude. It was a sort of "breathing allowance". What we felt
> was, "well, if they have to bring in so many Chinese in order, as
> they kept telling us, to help the Tibetans, why couldn't they train
> Tibetans to do the job? At least they wouldn't have to pay them
> to breathe."[28]

For Tibetans this new development was catastrophic.

Remaining forests were being cleared to house exclusively Chinese communities; Chinese settlements, five-to-ten-storey blocks of flats (with electricity and running water, naturally) were constructed alongside all major Tibetan cities and towns. Tibetan towns became shanty towns overnight; where electricity *was* available (i.e. if there were Chinese living in the village) it was available to Tibetans for only three or four hours in the evening. No Chinese, no electricity. In the fertile river valleys of Kham the Chinese set up agricultural settlements, forcing the Tibetans to move off the arable land and find shelter in the high, nomadic pastures.[29] In Lhasa, the influx of Chinese inevitably caused food shortages, sent prices soaring and, in flooding the job market with Chinese labourers, put countless Tibetans out of work. Chinese workers were given automatic priority (and higher pay) in the job market. About 30,000 Tibetans employed in state work-units in Lhasa were replaced by immigrants and sent home to their villages to look for work.[30]

Gradually the Chinese immigrants, with their government subsidies and easy access to cheap raw materials from China – these came in daily by the lorry-load – began taking over Tibetan restaurants and such traditionally Tibetan work as tailoring, building, car maintenance and carpentry. As almost all factory workers were now Chinese, only the unskilled jobs being reserved to the Tibetans, there was not much left for the natives but street-hawking. The number of beggars grew daily.

The inevitable effect of all this was to make the Tibetans doubt their own culture and even be ashamed of it. Their self-image plummeted. "What's it like", queried John Avedon blisteringly,

> if you're a Tibetan lucky enough to get a job removing debris from mining, doing road-repair, sweeping or pig-feeding in a Chinese compound? You're likely to get one-to-two yuan a day – about seventy cents. What's your paycheck if you're a newly arrived Chinese immigrant? To begin with, you'll receive a guaranteed supplement of twelve dollars a month, issued, the Government states, to meet your need for a healthier diet in the

trying altitude. That's on top of free furniture, household items and clothing.[31]

The discrimination was keenly felt by the cadres, said Kelsang Namgyal:

> All the newly arrived Chinese officials were given an apartment, or at least a decent room, while we Tibetans who had worked for them for eight or ten years were still without one. (When I first began working, I had to share a room with six others and there were no cooking facilities.) If a Han cadre's light bulb fused, he would get an instant replacement. They even gave him a broom for sweeping his place, because, they explained, "he came all the way from the mainland to help Tibet".
>
> The Han cadre who has worked for eighteen months in Tibet, gets six months holiday with pay, and his air travel to the mainland is provided free. Tibetans working in Lhasa but coming from, say, Chamdo, were entitled on paper to a month's holiday at that stage, but in practice, that was all eyewash, we didn't get anywhere near that much. In any case, we had to make our own way home and pay our own expenses. And when we came back, the hard way, by truck, on a journey lasting several days, we were allowed only twenty-four hours in which to recover. If we took more, our pay was docked. But when the Han officials returned after their six months, they were given seven days paid leave in which to recover from a short journey by air. "He must have rest after coming so far", they explained, "he has to readjust to the altitude."[32]

When the Chinese immigrant finally returns home:

> they give him a housing allowance, a furniture and furnishing allowance and a lump sum, plus quantities of wood. They give them a truck and pay all the loading and unloading costs. The Chinese cadres make huge crates and fill them so full of possessions they have to hire a crane to load them into the truck.

Dorje Tsephel, a Tibetan who actually worked for the security police – "I had to earn a living somehow" – is equally bitter:

The Chinese claim they've come to help the Tibetans, but all they do is rob us and take all our natural wealth to China. When they arrive, they come with empty bags, but they go away with two or three truckloads of possessions. A posting to Tibet is a guarantee that they will make their fortune.[33]

Lobsang Nyima, fully dedicated now to the cause of Tibetan independence, arrived in Lhasa at this difficult time:

I kept myself alive as a street hawker. Living conditions were terrible. Meat and butter were prohibitively expensive; and even tsampa was too dear for Tibetans to buy. Lhasa was flooded with Chinese, and there was nothing left of the old city except the tumbledown Barkor area. The Tibetans were being treated as though they were animals or ignorant savages and they resented it bitterly. I tried to tell the younger ones what the Chinese were up to and how they ought to join the resistance.[34]

When Catriona Bass saw the Holy City of Lhasa for the first time, she was horrified to find:

Chinese suburbia. All around us, high-walled compounds, characterless blocks, broad lines of streets stood out with the same desolate symmetry. Despite the miles and mountain ranges separating Tibet from Central China, it seemed to me as we neared the centre, that Lhasa had nothing to distinguish it from Wuhan, Chengdu, Xian or Peking. Even the shadows cast by the street lamps were the same.

The tannoy system, continuously blaring out exhortations to love the Party, serve the people and work hard for the socialist faith completed the disillusion. In the Barkor, "historic buildings and winding alleys had been swept away and replaced by baubled lamps and concrete flowerbeds to give the view of the temple more grandeur."

The spectre of apartheid was thriving in the Chinese People's Republic as most Tibetans huddled in their slums, discriminated against at almost every turn, and with few of the amenities that might have made life bearable.

CHAPTER 16

The "Final Solution", 1985

For the last twenty-seven years there has been a systematic exploitation of Tibet's natural resources. More than anything else, Tibet was made the source of raw material for the economic development of China. If the present trend continues and also if the Chinese hastily and haphazardly plan the economic development of Tibet to meet their overall modernization target without taking into consideration the conditions of the country and the needs of the people, there is the danger that not only economic chaos but economic disaster will befall Tibet.

THE DALAI LAMA, 1986

Early in 1985, a fourth delegation sent by the Dalai Lama arrived in Beijing, to negotiate the terms for the Dalai Lama's return. To their dismay, the Chinese government announced again that their administration of Tibet was non-negotiable; that if the Dalai Lama returned, it would be to Beijing, not Tibet. One day, this group was addressed by Ngabo Ngawang Jigme, the man whom most of them regarded as an arch-traitor and who now lived in Beijing. "He began with all the usual sloganizing," says Tenzin Atisha, a member of the delegation:

Well, he had to. The Chinese were listening. But suddenly, to our amazement, he leaned forward and said urgently: "The

proposal to bring the Dalai Lama here is of tremendous importance. You must all go away and think it over *very carefully indeed.*"
We were quite startled, we sensed he was warning us that the
Dalai Lama must not come to Beijing. I now believe that Ngabo
was a coward and a weak man but never a traitor. He has
Tibetan interests at heart. Look how the Chinese keep him
under wraps in Beijing. If they'd really believed he was their
man, they'd have paraded him all over the world as a Tibetan
who loved and admired them.[1]

The Dalai Lama did not lose heart at this setback. "I still
believe it is better to talk face to face", he said, "than to keep
standing with our backs to each other ... Politics is like Judo,
you have to be always alert. The Chinese have given us plenty of
experience in this game."[2]

When the delegates reached Amdo and Kham in the summer
of 1985, they were shocked by the unprecedented influx of
Chinese settlers. The Tibetans were the new aborigines,
engulfed by Chinese and, unable to compete commercially with
them, squeezed out of employment. Out of forty families in
Taktser, home village of the Dalai Lama, only eight were
Tibetan.

The delegates were not allowed to enter the TAR, because
special festivities were impending there. 1 September 1985 was
the twentieth anniversary of the Tibetan Autonomous Republic
(TAR) and there were to be spectacular celebrations in Lhasa,
wth the foreign press in attendance. Lapel badges with pictures
of the Potala were handed out; and the reluctant Tibetans were
dragooned into endless rehearsals of flag-waving and flower-
strewing. But as the day drew near, the Chinese got cold feet,
realizing that the Tibetans would in any case turn up only under
duress, and might well use the occasion to protest against
Chinese rule. Thousands of extra troops and plain-clothes policemen were brought in from other areas, together with two
hundred Public Security Bureau surveillance men from Beijing.
No more foreign journalists were allowed to visit the city, which
was then sealed, with checkpoints set up on all the major roads.

A nine to seven curfew was imposed and ninety potential troublemakers were arrested.

This time there was little to justify the paranoia. Someone did, it is true, smear excreta over the doors of some Chinese offices; and, three days before the festivities three homemade bombs were found, one outside the new Post Office, and two at the stadium where the ceremony was to take place. It was enough to panic the Chinese into changing the location, curtailing the celebrations to a brief half-hour ceremony (with Tibetans trucked in and trucked out again), and cancelling all the victory parades. The Tibetans cared little one way or the other. For them, the only event worthy of note was a visit by the Panchen Lama, only his second since before the Cultural Revolution. They received him with rapture, for, though living in Beijing and said to be married, the Panchen Lama was the nearest they had to a spiritual leader and they had long since forgiven him for the past. "People had changed their minds about him", said Tenzin Atisha who had met him in Beijing that July:

> When we saw him in Beijing, he told us quite plainly that he couldn't speak what was in his mind, and he hoped we'd understand. It was only an accident of fate that had made him serve the Chinese. We celebrated the Dalai Lama's birthday with him and there – in front of all the Chinese dignitaries – he prayed the long life prayer for His Holiness, for the fulfilment of all his wishes. He went on saying what the Chinese ordered him to say, that Tibet was a part of China and so on, just as a sort of formula. He was in a Chinese cage. But he was active in reviving Tibetan culture and preserving Tibetan traditions. When he visited towns in Kham and Amdo which were completely sinicized, he urged the Tibetans there to wear Tibetan clothes and speak the Tibetan language. His words carried a lot of weight.[3]

The Chinese did their best to pull the wool over the Panchen Lama's eyes about life in present-day Tibet. As Catriona Bass was told in Lhasa:

He was taken to a village where everyone had been dressed in new clothes; new thermos flasks and radios were put in their houses. But they couldn't trick Panchen Rimpoche. He knew it wasn't real. He was very outspoken; in a big meeting, he told everyone that there were many things wrong in Tibet, that Tibetans were suffering.[4]

The Panchen was not alone in refusing to be taken in. If the Chinese had hoped to impress the foreign journalists, their hope had certainly backfired. The journalists had seen and heard enough in their short time in Lhasa to convince them that the Tibetans were an endangered species. An article in the London *Spectator* entitled "Tibet's Barbaric Conquerors" referred to the flood of Chinese manpower and propaganda which filled the cities of Tibet and concluded:

> Chinese cinemas, Chinese television – a particularly potent weapon in Tibet – Chinese hotels, customs houses, theatres, all these, if not in the course of construction already, will envelop Lhasa within the next two years, leaving only pockets of the city with any distinctive Tibetan character.[5]

Worse still, the author found, was the attempt to sinicize Tibetan youth, not only through the lure of cassette recorders and television sets but, more worryingly, through

> the barbaric practice of removing children from their families for several years at a Han Chinese school. The Tibetan parents rarely have any say in this and several Tibetan mothers in Lhasa described how they watch their sons day and night in case they, too, disappear. This may be fanciful superstition, but there are few Tibetans between the ages of fifteen and twenty-one on the streets of Lhasa.

Women generally were bearing the brunt of the new repression. When the Chinese had introduced stringent birth control measures in central China in the 1970s, the policy, though harsh, had seemed understandable. When, however, the law was applied to Tibet, which has seventy-five times more land space per person than China, it seemed perverse.

Throughout the Seventies the rules were, in fact, only loosely applied. But from 1983 onwards they began to be enforced in some Tibetan areas. A testimony submitted to the Dalai Lama by one Tenzin from Amdo describes how one day, in his township of 400 people, a nine-man team arrived to set up a birth control centre for the area. They took down the names of all the women, divided the people into small groups and "went to more than forty households, terrorizing their women into submitting to birth control operations. Those who resisted or protested were tied up, thoroughly beaten and then taken away to be forcibly operated upon. In addition, the Chinese authorities killed their hens, sheep and goats for their own consumption."[6]

Ordinary Tibetan families were allowed two children, employees of the state only one. In fact, at this stage, a state-employee who was already pregnant with a second child could go ahead and give birth, but as a woman cadre told Catriona Bass,

> If you have more than one, they make you lose out on all sorts of benefits. Without a "one-child certificate", you don't get a bonus every month. Also, when new houses are allocated and when the leaders decide who should get a rise in salary, you have a much better chance of being chosen if you have a one-child card.[7]

Families outside the state system who exceeded the two-child threshold had to pay heavily. Tashi Dolma, a doctor working in Amdo, told me of her mother's cousin, a nomad, who already had the statutory two children:

> When she had a third, she had to pay a huge fine. The child is now four-and-a-half. When he is six, he will be barred from receiving an education and will not be given a food ration card. The family will have to share their own rations with him, and in addition pay 500 yuan a year as a penalty tax.[8]

There was one practice which few people came to hear about: the degradation of Tibetan girls from rural areas who are lured into joining the People's Liberation Army. The story of Lhakpa Chungdak is an example, and I propose to tell it at some length.

Lhakpa, from the village of Meldrogungkar, near Lhasa, was a bright fourteen-year-old when one day in 1983 a recruiting officer came to her middle school searching for thirty Tibetan boys and one girl for the PLA. He promised that any recruit who stayed in the army for three years would not only be guaranteed a job in government service afterwards, but would have his/her family taken care of for the rest of their lives. It was an enticing prospect for poor villagers, and there was considerable rivalry for the places. To Lhakpa's delight, after an intensive physical examination, she was chosen.

She left home in 1984, with a promise that she could be trained as a doctor in a military hospital. But first she must be a dancer in the PLA's dance troupe:

> It was the top military barracks in Lhasa. We Tibetan girls were told to serve the officers, bringing them water, making their beds and so on. They apparently preferred the new recruits to the older girls. On my first evening, one of these officers (they all seemed to be old men) sent for me. I thought it would be for some official duty. He had grey hair and had taken his false teeth out. He said, "You're my little girl now and must do whatever I say". He began to fondle me, so I screamed and kept on screaming. He let me go, and I went back to my room, shaking.

At this point in her narrative, Lhakpa had gone pale. Her distress was obvious and she continued with difficulty:

> Three hours later, he summoned me again and began asking me about my family. He gave me a sweet. I was nervous but took it. Then he gave me an orange drink. When I drank it, I immediately felt dizzy, and fainted. I remembered nothing more. When I came to, I was naked and bleeding, and I began to cry. The officer shrugged and said: "I raped you. So what? I'll go on

doing it as long as you're here. You'll have to understand that
that's what you're here for."

Soon after that, a lot of officers came from central China and
there was a reception for them. I was frightened when I was told
to take water to one of their rooms after dinner. But when I went
in and saw three high-ranking officers with stars, I heaved a sigh
of relief. With three of them, I'd surely be safe. Then they all
began stroking me at once, and they made me take a sweet. It
must have been drugged. I didn't actually lose consciousness, I
could see everything they did, but I lost all sensation. They went
on raping me for three or four hours. Then I really did freak out.
I wanted to die. I saw a fruit-knife on the table and tried to stab
myself. The officers couldn't have cared less, but one of the
bodyguards outside rushed in and grabbed the knife.

Lhakpa was taken to a military hospital, given a blood transfusion and a glucose drip and after five days was sent back to the
barracks. Over the next eighteen days she was assaulted by a
variety of men. She told her superiors that if they insisted on
keeping her in the dance troupe she would run away home and
tell everyone what had been done to her. They then transferred
her to a large military hospital near Sera monastery, along with
twelve other Tibetan girls. They again promised her a training,
but this amounted to no more than physical training in the
mornings and political theory in the afternoons:

There was a girl from Chamdo, Tsewang, a fourteen-year-old
like me. While we were resting from the PE, some officers called
her out. She was away for three hours and when she came back
she was crying. I asked her why and she said at first she was
homesick. But then she admitted the officers had gang-raped
her. During the next PE session, she began to bleed from the
vagina. The instructor said it was just her period starting and
she should ignore it. After all, he said, "If we were at war, you
wouldn't be able to take time off to have a period".

It was my turn next. An officer told me to go and wash vegetables in his kitchen. In the next room he was watching blue
movies and he called me in to watch. He told me that the duties
of a woman soldier were different from a man's. "It's part of
your training", he said, explaining that during the war with
Japan, women soldiers had been raped by the Japanese. "You
have to learn how to deal with that sort of thing." He was getting
excited, and as the movie progressed, he tried to rape me. I
struggled, but he threw an impregnated cloth over my head. So I
was raped yet again. He proceeded to give me a lecture on the
duties of army women. "In any case, I don't need to explain
myself to you", he said. "You're not a virgin, you've been with a
lot of men. You're just a whore."

Lhakpa wiped a hand over her prematurely-aged face. She was
now twenty-two, but looked twice as old. Over the next six
months she was raped continually. "The Chinese said it was no
use complaining, it was what being in the army was all about for
a Tibetan."

The military top brass paid frequent visits to the hospital to use
the Tibetan girls. Those who refused were given the filthiest of
jobs, like disposing of the effluent. Two of the girls got pregnant.
One of them, a girl from Shigatse, was forcibly aborted and
made to say that a Tibetan boyfriend was responsible. When I
went to see her, I saw many aborted foetuses lying around in
buckets. The second girl threw herself out of a second-storey
window. But she only broke a leg, and they took her to the
hospital and performed an abortion.

Just before the end of the three years "training", all thirteen
girls got together to pool their experiences. They had all suffered
the same treatment: drugged, then raped. Some had suffered
multiple rape by as many as ten officers at a time:

Some had even had their vaginas stitched to make them smaller
for Chinese penises. We were all bitter, because we had been

promised so much and had hoped to be able to help our families.
We decided then on mass suicide because our lives were ruined.
We'd never find a husband now. But before dying, we vowed
we'd tell our families the truth. We wanted to warn Tibetan girls
on no account to join the PLA.

Unfortunately, two of the group were informers, and they
betrayed the plan to the Chinese. The girls were surrounded by
thirty or forty soldiers who beat them with rifle butts before
arresting them. Lhakpa was accused of being the ringleader:

> They beat me till I "confessed". We were then all sent to dif-
> ferent units within the hospital. My posting – and I'm certain it
> was deliberate – was to an infectious diseases unit. The only
> thing that changed was that here it was the Chinese doctors (also
> in the PLA) who assaulted us. Nine months later they dis-
> charged us and ordered us back to our home villages. There was
> no mention of that promise to train us as doctors. Two girls
> managed to get a job as army cooks, one or two as hospital
> cleaners. Six girls were so traumatized that they couldn't go back
> home. They drifted onto the streets of Lhasa as petty thieves and
> prostitutes, no use to anyone, least of all to themselves.
>
> But they weren't going to get rid of me so easily. I went to the
> medical authorities and threatened I'd tell everyone how they'd
> abused me and turned me into a physical wreck. I was pregnant
> and accused one of the doctors of being responsible. This man
> immediately took me off and aborted me. But at last they began
> to give me some kind of training – for two months as a nurse,
> along with two others from our group.

It was while doing this training that Lhakpa discovered another
practice which she believes was widespread:

> The Tibetan patients in the hospital were being used as guinea-
> pigs for the Chinese medical students to practise on. One day a
> Tibetan boy called Tenzin, a messenger with the PLA, was
> brought in with a bullet wound in his leg. He was a small boy,

about eighteen years old. When he was well on the way to recovery, for some unexplained reason they took him away and performed an abdominal operation. It became clear that the medical trainees had been practising on him. He got weaker and weaker and finally became delirious. He beckoned me over and I went to his bedside. "When I'm dead", he whispered, "tell the people outside I was murdered." Three days later he died.

Initially all the patients were PLA people. Then it was decided to admit Tibetan patients who could afford to pay the very high fees in advance. Once a woman from Ngari was brought in suffering from head pains. A thick needle was inserted at the base of her spine from which fluid was to be extracted. One by one, using a microscope, the medical students all inspected the "needle", each one turning, twisting, removing and replacing it in the woman's body. Her condition began to deteriorate, she shivered uncontrollably and lost consciousness. She could not even turn her head without moving her whole body. Yet when she came in, she had only had head pains. Soon afterwards, she died.

When a Chinese officer was to be treated, the operation was "rehearsed" on a Tibetan patient suffering from a similar complaint. If the operation on the Tibetan was satisfactory, they went ahead and operated on the officer. When an officer needed a blood transfusion, they took the blood from the Tibetan patients.

It sometimes happened that the girls had to take away unclaimed Tibetan corpses for disposal. The men who prepared bodies for sky-burial* used to spit and snarl at them, says Lhakpa, accusing them of murdering healthy people: "They said the bodies had vital organs missing or in the wrong place, and that even the vultures refused to eat their flesh."

By 1985, Lhakpa could stand no more and applied for a discharge on grounds of family hardship. Though this was regarded as a serious breach of military discipline, in time she found work as a filing clerk in a police department dealing with divorce cases.

---

* The ancient ritual of sky burial (Jhator) in which the corpse is cut up and left on a high rock for the vultures is the commonest form of burial among Tibetans.

*   *   *

Nevertheless, there were some instances of genuine liberalization. As the result of a major concession by the Chinese (which they may afterwards have regretted), in December 1985 10,000 Tibetans were given leave to attend the important Kalachakra ceremony conducted by the Dalai Lama at Bodh Gaya in India.* Five hundred pilgrims took their children along – and left them behind in India to get the education denied them at home. The pilgrims' message for the exiles was bleak. Liberalization was largely illusory, they said, the future was once again dark.

Yet in the early part of 1986, there was a last flicker of hope. Monlam Chenmo, the centuries-old Great Prayer Festival which traditionally followed the New Year, was permitted for the first time since 1959. In March 1986, pilgrims poured into Lhasa from all over Tibet for the festival, some having taken weeks to get there. Beijing TV showed scenes of Tibetan cadres distributing alms to the 1,000 monks taking part, and remarked on the 100,000 gaily-dressed Tibetan pilgrims "enjoying their quaint culture and religion".[9]

Tourists were there too. The trickle of foreign visitors had become a flood; and since the end of the previous year even individual "backpackers" had been allowed. The Chinese immigrants continued to arrive in droves, no longer claiming to be sacrificing themselves for the sake of the barbarians, but openly pursuing the rich pickings to be found in Tibet. Lhasa's streets teemed with Chinese hawkers and shopkeepers. Restaurants, with names like "The Tasty Restaurant" and "The Merry-Making Dining Room" offered Western-style meals to tourists, reported Catriona Bass; "one day, with a salvo of fire-crackers and Western disco music a shop opened in Happiness Rd flaunting Tibet's first can of Coke."[10]

---

* Last held by the Dalai Lama in Tibet itself in 1957.

As journalist Nick Danziger found, it was an anything but egalitarian society, with little contact between "what I can only describe as the colonial Han Chinese and the Tibetan 'natives'. The elite were swept along in chauffeur-driven cars to feast themselves on delicacies specially flown in from China proper ... It would have been easy to forget the harsh poverty outside the restaurant's windows."[11]

Thirty thousand more tourists were expected that summer: a blood transfusion for the moribund economy, though many suspected that the Chinese would have liked tourism without the tourists. For the latter were disposed to talk to Tibetans, and the Tibetans made the most of every opportunity. One of Catriona Bass's students, a young monk, showed her a message he had sent to the UN via a Western tourist:

> The Chinese talk about liberalization, they say that Tibetans have never had it so good, but Tibetans are still unhappy. We have no real freedom ... Many Tibetans are still suffering in prison for their beliefs ... They are beaten and tortured and treated worse than ordinary criminals ... the Tibetan people are certain that if Western countries knew of the real suffering of Tibetans, they would help them in their struggle.

He had not written out of naivety, he said, but out of desperation: "We *must* talk to tourists, tell the outside world about Tibet. Maybe it will change something. Maybe it won't. But there is no other way."

Already by that summer, there were ominous signs that the apparatus of political control hadn't been dismantled at all, wrote Catriona Bass; "political study became serious again. People were told that they should 'unify their thinking', that ideological education should be improved. It was a foretaste of things to come".[12] In May, about 250 young Tibetans known to have friends or relations in Dharamsala were arrested in Lhasa as "anti-social elements" and paraded through the streets. In Amdo, six people, condemned to death during a public sentencing rally, were executed.

In July 1987, Yulu Dawa Tsering, a Tibetan who had spent twenty years in prison after 1959, had supper at his cousin's house in Lhasa. Here he met an Italian dentist on holiday from Milan. The conversation turned to politics. What did his hosts think of the Dalai Lama, the dentist asked, did they want him to return? What about the Chinese? And so on. Yulu answered:

> May Tibet be released from the mouth of the wolf . . . We are six million Tibetans whose only leader is the Dalai Lama. If his wishes are fulfilled then the needs of the Tibetan people are met . . . What we all hope and wish is that His Holiness should stay abroad and all the nations of the world should support him in his work, and peacefully achieve Tibetan independence.[13]

Six months later, Yulu Dawa Tsering and his cousin, Thubten Tsering, were arrested, accused of talking to "reactionary foreigners posing as tourists"[14] and of spreading counter-revolutionary propaganda on that night.* By then, the situation had deteriorated beyond hope of saving. And it was the Dalai Lama himself who would inadvertently light the fuse to the next explosion.

---

* The Chinese government came to portray Yulu Dawa Tsering as one of the key figures behind the Tibetan independence movement. He received an exemplary ten-year sentence, double the usual maximum for this kind of offence.

CHAPTER 17

Battle is Joined, 1987

Six months later Yulu Dawa Tsering was arrested. No-one has seen him since. Police have accused him of spreading counter-revolution on that night: they say he criticized the Chinese presence in Tibet. If he did so, he was not alone. Since September 1987 thousands of Tibetans have taken part in anti-Chinese demonstrations; thirty died in police attacks on protesters. Two thousand are believed to have gone to jail for demonstrating, speaking privately or reading books critical of China.

Tibet Support Group UK Leaflet, 1988

The exiled Dalai Lama had become a tireless traveller; a spokesman for the cause of Tibet, winning a sympathetic hearing wherever he went. After visits to the USA in 1979, 1981 and 1984, the Tibetan leader had become a popular figure there, so well respected that in 1986, ninety-one members of Congress wrote to the Chinese President urging him to resume direct talks with the Dalai Lama's representatives. The request was ignored. But the Americans persisted and in June 1987 the House of Representatives unanimously condemned China's annexation of Tibet and the loss of over a million lives under the Chinese occupation.[1]

In September 1987 the Dalai Lama was invited to address the US Congress. This historic event would prove also to be a catalyst for the Tibetans. In a Five Point Peace Plan, the Dalai Lama outlined a peaceful, Buddhist charter for his country:

1   The whole of Tibet to be designated a "Zone of Peace".

The entire plateau – including Kham and Amdo – would become an area without weapons. In this Zone of Peace, the manufacture, testing and stockpiling of nuclear weapons and other armaments would be banned. The use of nuclear power even for peaceful purposes would be prohibited, because of the poisonous waste it produced. The plateau would become the world's largest natural park, in which plant and animal life would be legally protected; the exploitation of the environment would be carefully regulated; and the process of social development would be attuned to the needs and possibilities of the people. National resources and policy would be directed to the active promotion of peace and the protection of the environment. Organizations which promoted peace and supported the environment would be able to find a natural home in a Tibet where human rights also would be sacrosanct.

With Tibet established as a peaceful, friendly buffer zone separating India from China, Indian troops would be able to go home from the Himalayan borders. The Chinese would feel more secure, and trust could be re-established between the peoples of the area.

But the important precondition for this trust, said the Dalai Lama, was the withdrawal of Chinese troops:

> After the holocaust of the last three decades during which, incredibly, almost one and a quarter million Tibetans lost their lives from starvation, execution, torture and suicide, and tens of thousands lingered in prison camps, only a withdrawal of Chinese troops could start a genuine process of reconciliation.[2]

2   China to abandon its population transfer policy which threatens the very existence of Tibet.

Calling this policy a "final solution" by stealth, the Dalai Lama

RIGHT *Tashi Dolma, a young doctor from Amdo*

BELOW *Lhakpa Chungdak, taken into PLA at age of 14*

BELOW RIGHT *Lobsang Jimpa, winner of the 1988 Reebok Human Rights Award - given to individuals under the age of 30 who in their early lives and against great odds have significantly raised awareness of human rights*

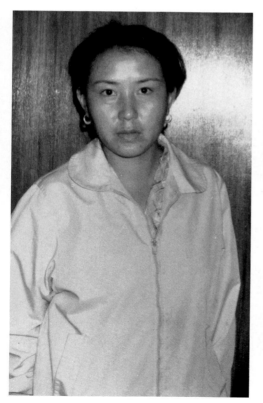

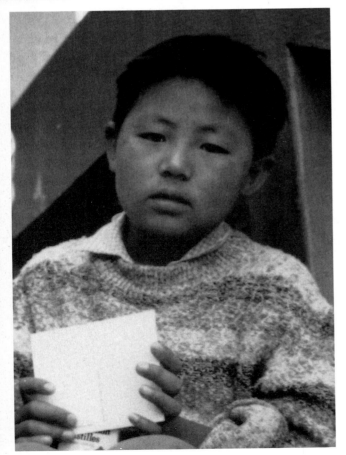

ABOVE *On 1 October 1987, the monk Jampa Tenzin ran through flames to rescue prisoners being held inside a burning police station (pp 260-261). Though badly burned, he was later carried shoulder-high round the streets by other demonstrators. This photograph of him raising his burned arms and waving a white Tibetan scarf became a symbol of the Tibetan Independence movement. On 22 February 1992, Jampa Tenzin was found dead in mysterious circumstances in his cell at the Jokhang Temple*

ABOVE RIGHT *India October 1987. Tibetan demonstrators in Dharamsala protest against the Chinese occupation of their country*

RIGHT *Lhasa, March 1988. Monlam Chenmo; monks calling for Independence*

LEFT *Sonam Tseten, aged 11, in Dharamsala – 1989*

ABOVE *Lhasa, March 1988.*
Monks loaded into trucks after
Monlam Chenmo protest.

LEFT *Christa Meindersma,*
the Dutchwoman shot during
demonstration in Lhasa,
December 10, 1988

ABOVE *March 1989 - May 1990. PLA soldier on roof top, northern side of Jokhang Square, Lhasa, with machine gun trained towards Jokhang temple*

BELOW *Martial law: Chinese armoured personnel carriers in the streets of Lhasa*

BELOW *Tashi Dolma from Kham*

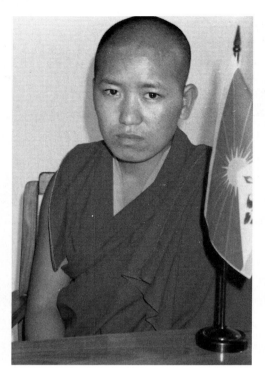

ABOVE *23 year old nun Gyaltsen Chodon, arrested and tortured by Chinese in April 1988, after calling for the release of political prisoners*

ABOVE *HH the Dalai Lama holding his Nobel Peace Prize, 10 December 1989*

BELOW *President George Bush receives the Dalai Lama at the White House, April 1991*

ABOVE *2 December 1991. The Dalai Lama accompanied by the Archbishop of Canterbury, Dr George Carey (left), meeting with Prime Minister John Major at 10 Downing Street*

BELOW *Lhasa, May 1991. Giant gilded yaks erected by the Chinese to commemorate their forty-year occupation of Tibet*

ABOVE *Fireworks at the Potala, 23 May 1991, marking the 40th Anniversary*

BELOW *Members of the Tibetan Youth Congress demonstrate in India*

drew a comparison with Manchuria, Inner Mongolia and Eastern Turkestan where the indigenous populations had been extinguished. For the Tibetans to survive as a people, he said, "it is imperative that population transfer be stopped and that Chinese settlers be allowed to return to China. Otherwise, Tibetans will soon be no more than a tourist attraction and a relic of a noble past".[3]

3 Human rights and democratic freedoms in Tibet to be respected.

"Human rights violations in Tibet are amongst the most serious in the world", he said:

> This is attested to by Amnesty International and other such organizations. Discrimination is practised in Tibet under a policy of outright apartheid which the Chinese call "segregation and assimilation". In reality Tibetans are, at best, second-class citizens in their own country.[4]

4 Tibet's natural environment to be restored and protected. Nuclear weapons no longer to be manufactured in Tibet and the country to cease to be a dumping ground for nuclear waste.

"Tibetans have a great respect for all forms of life," the Dalai Lama said.

> This inherent feeling is enhanced by our Buddhist faith which prohibits the harming of all sentient beings, whether human or animal. Prior to the Chinese invasion, Tibet was a fresh, beautiful, unspoiled wilderness sanctuary in a unique natural environment.
>
> Sadly, during the past decades, the wildlife of Tibet has been almost totally destroyed and, in many places, irreparable damage has been done to its forests. The overall effect on Tibet's delicate environment has been devastating.[5]

5 Serious negotiations to take place between the Tibetans

and Chinese, not only about the future of Tibet but also about relations between the Tibetan and Chinese peoples.

In this, the last of his five points, the Dalai Lama stressed that in seeking regional peace he was aiming at world peace, that he sought a solution which would be in everyone's long-term interest. He was not surprised, however, when the Chinese denounced his speech, alleging that it was a deliberate call to separatism.

They were outraged. "In Tibet, we heard about the peace plan through the Chinese", the young monk, Lobsang Jimpa,* told me. "They were absolutely furious, and began accusing the Dalai Lama of trying to split the Great Motherland. This made us *very angry*." Three days later, on 24 September, the Chinese in Lhasa ordered 15,000 people† to attend a mass political rally at which eight dissidents were sentenced to imprisonment and three to death. One of them was shot immediately outside the stadium; a second two days later. The logic, according to Indian journalist Amit Roy, was that of an old Chinese proverb: "Kill the chickens and warn the monkeys", the sight of headless chickens being calculated to frighten off any monkeys bent on trouble.

The threat, however, did not work. On the morning of 27 September, following a discussion in Lobsang Jimpa's room at Sera monastery, a group of thirty monks turned an act of traditional piety – circumambulating the Jokhang temple – into a symbolic act of defiance. "We decided", said Lobsang Jimpa:

> to stage a peaceful demonstration in favour of His Holiness's peace plan and to protest against the executions. We declared

---

* Winner of the 1988 Reebok Human Rights award in the USA – for individuals under thirty who against overwhelming odds have raised the world's awareness of human rights issues.
† Some accounts say 14,000.

firstly that Tibet was supposed to be independent but had no freedom. Secondly, that there was a danger of enmity developing between the Tibetans and the Chinese, and only if Tibet became independent again would that danger disappear. Thirdly, we supported the Dalai Lama's concept of Tibet as a zone of peace. We sent these declarations anonymously to the Chinese, and also stuck up homemade posters on Lhasa walls.

We had three self-imposed rules. 1) We were determined to be non-violent, even when threatened by death. 2) We would welcome lay people to join us, but would not try to persuade them. 3) If any of us was caught, he must not reveal the names of the others even under threat of torture. As we were all monks, these rules had the force of solemn vows.

We had managed to make a few Tibetan flags – a criminal offence in the Chinese book. On the morning of the 27th, carrying the flags, (no guns, only flags), the first group of thirty made three circuits of the Jokhang shouting five different slogans: "INDEPENDENCE FOR TIBET", "THE DALAI LAMA IS TIBET'S TRUE LEADER", "CHINESE, GO HOME", "RELEASE ALL POLITICAL PRISONERS", and "RESPECT THE UNIVERSAL DECLARATION OF HUMAN RIGHTS".[6]

The monks, joined by a crowd of about 200 bystanders, continued their demonstration in front of the TAR government building. Twenty-seven of them were immediately arrested and viciously beaten.

Rumours that the arrested monks had been tortured and condemned to death spread rapidly. Four days later on 1 October, China's National Day, Lobsang Jimpa was himself one of a second group of thirty-four monks who circled the Jokhang chanting pro-independence slogans and waving Tibetan flags. They were joined by a few score ordinary Tibetans. On their fourth circuit, about sixty of the protesters, including all the monks, were arrested and taken to the police station immediately opposite the Jokhang. Eyewitnesses testified that while still outside, the detainees were beaten by the security forces with clubs, rocks, fists and shovels.

A large and angry crowd of 2–3,000 gathered outside the police station, shouting for the release of the demonstrators, while police tried to arrest individuals among them. According to a pooled eyewitness account given to the Dalai Lama by forty-five Western tourists:

> dozens of security men arrived with video cameras and began filming the crowd. Fearing subsequent identification, several people began throwing stones at the police as they filmed. A few Tibetans panicked and began overturning police vehicles and setting them alight, whereupon armed members of the security forces started shooting.[7]

Eleven police vehicles were overturned and set on fire, and "in an attempt to release those detained inside, the crowd tried to smash down the door of the police station. They then used blankets, tables and kerosene to set fire to the door".[8] The first shots were fired by police at about eleven a.m. At the same time about ten monks ran into the building through the burning doorway, apparently to rescue their arrested colleagues. The police and cameramen reappeared on the roof of the building, threw rocks and fired into the crowd. While a few policemen fired into the air, several of the eyewitnesses saw police take aim and fire directly into the crowd with pistols and automatic weapons. "One police officer stepped forward from the group on the rear of the police station roof", a British tourist recalled in a sworn statement; "he took careful aim and, using his right hand, fired his pistol. He did this repeatedly and without haste. I was able to see from where I was standing about thirty yards away that he was firing low, deliberately and into the crowd."[9] Later these eyewitnesses saw rows of multiple bullet holes (apparently from automatic weapons) in the wall of the Jokhang, at a height of about six feet, near where Tibetans had sheltered from the firing.

Two young Americans, John Ackerley, an attorney, and Blake Kerr, a doctor, who had come to Tibet to climb Mount Everest, witnessed the deaths of several Tibetans, including a boy of about eight who was shot in the back and a man aged twenty-five to thirty, shot in the heart.[10] They were able to administer first aid to some of the wounded, though one (anonymous) European doctor reported that the people were often too terrified to let them through: "It was a terrible shock to realize that people would not go to the hospitals for fear of being arrested there."

Several Tibetan sources claimed that up to three of the demonstrators held in the police station were shot dead, possibly as they tried to escape through windows while the building burned. One Tibetan who escaped said later of their time in the police station; "The monks then prayed together for about twenty minutes. Four policemen armed with pistols stood guard over us. Suddenly four shots were heard. A Nechung monk who was standing near me was shot through the roof of his skull, blood gushed from his head and spilled all over me."[11]

Sonam Tseten, a nine-year-old Tibetan boy, had come up from the country with his father to stay with an uncle in the Barkor and to see his older brother Kunga, a sixteen-year-old Sera novice. When the demonstration began, they all rushed to the window to see what was happening. They were astonished to see Kunga, and his two maternal uncles, Karsel and Gyaltsen, circling the Barkor with a number of other monks. Then to their horror, as a still-dazed Sonam Tseten told me, "the Chinese came and arrested them. Later they opened fire. One fired straight at Kunga and we saw him fall with a bullet in his head. I saw the bullet come out at the front of his head. The Chinese came running up with a handcart and took the bodies away."[12] Karsel too was killed, Gyaltsen was arrested. When the nine-year-old saw these things happen, "I threw stones at the Chinese trucks, and one of my friends set fire to a jeep. We were so upset, we had to do something." Next day at the police station, the Chinese charged the family 330 yuan for Kunga's body:* "All the bodies had been thrown into various rooms. We

---

* The going rate seems to have been between 300 and 600 yuan, almost a year's salary, with most town-dwellers earning between 300 and 1,000 per year. A *New York Times* editorial in October 1987 put the annual per capita rural income at 110 dollars or 385 yuan.

found Kunga in the third room we looked in, in a drawer. We took him away to the Sera monastery."[13]

It was only the beginning. On 6 October, about ninety Drepung monks who walked – completely unarmed – to the Party offices, shouting for the release of their colleagues, were met by 250 Chinese armed militia carrying shotguns. Eye-witnesses reported that the monks were beaten with rifles, truncheons and studded leather belts on both hands and feet; they were then bundled into trucks and taken away.[14]

Both Tibetans and Western tourists were convinced that but for the presence of so many foreigners there would have been a massacre. To the Chinese, the tourists were a mixed blessing: their hard currency was welcome, but not their sympathy for the Tibetan cause. "The Chinese are afraid of the foreigner", said a Tibetan woman. "The foreigner goes home and tells the truth."[15] To the Tibetans, in this hour of danger, the presence of the tourists was a protection, but when they had gone, what then?

They would not be left to wonder for long. Though the Chinese had been caught unawares, they lost no time in cutting communication lines with the outside world. But news of the demonstrations had already flashed round the world – one Englishman had fortunately managed to contact Reuters in Beijing before the Chinese cut the outside lines. As another British visitor remarked:

> We were more-or-less certain that if Westerners – or someone – had not succeeded in leaking the news of the demos to the world press, the Chinese would never have admitted they'd happened ... It would have been much as it was described at the time to tourists at the Lhasa Hotel on 1st October: "Due to traffic problems in the city, the shuttle will not run to-day".

For the first time since 1959, Tibet was headline news again and was engaging the sympathies of the outside world. The US

Senate unanimously and strongly condemned China over human rights in Tibet; and similar votes of censure were passed by the West German Bundestag and the European Parliament.

In the face of this massive disapproval, Beijing remained unmoved, replying that this was an internal matter and no business of anybody but themselves. They insisted that the demonstrations had been stage-managed by a handful of "splittists" of whom the majority of Tibetans disapproved. They denied that there had been any deaths caused by the police in the 1 October riot, claiming that the police had not even used their weapons. (They said the demonstrators had seized the police guns and used them on each other!) Not until March 1988 did they admit (after a foreign witness had testified at the UN Human Rights Commission in Geneva) that the police had indeed opened fire. Though this represented a considerable climb-down, even then the Chinese spokesman, Chen Shi-qiu, continued to prevaricate. He declared that the demonstrators had merely been taken into the police station to be given advice; that a woman had been knocked down by demonstrators and that the police had then fired into the air, accidentally killing two Tibetans and one Chinese. Another Tibetan was killed, he claimed, by falling masonry, and a third by falling off the roof of a building. Mr Chen would admit to no more casualties than that. He was saddened, he said, that China was being rebuked at a time when "Tibetans and Hans are working hard to build a beautiful new Tibet together".

There was little enough sign of that beautiful new Tibet in the days following the riots, when journalists and tourists were expelled (their film confiscated), and the arrests began. The Chinese had set a 15 October deadline for anyone taking part in the demonstrations to turn themselves in. Once the deadline had passed, there was a brutal crackdown. Whole areas were sealed off by detachments of armed police. Houses were raided at night and hundreds – mostly young people – were taken away. (Film taken from the departing foreigners had helped in their identification.) Reports suggested that well over a thousand Tibetans were imprisoned, and most of them were subjected to torture. This new policy of indiscriminate torture was designed to extract confessions from the guilty and frighten off the rest – another twist in the "kill the chickens and warn the monkeys" policy.

The monasteries of Drepung, Sera and Ganden were occupied by plain-clothes police; the monks were subjected to an intensive campaign of political re-education and forbidden to leave or communicate with other monasteries without official permission. Security forces armed with truncheons and electric stunner rods were increased, police cars with wailing sirens criss-crossed the city and heavily-armed troops patrolled the streets. Chinese troops marching in desultory but menacing fashion anti-clockwise around the Barkor symbolized the new "politics of fear".

Everyone was afraid. The night the arrests started, Sonam Tseten lay awake listening:

> I began to be terrified and so did my dad. The Chinese had videoed everything from the roof of the police station, and that night they began arresting everyone they recognized. My dad was afraid they would recognise me as having thrown stones and would come and take me away. So he said I had to leave the country. We went next day hidden in a truck under a load of vegetables, and we travelled all day and all night until we reached the border with Nepal. There, my dad made an arrangement with some coolies. They dressed me like a coolie and took me with them.[16]

Thus did a terrified nine-year-old boy leave his home, family and country, to go into exile alone.

Thirteen-year-old Pemba was detained. One of that new generation that had never known Tibet without the Chinese and who had been born after the horrors of the Cultural Revolution, he had joined in the demonstration on 1 October with a friend, because he had nothing better to do:

> We only went to shout the slogans: "FREE TIBET", and so on. We were bored and it seemed like a bit of fun. Until then I

hadn't really given any thought to Tibetan independence. But suddenly on that day I realized it mattered to me. The Chinese loudspeakers were blaring out insults to the Dalai Lama, and that really infuriated me. I was so mad I set fire to a Chinese jeep with some matches.[17]

Despite his youth, Pemba was sent to the infamous Gutsa prison in Lhasa and put in a cell with nine men:

During the interrogation, the police hit me and threatened me with a gun. They slapped my face and boxed my ears so hard that I got abscesses in my ears. Then they used electric cattle prods which sparked on my skin. They wanted to know if I was a resistance fighter, but I hadn't known there were any. They kept on asking who had incited me to join in the demonstration, and where these criminals were hiding. They gave me photographs to identify. I didn't tell them anything. In any case, I had nothing to tell them. They charged me with snatching a gun from a Chinese official as well as with setting fire to the jeep. My friend was interrogated too. They charged him with unscrewing the cap of the petrol tank.

We were hungry. In the morning they gave us a small bowl of thin porridge and a cup of black tea. At lunch there were two ravioli and a ladleful of vegetable water. Dinner was the same: ravioli and black tea. We had to be asleep by nine and up at dawn. Once a day we were allowed to use the urine bucket. Apart from that, we had to stay in the cell waiting for the interrogations. We were chained to a wall with our hands tied behind our backs for twenty-four hours at a stretch. The chains were at different heights on the wall, those for children like myself being lower down. During the interrogations, the Chinese threatened that if I took part in any more demonstrations, I would be sent to prison for life. They said independence was a dream, Tibet had always been part of China and always would be.[18]

Pemba was released after a few days, to face a massive new

programme of political re-education. Liberalization went out of the window as ideology returned in force and 600 propaganda squads conducted re-education classes all over Tibet. As Pemba told me,

> We had to attend political indoctrination classes three times a day, nine thirty, twelve o'clock and two o'clock. There were about twenty-five of us, aged between fifteen and thirty-five, all of us just out of prison. They taught us about the Communist Party and about Tibet being part of China for seven centuries. And we had to confess our faults, make reports on each other, denounce each other. But our blood was up, and in spite of them, we sneaked out at night to stick up posters saying things like: "BLOOD FOR BLOOD", "WE SHALL HAVE OUR REVENGE".

"We were all conscious of a new sense of unity", said Pema Saldon:

> Nationalist sentiment had begun to grow, now that people fully understood the enormity of what had been done to them. Even those who were employed by the Chinese, who were brought up by the Chinese and had up to that time supported them, were beginning at last to reject the regime.
>
> People were totally disenchanted with the regime. Everyone wanted freedom and the return of the Dalai Lama. Those demos were not organized, they just happened spontaneously, and everyone joined in, from small children throwing pebbles to old people breaking up paving stones and handing them to those who were strong enough to throw them. It was an absolutely universal rejection of the regime.[19]

While still detained at the police station, the young monk, Lobsang Jimpa, had been beaten unconscious, then rescued by the crowd when they stormed the building. When he came to, he was being cared for by unknown people. From then on, he was passed from one house to another, hiding "in latrines, under beds, anywhere I could think of", while the police searched for him, believing him to have been the instigator of the revolts: "They interrogated all my relatives and friends and searched their homes. They manhandled my mother so badly that she had a heart attack and died."[20] To escape detection, he had discarded his monk's robes and grown his hair. On 15 November, he saw a "Wanted" poster, offering a reward to whoever would hand him over – alive or dead. "Anyone doing so was promised a new truck and a cash reward of 1000 Chinese yuan. Or even a jeep."[21] But no-one betrayed him: "I was able to survive because so many people went on helping me".* For eight months he stayed in hiding – in seventy-two different homes – increasingly aware that "the Tibetans were being forced to live like animals".

News of the Lhasa revolts spread rapidly throughout Tibet. In Amdo, hundreds of secondary school students and monks demonstrated against the brutally enforced birth control programme and the swamping of their towns and villages by Chinese settlers.[22] In Lhasa itself, two more revolts took place before the year was out. One was in late November when eighty monks from Ganden demonstrated against the ad hoc work-teams stationed in their monastery to keep them in order. The second was in mid-December when twenty Tibetan nuns marched around the Jokhang and were arrested. They were straws in the wind, a foretaste of what was to come, now that the Tibetans had allowed themselves to dream of freedom. They had, after all, nothing to lose but their chains.

---

* When he eventually returned to Lhasa, friends persuaded him to escape. With the aid of the Tibetan resistance movement, he crossed the Himalaya by a secret route and came to Dharamsala.

CHAPTER 18

Crackdown, 1988

The Chinese are tearing our hearts out.

WOMAN IN LHASA, 1988

In Lhasa, there was an awful sense of approaching doom; of being locked into a spiral of violence in which matters could only get worse. Tension between the Chinese settlers and the Tibetans was running high. Tibet was now virtually out of bounds to foreign journalists, individual travellers and human rights groups. A few well-supervised tour groups had arrived, but even these were regarded by the Chinese with increasing mistrust and xenophobia. One Western student in Lhasa reported that there were spies everywhere and that the Tibetans dared not talk openly to foreigners. Uniformed police swarmed over the city and were posted on rooftops with binoculars and machine guns.

Steve Myhill of the British Museum reported that monks in the Jokhang whispered "Freedom for Tibet, Chinese no good", as his tour group passed; and that hundreds of sightseeing Chinese troops in the temple "pushed and joked and jostled as they followed the pilgrims through the chapels, and so infuriated one caretaker-monk that he kicked a soldier down a flight of stairs and smeared another with yak butter."[1]

As the Tibetans grew more desperate, and as world sympathy focused on their attempts to be rid of their oppressors, the Chinese sought to tighten their grip. Hard-line officials urged a ruthless crackdown. But Tibetans in the administration, among them the Panchen Lama, contended that it was the Chinese failure to consider the real needs and hopes of the Tibetan people which had led to the present crisis; and warned that it would be catastrophic to introduce even more repressive measures.

It was not so much ruthlessness as crass insensitivity which precipitated the next revolt, the most serious since 1959. It was March 1988 and Monlam Chenmo, the Great Prayer Festival, was again approaching. With hundreds of monks in prison since the October riots, their colleagues were in no mood for celebration and feared trouble if Monlam took place as usual. They urged a boycott, claiming that in any case the festival was being staged only as "eyewash" for the tourists. But the Chinese, smarting from foreign accusations of human rights abuse, were not going to pass up this opportunity of demonstrating to the world how they had restored religious freedom to Tibet. Unaware of the irony that to force monks to celebrate a Prayer Festival against their will was actually to deny religious freedom, they continued to insist that it should go ahead. The monks protested, but when the Chinese threatened bloody reprisals, they had to give in.

But their resistance had made the Chinese uneasy. One week before Monlam, Reuters reported from Beijing that fifty military vehicles and more than 1,000 Chinese police, many in riot gear, were practising manoeuvres in front of the Jokhang. On 28 February, the BBC reported that:

> Thousands of Chinese security forces have been moved to the Lhasa area – road blocks are in force all over the city. Long convoys of armoured vehicles patrol the streets at night, and people are advised through loudspeaker announcements to stay at home. One message said bluntly, "If you misbehave, we will kill you".[2]

The Great Prayer Festival began on 3 March, with heavily armed police and soldiers, some of them in civilian clothes, blending into the crowd, to keep control without appearing on tourists' film wearing uniform. Some of the policemen in the crowd had shaved their heads or put on wigs, "to give the impression either that they were monks or that they were from outside Lhasa".[3] As one British tourist commented, "What should have been a solemn religious ceremony of the Tibetan people had been perverted into a pathetic bit of theatre to further Chinese propaganda aims".

On the first day, the ceremonies went ahead without mishap; and by the third day, 5 March, the military presence had been slightly relaxed. But that was when things started to go badly wrong. Early that morning, the statue of Maitreya, the Buddha-Who-Is-To-Come, was carried in solemn procession around the Jokhang. The procession had just reached the south side of the temple when about 300 young monks began calling for the release of Yulu Dawa Tsering, the lama who had been arrested two days earlier* (see pp. 254 and 255). Afterwards, they shouted independence slogans, and climbed onto a stage and jostled an invited audience of Chinese and Tibetan government officials sitting there.[4] When the protesters were dragged off into custody, monks on the ground and on the Jokhang roof began throwing stones at the Chinese cameramen videoing the proceedings from the roof of the police station.

Reports vary and it is difficult to be sure of what happened next. According to some accounts, the group of officials rushed for shelter into the Jokhang from where they radioed for help. Agence France Presse reporter, Patrick Lescot, the only foreign journalist present in Lhasa that day, said that as the monks moved to the square in front of the temple, several thousand onlookers and pilgrims began throwing stones at a small force of about fifty uniformed police.[5] "At first", stated a British tourist, one of about thirty who were in the crowd, "police just returned stone for stone. But then truckloads of police reinforcements arrived. Tibetans in the crowd told me that one Chinese officer was shouting to his men, 'Kill the Tibetans'".

---

* Five days later, on 10 March, Radio Lhasa would announce that Yulu Dawa Tsering had been accused of plotting with "reactionary foreigners posing as tourists".

It was two hours later, at around eleven thirty in the morning, that about 2,000 armed police stormed the Jokhang en masse, using tear gas and clubs. Matters then really got out of hand. According to a Tibetan eyewitness, "Thousands of fully-armed PLA started arriving in trucks from all directions. Throwing tear gas, soldiers poured into the Jokhang, the most sacred shrine."[6] "The place was full of smoke and we were all choking", said the young nun, Gyaltsen Chodon, who, with a friend, had followed the monks around the Barkor. Next, as a frightened monk told *Observer* journalist, Jonathan Mirsky, "They began beating everyone who looked Tibetan, including some of the regional leaders, with clubs. By ten fifteen, it was finished.They killed thirty monks. Later in the day they carried the bodies outside like dead animals and threw them in the back of two trucks."[7] "Thirty" may have been an exaggeration. Some say it was sixteen, plus two lay Tibetans. (An article in the Asian *Wall Street Journal* claimed that in the numbers game there was a crucial difference between the Tibetans and Chinese: "The Tibetans exaggerate; the Chinese simply lie".[8]) According to his memoirs, the Dalai Lama believes it was "at least twelve", adding, "One they beat severely, before tearing both his eyes out and hurling him from the roof. Tibet's holiest shrine became like a butcher's shop."[9]

The violence of the Chinese response marked a crucial shift in policy. In 1987 they had been taken by surprise and had left it to the regular police to quell the demonstrations. But in 1988 they were ready, and it was no longer the regular police but specially trained riot squads who were brought in. Terrifying in appearance and brutal in behaviour, they would shoot to kill or beat people up without mercy, bashing in heads and rupturing kidneys. Their main purpose seems to have been intimidation.

News of the temple invasion swept through the city in the afternoon, and threw the Tibetan sector into uproar. In the sixteen hours of street-fighting which followed, a Chinese policeman was thrown out of a second-storey window and killed; cars were set on fire and around twenty Chinese shops and restaurants were burned down. The riot police attacked the

crowd with rifles, tear gas, electric rods and iron bars, dragging·
away men, women and children.* "People were incensed",
reported a foreign eyewitness:

> Some cried and sank into a quiet despair. Others responded in
> more dramatic fashion ... The Chinese claimed later that the
> riots were instigated by a handful of "splittists", but I saw with
> my own eyes how the whole Tibetan sector, as many as maybe
> 10,000 people, rose up against the Chinese. It was as though
> years of pent-up frustration suddenly came to the surface. I
> witnessed one skirmish just to the north of the temple, in which a
> young nun – herself throwing stones – screamed to me, "My
> God, they're killing the monks in the temple", and desperately
> begged me to help.
>
> But it seemed so hopeless. There were the tin-hatted Chinese
> soldiers, thousands of them, with tear gas and machine guns,
> and all the Tibetans could do was throw stones.[10]

By midnight fresh Chinese troops had arrived in strength and
the military had regained control of the city.

The Chinese revenge was terrible. The New China News
Agency announced that religious leaders in Tibet had voiced
"dissatisfaction" with the central authority's "leniency" and
were requesting "firmer measures" to control the situation.[11]
Obviously the hard-liners had won the day. A curfew was
immediately imposed. "In the days which followed", the British
eyewitness quoted earlier reported:

> At least 1000, probably many more,† were arrested. Reports of

---

* A police video of these events was smuggled to the West and shown
widely there. It shows the police ferociously beating up demonstrators,
forcing them to kneel with their hands tied behind their backs, high in the
air while being beaten. One Chinese police officer is heard to say, "Don't
beat them now, you can do what you want when you get them to the
police station", or words to that effect.
† In his memoirs, *Freedom in Exile*, the Dalai Lama claims it was "at least
2,500".

summary executions abounded. At least once a day for the next two weeks, long Chinese army motorcades of as many as 122 trucks, each with twenty-five to thirty soldiers armed with machine guns circled and then drove right through the Tibetan sector of Lhasa, clearly a show of force intended to terrorize the populace.

In monasteries, work units and neighbourhood committees, political re-education was stepped up. Monks were forced, under threat of violence, to attend regular indoctrination sessions; and official work teams were charged with identifying those whose political loyalties were suspect. On 5 September, after a 45-strong work team had moved into Sera monastery, the monks were told: "Confess your participation in the demonstrations. If you do not confess and if you do it again, we will kill you; we will execute you; we will put you in prison for life".[12]

Intimidated and harassed though they were, the Tibetans would not give up. Pasting their illicit freedom posters up on the walls in the Tibetan sector, handing out leaflets in the market place, scrawling independence slogans in the dust of Chinese vehicles, they showed their defiance. They listened to recordings of the Dalai Lama's sermons despite a ban on all audio, visual or written material which so much as referred to His Holiness.[13] Punishment for ignoring this ban was severe. Twenty-eight-year-old Tashi Dolma, an illiterate nomad girl from Kham, had gone on pilgrimage to Lhasa in 1987 and had stayed for a year, hawking goods on street pavements. Frightened by the Monlam demonstration, she set off for home two days later. When someone handed her a Dalai Lama audiocassette and some pro-independence leaflets to take with her, she wrapped them in her few belongings without a qualm. "I suppose I knew it was a bit dangerous", she admits, "but I didn't really know what I was doing, and I never expected to be caught". At the first checkpoint outside the city, all the Tibetans were taken aside and searched. No-one believed Tashi Dolma's protests that she'd bought the cassette to help her with her prayers, and that she'd found the bundle of leaflets lying around on a pavement. She was arrested and taken back to Lhasa to prison:

> I was put in a very dark windowless cell with a cement floor and they left me there for nine days, interrogating me at all hours of the day and night, beating me and torturing me with electric cattle prods. They wanted to know who had given me those leaflets and told me I'd be shot if I didn't tell them. I didn't tell them anything.

Tashi Dolma was moved to a prison in Chamdo where she was interrogated for one month and sixteen days, chained either by hands or feet. Then they took her back to Gutsa prison in Lhasa, putting her first in solitary for four months and then into a cell occupied by four young nuns:

> It was the middle of winter. The Chinese poured several inches of water onto the cement floor of the cell and made us stand in it for twelve hours at a time. We suffered excruciating pain in the ankle bones, though mercifully after a time our feet went numb. They repeated this torture eight times in all. I still have pain in my knees and back as a result. At other times they made us spend hours with our feet on a table and our hands on the floor. Of course, as well as this, there was the daily routine of kicking and using the cattle prods.

Tashi Dolma was at the point of death when quite suddenly she was released. Most of her hair had fallen out. "The Chinese obviously thought it better for me to die outside the prison than in their charge", she reflected:

> They gave me a bill for 1000 yuan: two yuan a day for the food I'd consumed in prison. If I didn't pay within a certain time, they said they'd arrest me again. I told them I had no money – when I was arrested I had 200 yuan but they'd taken that – and no relatives in Lhasa to help me. All I would be able to do was beg in the streets. They didn't care and simply handed me a note confirming that I'd be rearrested if I didn't pay up.

I knew I'd have to try and escape – there was no other way.*

"But", Tashi insisted, "it was far worse for the nuns than for me":

> They set trained killer dogs onto them and emptied urine buckets over their heads. They applied their electric prods to their private parts. One of them went blind and another was made permanently incontinent. They strung them up to the ceiling by their thumbs. Oh, it was terrible what they did to them.[14]

With so many monks already in prison, the nuns had taken on themselves the burden of protest. Two young nuns from the Chupsang nunnery who escaped to India in the middle of 1990 told of how the work team stationed in the nunnery constantly harassed them:

> They said: "You keep saying Tibet is an independent country. For many years you have been shouting this. When was Tibet ever independent and who has put these words into your mouths? Today you should confess your crimes and dedicate yourself to the nation and you will be given ration cards and allowed to stay in the nunnery."[15]

The girls were ordered to swear they would have nothing to do with the "Dalai Lama's splittists"; and told that if they did not conform, "so many restrictions will be enforced here that not even the birds will be able to sing".[16]

Undaunted, on Sunday 17 April, thirteen nuns processed round the Barkor calling for the release of political prisoners. They fled when the police attacked, only to be arrested later in

---

* A monk took Tashi Dolma to the Tibetan Hospital where she slowly regained her strength. Then she joined a group of Khampas on a trading mission to Western Tibet. Leaving them, she joined another group trekking south to Kathmandu. She walked non-stop for a month, avoiding the ice-caps and begging her food all the way.

the day. One week later, a group of five young nuns carrying a Tibetan flag managed to circle the Jokhang three times before the police swooped. One of these, twenty-three-year-old Gyalt-sen Chodon from a hermitage near Sera monastery, claims she was still shouting "FREE TIBET" when they hauled her away. Her horrifying story is typical of many. (Gyaltsen was too ill to be interviewed when filmmaker Vanya Kewley talked to the other four in what she described as one of the most painful interviews she had ever recorded. "Several times their testimony was inaudible through their sobs".[17])

Gyaltsen, too – sick and in need of hospital treatment – trembled and wept as she recounted her painful experiences to me in Dharamsala:

> They threw us into the truck like so many stones, and took us to prison, twisting our arms behind us. They took away our belts and body-searched us. Then they beat us and chained us to the wall. Later they stripped us and used electric prods* all over our bodies, several men at a time, eyes, mouth, vagina, everywhere. They used those cattle prods as though they were toys, enjoying themselves, especially when they applied them to our private parts. They weren't human beings, they weren't animals, they were machines. They actually laughed and joked among themselves while they were doing these things. "You're not nuns now", they told us. "You're just garbage". They never called us by our names, but made us answer to names like: pig, horse, donkey and so on.
>
> When they interrogated us, they ordered us to confess who'd put us up to it. When we stayed silent, they took us outside the prison and left us standing for a night and a day, in chains with our hands in the air. While we were standing there, they beat us with sticks and set their dogs on us.

---

* The use of electric cattle prods was widespread. Their use was first reported in an Asia Watch report, "Human Rights in Tibet", in February 1988. The US Department of State substantiates the claim in "Country Reports on Human Rights Practices for 1988", p. 765.

"At times", she continued:

> they laid us face down on the ground, stripped to our underwear, hands outstretched, and beat us. More than once they dropped a huge iron rod from a great height onto our backs. My spine was severely damaged in the process.
>
> Sometimes, when they had thrown us on the ground, they would trample on our hands with their huge iron-tipped boots. They kicked us in the face and stomach. Buckets full of urine were put on our heads, while the guards hit the bucket with sticks, roaring with laughter as the urine and excrement streamed down our faces and bodies. They would take the *momo* (ravioli) that was for our lunch, dip it in the filth and force us to eat it.[18]

Phurbu Tsering, a twenty-seven-year-old house painter, was accused of helping to burn down a Chinese restaurant on 6 March. He was "stripped naked and hanged from the ceiling for an entire night". Jampey Losel, a twenty-three-year old monk from a small temple in Lhasa was also hanged upside down by the legs.[19] An interview with a former Tibetan policeman is highly instructive.[20] He confirmed that prisoners were nearly always beaten and that he himself had tortured his own people. "If a prisoner dies during the beatings", he told the two Americans, John Ackerly and Blake Kerr, "the police are not responsible because it is the prisoner's fault."[21]

The official Chinese accounts of the Monlam demonstration made no mention of Tibetan casualties, of the massacre which had sparked the riot, of the countless arrests, or of the torture of prisoners. They centred on the death of the one Chinese policeman, killed by a few "criminal splittists". In fact the Chinese behaved as though the murder of that policeman was the only act which made 5 March infamous. For weeks afterwards, the photograph of his mutilated corpse was shown and reshown on television. He was hailed as a national hero and martyr, and four Tibetans were arrested for his murder.

The Tibetans were sickened by this illustration of Chinese

tunnel-vision, this failure to so much as mention their own dead and wounded, this total lack of concern for their human rights. There were indeed glaring abuses. When an independent delegation from Britain, sanctioned by Beijing and led by Lord Ennals, arrived in Lhasa in May to investigate the human rights situation, its members were shocked by what they found:

Individuals are arrested during the night by the Public Security Bureau and are kept incommunicado for weeks, with their families not knowing the charge or what has happened to them.

Individuals in great distress told us of relatives who had disappeared. Monks we were due to see had disappeared during the night. In another case, so many had been detained at the monastery that we were asked not to speak to anyone in case it led to further detentions.

There is a steady stream of notifications to relatives asking that they come and collect bodies of detained relatives for which they have to pay a collection fee, sometimes in the region of 600 yuan.[22]

Those who were summoned to collect a corpse were shaken by the condition in whch they found it. The relatives of one man, Tenzin Sherap, could only identify him by his clothes, so badly battered was his face. All his bones had been broken. Yet they were still charged a 600 yuan storage fee, more than they earned in a year.[23] When Kelsang Wangyal, a twenty-two-year-old Jokhang monk went with a group of friends to the police station to claim the body of a colleague,

we were told we had to pay 600 yuan to cover the cost of medicines and an operation. We said we did not have that much money and our names were recorded. Then the police said that if we did not come up with the money, we would all go to prison. We returned the next day with the money and recovered the body.[24]

As a delegation of US Senators, visiting Lhasa for three days in

August, reported, it was "painfully clear that there is a human rights problem in Tibet".[25]

In the face of such horrors, it infuriated the Tibetans that the Chinese were portraying themselves to the outside world – and particularly to an increasingly worried Hong Kong – as victims of ungrateful barbarians whom they had tried to help. Why should the Tibetans feel grateful for all the years of oppression and misery? The progress that had supposedly come to Tibet in the wake of the Chinese invasion, the roads, the schools, the hospitals, were, as far as they could see, almost exclusively for the benefit of the Chinese – who were now, to cap it all, squeezing them out of existence. This attitude was incomprehensible to the Chinese, as Paul Theroux discovered when he visited Tibet in 1988. For they believed they *had* brought progress:

It seems like proof to the Chinese that they are dealing with sentimental savages when Tibetans say the roads and schools are just another Chinese outrage. But that doesn't weaken the Chinese resolve – quite the opposite. It just means there is much more work to do in this benighted place, they say, echoing missionaries and colonizers and imperialists and encyclopaedia salesmen the world over ... The Chinese have a fatal tendency to take themselves and their projects too seriously ... What the evangeliser in his naive seriousness does not understand is that there are some people on earth who do not wish to be saved.[26]

One had to see Tibet in order to understand the Chinese, concluded Theroux. "And anyone apologetic or sentimental about Chinese reform has to reckon with Tibet as a reminder of how harsh, how tenacious and materialistic, how insensitive China can be".[27] As the exasperated head of China's security apparatus, Qiao Shi, is reported to have complained to local officials during a visit to Lhasa in July,

We have implemented the policy of liberation in Tibet. We have restored many monasteries. The monks have been allowed to practise religion according to their wishes. Livestock and agricultural lands have been decollectivized. Now, if this is not liberalization, what is? Where else in the world would you find more liberalization? These monks, instead of being grateful to the government for its generosity, have sought to destabilize the nation.[28]

Qiao Shi could not grasp that what the monks and most Tibetans wanted was self-determination, the freedom to be Tibetan. Now, he concluded, proving how little he had understood, the time for softness was over. The time had come for a "merciless repression in handling anti-Chinese activities".

As the first anniversary of the October protests approached, security was stepped up. Despite the ban on individual travellers, many backpackers had sneaked into the city, often arriving with the tour buses and then breaking away. John Billington, a Tibetan-speaking British teacher who was in Lhasa for the whole of September and October, says that on 25 September a curfew was imposed on Tibetans and foreigners alike. The security forces engaged in a massive show of force – a public trial of about thirty petty criminals, paraded through the streets, flanked by a military convoy: "about twelve minibuses of PSB officers, forty motorcyclists with armed pillions and four truckloads of steel-helmeted militia".

But the protest to mark the anniversary could not be stopped. Billington was an eyewitness:

The Barkor stalls closed suddenly at around ten forty-five a.m. A group of between eight and twelve monks ... shouting slogans, carrying a Tibetan flag and a photograph of the Dalai Lama began circumambulating the Jokhang temple. I learned later that the monks were not protesting, but shouting support for the Dalai Lama's Peace Proposals. At the beginning of their second circuit, they were rushed by about 300 steel-helmeted PSB men who were deployed inside the Jokhang. The monks melted into the crowd. It was ten fifty-five a.m. The PSB made repeated charges down the Barkor in both clockwise and anti-clockwise directions. The Tibetan crowds repeatedly fled only to surge back again. One sixteen-year-old youth was arrested for throwing stones. He could not have been a monk, for he was dragged away by the hair.

The continued jeering and protests from the Tibetan crowd resulted in the firing of one round ... It was either tear gas or possibly a stun grenade. The trouble stopped when the PSB withdrew at eleven twenty-nine a.m.[29]

That afternoon, 400 women kept a silent prayer vigil outside the Jokhang. Although Western visitors had been ordered to stay away from – or ignore – any trouble, a few of them joined in the prayer meeting. They reported that emotions were running high, with the women crying out: "The Chinese are eating us alive", or "They are tearing our hearts out".

On the eve of the 1 October anniversary, the Chinese warned the Westerners more explicitly, threatening them with deportation – or worse – should they go near the Barkor. Police were deployed around all the monasteries to prevent any activity by the monks; and, to make assurance doubly sure, monks in the Jokhang were locked in. No visitors were allowed into the temple, and anyone seen filming or taking photographs had both film and camera confiscated. Truckloads of militia remained stationed in the Jokhang Square on the 1, 2 and 3 October, with large contingents of men armed with riot-shields, truncheons, bayonets and sub-machine guns taking it in turns to patrol the pilgrim circuit. Police personnel constantly videoed the square and surveyed it with binoculars from the police station roof. In the circumstances the only protest the Tibetans could make was to keep the Barkor stalls closed on the 1 and 2 October. On the evening of the 1st, a small Tibetan flag was briefly hoisted on a young willow tree in front of the Jokhang. This tiny symbol of Tibetan defiance – and of Tibetan powerlessness – was quickly taken down.

Since the Chinese themselves are much given to celebrating every anniversary in their revolutionary story, they could hardly be surprised at the Tibetan desire to commemorate their own landmarks. The next major one was 10 December 1988, the fortieth anniversary of the UN's Universal Declaration of

Human Rights. Christa Meindersma, a twenty-six-year-old Dutch woman, was in Lhasa at this time. Tension had been growing throughout December, she told me, as the Chinese brought in so many specially trained riot police that they almost outnumbered the inhabitants. Just days before, the relatively sympathetic Wu Jing-hua had been replaced by Hu Jin-tao as the TAR Party leader, and it was becoming clear that the policy of "merciless repression" was to be enforced. There was a terrible atmosphere of fear everywhere – people were walking with their heads down, terrified of talking to a foreigner.

Security forces in Lhasa were deployed from the evening of the 9th and groups of armed militia were on non-stop patrol. On the morning of 10 December, said Ms Meindersma, about 100 monks and nuns converged on the Barkor from the Ramoche Temple in the north of Lhasa, joined on the way by a crowd of ordinary Tibetans. She herself was sitting having a drink in the Jokhang Square when,

> Suddenly a group of about thirty young monks appeared, one of them with a Tibetan flag. They looked scared and not sure what to do. When the crowds began to gather encouragingly round the group, without any warning the police opened fire, shooting quite indiscriminately into the crowd. They didn't seem to mind who they hit. People began to scatter in all directions, trying to escape. I decided to do the same, but as I turned to run I was shot in the shoulder.

The behaviour of the police squads on this occasion was, in fact, quite different in kind from anything that had gone before. Within two minutes of arriving on the scene, they had opened fire, killing the two flag-bearers, Gyalpo and Kelsang Tsering. As these were blatantly executions, it must be presumed that the police were indeed carrying out Qiao Shi's policy of "merciless repression".

Christa Meindersma's ordeal was far from over. "The police pursued all the bystanders like myself who were trying to run away", she continued. "They were shooting at us all the time":

Despite the pain in my shoulder, I managed to keep running. At first I found shelter with a Tibetan family but I knew that I couldn't stay there – it would be dangerous for them. They found a friend of mine, a Canadian, who carried me on his back towards the hospital. Unfortunately the police appeared again and began to chase us, so I had to get down and run although I had hardly any strength left.

"People were falling and screaming", reported Ron Schwartz, a Canadian sociology professor; "I saw people carrying wounded Tibetans on their backs, running into their houses and trying to find some place to hide."[30] A British tourist ran away from the firing and found himself in a narrow alley with about fifty Tibetans. "The police fired tear gas at both ends of the alley", he said.

At the hospital, a Tibetan doctor whispered to Christa that she had only a flesh wound and must on no account let the Chinese operate on her. The whole thing would take just twenty minutes to bandage and clean up, he said. But then she was taken to a Chinese surgeon who, pronouncing a five-hour operation to be necessary, prepared to give her a preliminary injection. Christa, however, declined with such determination that he simply cleaned the wound and let her go.

Because Christa Meindersma, a Westerner, had been shot during the demonstration, another quite different factor had entered the equation. Tibet again became the focus of Western media attention. Together with other Western friends, Christa returned not to her own modest lodgings but to the main Lhasa hotel, which had a telephone in all the bedrooms. Managing to let foreign news teams know where she was, she gave them a full account of the day's events. The Chinese, meanwhile, were claiming that she and her friends had instigated the riot. Realizing that she might be arrested at any minute, Christa telephoned the Netherlands Embassy in Beijing. She was actually on the telephone to an official there when the police burst in to search her room. They took away all her photographs, recordings and films, a photo of the Dalai Lama and her passport – with the embassy official in Beijing listening in. When the Netherlands Government heard about the passport being confiscated, they officially protested at this breach of international law. The Canadian Government made even more of a fuss, since several of their nationals had had their passports taken away. The international furore was too much for the Chinese, who reluctantly climbed down and returned the passports to their owners.

But if the publicity was good for Tibet, it was bought at a heavy cost. For up to eighteen people are believed to have been killed that day, over 150 seriously wounded, and hundreds more arrested. With very little hope of an end to the killing, the Tibetan determination to remain non-violent must surely have been hanging in the balance.

The Dalai Lama was well aware of this danger and had been seeking ways to avert a clash. In a historic speech before the European Parliament in Strasbourg on 15 June (and encouraged by calls from various Western leaders for China to resume talks on the future of Tibet), he restated and elaborated his Five Point Peace Plan. Seeking to make an opening for the negotiations with China, he stated his readiness to abandon claims for full Tibetan independence, and to be willing to leave foreign policy and defence in the hands of the Chinese. It seemed that he was effectively offering China "suzerainty" in return for internal Tibetan autonomy.

It was not only Beijing which returned a dusty reply to these staggering proposals. In Dharamsala the suggested compromise sharpened the argument between those Tibetans who shared the Dalai Lama's pragmatic approach and those – particularly the young – who were becoming more and more belligerent. To them, what the Dalai Lama had proposed was a sell-out. Phuntsog Wangyal, who was running the Tibet Foundation in London (and was, according to Jonathan Mirsky "the best-known Tibetan west of Dharamsala"[32]) was increasingly identified with the militant point of view. "We outside Tibet," he said, "have no right to give away independence without the completely free agreement of Tibetans inside Tibet". Tibetan exiles elsewhere were largely opposed to the Strasbourg proposals. They feared that the Chinese could not be trusted, that once Tibet had conceded its claim to full independence, they would dismiss its fate as merely "an internal matter".

The Chinese denounced the Strasbourg speech as "an attempt to split the Motherland" and castigated the European Parliament for allowing it to be made on their premises. Nevertheless, during the autumn they professed themselves willing to reopen the dialogue with the Dalai Lama. Wasting no time, the latter nominated a five-member team and proposed a meeting in Geneva in January 1989. The Chinese had not perhaps expected so prompt a response, and they stalled for time. First, they objected to Geneva and said the meeting should take place in Beijing. Next, they refused to accept any member of the Tibetan government-in-exile because they did not recognize it. And finally, to give the talks the kiss of death before they had begun, they announced they would not talk with anyone who had ever called for Tibetan independence. They were, in fact, saying that they would talk to the Dalai Lama or no-one. For the umpteenth time there was stalemate. January came and went, but no talks took place.

But one event that January deeply saddened the Tibetans. The Panchen Lama died, aged only fifty-three, on one of his rare visits to Tibet from Beijing. In his own way, he had continued to uphold the Tibetan cause. Reliable sources informed Dharamsala that just before he left Beijing for the last time, he had attended a high-level meeting with the Chinese Government and had asked his masters what benefits they thought the Seventeen Point Agreement had ever brought to Tibet. At that meeting, he had "expressed his anger by hitting the table with his fist". A week before he died he took up this theme again in a public speech in his homeland. Whatever benefits the Chinese may have brought to Tibet, he said sadly, they were not worth the high price which the Tibetans had paid for them.

It was courageous of him to speak out, and some say his daring may have cost him his life. For shortly after arriving at his own Tashilhunpo monastery, the Panchen Lama suffered a

heart attack and died. Many in Tibet were – and are – convinced that he was poisoned by the Chinese. But Tenzin Atisha
does not agree. "He had always promised that he would die on
Tibetan soil, and I think he had come home to die – peacefully,
in his own monastery. It was a symbolic death".

The Dalai Lama was generous in his appreciation:

> In his whole life the Panchen Lama never enjoyed any freedom.
> But we always consider him to have been a freedom fighter. I
> think the clearest indication was his last speech ... when he
> quite daringly said that the Chinese had brought some progress
> to Tibet, but at a terrible cost. It took a lot of courage to say that,
> and to me it indicated that he had remained a true Tibetan. I
> feel that in very difficult circumstances he acted like a politician.
> To please the Chinese, he always stated that Tibet was a part of
> China, had always been a part of China, and always would be.
> Consequently, the Chinese leaders praised him. But he made
> some quite tough speeches in favour of preserving Tibetan
> spiritual life, culture, dress and language. He did this very
> cleverly, much more cleverly than I could have done. And
> there's another thing. If *I* had fallen into Chinese hands, I don't
> think I could have been as brave as he was. In the end, he had to
> stand up to a great deal of torture. So we praise him.[33]

The Dalai Lama was officially invited to attend the funeral. But,
in the absence of any agreement about the Geneva talks, he did
not feel able to do so. The Panchen Lama's death meant that it
would be more difficult than ever to negotiate with the Chinese.
For he had been a valuable mediator, one who could at least try
to explain his country to its uncomprehending overlords.

CHAPTER 19

"Kill the Chickens and Warn the Monkeys", 1989

Beijing's policy has been based on an old Chinese proverb, Kill the chickens and warn the monkeys. The logic is that the sight of headless chickens flapping about in front of monkeys will frighten them out of their wits.

AMIT ROY

Nineteen-eighty-nine – the memorable year in which the nation states of Eastern Europe finally sloughed off their totalitarian regimes and began the long search for democracy.

It was also the year of Tiananmen Square. In June the whole world watched in appalled helplessness as the tiny flame of Chinese democracy was snuffed out.

Three months earlier, there had been a similar outrage in Lhasa. But fewer people noticed.

Yet, though something like 2,000 miles separated Beijing from Lhasa, the two events were connected. What happened in Lhasa was critically important for what happened later in Beijing. For after March 1989 in Lhasa, the central government in Beijing knew that its very existence was threatened and that it could tolerate no further attacks on its authority. It was this knowledge which doomed Tiananmen Square in advance. For, "under Deng, as under Mao and under the emperors before them, the primary purpose of China's capital city had been to manifest the authority of the ruler who dwelt within it".[1]

Although people in China and Tibet had been told almost nothing of the political whirlwind which had scythed through Eastern Europe, they had discovered enough to make their own leaders tremble. In Beijing, the citizens had let off firecrackers to celebrate the execution of the Ceaucescus in Romania. China's students, teachers, writers and other intellectuals began calling for democracy, freedom and the rule of law. As the momentum of dissent built up, the fledgling pro-democracy movement flexed its muscles.

In Tibet, it was the monks who had begun to think seriously about democracy. Already in the previous year, a group of Drepung monks had explored the true meaning of the word in an important document printed on wood-blocks and distributed in villages around Lhasa.[2] They had sketched out a blueprint for a Tibet free of Chinese domination and living according to the constitution drawn up by the Dalai Lama in exile. No question here of restoring the *status quo ante*, of bringing back the old Tibet. The monks went out of their way to break with the past: "Having completely eradicated the practices of the old society with all its faults, the future Tibet will not resemble our former condition and be a restoration of serfdom, or be like the so-called 'old system' of rule by a succession of feudal masters or monastic estates." To the authors of the document, democracy was rule by all the people of Tibet, not an oligarchy based on class or power or wealth. In this state, the will of the people would be paramount and all shades of opinion possible "without need of fear, hypocrisy and concealment". In the name of this future Tibet, the monks called on Tibetans young and old to unite, to do whatever they could, directly or indirectly, to assist the movement to restore Tibetan freedom.

It was a heady call, and it met with an enthusiastic response. As a first step, the monks again refused to celebrate Monlam. (At least two senior monks were arrested for failing to persuade their colleagues to take part.) Next, on 5 March, came a demonstration to mark the thirtieth anniversary of the Lhasa Uprising on 10 March, and the first anniversary of the 5 March 1988 demonstration. It was a small, defiant protest by thirteen Buddhist monks and nuns marching round the Jokhang carrying a paper Tibetan flag, its hand-drawn snow lion rearing proudly against a backcloth of mountains. Along with the usual slogans they shouted, "This is a peaceful demonstration, please do not use violence", and, in English, "Freedom! Freedom!"[3]

The Chinese had been expecting trouble, and, in neighbourhood committee and work-unit meetings, had warned the Tibetans (as indeed they had on 10 December 1988) that anybody taking part in demonstrations risked being shot. Despite the warning, several score Tibetans joined in the protest, while hundreds more looked on. As the protesters approached the police station, a policeman on the roof threw a bottle at the crowd below, whereupon a Tibetan youth hurled a rock at the police station wall. Suddenly, reported an American bystander who was watching the roof of the police station: "I heard a dozen single gun shots coming from above my head".[4] The youth who had thrown the rock was shot, and two Tibetans who tried to pick him up were also shot and wounded. The crowd erupted in a hail of stones and catapults, but dispersed in panic when the police began using tear gas.

Chinese reports made no reference to the police opening fire, stating that "these nuns and lamas began to pick a quarrel. They spat at public security officers, started throwing stones at the police station and began smashing doors and windows".[5] In this version of events, the police had been goaded reluctantly into using tear gas. Only tear gas, of course.

The Tibetans knew otherwise; and this cold-blooded shooting of unarmed demonstrators acted as a powerful catalyst on public opinion. Over a period of three days, by a kind of spontaneous combustion, the peaceful demonstration ignited into an explosion of ethnic rage in which everyone joined in, from young children throwing pebbles to the elderly handing stones to the younger, stronger ones to throw. It seemed as if the whole of Lhasa was there, surging up and down, waving Tibetan flags and shouting for independence. Pemba, whom we last saw being re-educated after his release from prison in 1987, was there on the second day:

It was all very disorganized and chaotic, with sporadic outbursts all over the city. The Chinese started shooting indiscriminately and throwing tear gas canisters. People were throwing leaflets in the air, advocating Tibetan independence. One man brought out a huge Tibetan flag from the meat market, and a crowd followed him along the main road leading to a Chinese hospital. The Chinese blocked the road outside the hospital with armed police, so the Tibetans lifted the man with the flag shoulder-high and began shouting. The Chinese aimed their weapons; the police took up their riot shields and batons ready to charge.

The crowd then turned back towards the Tibetan Medical Institute, shouting and calling on all tsampa-eaters to join in. They marched into a Chinese street and began setting fire to Chinese shops.

I left this particular group after a time and went back to the Barkor where shops were also being set on fire. The riot police arrived and aimed their guns. The crowd retreated, still shouting.[6]

In different parts of Lhasa, Tibetans were breaking into Chinese shops, dragging the contents into the street and setting fire to them. The police made occasional sorties into the streets, allowing emotions to reach fever pitch before firing randomly at the unarmed crowd. Several witnesses said they had seen policemen firing automatic weapons into people's homes, killing whole families.[7]

Everyone sensed that this time was different from anything that had gone before. The Chinese themselves indirectly acknowledged the growing strength of the independence movement with a revealing comment on Lhasa Radio. After the usual accusation that the riots had been instigated and manipulated by a tiny handful of "splittists", or the "Dalai clique" masquerading as tourists, they described the struggle against such criminals as an "arduous, complex and long-term affair", for which party members were advised to prepare themselves.[8] It was clear that they were envisaging a fight to the death, in which the "merciless repression" policy would find its justification. Random shooting-to-kill would henceforth be the normal response to all public protest. A deeply shaken leadership appeared to have decided that their only hope of success lay in a terrifying display of naked power.

Estimates of casualties varied enormously, from the derisory Chinese figure of eleven, to one Tibetan Government figure of 400. A more conservative Tibetan estimate of between eighty and 150 dead is probably nearer the mark. But as Nyima Tsamcho, a nineteen-year-old Lhasa girl who was subsequently imprisoned, said, "Since the Chinese were shooting every Tibetan in sight, it was difficult for us to know the exact figures".[9]

At midnight on the evening of 7 March, martial law was declared – for the first time since 1959 – in order, the Chinese claimed, "to maintain social order and protect people's lives and property".[10] It seemed an extreme reaction to unarmed protest. The name of the game was terror. "It looked", wrote the Dalai Lama,

> as if the Chinese must be about to turn the place into a slaughterhouse, a Himalayan killing fields. Two days later, on the thirtieth anniversary of the Tibetan People's Uprising, I therefore sent an appeal to Deng Xiao-ping, asking that he intervene personally to lift martial law and end the repression of innocent Tibetans. He did not reply.[11]

A news blackout descended on Tibet, though thanks to the presence of a few foreigners at the time of the riots, reports of the outrage and its bloody aftermath had been transmitted to the outside world. The disturbances received copious coverage in Western news media, and there was a new onrush of sympathy for the Tibetan cause.

The Chinese were not about to risk any further criticism. Tourists and journalists alike were roused in the night by police and given thirty-six hours in which to leave. By 9 March they had all gone, their last haunting memory of Lhasa being of Tibetans, men, women and even children, being hauled out of their homes and driven away in military trucks. One West German traveller arriving in Chengdu said that the Lhasans were terrified that the foreigners were being expelled. "One Tibetan told me repeatedly, 'We are finished, we are finished'".[12] "The Chinese are just waiting to clean house, at least that is what the Tibetans think", said Steve Marshall, an American, "and they don't want any witnesses".[13] "The crackdown has started", said Chris Helm, another American; "who knows what will happen once the prying eyes of foreigners have gone?".[14] Others reported Tibetans, with tears in their eyes, begging them to stay. But go they had to. As they left, they were subjected to security checks every few yards. "There are green uniforms wherever you look. You can't move for men with guns".[15]

The martial law decree banned all meetings, strikes, parades and protests, with checkpoints everywhere to control movement in and out of the city. Non-residents like pilgrims and traders were refused entry into Lhasa without authority from their own district. Forty thousand who were already in the city were ordered to be expelled. Every weapon in the government armoury – the courts, police, army, armed militia, "patriotic organizations", media – was mobilized to "deal resolute, accurate and rapid blows at the serious crimes of a small number of separatists in sabotaging the unity, stability and solidarity of the motherland".[16] "The peoples will brook no interference", warned another editorial relayed on Lhasa TV:

> The great unity among the people of various nationalities cemented with blood brooks no sabotage and it is indestructible. Since the riots and rebellions were quelled ... the banner of national unity [in Tibet] has become even more dazzlingly beautiful and is shining with new radiance.[17]

But the "banner of national unity" was a tragic farce. Far from being "dazzlingly beautiful" and newly radiant, it was forced on a reluctant people by some twenty to thirty thousand heavily armed troops, arriving in convoys to supplement the thousands of paramilitary forces already in Lhasa. Trucks, each one loaded with twenty-five soldiers, patrolled the Barkor night and day. As it entered its latest nightmare, Lhasa was sealed off from the outside world.

When the isolation was complete, the crackdown began. Chinese security forces attacked by night, kicking in doors, conducting systematic house-searches, killing some inhabitants and dragging others away. A woman who later escaped to India told how her husband, two children and their baby-sitter were all shot dead in one of these night raids, while she herself was injured.[18] It is estimated that up to 2,000 Tibetans were arrested, either during the demonstrations or in the early days of martial law.[19]

"Pema", a twenty-four-year-old trader, was arrested at midnight on 5 March and taken to a police station in Lhasa.[20] Six policemen tied him up with rope, gave him shocks with electric truncheons and beat him into unconsciousness with sticks and rifle butts. Then he was taken to an interrogation centre and subjected to the torture known as "Airplane":

Two men asked me to stand up. When I answered that I could not stand up, they started kicking me with their feet from both sides. They attached another rope to the one which already secured my hands [behind my back] and they then hung me from the ceiling. After a few hours hanging like this my shoulders were dislocated. Every time they came around me, they started kicking me. The next morning they took me down. I could not move any more. I could not bring my arms back in front of me, they would automatically go to my back.

Shortly after this, Pema was transferred to Gutsa prison:

I was thrown into a kind of rectangular ditch about six feet by two feet with an opening on the top [that was normally covered]. It was about seven feet deep. I was pushed into this ditch handcuffed. There was no place to sit in it so I had to stand the whole time ... On each side of the ditch, there was a hole where they pushed two steamed breads ("momo") and a mug of black tea mixed with chilli powder so that after drinking the tea all your digestive system burnt. They kept me in this ditch for one week and during the whole week I had only one meal a day, always the same ... which I could not throw away as they would then start hitting me from the other hole.

Pema was released from Gutsa after two months and fourteen days, having spent his last days in a "normal" cell, chained to an iron chair which in turn was chained to a cement pillar. For the crime of taking part in the demonstration, all his property was confiscated, except for 150 yuan, his entire property amounting to 3,000 yuan in cash, a television set, a large Tibetan carpet, a tape recorder and a bicycle.

Namgyal, the farmer's son from the Lhasa area, had taken part in the demonstrations and was recognized from a police photograph:

They arrested me when I went shopping for vegetables in my lunchbreak. They took me to Gutsa and kept me for a night and a day half bent over, watched by a security guard. When interrogation followed this treatment and they asked me if I'd set any vehicle on fire, the pain in my legs was so excruciating that I confessed to whatever they wanted – setting trucks on fire, shouting for independence, the Dalai Lama, anything. They sneered at the Dalai Lama, saying, "He had all that wealth and he didn't even build you any roads. We came here on foot to liberate you, because Tibet is part of the Great Motherland. You think the Dalai Lama stands for peace, but you are wrong. He is directing the 'splittists'." I replied, "It's not the Dalai Lama I'm fighting for. Here in Tibet we have no equality. We're given no opportunities. I was refused my school certificates and have no chance of a proper job. I'm fighting for a proper livelihood for myself – and for the hopeless young people of Tibet." At that, they struck me on the mouth and broke all my front teeth.

Next day they offered me money if I would betray my associates, money for each one I would betray, plus the promise of a good job, better accommodation and so on. But even if I had been willing to betray anybody, I had no one to betray. There had been people in the demonstration from all over Tibet and most of them were complete strangers to me.

So they kept me chained up every night and released me each day. Then they sent me to a work unit, breaking up stones. I was there till March 1990. One day, during the New Year celebrations, there were no guards watching, and I managed to escape.[21]

Teenaged Pemba had been shot in the right arm on the third day of the demonstrations and was therefore in imminent danger of discovery. As he had been in prison before and knew what to expect, he too decided on escape. With some friends he tried to get to Nepal, but they were at first forced back by lack of food. On the second attempt they were successful. Lobsang Nyima also made it to the West, all his former resilience punctured. "If no-one will come to our aid", he lamented gloomily, "it would be better to drop a nuclear bomb on Tibet and be done with it. Anything, even that, would be better than this present slavery."

Tibetan aspirations to self-determination were denounced in Beijing. "The Lhasa riots have their own particular background", proclaimed a 14 March *People's Daily* editorial, "but they show how we must value a stable environment ... Haste and impatience for progress on the question of democracy will only increase the sources of instability".[22]

Nevertheless demonstrations continued both in Lhasa and elsewhere throughout May. Five hundred students and teachers in Amdo marched in protest against the repressive measures used to quell the March demos in Lhasa. Chinese youth's own pleas for democracy and freedom began in that same month, triggered by the death of Hu Yao-bang, the reforming one-time Communist General Secretary who, shortly after calling for changes in Tibet had been removed from office. When the Beijing students began their doomed protest, the students of Lhasa University went on hunger strike as a sign of sympathy.

All to no avail. March in Lhasa, June in Tiananmen Square: Beijing's determination at all costs to keep its grasp on power could never again be in doubt. As the Dalai Lama wrote, "They showed the world the truth about their methods: scepticism of Tibetans' claims about Chinese human rights abuse is no longer possible".[23] (Within six weeks of the Tiananmen massacre, the Chinese announced that they were willing to meet the Dalai Lama, with no strings attached. Then they spoiled the effect by adding that he must first give up all claims to Tibetan independence – and that they still wouldn't meet any members of the government-in-exile. Hardly a change of heart!)

The handful of foreign groups who were allowed into Tibet in July to shore up the ailing tourist trade found Lhasa outwardly calm, though soldiers still manned checkpoints at every major crossroads and at the entrance to the Tibetan sectors of the city. But the illusion that all was well was quickly dispelled whenever the groups visited the monasteries. An *Observer* journalist travelling as a tourist reported being "ushered into the shadows by whispering monks. Keeping a careful lookout for the government-employed 'watchers' posted at every key site in Lhasa, they told me of the 'problems' plaguing Tibet. A number of them passed me printed appeals."[24] These appeals were for the first time being printed in English, on the small squares of paper normally reserved for wind-scattered prayers. One such message ran:

> STOP GENOCIDE IN TIBET, STOP FORCED STERILIZATION, MEDICAL MALPRACTICES, RACIAL DISCRIMINATION AND ABOVE ALL POPULATION TRANSFER POLICY. WE ARE FIGHTING FOR OUR LEGITIMATE RIGHTS – THE RIGHT TO GOVERN OURSELVES AND DETERMINE OUR OWN FUTURE.[25]

In August, the Chinese said they had no plans to lift martial law, and underlined their resolve by sentencing ten Tibetans to three years in prison for "shouting reactionary slogans" and damaging property during the March disturbances. More seriously, two Lhasa men who had been detained after the riots were charged with being secret agents of the Dharamsala government and with instigating the riots. It was the first time that a charge of espionage (a capital offence in China) had been levelled in such detail against Tibetans. The prospects for negotiations with Dharamsala seemed to recede even further.

September 1989, with its post-Tiananmen backlash, brought a new horror, with the launch of a new re-education campaign for the Tibetans (but not for the Chinese immigrants). All over Tibet, people were summoned to three-hour meetings, in neighbourhood committees or in the monasteries, sometimes twice a week, sometimes five times, sometimes every day, in the evening, and often in the morning too. Sometimes the meetings lasted as long as eight hours, and on danger days, such as the 10 March anniversary, they might take the whole day! No excuses were accepted for non-attendance and every family had to send one representative. Refugees interviewed in India some months later said that it was like the Cultural Revolution all over again:

> You had to criticize one another, denounce demonstrators, people pasting up posters and so on ... if you don't want to denounce people during these sessions, there is a denunciation box which you can use in each part of the town, where you can denounce anybody without even mentioning your name. The person will be arrested without further checking.[26]

An office worker stated:

> We had to read the material the Chinese gave us and then confess everything we'd been doing wrong, and also denounce people working for the independence of Tibet inside and outside the country. We had to criticize the Dalai Lama and refer to him as "the Dalai-reactionary" or "the separatist troublemaker". We were forced to attend these sessions, or we would have been in trouble and our salary reduced.[27]

"They cut off your ration quota", said another, "or you do not get a permit to buy kerosene for cooking. Of course, it is a big problem if you do not get this oil, because then you can't cook".[28] To add insult to injury, these sessions were conducted in the Chinese language, even though scarcely any Chinese were present – and those few only as spectators.

Though stifled as never before, Tibetan determination was strong. There was a great sense of unity, of "You Chinese, We Tibetans". In the schools and colleges, children and students were writing songs and poems which expressed their longing for independence – and their willingness to die for it. Tibetan cadres and state employees, weary of being discriminated against, for the most part threw discretion to the wind. Lhakpa Chungdak, despite her job in the police department, had taken part in the demonstrations of '87 and '88 and was now putting up posters and singing independence songs with her friends. "There is an old Tibetan saying", Kelsang Namgyal told me, "'No matter how much you burn inside, don't let the smoke come out'. Well, this was the moment when we all began to breathe out smoke."[29]

Inside and outside Tibet, Tibetan youngsters were "breathing out smoke". Calls for violent action were increasingly being listened to. One young man to whom I spoke in Dharamsala that September had just arrived from Tibet and was in no mood for compromise: "The Dalai Lama calls for non-violence and I understand that. He is a bodhisattva, a man of peace. But I am not. When I think of the Chinese and what they have done, I know that if there's the slightest chance of fighting them, I'll be ready."[30]

It was in the same militant mood that young Tibetan exiles came together in September for their annual Youth Congress in Dharamsala. The atmosphere was tense with barely suppressed rage. The Dalai Lama opened their deliberations by yet again urging non-violence; but his audience was restive. His Holiness was optimistic, however, believing that, with time and patience, the situation would improve: "The old Chinese way of thinking is dying out. The next generation will almost certainly be quite different. Then there will be room for discussion. We are not anti-Chinese, we have no ill feeling towards the Chinese. We must talk to them."[31]

But the Youth Congress was unconvinced, he agreed when I

spoke to him on the afternoon of that first day. He was somewhat battered by his meeting with the young militants, aware that his arguments did not appeal to hot young blood, yet confident that reason was on his side:

> They say we must take violent action now. My argument is that, yes, I know things are serious, but if we take up arms they become even more serious. The Chinese will find it perfectly easy to send in an even bigger army. They would explain to the outside world that they had had to do this in order to keep law and order. And, again in the name of law and order, they could wipe out Tibetan villages. But if the Tibetans remain silent and adopt non-violent tactics, the Chinese will find it very difficult to wipe us out. If they *did* send in military reinforcements, they would have to explain their behaviour to the outside world. World opinion does have *some* restraining effect.
>
> There's another factor. Suppose the Tibetans do go in for violence – with a few guns, a few bombs – what difference will it make? It will merely create a crisis atmosphere. In order to have any real effect, we would need many more weapons and arms. But who would supply them?
>
> So there they were this morning, all saying we must take up arms and fight with the Chinese. It's very easy to talk like that. But if you come down to practicalities, it's impossible. For one thing, India wouldn't tolerate it. Nor America, Russia, France – nobody would help or supply weapons. And there's one more thing – if Tibetans turned to violence, they would no longer be special. Many countries support Tibet precisely because she is special, fighting for freedom through non-violence. Let us stick to our non-violence, because it is unique. It is something quite new on this planet, to fight for freedom through non-violence and human understanding.[32]

In the end, the Youth Congress, after considerable heart-searching, did not make a call to arms. It was an anguished decision, admitted Lhasang Tsering, the radical president who was re-elected for a second term. "We are not just struggling for freedom", he told me passionately after the closing session of the

Congress, "it is a question of our very survival". He explained why the desire to react was so strong:

> I am an ordinary human being. Separated from my parents at the age of eight, I don't even know my family name. Such is the Tibetan tragedy. When I was working in the Children's Village, there were many children who did not know their father's name, and among the delegates here today there are many who have never known their parents, who do not even know their names, who are even afraid to marry, in case they are marrying their own sister or brother.

"But when we make a call for arms", he exclaimed, "we are not talking about attacking other people, we are talking about the right of every individual, every nation to defend itself from annihilation".

Nevertheless he would not defy the wishes of His Holiness and was now searching for ways of treading the tightrope: discovering how to confront the immediate threat of extinction facing his countrymen, while keeping to the path of non-violence. Did he expect to succeed, I asked him. "I am hopeful", he replied vigorously:

> We will find ways – outside the boundaries of Tibet. Non-violent ways – *that* we have made very clear. We hope the world will help us. Today, many of our members were suggesting that all of us should go down naked into the streets, wearing animal masks, and ask the world to decide whether the Tibetans are humans or animals. We have not been recognized as human beings, with the same basic rights of honour and equality and dignity as are accorded to other people. We don't ask any more than that – we want to be treated like human beings.

Within a few weeks, some kind of recognition *was* given to Tibet, when the Dalai Lama's devotion to non-violence earned him the Nobel Peace Prize. He was in California when the announcement was made – on 4 October. His reaction, as he described it to me a few months later, was typical of the man:

It was late evening when I heard it rumoured. Then I was a little bit excited. Then I listened to the radio at eight thirty local time, and there was no mention of it. So I thought, "Oh well, it was only a rumour", and I went to sleep. Next morning as usual I got up at four. I heard then that the award had been confirmed. But I didn't feel excited any more.[33]

He boomed with delighted laughter at the memory. "The Dalai Lama has a wonderful laugh", the *Washington Post* had reported on his first visit to the USA: "It surprises itself in the act of delight and rings out round the room, as if all his past thirteen incarnations were joining in."[34]

By coincidence, on that same day, news came through of five Tibetan nuns sentenced at a mass public rally and sent to labour camps for taking part in a minor demonstration in September. (A sixth nun was still being investigated.) That brought to fourteen the number of those convicted within the last month. The five were said to have shouted "reactionary slogans" for an independent Tibet "in a frenzied way and hysterically" as they processed round the Jokhang on 22 September.[35]

The Nobel award was both a recognition of the Dalai Lama's legitimate claims and an implicit condemnation of the Chinese regime. In the wake of Tiananmen Square, it was a show of sympathy for the suffering peoples of both Tibet and China. China interpreted it as the direst of insults. From the Chinese Embassy in Oslo, the Counsellor, Mr Wang Gui-sheng, complained that the decision to give the prize to the Tibetan leader was "interference in China's internal affairs" and had "hurt the Chinese people's feelings". But in the Dalai Lama's view, the award signified:

international recognition of the value of compassion, forgiveness and love ... Chairman Mao once said that political power comes from the barrel of a gun. He was only partly right: power that comes from the barrel of a gun can be effective only for a short time. In the end, people's love for truth, justice, freedom and democracy will triumph. No matter what governments do, the human spirit will always prevail.[36]

According to a group of Tibetans who escaped to Nepal in November, Lhasans first heard the news about the award through the Tibetan language broadcasts on All-India Radio and the Chinese language broadcasts of the Voice of America, Radio Moscow and the BBC. But as few of them had ever heard of the Nobel prize, they did not realize how important it was until the Chinese started belittling it, saying for example that the Dalai Lama hadn't deserved this prize, but had used "back-door contacts" with the Americans to obtain it. Then their euphoria was so great that they surged onto the streets. Because of martial law, any large-scale demonstrations were impossible, but there was a spontaneous celebration in Lhasa which lasted all day and involved up to about 1,000 people. The Tibetans stopped work, stuck up posters wishing long life to the Dalai Lama, telling the Chinese to get out, and thanking the world for upholding the Tibetan cause. They celebrated in the traditional way with the burning of incense and the throwing of tsampa into the air and at each other.[37] Because they had really no idea what the Tibetans were celebrating the Chinese tolerated the goings-on until about seven in the evening. Then they tumbled to the truth and their attitude changed instantly. The Tibetans were prevented from erecting a small memorial in front of the Jokhang, and were threatened with a retribution so severe as to make the March crackdown look like a children's party.[38]

The euphoria over the award panicked the Chinese into banning all religious activities associated with the Dalai Lama. Practices such as the throwing of tsampa and the burning of juniper wood came into the category of superstition, and were therefore unconstitutional and easy to ban. In October, the *Peasants' Daily* linked Buddhism to feudal practices and warned:

Since these feudal and superstitious activities poison the minds of the masses, adversely affect the healthy growth of our younger generation, pollute the general mood of our society, and impede the building of socialist spiritual civilization in our rural areas, under no circumstances should we underestimate their seriousness and slacken our vigilance against them.[39]

The banning was made law in December. A committee was set up to investigate anyone who had celebrated the awarding of the Peace Prize; and anyone who had burned incense or thrown tsampa was arrested. (Lhakpa Chungdak was summoned by the head of her department, a Tibetan. He warned her that the Chinese had video proof that she had thrown tsampa and that she would face a fifteen year prison sentence if arrested. Shaken, she decided to escape while there was still time.)

The smallest sign of nationalist sentiment was stamped on. Nineteen-year-old Lhakpa Tsering and five other pupils at the Lhasa High School were arrested in November for making copies of a Tibetan flag and pasting up independence leaflets. A teacher at another school in Lhasa was detained for writing "reactionary" songs on the blackboard. After a ceremony of thanksgiving at a nunnery, seventeen nuns were expelled, two of them later being arrested and sent to Gutsa prison. One of these, eighteen-year-old Namdol Tenzin, told how she was given electric shocks while tied to a chair with wires around the fingers of both hands. Flung to the ground repeatedly by the force of the shock, every time she fainted she was revived so that the torture could begin again.[40]

In October, the government decreed that children of parents who had taken part in demonstrations were ineligible not only for education but also for any but the most menial job. This was the last straw for the married ex-monk Yeshe Gonpo, whose wife had been detained after the 1987 demonstrations. To make matters worse, the Chinese had demolished his house in the Tibetan part of Lhasa, ostensibly because it was old, "but they were making a habit of this sort of thing, because often they found silver, gold or other buried treasure in the rubble. Then they would rebuild the house and charge a much higher rent for it."[41] Residents were appalled by this new development. One man, waiting for his home to be destroyed, said, "It's like pull-

ing out a perfectly good tooth and putting a false one in its
place." Though the Chinese claimed that the changes would
benefit the Tibetans, it was yet another blow to Tibet's culture
and was generally seen as part of "the final solution". "The
Chinese are not doing anything useful for us", complained a
monk,

> the building programme in Lhasa is just superficial change
> designed to deceive people into thinking the Communists are
> helping us. It's all part of their main aim: to wipe out Buddhism
> and destroy our spirit. If it goes on like this, not just our houses
> will go, but Tibetans as a race will become extinct.[42]

For Yeshe Gonpo, his wife and their two sons, aged three-and-a-
half and seven, it was time to go. Sadly, they prepared for the
long, secret journey to India.

The day when the Nobel Prize was awarded in Oslo – 10
December – did not go unremarked in Lhasa. Monks at
Ganden, prisoners in their own monastery, claimed that when
they went out in the morning to collect the milk they were
beaten by soldiers with thirty inch iron bars, wooden clubs and
leather belts.[43]

In his Oslo speech, the Dalai Lama drew world attention to
the tragic fate of his country. But the award to "a simple monk
from far-away Tibet" was, he was sure, a hopeful sign:

> It means that, despite the fact that we have not drawn attention
> to our plight by means of violence, we have not been forgotten. It
> also means that the values we cherish, in particular our respect
> for all forms of life and our belief in the power of truth, are today
> recognized and encouraged.[44]

He promised (and almost immedately made the promise good)
to use the prize money (US$469,000) to help the starving, the
lepers in India and a variety of peace projects throughout the
world. Among the many donations to good causes was one for
$6,000 towards medical aid for Romania. And he urged China

to follow the reformist example set by Eastern Europe, in order to avoid a second Romania in the Himalayas.[45]

Making the most of his stay in Europe at a time when history was being made, the Dalai Lama visited Berlin just as the unpopular Communist leader, Egon Kranz, was overthrown. With the co-operation of the East German authorities, he was able to go right up to the Berlin Wall. As he stood there, in full view of a still manned security post, an old lady silently handed him a red candle:

> With some emotion, I lit it and held it up. For a moment the tiny dancing flame threatened to go out, but it held and, while a crowd pressed round me touching my hands, I prayed that the light of compassion and awareness would fill the world and dispel the darkness of fear and oppression.[46]

The Chinese rapped the East German government over the knuckles for this lapse of judgment.[47] Prime Minister Li Peng condemned the reforms sweeping Eastern Europe. Beijing, he said, had had the good sense to crack down on its own democracy movement in June, thus protecting China from the "chaos and confusion" now prevailing elsewhere.[48]

To underline how little had changed in Tibet, the Chinese masters ended this most infamous of years with a mass sentencing rally at which eleven Tibetan monks were jailed for terms of up to nineteen years for the "counter-revolutonary crime" of campaigning for Tibetan independence. Their leader, sentenced to nineteen years, was Ngawang Phulchung who had translated the UN Universal Declaration of Human Rights into Tibetan. He was the leader of the Drepung group of monks which had dared to draw up a charter for an independent, democratic Tibet.

CHAPTER 20

"A Volcano Ready to Erupt", 1990–1991

"They come at night", shuddered a refugee, recently arrived in India,

> usually between eleven p.m. and one a.m., and search the houses. If they find a visitor in the house who has no residence permit, they will fine him ten yuan and tell him to register the next day. They interrogate the suspect and if he does not give satisfactory answers, then they will arrest him. Any person on their black list is automatically arrested.[1]

That man left Tibet in February 1990 at about the same time as Pema Saldon too escaped. Pema had hitherto refused to consider escape, believing she could still be useful to Tibet. But when in November 1989, her husband, Phuntsok, was arrested and charged with inciting revolt, she knew it would be her turn next. After several unsuccessful attempts to find out where Phuntsok was being held, Pema fled to Nepal in February – just in time, as the police came for her only hours after she had gone.[2] She had become one of the 1,000 refugees annually making the dangerous journey across the Himalaya to safety. In those dark days of martial law, few exit permits were being issued for travel to India and Nepal, for the Chinese considered that contact with Tibetans on the other side had served only to fuel discontent. Permission, if granted at all, was taking up to two years to come through. Visas for the exiles to visit Tibet were virtually a thing of the past.[3]

Although the military presence was still pervasive and the atmosphere tense, martial law was lifted on 30 April. The move was almost certainly timed to impress President Bush who was considering whether or not to renew China's "most favoured nation" status with its billions of dollars' worth of trade concessions. (If so, the gamble paid off, for three weeks later, the coveted status was renewed.) The PLA soldiers withdrew, only to be replaced by thousands of armed plain-clothes police, an undisciplined paramilitary force known in Chinese as the Wu Jing. Control had merely changed hands. In fact it was widely believed that the PLA soldiers had simply changed uniforms.

Two weeks earlier, in an attempt to root out all possible sources of dissent, several hundred politically active nuns (and some monks) had been arrested or expelled from their monasteries and nunneries and ordered home to their villages. Monks at the Potala Palace could stay if they signed a two-year pledge to behave themselves.[4] Those at Sera and Drepung were given no such option, and among those expelled were some of the most advanced students and the most serious practitioners of Buddhism. "Who will be the teachers?" lamented one of the remaining monks. "They are trying to kill Buddhism ... The Chinese are pulling Tibetan Buddhism out by the roots." It was true. The enemy had been identified and targeted: the Chinese would go to any lengths to destroy this creed, the chief obstacle to their right to rule in Tibet.

Just two days before martial law was lifted, the citizens of Lhasa were ordered to attend an outdoor sentencing rally at which forty-three Tibetans were paraded through the main street and mercilessly humiliated at a public sentencing rally. It was a warning, for with the army's departure, the new civilian government unleashed a deluge of restrictions. A six-point decree authorized the Lhasa City Police to "resolutely crack down on activities that oppose the socialist system or are aimed at dividing the Motherland"; permission had to be sought for any kind of assembly; and even the most minor disturbance would be put down by force. The decree specifically urged informers to remember their duty[5] and reminded the populace that their constitutional rights did not include the right to criticize the system.

Hu Jin-tao, the new Party Secretary, announced that "Tibet

is still facing an arduous task in carrying out an in-depth struggle against splittism and in further stabilizing the situation in the next five years". Everything that had gone wrong in the past few years was the fault of a few "splittists" in the pay of Dharamsala and/or Washington, and they must be crushed, no matter how. To underline their determination to "stabilize" by terror, the government executed two Tibetans for attempting to escape from a Lhasa prison,* an act which aroused great bitterness throughout Tibet, and turned even long-time collaborators against the regime.

Meanwhile, other aspects of life were also coming under stricter control. A paper submitted to the Shanghai Academy of Social Sciences in 1989 had called for the setting up of a special police force to conduct abortions on women from minority nationalities with a population of more than 500,000.[6] And an article in *China Population News* described the relaxation of family planning because of "ethnic customs" as an "absolutely untenable proposition". Almost immediately, the birth control programme in Tibet was tightened, with birth control teams everywhere established to begin to implement the law.

On 29 May 1989, the Chinese authorities announced that 18,000 of the 600,000 women of childbearing age in the TAR had "volunteered" to be sterilized. Two Tibetan monks from Amdo, interviewed in Dharamsala, had seen something of this "volunteering", when a birth control team operated next to their monastery:

> The villagers were informed that all Tibetan women had to report to the tent for abortion and sterilization or there would be grave consequences. Those who refused were taken by force and operated on. We saw many girls crying, heard their screams as they waited to go in the tents.[7]

---

* Later Amnesty International (and Tibet Information Network) reports suggested that they were also accused of supporting independence. This was never admitted by the authorities but was known amongst Tibetans.

A 1989 report in the *Guardian* suggested that the birth control teams were given financial incentives to perform as many sterilizations as possible. This is borne out by many independent witnesses who describe women – girls of thirteen and fourteen allegedly among them – being dragged off, screaming, by the truckload.

Tashi Dolma was one of four Tibetan doctors at an Amdo hospital, all of whom eventually left their jobs in obstetrics in protest against the inhumanity of the birth control policies:

> No one can escape. In remote areas, where there is no hospital, teams of Chinese doctors and nurses arrive in two jeeps, one for themselves, the other for their equipment. They go from village to village and are on the road for about two or three months, performing on-the-spot abortions and sterilizations. By the end of each trip they have handled about 2000 cases.

A report on human rights in Tibet stated that:

> Abortion is usually performed in the morning, and the mothers must return home the same afternoon. Office workers receive two to three days paid leave, but those working on the land are forced to return to work as soon as possible to try to earn a living wage.
>
> Another refugee paints a harrowing picture of the situation in Chamdo: "You may find it hard to believe, but the Chinese also force abortions on women who are three, four and five months pregnant. I've seen foetuses of those three- four- and five-month olds lying in the storm drains and in the dustbins outside the (Chamdo Public Welfare) hospital."
>
> The process has even been taken one step further; to the slaughter of new-born babies belonging to mothers of two-child families: "Sometimes the mother will go through labour, give birth and hear the baby cry and then after fully awakening will learn that the baby died during childbirth".[8]

Tashi Dolma agrees that foetuses are aborted at an extremely late stage:

The foetus is often removed at twenty-eight weeks and over, when the heartbeat is already being heard. The woman is forcibly aborted and when the healthy foetus is removed, its head is immersed in a bucket of water. Healthy, well-formed babies. Some of them actually come to full term, but on being born they are drowned in the bucket of water. The mothers nearly go out of their minds.[9]

A refugee from a village near Shigatse told the Dalai Lama that a Chinese doctor had admitted to her that in order to fulfil his quota of abortions he was forced to resort to killing the new-born. A Tibetan married to a woman doctor at a maternity clinic in Lhasa, claimed that "birth control measures" were one of the hospital's main functions; and that lethal injections were frequently given to babies upon delivery.[10] Another hospital was known as "the butcher's shop", a man in Lhasa told Vanya Kewley,

> because that's where they take our women for forced abortions. And remember that we are Buddhists: we believe it's a terrible sin to take any life ... and to take the life of an unborn child ... As a Westerner you can't really appreciate how devastatingly traumatic it is for a Tibetan Buddhist to commit this crime ...[11]

The effect on the mother who is told she has to lose her baby is shattering, affirms the doctor, Tashi Dolma – whose own second child was forcibly aborted:

> I had a little boy of three and a half when I became pregnant again. The hospital director found out when I was eight weeks pregnant and threatened my husband and myself with the loss of our jobs, together with a huge fine. They made life so difficult for us that I knew I'd have to submit. In the end they didn't leave it to me. They forced me onto a table, inserted an electrical device into my uterus and left me like that for hours. I was bleeding profusely and the uterus was dilating. Then they came and inserted some kind of spatula and twisted it round and round, scraping the foetus out in small pieces.[12]

In the circumstances, it is not difficult to understand why, in that summer of 1990, the mood in Lhasa was dangerous. "We have been pushed too far", complained one Lhasa inhabitant, describing the situation as "a volcano ready to erupt, and when it does it will make Tiananmen look like a picnic".[13] Brave words, born of desperation; but by the end of May a new law had been passed making public protest almost impossible.[14] All demonstrations were to be notified in advance to the authorities, together with the names and addresses of the organizers – and the text of the slogans to be shouted! The new law increased the pressure on monks and nuns by forbidding the use of religion as a focus for "rallies, demonstrations or parades that will endanger the state's unification or destroy national unity or social stability". No protests were to be allowed within 300 yards of religious centres, making any demonstration near a monastery or in the Tibetan quarter of towns illegal. The Jokhang temple, scene of so many protests since 1987, would henceforth be out of bounds.

The country was closed now to foreign journalists and individual travellers. This was a serious blow to Tibetans most of whom approved of tourism – knowing that even a brief exposure to the sort of conditions in which they lived had gained many new supporters for their struggle. Apparently realizing this, the Chinese were trying to tempt a new class of tourist, the relatively well off in search of an off-beat holiday experience. "We want fewer but higher-paying guests than before", a senior tourist official in Chengdu told the *South China Morning Post*. "Backpackers spend almost nothing, stay for a long time and stir up the Tibetans against us. We definitely do not want them".[15] "Backpackers", making up 65% of previous visitors to Lhasa, were *personae non gratae*, unless they joined up with an official tour group.

I joined one of these (still relatively uncommon) tour groups in September 1990, given no option but to stay at the expensive Chinese-owned Holiday Inn, where most of the staff were Chinese, though some of them wore Tibetan dress. Outwardly, Lhasa was calm: the streets were choked with bicycles; the trinket-sellers competing noisily for customers on the Barkor were cheerful as well as picturesque; there were long lines of pilgrims queuing outside or shuffling inside the monasteries, prostrating their length, muttering their mantras, telling their prayer beads, twirling their prayer wheels, spooning rancid yak butter into the temple lamps – a picture of exotic contentment. As one writer described the scene, it was:

> Happy music gushing all day long on the banks of the Happy River, happy bees going about their little tasks, each contributing to the good of the hive, happy tourists, happy Tibetans, happy Han Chinese, everybody playing his part in the wary charade that life in Lhasa had become.[16]

It was possible to wonder what all the fuss was about. Until, that is, one began to notice other things: that in some quarters of the Tibetan capital, almost everyone on the streets was Chinese; that the oblong identikit apartment blocks and offices were all made of concrete, making Lhasa look like every other Chinese town; that the shops, the stalls, the merchandise were all cheap Chinese, and even on the Barkor itself many of the vendors were Chinese. Even the *khata*, the traditional Tibetan felicity scarves, had been made cheaply in China and were being sold to Tibetans by Chinese or Muslim merchants. Arbitrary taxes imposed on Tibetan traders and the sheer impossibility of obtaining goods and materials at a competitive price had reduced some of them to begging on the streets. "No matter how hard we work", a young man told us bitterly, "we Tibetans remain in a state of penury. Everything we earn is creamed off by top Communist officials, to pay for more and more high-level meetings, at which they talk a lot of hot air and decide absolutely nothing. Nothing is ever done to improve our lot."*

Always shepherded as a group, we visited the regular tourist sights, temples and monasteries foremost among them: the partly restored Jokhang, Potala, Ramoche, Drepung, Sera, Ganden, Samye, Mindroling, Sakya. It irritated us that we had to pay to take interior photographs, suspecting – rightly – that the money would fetch up in the pockets of the Democratic

Management Committee, rather than go to the monks. Such is the fate of all monies left by unsuspecting pilgrims in monasteries. We idly wondered why the monks were so thin on the ground at Drepung and Sera monasteries, not knowing then that several of them had just been arrested or expelled.

Confronted with the ruined Ganden monastery, we glimpsed a little of the horror that had befallen this ancient land. As we wandered through the partially rebuilt temple, (Ganden receives very little grant money from the government) a monk whispered a warning to us that our guide was a government spy. On no account must we display any pictures of the Dalai Lama, a seditious act for which one tourist had recently been detained by the police.

One afternoon, as we admired the frescoes in one of Lhasa's famous buildings, our monk-guide interrupted his commentary (as a be-medalled PLA officer moved out of earshot) to whisper that seventy nuns had been arrested in the city that week. We checked his story with a reliable source and found that seven monks from Jokhang, fourteen from Drepung, fifteen from Ganden had been imprisoned in the last seven days. And of ninety-two nuns expelled, twenty-eight of them were now in prison somewhere in Lhasa. I thought of the young nun, Gyalt-sen Chodon, whose story had moved me to tears a few months earlier in Dharamsala; and I shuddered for the fate of those courageous young girls.

In the countryside, Lhasa sophistication, such as it was, fell away and we were painfully aware of the Tibetans' poverty, the

---

* While we were in Lhasa, a great deal of interest was being aroused by the trial of 23-year old Tashi Tsomo, a bank clerk at the Bank of China. She had embezzled a large amount of money, much of which she had spent on a good time, but some of which she had given away. To the Chinese she was a "bandit", but the Tibetans saw her as a latter-day Robin Hood, recovering money from a thieving government which habitually bled the people white. To them she was a political hero. When, therefore, Tashi Tsomo was executed for this offence in December 1991, they regarded her execution as politically motivated, a further attempt to intimidate them.

harshness of their living conditions. Though Chinese settlements have electricity, there is none in the Tibetan villages. In
most cases, their living space has been reduced, and they do not
have enough to eat. Children, even at exposed altitudes of
15,000 feet and more, go barefoot and hungry, summer and
freezing winter alike. As I wrote in an article after my return:

> I am haunted by the memory of a picnic in a field near Sakya.
> Out of nowhere, a small crowd of skinny, dirty, ragged, snot-
> caked, snuffling children – and a few hopeless-eyed adults –
> gathered round us. They did not beg, as children have learned to
> do in the cities; they simply stared. Ashamed, we swallowed a
> token mouthful, then piled up the food in boxes. They waited till
> we'd gone a safe distance, then pounced on the remains like a
> flock of marauding starlings. It was a demoralising experience.[17]

Three months after this, in December, Lhakpa Tsering, the
teenaged boy arrested for putting up pro-independence posters
at his secondary school, was found dead in his cell in Lhasa's
Drapchi prison. He had apparently been beaten to death by
prison staff for refusing to keep his mouth shut during a visit of
foreign dignitaries. Ninety-three other political prisoners in the
jail held a silent human rights vigil round his body, holding, as a
symbol of solidarity, a string of strips of cloth torn from the
boy's bedding. (Following the protest, these prisoners were
themselves said to have been beaten or tortured. Visitors to the
prison on 20 December reported that almost all of them had
faces "swollen with scratches", and that many had bruises on
their heads.[18]) Amnesty International called for a full-scale
inquiry into the death; and thirty US Senators sent a letter to
the Chinese premier, protesting about such violent repression of
Tibetans who had expressed their views peacefully. Senator
Edward Kennedy called Tsering's death "yet another human
rights tragedy in Tibet, all too typical of the cruel Chinese
repression of the Tibetan people".[19]

When the then US ambassador to Beijing visited Drapchi
prison in Mar./Apr. 1991, in order to see political prisoners, the

Chinese did their best to fool him. According to a report received by the Tibetan administration, common criminals dressed up in new clothes were passed off as demonstrators "keenly undergoing re-education". The real political prisoners were prevented from getting near the ambassador.* The latter, however, was not fooled. The Chinese officials' presentation of prison conditions in Tibet was, he said, "as phoney as a three-dollar bill". "That prison was no Boy Scout camp", he added, "and we knew it".[20]

The year 1991 began quietly. It could scarcely have been otherwise, in view of the restrictions on movement and assembly. Chinese vigilance increased as 10 March approached and there were ominous signs of an even more stringent crackdown to prevent the Tibetans marking their precious anniversary. At two public sentencing rallies in February – one in Shigatse, the other in Chamdo – at least three Tibetans were publicly sentenced in front of conscripted crowds for supporting the independence movement; and another was denounced as a spy for the government-in-exile. A ten-day curfew imposed on 900 monks at Drepung, Sera and Ganden prevented them from leaving their monasteries and reaching the city. One monk was shot and wounded in the groin after attempting to leave. It seemed that the Chinese had not yet winkled out all their potential opponents from the monasteries.

Official media reports described Lhasa as "stable", but tourists saw large numbers of plain-clothes police on the streets, armed policemen on the roofs overlooking the main square, and convoys of police in armoured trucks patrolling the city. The most effective measure of all, however, was the unexpected digging up of the Barkor, the pilgrimage path around the Jokhang temple. The Barkor had always been difficult for the Chinese to police and control, and its narrow alleyways had often given

---

* Five of them *did* however get up to him and handed him a petition – which the Chinese immediately snatched away. The five were beaten, put in solitary confinement for up to three months, and moved to other prisons.

shelter to fugitives. In less than two weeks at the beginning of March, bulldozers had reduced the entire circuit to rubble; even the brand new paving stones in front of the Jokhang were torn up. All prospects of demonstration were thus thwarted. The Tibetans were devastated.*

Nevertheless, five monks (all said to be in their twenties) did manage to escape from their monasteries, avoid the road blocks which guarded all entrances to the city and complete a circuit of the ruined Barkor. The People's Armed Police arrived to arrest them, just as they were unfurling a Tibetan flag in the centre of a large and slogan-chanting crowd. It was only a token demonstration, not only because of the restrictions but because the Dalai Lama was cautioning his people against any public demonstrations, however peaceful. Too many Tibetan protesters had already been shot, he explained during a visit to Britain in March; the risk of losing any more was unacceptable. "For us every single Tibetan killed is a big loss".[21]

In his 10 March statement the Dalai Lama finally admitted that his Strasbourg proposal of 1988 had failed, and that, if there continued to be no response from China, it would be withdrawn. But he remained fully committed to non-violence and believed that the only way to a solution lay in dialogue and negotiation.

His people's commitment to non-violence was, however, sorely tested when the Chinese launched their "grand celebrations" for the fortieth anniversary of their "peaceful liberation" of Tibet on 23 May, the day on which the Seventeen Point Agreement had been signed. "They do not seem to realize the humiliation we must endure when they force us to celebrate their occupation", said a Tibetan intellectual, quoted in a Reuter report. Anticipating that the Tibetan response might be lukewarm or worse, the Chinese took the precaution of arresting 146 "criminals" on 10 April. The arrests were announced at a

---

* It should be noted that in due course the Barkor was repaired.

public sentencing rally at which the police ordered Lhasans "to take immediate action to fight against all criminal elements, to greet the great occasion of the fortieth anniversary of the liberation of Tibet with a good social environment".[22] A week later, a further forty-four "criminals" – none of whom had been brought to trial and most of whose offences were unspecified – were paraded through the city by way of deterrent.

A "frenzy of building" was going on, as Lhasa underwent a face-lift. Tibetan houses were demolished, roads widened, street lights installed and trees planted. Prominent buildings were whitewashed and on some of them the figure forty was painted in letters ten feet high. To Tibetan disgust, a seventy metre high metal spire was planned as a commemoration of the arrival of the Chinese in Lhasa. This plan was later cancelled and a giant statue of two gilded yaks was erected instead.

Such insensitivity and bad taste were too much for some Chinese, especially those with a sense of history. "I am very worried about what the future holds for Tibet", one of these, a technician posted a few years earlier to Lhasa from China, wrote in March to a Western friend. "As I write, I find I can hardly recognize Lhasa. How I will miss the old Tibet ... Come back and have a last look at the old Lhasa before it goes. Come quickly ... There is no question that a new Tibet, a new Lhasa will appear soon."[23]

I was reminded of my conversations with Tibetan ex-cadres in Dharamsala, who had found sympathy and understanding among many of the older Chinese who had lived for some years in Tibet and developed an affection for the Tibetans. (It was the newer arrivals who cared little or nothing for them.) Tsering Wangchuk had no doubts that the Chinese cadres, too, were reluctant victims of the Communist regime. "Many of them are disillusioned and hate the system", he said.

All through April and May, thousands of pro-independence posters and printed slogans appeared on walls and telegraph poles and inside the monasteries in Lhasa, despite increased police surveillance. Forbidden Tibetan flags flew defiantly. One underground group – the Tiger Dragon Youth Organization –

produced tiny leaflets like prayer flags under the slogan "Tibet
for the Tibetans", asking Tibetans everywhere to shout it at the
top of their voices. Forty years of Chinese rule, they asserted,
had meant "wanton destruction and exploitation of both land
and people"; Chinese policy was "to turn Tibet into a part of
China, to turn Buddhism into a blind faith and to turn the
Tibetans into a stupid race".[24]

The "stupid race" was to be either bribed or threatened to
celebrate its national downfall with every appearance of unin-
hibited joy. A source in Lhasa claimed that about 1.5 million
yuan (US$300,000) had been set aside for the celebrations. A
large portion of that amount would be earmarked for firework
displays and the floodlighting of historic buildings. Work stopped in Lhasa a week before the 23rd, schools and factories were
closed, their occupants plunged into compulsory rehearsals.
Hundreds of "joyful" Tibetans reluctantly "volunteered" to
take part in the spectacular parades and lavish song-and-dance
routines, reminiscent of the Mao-worship of the Sixties. More
realistically, five field guns were towed through the streets of
Lhasa, and fourteen truckloads of soldiers were brought in.

On Sunday 19 May, top Chinese officials from the Party
Central Committee arrived, led by Li Tie-ying, whose father
had led the original delegation which in 1951 had enforced
Tibet's signature to the Seventeen Point Agreement. Though
the Tibetans felt the insult keenly, large numbers of "volunteers" were dressed up in brightly coloured national costume to
greet the VIPs at the airport with song and dance. Some areas of
the city had been completely closed off for the officials' greater
safety, and PLA troops were stationed every twenty yards along
the road from the airport to Lhasa.

On the anniversary itself, the Chinese authorities reduced the
price of liquor in Tibet by half. "Someone high up in the
administration has realized that there are more artful ways of
subduing people than shooting or jailing them," suggested a
report in *The Economist*.[25] Many Tibetans, disoriented and
wretched from years of suffering had turned to alcohol as an
escape, not the home-brewed Tibetan beer but Chinese spirits

trucked thousands of miles from China to all parts of Tibet. Some of the varieties are downright dangerous, with, says Jamyang Norbu, "the potency of rocket fuel". "The Chinese intention is to weaken our people", commented an official of the Health Department in Dharamsala. "The effects of alcohol on health are easily seen. Selling cheap alcohol and cutting the price by half on 23 May is a deliberate step. If they wanted to do so much for the Tibetans, why didn't they reduce the price of food on that day? Why alcohol?"[26]

But in spite of everything, the celebrations backfired. Foreign governments simply declined to attend. The guests did not come to China's party because no one but the host felt there was anything to celebrate. The international community was no longer uncritical of China and was looking with a great deal more sympathy on Tibet. In the wake of Tiananmen Square and the recognition that China had been selling weapons and nuclear equipment to Pakistan, Syria (and possibly Iran and Algeria), attitudes were changing.

Before March 1990, Western parliaments had occasionally protested against human rights violations in Tibet, but had been careful to avoid all mention of Tibetan independence. Only the Norwegians and President Vaclav Havel of Czechoslovakia had dared (in defiance of the usual Chinese protests) to receive the Dalai Lama on his travels. In March the British Prime Minister, John Major, on Foreign Office advice, declined to meet the Tibetan leader*, though he did not debar him from making political statements, as Margaret Thatcher had in effect done in the previous year.

But a sea-change in the international perception of Tibet was about to take place. West Germany and Costa Rica led the way by receiving the Dalai Lama. In April 1991, US President George Bush received His Holiness at the White House and for the first time the US Senate declared its unqualified support for

---

* John Major did, however, receive the Dalai Lama at Downing Street in December 1991 (see photo).

"freedom for Tibet". (China was mightily displeased, though Bush himself would shortly – in the teeth of Congressional opposition – cushion the blow by renewing her "most favoured nation" status, optimistically claiming that trade was a lever that could persuade China to improve its human rights record). On 23 May, the very day of the jamboree in Lhasa, the Senate passed a further resolution declaring Tibet – including those areas now incorporated into the Chinese provinces of Yunnan, Gansu, Qinghai and Sichuan – to be a state under illegal occupation by China. The true representatives of Tibet, they added, were the Dalai Lama and the Tibetan government-in-exile. These historic resolutions by Congress, whether or not supported by the President or the State Department, acknowledged that Tibet had functioned as an independent state before the Chinese invasion of 1950 and thus directly challenged China's territorial claims.[27]

It was a major shift of policy at a crucial time. Probably aware that foreign diplomats would not be attending the celebrations in Lhasa, China banned all the Beijing-based Western journalists and diplomats from coming. For their part, they filed reports telling not of China's "peaceful liberation" of a backward country forty years earlier but of her destruction of a small and independent state; and of the efforts of a growing independence movement to dislodge her.

One by one, the diplomats let it be known that they would not be attending the 23 May festivities in Lhasa. On 22 May, *The Times* reported:

> As a nervous Peking pours troops into Tibet in anticipation of tomorrow's fortieth anniversary of its annexation, Britain and the United States are leading a diplomatic boycott of celebrations. Diplomats from several European countries are also failing to respond to invitations to celebrations in Lhasa, the Tibetan capital, and at Chinese embassies. Receptions featuring film shows and propaganda booklets are being used to try to counter sceptical world opinion.

As yet, no happy ending is in sight. The bitter, unequal

struggle goes on. On 22 May, Li Tie-ying warned an assembly of soldiers in Lhasa: "You are engaged in an arduous struggle against splittist activities. We must maintain a high state of alert against our enemies. We cannot allow their plot to succeed."

Those who wish the Tibetans well and admire their indomitable spirit can only hope that, on the contrary, it is Li Tie-ying and his like who are stopped before it is too late. Only the international community can bring the right sort of pressure to bear on China to achieve this. The Tibetans are hoping against hope, sensing the tide of history flowing at last in their favour. For the moment, as for the last forty years, they are still alone. But they are united as never before. A song is current on the streets of Lhasa which reflects their awareness that – whatever happens – they are all in this together. "In the Norbulingka", they sing, "many very different flowers have bloomed. But neither hailstorm nor winter frost can ever weaken the bond that unites us".

The Exiles: Dharamsala, Himachal Pradesh, India, September 1991

Today Tibet lives, not within Tibet but outside Tibet. Everything that is Tibet – the culture, the religion, every aspect of Tibet lives outside of Tibet.

KASUR LODI GYARI, the Dalai Lama's Special Representative in Washington

And still they come, the refugees from hopelessness. Today, there are over 110,000 Tibetan exiles in sixteen different countries. The majority – 100,000 – are in India, but there are 6,000 in Nepal, 1,500 in Bhutan, 1,700 in Switzerland, and smaller groups in other countries such as the USA (where the number is growing) and the UK. For the most part, they have not accepted citizenship of their host countries; retaining their refugee status is their way of affirming that one day they will go back home.

They arrive, destitute and footsore, with over thirty years between the oldest and newest arrivals.* (Thirty years and an

---

* Since the last wave of terror began in 1987, thousands have fled, but not all have been successful. Many still die on the way. Others suffer a different fate. In May 1990, for example, the Nepalese authorities handed over forty-three Tibetan refugees to the Chinese who imprisoned them for attempting to leave illegally. Reports from the Tibetan regions near the Nepalese border say that the Chinese have imposed a fine of 2,000 yuan on any Tibetan caught in the act of escaping.

abyss of differing experience.) And by their own choice most of them come first to this isolated place, perched on the spur of a ridge overlooking the beautiful Kangra Valley. Though it may sound idyllic, Dharamsala itself is unlovely. A Tibetan friend has just described it with a shrug: "It's the end of the world. The bus turns round here: there's nowhere else for it to go". As everyone complains, "When you come out of your house, you can only go up or down". Either way, walking is difficult and rapid progress impossible. Dharamsala is "too hot in summer, freezing in winter, the only pleasant months being August and September, but then it rains all the time", says another friend. It has the second highest rainfall in the whole of India, a statistic not difficult to believe, since, even as I write, the monsoon downpours are churning the unpaved paths into rivers of mud. The Dalai Lama himself has been heard to compare the climate to Chinese policy in Tibet: unpredictable and unpleasant.   ·

Why then do the refugees choose to come to Dharamsala? To them, as to all Tibetans, this is a holy place, for it is here that the Dalai Lama lives, here that Tibet's future is being worked out by its government-in-exile. This is their place of once-in-a-lifetime pilgrimage. So after a stint in the transit camps – where they're medically inspected and given the necessary injections, they come here to a reception centre in McLeod Ganj, about 200 of them at any given time, dossing down on straw mats on a cement floor. Here they will have a roof over their heads and free meals for two weeks.

Some of the younger arrivals have doubted whether the Dalai Lama actually existed and are amazed to find he is real. "When I was young", a Khampa boy told me, "I used to imagine the Dalai Lama as some kind of ornate statue, so when I saw him as a living, breathing person, I was astonished. I told him so, and he rocked with laughter."

His Holiness sees them all, either in a group or individually, most of them weeping with emotion and fatigue, and with harrowing tales to tell. He mourns with them, consoles them and provides for them as best he can. But there are so many of them and the resources he can offer are temporary at best. Accom-

modation is the biggest problem. "At present", Tendzin Choegyal tells me, "there are refugees sleeping six to a bed, sideways
on. The resources that we have fall far short of the demand."

The summer of 1991 brought an unusually large number of
escapees, with over 376 reaching Dharamsala and several hundred more staying in Nepal. When a group of ninety nuns –
mostly in their teens and early twenties – arrived here and sixty-
six of them elected to stay permanently in Dharamsala, there
were no beds for them at all, and the Tibetan Women's Association appealed for help to friends and supporters abroad. Only
twenty-four of the nuns chose to go south, to the nunneries
established in Bylakuppe and Mundgod. The refugees are
always free to choose where they will go. About 60% of the
young men who come, particularly those from Kham and
Amdo, choose to go south, to one of the "Big Three" monastic
universities – Drepung, Sera and Ganden – which have been re-
established there.

Altogether more than 35,000 Tibetans have settled in the
south of India, the bulk of the refugee communty. They live,
mainly as agricultural workers, in five major resettlement
camps. Life here is "very simple, very decent", says Tenpa
Samkhar who for some years was head of the first settlement in
Bylakuppe (there are now two settlements there):

> It is a mini Tibet; they live their lives as they did back home.
> Most of them get up at four, say their prayers, milk their cows,
> go to the fields. They wear Tibetan dress, eat tsampa and drink
> Tibetan tea. What is different, of course, is that they also eat rice
> and maize. They help each other a great deal and are on good
> terms with the local Indian people. We have a co-operative
> society which looks after their welfare, helps them buy fertilizer,
> sell their products and so on. It has also opened shops which
> cater for their daily needs.

But good agricultural land is in short supply, and the settlements are having to support twice as many human beings as
had been bargained for. None of the settlements has proper

irrigation and they have suffered badly during the frequent droughts. But the refugees – including the monks who must work on the land in order to support themselves – have made the most of their talents and limited resources, establishing an agricultural research centre, dairy co-operatives, feed-grain processing plant, tractor repair and metalwork shops. In order to make a little more money, the exiles in Bylakuppe make the nine-hour journey to the Ooty Hills to sell sweaters to the tourists. Handicraft centres (where Indians and Tibetans together weave carpets), give employment to thousands. Refugees in Nepal have been particularly successful in this line. Carpet exports are the second largest source of hard currency earnings in Nepal. In that country, beloved of tourists and mountaineers, Tibetans have started up hotels, guest-houses, shops and restaurants, and many of them have prospered.

They have done the same in Dharamsala, though there are fewer tourists there, and those who come do so only because they are interested in Buddhism or Tibetans or trekking – or the Dalai Lama. In the late Sixties and early Seventies it was the hippies and flower children who came, hungry for the Dalai Lama's call to world peace through personal transformation. Some of them are still there, relics from the past, joining the handful of British left over from the Raj.

In Dharamsala's narrow, overcrowded, unpaved streets, the enterprising and hard-working Tibetans have built houses, small ramshackle hotels, cafés and tea-houses. Mr Nowrojee's General Emporium is still there, unchanged from the days of the Raj, but next to it are lively market-stalls offering trinkets, costume jewellery, ancient Tibetan artefacts, tee-shirts, Indian skirts, dayglo socks and Reebok trainers. There is a handicrafts centre selling Tibetan rugs, thangkas, sweaters; there are taxis, travel agencies, a post office and two bookshops. There is a home for the elderly; in the Delek hospital, Tibetan and Indian patients are nursed in caring but overcrowded conditions; while at the Tibetan Medical and Astro Institute traditional Tibetan medicine is available for those who prefer it.

Visitors to Dharamsala admire the Tibetans for their

resourcefulness, for having overcome the odds against them and for being such "good" and uncomplaining refugees. But Dharamsala is beset by problems, not least that with the never-ending influx of destitute refugees, there are acute shortages of water and electricity. Even in the better accommodation, there is no heating for the bitter winters and running water is a rarity. Because they are under the protection of the Indian government, Tibetans may not levy any taxes of their own to deal with the situation. Everyone does what he/she can, handing in cast-off clothing and shoes to a central depot and contributing at least a little to the refugee fund.

The Tibetan Women's Association and the Youth Congress (which has members in all the different host countries) provide much of the rest. The Indian government gives relief and there are many private benefactors from the West. People in different countries, for example, will sponsor children to receive an education. There are now eighty-two schools for Tibetan children in India, Nepal and Bhutan. Of these, thirty are under the Central Tibetan Schools Administration supported by the government of India; forty-three, including nine TCV schools and the Tibetan Homes Foundation are run under the direct control of the Department of Educaton of the Central Tibetan Administration. In addition there are nine autonomous schools mostly in Uttar Pradesh and Sikkim.

The TCV houses, educates, feeds and clothes about 8,000 refugee children, nearly 2,000 of them in Dharamsala, many of them orphans, or brought to India by parents who, for the sake of their other children, must immediately return to Tibet. "They are coming all the time", says Tsewang Yeshi, the Village Director in Dharamsala, "about 200 of them every year, so that Homes designed to take twenty-five children each now have about fifty. Most of the smaller children share beds." I ask him what he will do when the TCV reaches bursting point. "Well, we'll never turn any of them away", he replies. "Even if we have to house them in tents or shacks, we'll manage somehow."

On a seven-and-a-half acre site at Bir, in the fertile Kangra valley not far from here, there is a Tibetan settlement based mainly round a handicraft centre. It also has a school for the youngsters who come out of today's Tibet to taste freedom – "I never had any in Tibet" – to learn about Tibetan culture and to study the English language. The Chinese don't like it. They are convinced that at Bir the Dalai Lama is training young Tibetans for military action; that this is a school for subversives; that all the fine words about non-violence are just a front. But they're wrong. "In Tibet, I learned nothing about Tibetan culture", one boy told me, "nothing but volume after volume of Chinese political theory. I led a deputation to the Chinese office asking for lessons in our own culture, but they broke bottles over my head. I still have the scars." "We need to be educated", said another boy (who had come from Amdo and had taken two months to reach India); "His Holiness tells us that the only way forward is through dialogue, but for dialogue you need to be educated. Education is the key to everything."[1] Most of the youngsters who receive an education at Bir have actually returned to Tibet, to tell Tibetans the truth about the exile community and to spread the word that an education is available for those brave enough to risk the hardships and dangers of getting to India.

Higher education for the exiles presents a pressing problem. Some young Tibetans do go on to college and university, but more would do so if they could afford to. The opportunities are limited, college fees are high and scholarships are few and far between. Then too, even those who have been lucky in this respect find it difficult to get jobs afterwards. It is a situation which may eventually force the younger Tibetans to leave the refugee community and seek Indian citizenship. And it is already happening to some extent in the south. "There is a big unemployment problem", admits Tenpa Samkhar:

When young people have been through the education system, they don't want just to work in the fields like their parents. They want a white-collar job, but they can't find any in the settlements. A few of them find work in the offices of the co-operative, some of them go off to sell sweaters.

Everywhere the problem of the young is acute. Young Tibetans in Dharamsala are growing up in a quite different culture from their parents'. They wear jeans and sweat shirts, they like pop music and fast food. Tendzin Choegyal believes that the greatest problem facing the refugees is how to integrate the young into Tibetan traditional values, how to convince them that Tibetan culture is worth saving:

> We have to be very clear about what we are trying to save, why we lead the life we do. I feel that our main task at present is to make our community self-sufficient, making the best use of today so that tomorrow can take care of itself. What we Tibetans have to preserve is the art of becoming happy, of making other people happy, the art of compassion. That's the crux of the special Tibetan concept based on Buddhism. The rest, the external manifestation of that concept as represented by the old feudal tradition, is unimportant.

Like his brother, the Dalai Lama believes that the Tibetan exiles must make the best possible use of their present situation so as to be ready for whatever tomorrow may bring. To this end, His Holiness continues to press for constitutional reform. In May 1990, at the time when the new civilian government in Lhasa was tightening the noose around the necks of its Tibetan subjects, in Dharamsala a quite different process – towards democracy and the rule of law – was being set in motion. At an Extraordinary Conference of nearly 400 delegates from all over the world, for the first time in Tibetan history a new Kashag (Cabinet) was elected not by the Dalai Lama but by the delegates themselves.

On the very day on which this historic election took place, the Dalai Lama told me of his deep desire for radical change. He wanted changes to the constitution he had drafted in 1963, and had no desire to continue as head of government. "The Tibetans", he conceded ruefully, knowing how much resistance he faced, "conceive of the Dalai Lama as the ultimate ruler of Tibet, but that concept must go. Otherwise we shall never have a democratic system. We should be drawing up a document about how precisely to elect the People's Deputies as well as how to appoint the Cabinet."[2] The time had come, he said, to appoint Kashag members by vote, not by his own diktat: "The people will accept the change because I've made it clear that I will remain as leader until we achieve liberation. As long as we remain refugees, I shall stay, but when the Tibetans have achieved their freedom, I will *not* participate in government any longer."

His determination to make the Tibetans come to terms with modern political realities was apparent in June of the following year (1991) when the newly elected Assembly of People's Deputies drew up a new Charter containing 115 Articles. One article in the old draft constitution had stipulated that if and when the support for the Dalai Lama should shrink to less than the required majority vote, then he must go. The Deputies, unlike the Dalai Lama, were appalled at being expected to take this seriously. "We actually took the clause out", says Tendzin Choegyal, one of the newly-elected Deputies, "but he made us put it back in, insisting that without it there would be no democracy."

Reluctantly, the Deputies agreed (solely to please His Holiness) that one day the Dalai Lama might be edged out. Such dithering on the margins of democracy annoys radicals like Lhasang Tsering "and Jamyang Norbu, both of whom feel that Tibetan society in exile is still mired too deeply in the past.[3] "If we go for democracy, there can be no half-measures", warns Lhasang Tsering; the present system is providing new shoes for walking along the same old road. We need to build a new road. Why not experiment more? We have nothing to lose, we have lost everything already."

Nevertheless, the democratic experiment, if too slow for some people's taste, is a genuine one. Most of the new Charter is devoted to the formation at grassroots level of the sort of system which would suit the settlements. "It's important for us to discover if this Charter can be made to work for us here and now", urges Tendzin Choegyal; "we don't want it to be a Charter in name only, but something living. Essentially what we Deputies have to do is protect the Charter, represent the people and watch over the administration, to see that it works properly." A draft constitution for "future Tibet" has already been prepared. And though there is still a long way to go, the Tibetans must surely be the only refugees in the world to be planning a precise constitutional framework for the future while still in exile.

Integral to the new Charter is a dedication to non-violence, a refusal to engage in armed struggle in pursuit of Tibetan independence. This too is challenged by Lhasang Tsering for whom the refusal is tantamount to renouncing the right to self-defence:

> Now I can understand renouncing war as an instrument of foreign policy, I can understanding renouncing aggression. But I cannot understand renouncing the right to defend ourselves. If we say that our goal of freedom and our goal of preserving our religion and culture are one and the same, then must we not conclude that the means we use to achieve the one are also the means we use to protect the other? Or are our religion and culture not worth preserving?

The dispute goes on, though Western friends continue to tell the Tibetans that it is their non-violence which attracts so many outside supporters to their cause. "It is very important to win our struggle for freedom through this non-violent path", the Dalai Lama assured me, "because then it will be an example to the rest of the world".

This autumn of 1991, with Communism fast disappearing from the European scene, there is a new hope about in Dharamsala. Ever since the Thirteenth Dalai Lama gave his dire warnings about Communism in 1931, the Tibetans had seen it as an irresistible negative force. But now that negative force is being routed. Even in China, the Dalai Lama is convinced, the situation is ripe for change. The old men are still in power and determined to go on imposing their hard-line ideology, he agrees:

But outside pressure does make an impact on their policies. For instance, in the matter of human rights, they used not to care at all. But today, whatever the actual violations, they have to convince the outside world that they take note. The Australian parliamentary delegation which recently visited China and Tibet laid stress on the human rights issue. And I'm told that an Italian delegation is on its way. The Chinese are compelled now to receive delegations like these, the main purpose of whose visit is to investigate human rights abuses.[4]

In any case, China is no longer a monolith, and the situation inside that country is very unstable. "It's not just a question of a leadership struggle", suggests Lhasang Tsering:

There are tensions within the Party, tensions between the Party and the army, tensions within the army itself. Tiananmen Square was the real turning-point. After that I met many Chinese students across North America, Europe, Australia. Even those of them who still believe that Tibet is part of China, at least now believe what the Tibetans have long been saying. "If our government can do this to us", they say, "why should we not believe they do even worse to the barbarians?" You know, there were certain sections of the army which did not obey Party orders in June 1989. In a similar situation in the future, would the leadership have the confidence to give those same orders? And if they do, what will happen?

This, together with a conviction that Chinese Communism, like its Soviet counterpart, will eventually disintegrate into economic chaos, ("Like the Manchus and the Nationalists before them, the Communists will have to realize that they can't have Western science and technology without Western liberal thinking"[5] leads many Tibetans to believe that they are going to be given another chance.

Much of the hope lies with the courage and determination of the ordinary Tibetans still trapped inside the Chinese web. There is not one family in Tibet which has remained unscathed,

not even the families of cadres and fellow-travellers. Yet, as the
Dalai Lama points out, the people have an absolutely unshake-
able will to be free. And, one might add, an absolutely unshake-
able faith in the Dalai Lama himself. This, acknowledges
Lhasang Tsering, "is our greatest strength. There are many
freedom movements throughout the world, but none of them has
the advantage of a single leader loved by all the people without
exception".

Their fate is still in the melting-pot, and much suffering may
lie ahead. But the world has begun at last to take notice of Tibet.
Interest, sympathy and support are now widespread. The
people here are convinced now that they will return to Tibet,
and that it will be sooner rather than later. The talk is of
"when" rather than "if". "It seems that now the time is drawing closer", the Dalai Lama tells me. "I have started telling
Tibetans that within five to ten years, everything will have
changed". One can only hope that he is right.

Afterword

In the seven years that have elapsed since this book was first published, the situation inside Tibet has gone from bad to worse. Caught in a fresh tidal wave of repression, the country seems to be battling now for its very existence.

The knell was first sounded in 1994. The Third Forum on Work in Tibet held in Beijing that year determined to root out separatism, (or, as the Chinese call it, "splittism") by undermining once and for all the Dalai Lama's political and religious influence on the Tibetans; and by forcing the outward and visible signs of Tibetan-ism (whether language, ideas, customs or religious beliefs) to adapt themselves to Socialist society or die. Exasperated by more than forty years of failure to win the hearts and minds of the Tibetans, the Chinese had decided at last to go for the jugular.

These policy objectives found expression two years later in the launch of three major campaigns with a distinctly political agenda. The "Spiritual Civilization" (1996), "Strike Hard" (1996) and "Patriotic Education" (1997) campaigns, all of them anti-Dalai Lama and anti-Splittist, have dominated the Tibetan scene with increasing savagery ever since.

Thanks to these three largely overlapping campaigns, the most basic and integral aspects of Tibetan life and culture (religion, the Dalai Lama, the Tibetan language) have come under attack as splittism in another guise, and therefore as a threat to the unity of the Chinese motherland. Increasingly hardline policies designed to counteract this dire threat—the indoctrination imposed by the Patriotic Education Campaign, for example—have been extended to all Tibetan-inhabited areas, even those

outside the Tibetan autonomous Region (TAR), which were
long ago absorbed into China proper. Since November 1997,
indoctrination has proceeded apace and according to plan, "in
agricultural communities, towns, cities, government organs and
schools." Party control has been tightened, even in the villages
and rural areas, most of which are now said to have been
brought into line. Towns are no longer recognizable as Tibetan;
Tibetan buildings having been torn down to make way for endless vistas of ugly concrete. "Sprawling Chinese concrete new
towns," remarked a friend of mine who knows Tibet well and has
recently returned from there, "tannoy systems blaring out propaganda, so much begging, and the very worst aspects of modern urban civilisation. Discos, gambling dens, brothels
everywhere, are insidious ploy by the Chinese to promote deca-
dence and so to wean the Tibetans still further from their traditional way of life. Then, once they have been sucked into a
life-style that is totally dependent on drink and drugs, they are
no longer fit to be employed. They're finished." Resentment at
what is happening is deep and widespread.

"Spiritual Civilization" was the first of the campaigns in Tibet,
launched in May 1996. It targeted monks and nuns and proclaimed its intention of cleansing "the feudal, foolish and backward atmosphere poisoned by the Dalai clique."[1] Buddhism was
declared an alien import, no more native to Tibet than twentieth-century Chinese Communism (it had after all been brought
from India only in the seventh century!!!), and justifiable only
insofar as it may be tailored to serve Socialism. In January 1999 a
propaganda drive to promote atheism was launched; Chinese
cadres with their own brand of choplogic were assuring Tibetans
that "atheism hastens economic development and builds prosperity." They did not need to add that the adoption of atheism
would undoubtedly spell an end to the spiritual and moral leadership of the Dalai Lama.

Attacks on the Dalai Lama, not only on his political stance but
on his religious and personal integrity, have become virulent.
Religious history is being rewritten. In moves that recall the
worst days of the Cultural Revolution, teams of officials are dis-

patched to monasteries and nunneries in even the remotest areas of Amdo and Kham to expunge all references to the Dalai Lama from the Buddhist texts. "They came to the nunnery at night, to check if we were reading any words of His Holiness," wept one young nun shown on film.[2] Not only are books and articles about the Dalai Lama destroyed, photographs and pictures of him torn down, but every monk and nun must now formally condemn and abjure him—and sign a document to that effect. Any who refuse to do so are expelled or arrested or both. "Those who refused were simply dragged away," the same young nun reported. "They were shouting 'Tibet is independent,' and the Chinese stuffed gags in their mouths and beat them." As support for the Dalai Lama is now a criminal offense (in accordance with the 1997 Strike Hard Campaign against splittism), the penalty for refusal announced on posters prominently displayed throughout the monasteries, is a seven-year prison sentence. If no monk or nun will sign, the house is closed down permanently or, as has sometimes happened, destroyed. The Jonang Monastery near Shigatse, for example, has been completely dismantled, its renowned artifacts sold in the bazaar. The Rakhor Nunnery outside Lhasa has been desecrated. It follows that the religious houses of Tibet, places which once teemed with life and resounded with prayer, are ghost towns, inhabited only by those monks or nuns who have renounced all allegiance to the Dalai Lama, and controlled by Communist officials. The spiritual heart is being ripped out of the country.

Knowing the pressure being put on the monks and nuns in Tibet, the Dalai Lama has urged them not to hesitate to denounce him, but it is doubtful whether they will heed his plea. The fact is, although many Tibetans have finally accepted that further struggle is futile and are opting for a life-in-exile beyond the Himalayas, a new mood, part desperation, part determination, is gripping those who remain, particularly those who are incarcerated for their beliefs.

Monks and nuns in prison, subjected to political re-education, exhausting "forced exertion"[3], solitary confinement and extreme torture know they will never be allowed to return to their religious houses and that the survival of religion is, in any case, under terminal threat. Lay prisoners know that even when they are released they will never again be free of surveillance. It seems that this knowledge is driving prisoners to a kind of fatalism in which they take extraordinary risks to show the authorities that their repressive policies have failed, that, even if Tibetan prisoners have to die for it, they will never renege on their beliefs, never be brainwashed into denying them.

Five (maybe more) demonstrations have occurred in Drapchi Number One Prison in Lhasa in the last five years, and the consequences of each have been bloody. Shouts of 'Long Live the Dalai Lama' and 'Free Tibet' at Drapchi in May 1998 were followed by the most severe repression since the imposition of Martial Law in 1989. At least ten prisoners, including six nuns, died following beatings and torture. (Torture, more sophisticated and abhorrent than ever, is now systematic in Tibetan prisons, especially in the case of political prisoners, who are, for the most part, monks and nuns.) The nuns were singled out as ringleaders and given especially severe treatment; on June 7 of this year, five were found dead in their cells. One had hanged herself. The other four, claimed the authorities, had suffocated themselves by stuffing scarves into their mouths. The question arises—if these deaths were indeed suicide, why did they all happen on the same day, a month after the original protest, in different cells, with the girls all in solitary confinement and unable to communicate with each another?

A sixth nun died later. A seventh, Ngawang Sangdrol, went on resisting even after, or out of despair at, the death of her comrades. She is serving an eighteen-year sentence, an original three years in 1992 for taking part in a demonstration, an extra six when she and thirteen other nuns dared to sing and tape-record independence songs in prison, and a final nine in 1996 when she and others protested the Chinese choice of the Panchen Lama. A former prisoner now in exile has told of the petty new disciplinary measures that followed the nuns' protest. "Under the pretext that beds had not been properly made, they beat the women severely," he reported, adding that police armed with bamboo sticks and belts were sent into the cells to check the beds, and that Ngawang Sangdrol was among those singled out for kicking and beatings. More than eighty female political prisoners went on hunger strike for four days in protest at the severity of the punishments. Today no one knows whether Ngawang Sangdrol is alive or dead. The latest reports tell of prison guards beating her and stamping on her head.

The outlook for any Tibetan who expresses a political view contrary to the one demanded by the state is incomparably worse now than it was five years ago. It is true that political prisoners are no longer being executed by court edict—equally true, however, that they are being killed by or as a result of serious abuse in prison. A female Tibetan prisoner has a one in twenty chance of dying in prison or shortly after release, a male, one in forty. The Chinese have eliminated the term "counter-revolution" from the criminal statute books, replacing it by the offenses of "endangering state security," "subversion," and "attempts to overthrow the state," which foreign governments are more likely to understand and sympathise with and therefore less likely to challenge. But what the foreign governments perhaps do not realise (or do not care to think too closely about) is that a Tibetan caught singing or playing a cassette of national songs, reading a book about or by the Dalai Lama, putting up his picture, or writing a leaflet in praise of freedom whether civil or political, is "endangering national security." A tortured monk or nun enduring long solitary confinement in prison shouts an independence slogan and has his or her sentence prolonged by a number of years for "attempting to overthrow the state." It's a question of semantics. China, denying torture, denying in fact that there are any political prisoners, since political offenses are *ipso facto* criminal, has skillfully managed to prevent information about political imprisonments from reaching the outside world. She is adept, too, at dissuading foreign governments from linking economic concerns to political issues. When President Clinton decided to restore Most Favored Nation trading status to China in 1994, after removing it a year earlier because of that country's appalling human rights record, it was a kick in the teeth for the Tibetans. Police in Lhassa began taunting them: "If America dares not oppose us, how can you?"

It is hard to credit that in 1980 China signed an *International Convention on the Elimination of All Forms of Discrimination Against Women* and in 1988 ratified a *Global Convention Against Torture and Other Cruel, Inhuman or Degrading Treatment or Punishment.* In its most recent (1988) reports on the implementation of these conventions, China claims to have abided by these agreements, yet makes no reference to the issue of torture.

The continuing attack on Tibetan women's reproductive rights possesses a horror all its own. Recently (early 1999), a report was produced in the United States entitled *Violence and Discrimination Against Tibetan Women.*[4] It points out that whatever the excuse for birth control in China proper, Tibet never had, and still does not have, a population problem. Its territory is vast, its populations sparse, and policies aimed at making it sparser still cannot be justified.

The number of children that Tibetan women are permitted to bear varies from district to district. In Phenpo County, for example, woman are allowed two children, and may not marry until they are age 25, though in other areas they may do so at 22. In some parts of Amdo, government workers are allowed two children, nomads and farmers three, while elsewhere a one-child policy is rigorously enforced. Women are threatened with losing their jobs or homes if they have an extra child, and face a crippling fine, far beyond their ability to pay. If they go ahead and give birth anyway, no ration cards or identity papers will be made available for the child who will be a nonperson, barred from both schooling and health care.

A three-year gap between pregnancies is insisted upon, and many women reported regular pregnancy checks, weekly or monthly vaginal examinations in their own homes or at compulsory public meetings held specifically for this purpose. Sterilisation teams police the country and bring women by the truckload for treatment. An official document issued in Amdo in 1991 complained of Tibetan women's "stubborn adherence to old customs and traditions," their "resistance to birth prevention operations," and stated that when a new birth-control program was introduced in the following year "no excuses or pretexts [would] be entertained as any reason for staying or postponing the operations any further." In one village where a woman had given birth to three children, the team sterilized her still-childless sister. One village reported nine women being trucked away to a nearby town for sterilisation—one of them being pregnant at the time. In Nyemeo a male witness saw thousands of women literally dragged to the sterilisation center in the summer of 1996. About 300 were sterilized that day, including, he said, women with three-month old fetuses. "They were bleeding like animals, and many of them were too weak to even move." Afterwards, he said, they were made to pay for the operation.

Abortion is being forced on Tibetan women who regard the taking of all sentient life as a sin. A thirty-seven-year-old Khampa woman witnessed nomad women being rounded up for abortions, two hundred at a time. There is evidence of a similar roundup in Amdo in 1997, when 113 forced abortions were performed in one district alone. A nun from a village not far from Lhasa claims that most women in the village had been forced to abort their children. (Leaving the CEDAW Report for a moment, I recall a harrowing scene in that BBC TV film referred to above. A woman crying "They come and drag us from our homes, they throw stones at our husbands, they terrorize our children." This woman, who was ordered to hospital for abortion and sterilisation, said "The woman in the next bed to me was eight months pregnant, but they killed the baby and threw it to the dogs.")

Several women reported late-term fetuses being killed in the womb before being extracted from it. One woman wept as she told how she witnessed the late-term abortion of a friend. "They injected a needle where the baby's head was. She was in labor for one hour. The baby was born and it cried. Then it started bleeding from the nose and died." Another was present at an abortion performed on a woman six-months pregnant: "They injected a needle into her stomach, and she gave birth. The baby was delivered and put into a bowl. It moved for a few minutes, then died. It had a hole in its head."

The CEDAW report concluded that not only was there widespread abuse of women's reproductive rights in Tibet but also that the measures taken by the Chinese to limit Tibetan births break the international law on genocide, there being no possible justification for limiting the size of the Tibetan population while at the same time urging thousands of Han Chinese entrepreneurs to go and settle in Tibet. (Han Chinese outnumber Tibetans in Lhasa now, and they take all the best jobs.) The present birth-control clampdown must be seen in the context of fifty years of attempted sinicisation in Tibet and of the present determined effort to stamp out all remaining Tibetan-ness. As such, it is indeed genocidal.

Is the end game now really being played out? Formal discussions between the Dalai Lama and the Chinese came to an end in August 1993, but until quite recently a few informal channels remained open. The Dalai Lama remained optimistic, always talking of 'when' rather than 'if' the Tibetan exiles would return to their country. When President Clinton visited Beijing in June 1998, his talks with his Chinese counterpart, Jiang Zemin, seemed to hint at the possibility of renewed dialogue, and His Holiness signaled his willingness to start talking again.

Since the late autumn of 1998, however, the Chinese position has hardened again, their attitude toward the Dalai Lama settling into one of unremitting hostility. It is as though, maddened by the Tibetan refusal to come to heel and consider themselves part of the Chinese Motherland, infuriated by their refusal to accept the Chinese choice of Panchen Lama, and by their continuing stubborn loyalty to their exiled leader, the Chinese have now declared open season on all things Tibetan.

In Lhasa, as the fortieth anniversary (March 1999) of the Tibetan Uprising approached, the hundreds of armed police on the streets, the antiriot armoured cars, the high-pressure water-cannon bore witness to the three essential factors in this continuing sad saga of Tibet: the very real Tibetan resentment and despair, the Chinese terror that the resentment will spill out onto the streets again, and their determination—at whatever cost—to make sure that it does not.

Afterword Endnotes

[1] *Hostile Elements: A Study of Political Imprisonment in Tibet 1987–1988*, Steven D. Marshall, Tibet Information Network (TIN), London 1999. I am indebted to this up-to-the-minute document for much of the information in this Introduction. Also to two companion TIN publications, *Background Briefings from Tibet, 1998*, London 1999. These and any information required are available from TIN USA PO Box 2770 Jackson, WY 83001, USA. Telephone: 307-733-4670. Fax 307-739-250. Email: tinusa@ wyoming.com.

[2] Film made by Sue Lloyd Roberts shown on BBC 2 TV.

[3] TIN (see above) reports the prevalence now, for both men and women prisoners, of "a martial routine in which People's Armed Police guards compel prisoners to perform two three-hour sessions of drills daily."

[4] Presented to the Committee on the Elimination of Discrimination Against Women (CEDAW) by three official groups, the International Committee of Lawyers for Tibet, the Women's Commission for Refugee Women and Children, and the Tibetan Centre for Human Rights and Democracy. It has also been endorsed by the National Association of Women Lawyers in America.

Notes

Prologue
1 *Asia Watch*, an American human rights group report, February 1990.
2 Speaking in Tokyo, 1982.
3 16.3.91.
4 ABC TV film, *Lost Horizons*, July 1991.
5 House of Lords debate on Tibet, 13.12.89.

Chapter 1
1 Roger Hicks, *Hidden Tibet: The Land and Its People* (Element Books), p. 31.
2 Heinrich Harrer, *Seven Years in Tibet* (Paladin/Grafton Books 1988), p. 143.
3 Michael Harris Goodman, *The Last Dalai Lama* (Shambhala, Boston and London 1984), p. 23.
4 Harrer, p. 168.
5 Chris Mullin and Phuntsog Wangyal, *The Tibetans: Two Perspectives on Tibet–Chinese Relations* (Report No. 49, Minority Rights Group Publication, 1983), p. 6.
6 Lama Anagarika Govinda, *The Way of the White Clouds: A Buddhist Pilgrim in Tibet* (Rider Publication 1966).
7 Mullin and Wangyal, p. 16.
8 Harris Goodman, p. 27.
9 Author interview 1989.
10 Author interview, Dharamsala, 1989.
11 Author interview, Dharamsala, 1989.
12 Author interview, Dharamsala, September 1989.
13 Hugh E. Richardson, *Tibet and Its History* (Shambhala 1984), p. 12.
14 John Avedon, article in *From Liberation to Liberalisation: Views on "Liberalised" Tibet* (Dharamsala 1982).
15 Tsepon W. D. Shakabpa, *Tibet: A Political History* (Potala Press), p. 204.
16 Shakabpa, *op. cit.*, p. 219.
17 See Peter Hopkirk's *The Great Game: On Secret Service in High Asia* (Oxford University Press 1991).
18 For a full account, see Edmund Candler, *The Unveiling of Lhasa 1905* and Peter Hopkirk, *Trespassers on the Roof of the World* (Oxford University Press 1982), Ch. 10.

19 Shakabpa, p. 230.
20 K. Dhondup, *The Water-bird and Other Years* (Rangwang, New Delhi), p. 1.
21 *My Land and My People: Memoirs of the Dalai Lama* (Potala Press 1962), p. 79.
22 Richardson, p. 188.

Chapter 2

1 According to Shakabpa, in 1922, the British Government asked permission to build a road from India to Gyantse, to facilitate trading. A temporary road was built, three cars were put into use and made the trip twice. But the local people who earned a livelihood providing animals for transport objected and the project was abandoned.
2 *My Land and My People*, p. 85.
3 Author interview, Dharamsala, September 1989.
4 Richardson, p. 33.
5 Vijay Kranti, *Dalai Lama: the Nobel Peace Laureate Speaks* (Centrasia Publishing Group, New Delhi 1990), p. 126.
6 Harris Goodman, pp. 146–7.
7 Hopkirk, Ch. 15.
8 John F. Avedon, *In Exile from the Land of Snows* (Michael Joseph 1984).
9 Harrer, p. 239.
10 Harrer, p. 240.

Chapter 3

1 Author interview, Dharamsala, September 1989.
2 Author interview, Dharamsala, September 1989.
3 Harris Goodman, p. 156.
4 Author interview, Dharamsala, September 1989.
5 Avedon, p. 32.
6 Harris Goodman, p. 160.
7 *My Land and My People*, p. 83.
8 Harrer, p. 277.
9 Author interview, Dharamsala, May 1990.
10 *My Land and My People*, p. 88.
11 Alexandra David-Neel, *My Journey to Lhasa* (Virago/Travellers).
12 *Buddhism under Mao*, Holmes Welch, 1972, pp. 18–25.
13 Author interview, Dharamsala, May 1990.
14 *Freedom in Exile*, p. 80.
15 Quoted in Harris Goodman, pp. 189–90.
16 *Freedom in Exile*, p. 86.

Chapter 4

1 Author interview, Dharamsala, September 1989.
2 Author interview, London, 1989.
3 Author interview, London, 1989.
4 Jamyang Norbu, *Horseman in the Snow: The Story of Aten, an Old Khampa Warrior* (Dharamsala), p. 70.
5 Jamyang Norbu.
6 From eyewitness accounts supplied by Tibetan refugees in India to the Legal Inquiry Committee on Tibet of the International Commission of Jurists, and quoted by Michael Harris Goodman in *The Last Dalai Lama*, ch. 16. The committee found that acts of genocide had been committed by the Chinese occupation forces "in an attempt to destroy the Tibetans as a religious group".
7 Author interview, Dharamsala, September 1989.
8 Christoph von Fürer-Haimendorf, *The Renaissance of Tibetan Civilization* (Oxford India Paperbacks), p. 92.
9 Jamyang Norbu.
10 Harris Goodman, p. 197.
11 Harris Goodman.
12 Interview with author, 1989.
13 Harrer, p. 169.
14 Author interview, Dharamsala, September 1989.
15 Mullin and Wangyal, p. 16.
16 *Tibet under Chinese Communist Rule: A Compilation of Refugee Statements, 1958–1975*, Information Office, Dharamsala.
17 Avedon, p. 44.
18 Jamyang Norbu, p. 76.
19 Author interview, Dharamsala, May 1990.
20 Harris Goodman, p. 255.
21 Vanya Kewley, *Tibet: Behind the Ice Curtain* (Collins/Grafton 1990), pp. 270–1.
22 Avedon, p. 47.
23 Avedon, pp. 44–5.
24 Jamyang Norbu, p. 91.
25 Harris Goodman, p. 232.
26 Vanya Kewley, p. 91.
27 See Nien Cheng's moving and horrifying autobiography, *Life and Death in Shanghai* (Collins/Grafton 1986).
28 Fredrick Hyde-Chambers, *Lama, A Novel of Tibet* (Souvenir Press 1984).
29 Author interview, Dharamsala, September 1989.
30 Jamyang Norbu, p. 122.
31 Jamyang Norbu, pp. 102–3.

Chapter 5

1 Author interview, Dharamsala, May 1990.
2 Author interview, Dharamsala, September 1989.
3 *My Land and My People*, pp. 117–8.
4 Author interview, Dharamsala, May 1990.
5 Harris Goodman, p. 218.
6 Dawa Norbu, *Red Star over Tibet* (Envoy Press, New York 1987), p. 132.
7 Dhondup, p. 136.
8 *My Land and My People*, p. 137.
9 Avedon, pp. 227–8.
10 *My Land and My People*, p. 129.
11 Author interview, Dharamsala, May 1990.
12 Author interview, Dharamsala, May 1990.
13 *My Land and My People*, pp. 147–8.
14 Gompo Tashi Andrugtsang, *Four Rivers, Six Ranges: A True Account of Khampa Resistance to the Chinese in Tibet* (Dharamsala 1973), pp. 42–3.
15 Harris Goodman, p. 263.
16 John Prados, *The President's Secret Wars CIA and Pentagon Covert Operations from World War II through Iranscam* Quill/William Morrow, p. 149–170.
17 Avedon, p. 48.
18 *Freedom in Exile*, p. 136.
19 *My Land and My People*, p. 137.

Chapter 6

1 Author interview, Dharamsala, September 1989.
2 Author interview, Dharamsala, September 1989.
3 Testimony before the March 1989 Bonn Tribunal on Human Rights; and author interview, Dharamsala, September 1989.
4 Victor Gollancz 1990.
5 International Commission of Jurists report, July 1960.
6 Harris Goodman, p. 234.
7 Jamyang Norbu, p. 122.
8 Author interview, London, 1989.
9 Author interview, Dharamsala, September 1989.
10 Jamyang Norbu, p. 128.
11 Andrugtsang.
12 *My Land and My People*, p. 162.
13 *My Land and My People*, p. 160.
14 *My Land and My People*, p. 163.

Chapter 7

1 Author interview, Dharamsala, September 1989.

2   *My Land and My People*, p. 173.
3   Author interview, Dharamsala, May 1990.
4   Author interview, Dharamsala, September 1989.
5   Author interview, Dharamsala, September 1989.
6   Author interview, London, June 1991.
7   Author interview, London, June 1991.
8   Author interview, Dharamsala, September 1989.
9   *My Land and My People*, pp. 198–9.
10 *Freedom in Exile.*
11 *My Land and My People*, pp. 198–9.
12 Author interview, London, June 1991.
13 *Freedom in Exile*, p. 152.
14 *Freedom in Exile*, p. 152.
15 *Freedom in Exile*, p. 154.
16 *Freedom in Exile*, p. 154.
17 *My Land and My People*, p. 207.
18 Dawa Norbu, p. 154.
19 Author interview, Dharamsala, May 1990.
20 *Tibet under Chinese Communist Rule*, p. 33.
21 *Freedom in Exile*, p. 156.

Chapter 8

1   Author interview, Dharamsala, September 1989.
2   Author interview, Dharamsala, September 1989.
3   Author interview, Dharamsala, May 1990.
4   *Tibet under Chinese Communist Rule*, p. 34.
5   Tsering Dorje Gashi, *New Tibet* (Information Office, Dharamsala 1977).
6   Catriona Bass, *Inside the Treasure House* (Victor Gollancz 1990), p. 200.
7   Bass, p. 200.
8   Avedon, p. 226.
9   Avedon, p. 228.
10 Avedon, p. 230.
11 *Tibet under Chinese Communist Rule.*
12 Gashi.
13 Vanya Kewley, p. 121.
14 "Tibet's Top Physician describes Chinese Prison Conditions" in *Tibetan Review*, March 1981, pp. 4–5, quoted by Phuntsog Wangyal in *The Tibetans.*
15 Dawa Norbu, p. 219.
16 Author interview, Dharamsala, May 1990.
17 *Tibet under Chinese Communist Rule.*
18 Dawa Norbu, p. 222.

19 Mullin and Wangyal.
20 *Tibet under Chinese Communist Rule*, p. 87.
21 Hugh E. Richardson, p. 213.
22 From the private correspondence of Llewellyn Wyn Griffith, 5.1.1948.
23 Dawa Norbu, p. 167. Buddhists express allegiance to "the Three Jewels": the Buddha (the Enlightened One), the Dharma (his teachings) and the Sangha (the community of Buddhists, especially the monks).
24 Gashi, p. 80.
25 Avedon.
26 *Tibet under Chinese Communist Rule*.
27 Paul Theroux, *Riding the Iron Rooster* (Penguin 1989).
28 Avedon, p. 237.
29 Dondub Chodon, *Life in the Red Flag People's Commune* (Dharamsala 1978), p. iv.
30 Dawa Norbu.
31 Gashi.
32 Dawa Norbu, p. 185.
33 Author interview, Dharamsala, September 1989.
34 Author interview, Dharamsala, September 1989.
35 Dawa Norbu, p. 206.
36 *Tibet under Chinese Communist Rule*.
37 Dawa Norbu, p. 206.
38 Author interview with Pema Saldon, Dharamsala, May 1990.
39 Kewley, pp. 250–1.
40 *Tibet Society and Relief Fund Journal*, Winter 1983/4.
41 *Tibet under Chinese Communist Rule*.

Chapter 9

1   Dawa Norbu, p. 148.
2   *My Land and My People*, p. 219.
3   Author interview, Dharamsala, May 1990.
4   *Freedom in Exile*, p. 166.
5   Mullin and Wangyal, p. 21.
6   From the report of the International Commission of Jurists 1959.
7   Dawa Norbu, p. 155.
8   Author interview, London, 1989.
9   Avedon, p. 72.
10 Author interview, Dharamsala, May 1990.
11 Author interview, London, 1989.
12 *Freedom in Exile*, pp. 173–4.
13 Avedon, p. 82.
14 Avedon, p. 84.
15 Avedon, p. 88.

16 Avedon, p. 88.
17 Harris Goodman, p. 324.
18 *My Land and My People*, p. 227.
19 *My Land and My People*, pp. 232–3.
20 Dawa Norbu, p. 243.

Chapter 10
1 Dawa Norbu, p. 158.
2 For information on this subject, see Avedon, pp. 118–25.
3 Avedon, p. 267.
4 Avedon, pp. 270–1.
5 See *The President's Secret War*.
6 Kewley, p. 123.
7 Avedon, p. 249.

Chapter 11
1 Avedon, p. 271.
2 Author interview, Dharamsala, September 1989.
3 From "The Panchen Lama, 'A True Tibetan'" in *Tibetan Review*, August/September 1969, p. 11.
4 Avedon, p. 274.
5 *Tibet under Chinese Communist Rule*.
6 Author interview, Dharamsala, September 1989.
7 Avedon, p. 275.
8 Dhondup, p. 140.
9 *Peking Review*, Vol. VIII, no. 37, 10.9.1965.
10 Bass, p. 117.
11 Quoted in Avedon, p. 277.

Chapter 12
1 "Hell – and Hope – in Shangri-La" in *From Liberation to Liberalisation*, p. 184.
2 Inaugural Declaration of the Lhasa Revolutionary Rebel General Headquarters, 22.12.66.
3 Gashi, pp. 24–5.
4 Chodon.
5 Wangdu Dorje in *Tibet under Chinese Communist Rule*, p. 110.
6 Chodon, p. 64.
7 Chodon, p. 64.
8 *Freedom in Exile*, p. 260.
9 *Tibet under Chinese Communist Rule*.
10 Author interview, Dharamsala, September 1989.
11 Bass, p. 142.

12 Kunga Thinle in *Tibet under Chinese Communist Rule*.
13 *Tibet under Chinese Communist Rule*.
14 Author interview, Dharamsala, May 1990.
15 Chodon.
16 Author interview, Dharamsala, May 1990.
17 "Why Pictures of the Dalai Lama are Back on the Parlour Wall" by Alan Hamilton, in *From Liberation to Liberalisation*, p. 170.
18 Chodon.
19 Chodon.
20 Pema Lhundup in *Tibet under Chinese Communist Rule*.
21 Gashi, pp. 128–9.
22 Avedon, p. 289.
23 Author interview, Dharamsala, May 1990.
24 Author interview, Dharamsala, September 1989.
25 Author interview, Dharamsala, September 1989.
26 "Hell – and Hope – in Shangri-La", by Harrison Salisbury in *From Liberation to Liberalisation*, p. 185.
27 Avedon, p. 290.
28 Avedon, pp. 290–1.
29 Sanlang Tungchou, "Emancipated Serfs will Never Tolerate Restoration" in *Beijing Review*, 19.7.74, p. 11.
30 *Tibet under Chinese Communist Rule*.
31 Author interview, Dharamsala September, 1989.
32 Chodon.
33 *Freedom in Exile*, p. 199.
34 Author interview, Dharamsala, May 1990.
35 Gashi.
36 Gashi.

Chapter 13
1 Testimony given to Human Rights Tribunal in Bonn, April 1989. Also in conversation with author, September 1989, in Dharamsala.
2 Avedon, pp. 316–18.
3 Avedon, p. 301.
4 Avedon, p. 301.
5 Author interview, Dharamsala, September 1989.
6 Author interview, Dharamsala, September 1989.
7 Author interview, Dharamsala, May 1990.
8 Author interview, Dharamsala, September 1991.
9 Avedon, p. 302.
10 Avedon, p. 303.
11 Author interview, Dharamsala, May 1990.

12 Kewley, p. 124.
13 Author interview, Dharamsala, September 1989.
14 S. Bhushan, *China: The Myth of a Superpower* (Progressive People's Sector Publications, New Delhi 1976). Quoted by Phuntsog Wangyal in *The Tibetans*.
15 22.11.72.
16 Author interview, Dharamsala, September 1989.
17 Avedon, p. 313.
18 Mullin and Wangyal, p. 10.
19 *The Quest for Universal Responsibility: Human Rights Violations in Tibet*, Howard C. Sachs 1983, pp. 20–1.
20 Chodon.
21 *Tibet under Chinese Communist Rule*, p. 155.
22 Author interview, Dharamsala, September 1989.
23 Author interview, Dharamsala, September 1989.

Interlude

1 Author interview, Dharamsala, September 1991.
2 Author interview, Dharamsala, September 1991.
3 "Opening of the Political Eye: Tibet's Long Search for Democracy" by Jamyang Norbu, *Tibetan Review*, November 1990.
4 Author interview, London, 1989.
5 Author interview, Dharamsala, September 1989.
6 Avedon, p. 127.

Chapter 14

1 Avedon, p. 327.
2 *Freedom in Exile*, p. 248.
3 Avedon, p. 328.
4 Avedon, p. 329.
5 Author interview, Dharamsala, September 1989.
6 Author interview, Dharamsala, September 1989.
7 Testimony to Bonn Tribunal of Human Rights, 1989, and author interview.
8 Author interview, Dharamsala, September 1989.
9 Author interview, Dharamsala, September 1989.
10 *Freedom in Exile*, p. 254.
11 Author interview, Dharamsala, September 1991.
12 Heinrich Harrer, *Return to Tibet* (Weidenfeld & Nicolson 1984), p. 47.
13 Avedon, p. 333.
14 Avedon, p. 419.
15 Avedon, p. 337.

16 "Letter from Tibet" by A. E. George in *From Liberation to Liberalisation*, p. 177.
17 *Freedom in Exile*, p. 255.
18 Author interview, London, 1989.
19 *Freedom in Exile*, p. 256.
20 Author interview, London, June 1991.
21 Avedon, p. 337.
22 W. P. Ledger, *The Chinese and Human Rights in Tibet*, a report to the Parliamentary Human Rights Group 1988.
23 Author interview, Dharamsala, September 1991.
24 *Freedom in Exile*, p. 263.
25 Avedon, p. 344.
26 Author interview, Dharamsala, September 1991.
27 *From Liberation to Liberalisation*, p. 133.
28 Author interview, London, 1989.
29 Author interview, London, June 1989.
30 *From Liberation to Liberalisation*, p. 96. Also Mullin and Wangyal, p. 18.
31 Author interview, London, June 1989.
32 Author interview, London, June 1989.
33 Harrer, p. 48.
34 *From Liberation to Liberalisation*, p. 113.
35 Mullin and Wangyal, p. 18.
36 *Freedom in Exile*, p. 263.
37 John Avedon, *Tibet Today* (Wisdom Publications 1987).
38 Avedon.

Chapter 15

1 Mullin and Wangyal, p. 21.
2 *The Times*, 27.7.83.
3 Author interview, Dharamsala, September 1991.
4 Bass, pp. 80–1.
5 Author interview, Dharamsala, May 1990.
6 Author interview, Dharamsala, May 1990.
7 *Forbidden Freedoms: Beijing's Control of Religion in Tibet*, a report by the International Campaign for Tibet (Washington DC, September 1990), p. 14.
8 Author interview, London, May 1991.
9 His Holiness the Dalai Lama, *Five Point Peace Plan for Tibet*.
10 *Freedom in Exile*, p. 167.
11 Nick Danziger, *Danziger's Travels: Beyond Forbidden Frontiers* (Paladin/Grafton Books 1987).
12 Avedon.

13 "The Report from Tibet" by Phuntsog Wangyal in, *From Liberation to Liberalisation*, pp. 143–5.
14 "Trouble in Shangri-La" by Tory Stempf in, *From Liberation to Liberalisation*, p. 68.
15 W. P. Ledger.
16 *Forbidden Freedoms*, p. 43.
17 Vikram Seth, *From Heaven Lake: Travels through Sinkiang and Tibet* (Abacus 1983).
18 Harrer.
19 *Population Transfer and the Survival of the Tibetan Identity*, Michael C. van Walt van Praag, for the US Tibet Committee (New York, 1986).
20 "Tibetans Struggle for Identity", 9.9.81.
21 Michael Weisskopf in *International Herald Tribune*, 15.8.83.
22 15.8.83.
23 Newsletter of Tibet Society and Relief Fund of the UK, Winter 1983–84.
24 *Tibetan Review*, January 1985.
25 *Tibet: The Facts*, a report by the Scientific Buddhist Association, London 1984, p. 29.
26 Kewley, p. 253.
27 van Walt van Praag, p. 18.
28 Author interview, Dharamsala, September 1991.
29 van Walt van Praag, pp. 13–14.
30 van Walt van Praag, p. 20.
31 Avedon.
32 Author interview, Dharamsala, September 1991.
33 Author interview, Bir School, May 1990.
34 Author interview, Dharamsala, September 1989.

Chapter 16

1 Author interview, Dharamsala, September 1989.
2 Vijay Kranti, *Dalai Lama: The Nobel Peace Laureate Speaks* (Centrasia Publishing Group, New Delhi 1990).
3 Author interview, Dharamsala, September 1989.
4 Bass, pp. 116–17.
5 Richard Bassett in *The Spectator*, 14.9.85.
6 *Forcible Birth Control Policy in Communist Chinese-Controlled Tibet from 1983*, a testimony given in Chinese by Tenzin, aged twenty-five, native of Drukchu, on 27.5.91. Held by the Office of Information and International Relations, Dharamsala.
7 Bass, p. 133.
8 Author interview, Dharamsala, September 1991.
9 Bass.

10 Bass, pp. 135–6.
11 Danziger.
12 Bass, p. 71.
13 *Defying the Dragon: China and Human Rights in Tibet*, a report issued jointly by The Law Association for Asia and the Pacific Human Rights Standing Committee and the Tibet Information Network, March 1991, pp. 40–1.
14 Radio Lhasa, 10.3.88.

Chapter 17

1   Avedon.
2   *Freedom in Exile*, pp. 175–6.
3   *Freedom in Exile*, p. 277.
4   *Freedom in Exile*, p. 277.
5   *Freedom in Exile*, p. 178.
6   Author interview, Dharamsala, September 1989.
7   *Freedom in Exile*, p. 281.
8   This account of 1.10.87 is taken from *Defying the Dragon*, and is based on interviews with Western and Tibetan eyewitnesses; one sworn and seven unsworn Western eyewitnesses (which were referred to in submissions made to the forty-fourth session of the United Nations Human Rights Commission, Geneva, February 1988); a pooled account written on 2.10.87 on behalf of forty-five Western eyewitnesses and an eleven-page telex written in Kathmandu in November 1987 by two of the Western eyewitnesses.
9   From *Defying the Dragon*.
10 Two years later, under the auspices of the American Physicians for Human Rights, they published a document entitled: *The Suppression of a People: Accounts of Torture and Imprisonment in Tibet* (November 1989).
11 *Defying the Dragon*.
12 Author interview with Sonam Tseten, September 1989 in Dharamsala.
13 Author interview, Dharamsala, September 1989.
14 *Defying the Dragon*, p. 23.
15 *Asian Wall Street Journal*, 14.4.88.
16 Author interview, Dharamsala, September 1989.
17 Author interview, Dharamsala, May 1990.
18 Author interview, Dharamsala, May 1990.
19 Author interview, Dharamsala, May 1990.
20 Author interview, Dharamsala, September 1991.
21 Author interview, Dharamsala, September 1989.
22 *Defying the Dragon*, p. 24.

Chapter 18

1 Steve Myhill of the British Museum, writing in *The Voice of Tibet*, London, Summer 1988.
2 Quoted in *Freedom in Exile*, p. 282.
3 *Freedom in Exile*, p. 283.
4 *Defying the Dragon*, p. 25.
5 "A Lost Horizon" by Robert Delfs in *Far Eastern Economic Review*, 17.3.88.
6 *Tibet in China: An International Alert Report* (August 1988), Document 4.
7 The *Observer*, 8.5.88.
8 *Asian Wall Street Journal*, 14.4.88.
9 *Freedom in Exile*, p. 283.
10 Unattributable source. Testimony held at the Information Office in Dharamsala.
11 Avedon, p. 32.
12 *Defying the Dragon*, p. 17.
13 *Defying the Dragon*, p. 43.
14 Author interview, Dharamsala, May 1990.
15 *Defying the Dragon*, pp. 17–18.
16 *Defying the Dragon*, pp. 17–18.
17 Kewley, p. 114.
18 Author interview, Dharamsala, May 1990.
19 John Ackerly and Blake Kerr M.D., *The Suppression of a People: Accounts of Torture and Imprisonment in Tibet* (Physicians for Human Rights, November 1989), p. 37.
20 Ackerly and Kerr.
21 Ackerly and Kerr.
22 *Tibet in China*, p. 36.
23 "Forbidden Tibet Looks Outward" by William McGurn in *Asian Wall Street Journal*, 14.4.88.
24 Ackerly and Kerr.
25 *Tibetan Review*, December 1988.
26 Theroux, p. 481.
27 Theroux, p. 485.
28 Information sheet no. 4 1989, Office of Information and International Relations, Dharamsala.
29 *Tibetan Review*, Vol. XXIII no. 12, December 1988.
30 *Defying the Dragon*, p. 26.
31 *Tibetan Review*, January 1989.
32 The *Irish Times*, 9.3.89.
33 Author interview with the Dalai Lama at Thekchen Choeling, Dharamsala, September 1989.

Chapter 19

1 Michael Fathers and Andrew Higgins, *Tiananmen: The Rape of Peking* (*The Independent* in association with Doubleday, 1989).

2 *The Meaning of the Precious Democratic Constitution of Tibet*, written and produced by a group of Drepung monks. See *Defying the Dragon*, Appendix C, p. 115.

3 *Defying the Dragon*, p. 27.

4 *Time*, 20.3.89.

5 *Defying the Dragon*, p. 27, quoting Shi Ming, "Lhasa: From Riots to Martial Law", *Beijing Review*, 27.3.89–2.4.89.

6 Author interview, Dharamsala, May 1990.

7 *Freedom in Exile*, p. 287.

8 *Irish Times* editorial, 9.3.89.

9 *Present Conditions in Tibet* (Dharamsala 1990), p. 10.

10 From text of State Council order imposing martial law, and *Defying the Dragon*, p. 29.

11 *Freedom in Exile*, p. 288.

12 *Time*, 20.3.1989.

13 *Irish Times*, 9.3.89.

14 *Irish Times*, 9.3.89.

15 *Irish Times*, 10.3.89.

16 "Hit Hard at the Small Number of Separatists" in *Tibet Daily*, 13.3.89. Quoted in *Defying the Dragon*, p. 5.

17 "Hold Aloft the Banner of National Unity and Advance on the Crest of Victory" in *Tibet Daily*, 4.9.90, as read out on Tibet TV 4.9.90. See *Defying the Dragon*, p. 6.

18 *Present Conditions in Tibet*.

19 *Defying the Dragon*, p. 37.

20 The following account is taken from *Defying the Dragon*, pp. 48–9.

21 Author interview, Dharamsala, May 1990.

22 Fathers and Higgins, p. 11.

23 *Freedom in Exile*, p. 289.

24 "Rule by Kalashnikov" by Arthur Kent in *The Observer*, 23.7.89.

25 Fathers and Higgins, p. 11.

26 T.I.N. Summary, 25.5.90, p. 5.

27 Arthur Kent in *The Observer*, 23.7.89.

28 T.I.N. Summary, 25.5.90, pp. 4–5.

29 Author interview, Dharamsala, September 1991.

30 Author interview, Dharamsala, September 1989. It was no secret that a Tibetan force of 10,000 men formed part of the Indian Army stationed near Dehra Dun. The Indians, however, were unwilling to accept new arrivals for fear of their being spies sent by the Chinese.

31 Author interview, 11.9.89, the day the Youth Congress opened in Dharamsala.
32 Author interview, September 1989.
33 Author interview, May 1990 in Dharamsala.
34 Quoted by Alex Shoumatoff in *"Letter from Lhasa: The Silent Killing of Tibet"*, in *Vanity Fair*, May 1991.
35 "China scorns Nobel peace award to the Dalai Lama" in *The Times*, 6.10.89.
36 *Freedom in Exile*, p. 290.
37 *Defying the Dragon*, p. 30.
38 *Tibetan Review*, November 1989.
39 *Defying the Dragon*, p. 11.
40 *Tibet Support Group UK Newsletter*, March 1991.
41 Author interview, Dharamsala, May 1990.
42 *Tibet Support Group UK Newsletter*, March 1991.
43 *Defying the Dragon*, p. 17.
44 Nobel Lecture, University Aula, Oslo, 11.12.89.
45 *The Times*, 6.12.89.
46 *Freedom in Exile*, p.290.
47 Reuter report, quoted in *The Daily Telegraph*, 7.12.89.
48 Stephen Vines in Hong Kong. Article in *Guardian*.

Chapter 20

1 Interview reported in T.I.N. Summary, 25.5.90, p. 2.
2 It took her fifteen days to reach Nepal, nine of them spent walking non-stop night and day, frequently over high passes, without food, shelter or a change of clothing. It was, she said, "the hardest thing I have ever done".
3 *Defying the Dragon*, p. 93.
4 *Defying the Dragon*, p. 20.
5 T.I.N. News Update, 30.5.90. "An already extensive network of inform-ers is said by escapees to have been set up by the security forces in Lhasa during the thirteen months of martial law. Informers, often people whose relatives are still in prison, are paid cash sums – said to average about 400 yuan (60 US dollars), equivalent to about three months salary – for denouncing political suspects. Boxes have been installed in schools, colleges and public places for written denunciations to be posted."
6 *The Star*, Penang, 25.8.89, quoting Kyodo News Agency, Shanghai. See *Defying the Dragon*, p. 91.
7 "The Systematic Annihilation of the Tibetan Race and Civilization by the People's Republic of China, by Pema Dechen, Vice President,

Tibetan Women's Organization, in *Dolma: The Voice of Tibetan Women*, Summer 1991.

8   W. P. Ledger, p. 25.
9   Author interview, Dharamsala, September 1991.
10 Pema Dechen, "The Systematic Annihilation" etc.
11 Kewley, pp. 105–6.
12 Author interview, Dharamsala, September 1991.
13 "China's Own Kuwait" by Robert Barnett in *The Spectator*, 16.3.91.
14 T.I.N. News Update, 30.5.90.
15 T.I.N. News Update, 30.5.90, p. 4.
16 Alex Shoumatoff in *Vanity Fair*, May 1991.
17 *Independent Magazine*, 27.10.90.
18 T.I.N. News Update, 3.3.91.
19 Tibet Support Group Newsletter March 1991; and T.I.N. News Update, 3–22 March 1991.
20 *Tibetan Bulletin*, September/October 1991.
21 T.I.N. News Update, 21.3.91. Also "Shoulder for a Nation to Cry on" by George Hill in *The Times*, 22.3.91.
22 *Tibet News*, No. 6, July 1991.
23 T.I.N. News Update, 17.5.91.
24 T.I.N. News Update, 20.5.91.
25 *Tibetan Bulletin*, September/October 1991.
26 *Tibetan Bulletin*, September/October 1991.
27 T.I.N. News Update, 30.8.91.
28 *The Voice of Tibet*, Vol. 1/6, August 1991.

Epilogue

1   Author interviews, Bir School, Kangra Valley, India, September 1989.
2   Author interview, May 1990, Dharamsala.
3   "Opening of the Political Eye: Tibet's Long Search for Democracy" by Jamyang Norbu in *Tibetan Review*, November 1990.
4   Author interview, Dharamsala, September 1991.
5   Author interview with Lhasang Tsering, Dharamsala, September 1991.

Bibliography

I am indebted principally to the following:

My Land and My People: Memoirs of the Dalai Lama (Potala Press 1962).
Freedom in Exile: The Autobiography of the Dalai Lama of Tibet (John Curtis/ Hodder & Stoughton 1990).
John Avedon, *In Exile from the Land of Snows* (Michael Joseph 1984).
Michael Harris Goodman, *The Last Dalai Lama* (Shambala 1987).
Hugh E. Richardson, *Tibet and its History* (Shambala 1984).
Tibet under Chinese Communist Rule: A Compilation of Refugee Statements, 1958–1975 (Information Office, Dharamsala).
Chris Mullin and Phuntsog Wangyal, *The Tibetans: Two Perspectives on Tibetan–Chinese Relations* (Minority Rights Group report no. 49 1983).
Forbidden Freedoms: Beijing's Control of Religion in Tibet (a report by the International Campaign for Tibet. September 1990, Washington DC).
Defying the Dragon: China and Human Rights in Tibet (a report issued jointly by LAWASIA [The Law Association for Asia and the Pacific Human Rights Standing Committee] and T.I.N. [the Tibet Information Network], March 1991).

And also:

John Ackerly and Blake Kerr M.D., *The Suppression of a People: Accounts of Torture and Imprisonment in Tibet* (Physicians for Human Rights, November 1989).
Gompo Tashi Andrugtsang, *Four Rivers, Six Ranges: A True Account of Khampa Resistance to the Chinese in Tibet* (Dharamsala 1973).
Niema Ash, *Flight of the Wind Horse* (Rider Press 1989).
John Avedon, *Tibet Today* (Wisdom Publications 1987).
Catriona Bass, *Inside the Treasure House: A Time in Tibet* (Victor Gollancz 1990).
Elaine Brook, *Land of the Snow Lion: An Adventure in Tibet* (Jonathan Cape 1987, 1989).
Richard Cavendish, *The Great Religions* (W.H. Smith Publications).
Dhondub Chodon, *Life in the Red Flag People's Commune* (Dharamsala 1978).

Nick Danziger, *Danziger's Travels: Beyond Forbidden Frontiers* (Paladin/Grafton Books 1987).

Alexandra David-Neel, *Magic and Mystery in Tibet* (Dover Books 1971 [orig. 1932]).

Alexandra David-Neel, *My Journey to Lhasa* (Virago/Travellers).

Michael Fathers and Andrew Higgins, *Tiananmen: The Rape of Peking* (*The Independent* in association with Doubleday 1989).

Christoph von Fürer-Haimendorf, *The Renaissance of Tibetan Civilization* (Oxford University Press 1990).

Tsering Dorje Gashi, *New Tibet*, Published in Tibetan as *Ten Years in Communist China and Tibet 1956–1966* (Dharamsala 1977).

Lama Anagarika Govinda, *The Way of the White Clouds* (Rider 1966).

Heinrich Harrer, *Seven Years in Tibet* (Paladin/Grafton 1988) (originally published by Rupert Hart-Davis 1953).

Heinrich Harrer, *Return to Tibet* (Weidenfeld & Nicolson 1984).

Roger Hicks, *Hidden Tibet: The Land and Its People* (Element Books 1988).

Peter Hopkirk, *Trespassers on the Roof of the World: The Race for Lhasa* (Oxford University Press 1982). (Hardback John Murray 1982).

Peter Hopkirk, *The Great Game* (Oxford University Press 1991).

Fredrick Hyde-Chambers, *Lama: A Novel of Tibet* (Souvenir Press 1984).

Vanya Kewley, *Tibet: Behind the Ice Curtain* (Collins/Grafton 1990).

Vijay Kranti, *Dalai Lama: The Nobel Peace Laureate Speaks* (Centrasia Publishing Group, New Delhi 1990).

W. P. Ledger, *The Chinese and Human Rights in Tibet* (a report to the Parliamentary Human Rights Group 1988).

Claude B. Levenson, *The Dalai Lama: A Biography* (Unwin Hyman 1988).

Rinchen Lhamo, *We Tibetans* (Potala Press 1985 [orig. 1926]).

Andre Migot, *Tibetan Marches* (Rupert Hart-Davis 1955).

Dawa Norbu, *Red Star over Tibet* (Envoy Press, New York 1987).

Jamyang Norbu, *Horseman in the Snow, The Story of Aten, an Old Khampa Warrior* (Dharamsala).

Thubten Jigme Norbu (and Colin Turnbull), *Tibet: Its History, Religion and People* (Chatto & Windus 1969, Penguin 1976, 1983).

Marco Pallis, *Peaks and Lamas* (Cassell 1939).

John Prados, *The President's Secret Wars:* CIA and Pentagon Covert Operations from World War II through Iranscam (Quill/William Morrow).

Howard C. Sacks, *The Quest for Universal Responsibility:* Human Rights Violations in Tibet (Dharamsala 1983).

Vikram Seth, *From Heaven Lake: Travels Through Sinkiang and Tibet* (Abacus 1983).

Tsepon W. D. Shakabpa, *Tibet: A Political History* (Potala Press).

Paul Theroux, *Riding the Iron Rooster: By Train Through China* (Hamish Hamilton 1988, Penguin 1989).

Michael C. van Walt van Praag, *Population Transfer and the Survival of the Tibetan Identity* (a report published by U.S. Tibet Committee, 1986).

Reports and Pamphlets

From Liberation to Liberalisation: Views on "Liberalised" Tibet (Dharamsala 1982).

Government Resolutions and International Documents on Tibet (Dharamsala 1989).

Nobel Prize for Peace: Collected Speeches by the Dalai Lama in Oslo, December 1989 (Dharamsala).

Present Conditions in Tibet (Dharamsala 1990).

Search for Jowo Mikyoe Dorjee (Dharamsala 1988).

The Legal Status of Tibet: Three Studies by Leading Jurists (Dharamsala 1989).

Tibet and Freedom (a publication by the Tibet Society UK).

Tibet, China and the World: A compilation of Interviews with the Dalai Lama (Narthang, New Delhi 1989).

Tibet in China: An International Alert Report (August 1988).

Tibet: The Facts (a report by the Scientific Buddhist Association, London 1984).

Where Did Tibet's Forests Go? (Dharamsala 1988).

Journals

T.I.N.: Tibet Information Network, an independent information service, 7 Beck Rd, London E8 4RE.

Tibet Foundation Newsletter, published by the Tibet Foundation, 43 New Oxford Street, London WC1A 1BH. Quarterly.

The Tibet Society Newsletter, Olympia Bridge Quay, Russell Road (Westside), London W14. Quarterly.

Tibetan Bulletin, the official journal of the Tibetan Administration, Dept. of Information, Dharamsala 176215 (H.P.) India. Bi-monthly.

Tibetan Review, New Delhi. Monthly.

Index